RED DAWN

Alexandra Churchill

ISBN: 9781688600652
(c) Locket Publishing, 2019

For my mum.
Who has been heard to utter the words:
"If you wrote something a bit less miserable I might be able to get to the end."
Sorry, failed again.

War is boredom.

Endless, exhausting, incurable boredom.

I know what people at home think. They imagine charges against the enemy at the point of a bloody bayonet. They dream of brandishing regimental colours with the heel of one's boot driven into the vanquished foe underfoot. They hear of rampant cavalry charges mowing through the Hun ranks like a hot knife through butter. I blame the pictorials. Because what people don't realise is that the fools who draw those pictures have never been near a battlefield whilst there is a scrap in progress. I saw one yesterday from just before Christmas of a grinning Tommy with rosy cheeks and cigarette in one hand, thrilled with this life, and with a festive package from home in the other. 'I'll be home soon,' it said underneath.

Tommy lied.

Tommy is not going anywhere.

Shall I tell you what Tommy was doing at Christmas as far as this battalion was concerned? He was sitting up to the neck in rotting, stinking water, where he had been ever since the fight for Ypres. Tommy was cold, Tommy was wet, Tommy was caked in mud, Tommy had not had a bath in weeks. And do you know what else, dear brother of mine? Tommy never stops bloody moaning about it. Tommy endured all of the above with all the grace of Lizzie learning how to waltz. Do you remember that? I thought I should never feel my feet again after two weeks of them being trampled into the drawing room floor.

I wake up and Tommy is complaining about the weather. At breakfast he is bleating about how his tea tastes of petrol. When I do my rounds in the middle of the morning, he is annoyed about a lack of post, because the mud has ensured that none has been brought up. In the afternoon he is grousing because he has run out of cigarettes, despite the fact that the platoon has smoked in their entirety the contents of mother's last two replenishments for them. Then he is moaning about the desultory noise of the German guns. One thinks he would be rather more bitter if they managed to register their targets, (us) instead of the empty woods next door. As the light fades and the temperature drops, Tommy complains that he is cold. Tommy seems to forget on occasion that his officers, including myself, endure everything that he does, so that there is no point in vocalising his misery. If there was anything to be done, I should have done it for my own benefit as well as his.

Last night at least, Tommy and his friends found some amusement in singing lewd music hall songs, which I laughed at out of sight in my squalid dugout so that they did not think I had become a soft touch. They did a full repertoire for the pleading Germans across the way who are only a few yards from us and enjoyed the show very much. They applauded each turn and shouted 'encore'. But the devils booed the national anthem at the end of proceedings; when I told Tommy to shut up at 3 o'clock. However, for one or two hours, Tommy stopped complaining and took his bows proudly from inside the trench, where of course his audience could not see him. Otherwise it might not have ended quite so well.

Thus, Tommy has been rather more cheerful today. Of all our national traits, I admire the capacity of we Englishmen to complain incessantly both with a sense of humour and without actually losing one's temper the most. Where there is to be no restitution, there can always be a good whinge and a cup of tea instead. Even if it does taste of petrol.

What people at home don't realise, is that for every day of activity that is worthy of a rather loose illustration in one of their pictorials, there are perhaps one hundred of gloomy monotony. And digging. All we do in this war is dig. Dig new trenches. Re-dig trenches that have grown sodden and fallen in. Repair trenches that have been blown in by the enemy. Well, it is Tommy that digs, and I supervise. But you get the general idea. I am starting to sound like Tommy, so I shall desist from burdening you with any more of my woes.

One day soon I shall write you a letter that is remotely interesting.

We should come out of here in a few days at most, whence I hope to find a hot bath, a smiling French girl and something to eat that is not stale or saturated in muck. Send me some cake, won't you? Lots of fruit in it. You know the sort. I will sign off this pathetic effort as I must check on Tommy. He is currently engaged in an attempt to fart 'Tipperary' with his chums, so as you'll understand I have been reluctant to venture outside. You know the drill, old man. Tell mother I am having a gay time and that I should not want to be anywhere else, that I cannot wait to get at the beastly Hun again, etc., etc. Whatever rot you must.

My feet have been wet so long that my wrinkled big toe looks like Nanny's face.

Till we meet again, little Will. Look after Kitch, don't let the women make him fat. As ever, you know what to do with the enclosed.

Your most loving (and most filthy) brother, John.
28th January 1915

Monday, 8th March 1915

I.

If you shut your eyes, you can pretend that the war is not happening. You can imagine that everything in London is much the same as it always was. Such as sitting in a restaurant with a friend. There is the clinking of cutlery upon the china, the excited chatter, the popping of corks, and ambient music from a quartet upon a small stage on the other side of the room. There is also the smell of an assortment of fine food: a hint of roast beef, some sort of fish, something achingly sweet; like those little bags of warm sugared nuts sold by street vendors. All of it mingles with the passing exhalations of after dinner cigarettes.

"I say, Will! Hey, Stanley? My gosh you haven't fallen asleep have you?" Bunny punches me in the arm and laughs loudly.

I cringe. That Bunny works in intelligence is an oxymoron if ever I have heard one, for his head contains nothing but air. Nominally he belongs to my brother's regiment, but I suppose that matters at stake across the Channel were petrifying enough for the Grenadier Guards, without the idea of using him as a subaltern; giving him responsibilities over other mens' lives. He cannot take anything seriously. The army found other work for him here at home, and in fact he has proved himself to be more than satisfactory in his role. Bunny is an Earl, and so the fact that he is quite stupid and never applies himself fully to anything will never hurt him. He was threatened with being sent away from Harrow many times, but such punishment never materialised. He is one of those men who is going to breeze through life as if it is no effort at all.

Bunny is so attractive to look at, that to spend time with him is to accept that one will just be anonymous in his company. He has the build of an oarsman, big and solid, with a great mop of curly blond hair and blue eyes. In the restaurant all heads turn to watch him, not only on account of his Grecian appearance, but owing to his effervescently loud personality. Well. That and his absurd laugh, a high pitched, staccato noise like a machine gun; apt to go off at inappropriate times as if someone has accidentally pressed the trigger. It causes people to stop, startled, and try to account for where it has come from. Such embarrassment matters little to Bunny. He is a passionate dramatist and loves the attention. I think his name is Charles, but I have forgotten. A week after I met him in France last year, Bunny assumed his unfortunate nickname when a bullet pinged off a cart wheel, entered his boot at the heel and he was forced to hop some eighty miles during the retreat from Mons. He pretends to despise his new moniker, but he loves the attention, and needless to say that his theatrical indignance has ensured that he will never now be known as anything else. Bunny and I represent part of the Society of Socrates, a self-founded, condemned man's drinking club. The war will most probably claim us all at some stage, but we shall not go quietly to the other side. We intend to have the most fun we can on our way out. We do not curb our excesses, we will not go quietly in spite of our sentence. We will live life to the full, making no apologies for our careless convictions, offering no compromise.

Now that my eyes are open, in such close proximity to Whitehall the war is quite apparent. I can see that a great portion of the diners are clad in khaki or navy blue. The lighting is not quite right; dim. This is because above us, the resident, pretty bulbs that usually adorn the skylight have been taken down, lest we provide a marker for the German air menace that Londoners have actually yet to see above the capital. As if a Zeppelin would be guided into the heart of government nearby by a string of fairy lights. In actual fact at present, unless, it seems, one has the misfortune to live in precisely the wrong hamlet in darkest Norfolk, one that a zeppelin may stumble upon whilst it is ambling about bombing the odd cow or an empty field, one will be quite safe.

As a result of tonight's attempt to maximise the enjoyment of what remains of our existence, I am quite drunk. Bunny began ordering champagne as soon as we sat down, and then he began goading me about my inability to keep up with him glass for glass. I fell for this oft-used ploy and began pouring the stuff down my throat. My head is swimming as I survey our fellow diners. I can hear distantly the sound of my companion complaining about the quality of the service. It is a constant source of chagrin for him. About as much hardship as the poor lamb has suffered in the war, since the bouncing bullet episode.

"You know what it is, don't you, Will?"

My response is lazy and slurred. "German waiters." I have heard this diatribe many times before and so I simply close my eyes again as Bunny begins to lament that a little over six months ago, one would be treated like a king by one of a swarm of waistcoated Germans with silver trays in any one of London's finest establishments. Every place of repute had them. Quite understandably, they all left promptly last August, and we have not seen them since.

"Heinrich!" Bunny suddenly says a little too loudly. "Oh Will, do you remember Heinrich at the Cafe Royal? He was a master of choosing the correct wine for a meal. And he was as silent as a mouse but as sleek as a cat when it came to laying the table, or putting down dishes. It was as if he wasn't there." For a moment he swills a little champagne, his fingers lightly touching the long stem of his glass flute. He stares at it glumly. "Poor Heinrich," he says quietly. "I wonder where he is now?"

I push my chair away from the table. "I'd wager that Kaiser Bill has had him for his army." Poor Heinrich indeed. Pretty, foppish, graceful Heinrich. "And a jolly poor soldier he will make too," I say as I stand up, momentarily swaying back and forth until my balance is assured.

Bunny is still sulking. I rather suspect that Heinrich was providing more than wine as an accompaniment to dinner. "I say!" He brightens up suddenly. "You are not off to dog that dancer sort from the Palladium again are you?" He follows me to the nearby cloakroom.

"Shut up," I retort. "You make me sound like a seedy madman." I pull on my coat. "Dog indeed. I'd prefer something romantic, like… court, or… pursue."

Bunny does not care. "What was her name again? Daisy?"

"Doris, you fool, Doris Rosalie. She sounds like a beautiful flower."

Bunny lets out an ear-splitting cackle. "Well, beautiful or not, old boy," he says at the top of his voice, 'you mind you stay away from her flower. She's got a pile of brothers big enough to box your ears. Believe me. I've had one of the brutes chase me through Battersea."

I hand him a cigarette whilst I set about trying to light one for the walk home. My brain and fingers appear disconnected and Bunny has to take the match and do it for me. "Don't worry," I tell him. "I'm too fagged with my wretched cold and too addled, thanks to you and your champagne, to set about anything else tonight. I'm going to go home and sleep till noon tomorrow. The Germans could make landfall in Brighton and set the pier on fire and I should refuse to get out of bed."

He snorts and marches off with a smirk upon his face. "Cold, indeed, you idle bugger," are the last words I hear. As he strides confidently away towards Soho, Bunny's nose in the air and his head swings side to side, as if he is sniffing out his next destination like a contented basset hound with not a care in the world.

Within moments I am crossing Trafalgar Square, the darkened bulk of the National Gallery to my right, its dome blocking out the moon. Another snowstorm has begun, and dainty white flakes are beginning to catch on my eyelashes. A rare beneficiary of the war, the National was only able to reopen because on the declaration of hostilities against Germany, those in favour of women's suffrage who had grown fond of smashing up priceless pieces of art agreed to stop such violent acts. By the time I reach the Union Club, on the western side of the square, the bitterly cold air has caused my nose to begin streaming again. I deserve more sympathy for my ailment. Cold does not convey the gravity of how awful I feel or how I got it. Apparently I do not dress for the weather, and apparently all men over-egg such trivial matters. If my mother knew that an involuntary swim in the English Channel in the middle of the night was the cause of my malady, she might have more sympathy. But of course, she can never know.

I start as a taxi with its lamps switched off rumbles around a corner from the direction of Pall Mall and bumps past me, emblazoned with placards calling for recruits. Everyone drives about with their lights off now and it is liable to cause many an accident. Tramcars are at it, buses, motorcycles too. I wonder how many people have been knocked down already by unruly vehicles since lighting restrictions were brought into force in the capital. Sky-signs and bright advertisements must not be switched on either, a number of street lamps are no longer lit, and the ones that are have their tops painted black so that they cast no light upwards to guide the dreaded Zeppelins about. It hasn't plunged us into darkness, but these enforced measures have certainly robbed London of its lustre, and it makes one gloomy. My grandfather says that it reminds him of when the city was lit solely by gas lamps. This was quite a revelation considering that usually he cannot remember what he had for breakfast. At times, I feel as old and as befuddled as he is. I am 25, but the last few months have been tumultuous to say the least, and they show on my normally youthful face. I cannot decide whether trouble follows me, or whether I attempt to hunt it down, but as a result, I feel weary and quite entitled to be slack for now. I am extremely grateful to be back in London, and I mean to make my stay as long as possible. I began the war like a fool, bounding off to France to join the Intelligence Corps, which meant that I was vaguely entrusted to drag an extremely unreliable motorcycle through half of France. I sustained all manner of scrapes, bruises and blisters in trying to get the damned thing started again and again; never with a particularly inspiring destination ahead, nor anything useful behind. Now my role in this ongoing adventure is rather more ad hoc, but usually still tied to the flow of sensitive information. Odd things happen relating to the war effort, and now having pursued and solved several occurrences of such, my name gets thrown into the hat as the poor fool who has to pursue such cases discreetly. The rough is extremely rough, and more often than not carries the prospect of imminent death. In such an event, my godfather will have to devise some explanation for my mother about my end. It is he who sends me forth into ridiculous escapades. However, in between the bouts of unlikely madness there are weeks such as these, during which I can be blissfully idle, so I feel not an ounce of guilt in enjoying them.

Pall Mall is all but deserted and it is not even ten thirty. Even if the half full theatres were to turn out, London's West End would be a shadow of itself. There is not a soul to be seen as I round the corner at the end of the street, behind St. James's Palace. Built on the site of a leper hospital, the red-brick Tudor residence has been somewhat swallowed from this angle at least by more modern architecture and hardly befits the location of such momentous events as the place where Charles I spent the night before his execution; perhaps where Elizabeth awaited news of the Spanish Armada, and certainly where her catholic, bloodthirsty sister Mary passed away. Not only was the late Queen wed to her beloved Albert here, but her daughter, too, married a German prince at St. James's eighteen years later. To an extent we have the first product of that latter marriage, Kaiser Wilhelm II, to thank for the ghastly mess that Europe is in now.

I am an historian. That means that everywhere I go, I have one eye on those who walked these streets decades before I do so now; what transpired on them centuries before my existence was even a remote possibility. I am still surrounded by history as I make my way left down Piccadilly. It was never important as a thoroughfare until the main road from Charing Cross to Hyde Park Corner was flattened to make way for Green Park, which is now on my left. I think it used to be called Portugal Street, on account of Charles II's barren Queen. Galleries, mansions and arcades are not the sort of thing that ignite my imagination; but I wish the Old White Horse cellar had survived into my lifetime. It was once the most famous coaching inn in England, the start and end of all journeys between the capital and the west, where my family's estate lies. I have read all the family papers in our possession and many of them mention waiting for coaches there, eating a meal or huddling in the cellar for a merry evening with the other patrons. My grandfather was born in the year of Waterloo. He has told me stories of the nights that he spent in one of its numerous incarnations when he was a young man; which would have coincided with the beginning of Queen Victoria's endless reign.

Leaving Hyde Park Corner behind, I enter the maze of curved crescents, green squares and grand houses east of Buckingham Palace. I have not passed another soul in nearly half an hour. It is not only the sense of misery that keeps people at home, but also fear of the enemy. There is an anti-aircraft gun on top of Queen Anne's Gate nearby, but to my knowledge the cover has only been off it once so far. Paris was raided in August, so I have no doubt that these crimes are something of which the Hun is utterly capable of. Searchlights began doing sweeps in September, the Navy was placed in charge of protecting us from any airborne menace. A tiny proportion of locations in Norfolk and Essex have seen Zeppelins pondering aimlessly overhead, but word on the intelligence grapevine is that the Kaiser has now sanctioned bombing London's docklands and that his crews are interpreting that to mean that anything east of Charing Cross is fair game. Thus the threat to the capital is now apparently imminent. At the beginning I laughed at the populace walking about craning their necks, gawping skyward as if a Zeppelin were about to glide from the clouds. I am not laughing quite so hard anymore, but still, if this war is to begin raining fury on England from above, the Kaiser's men will have to learn the difference between East Anglia and the centre of the British Empire. Navigation does not yet seem to be their strong suit.

This last fact has not dissuaded our housekeeper, Mrs. Mitcham, from taking the matter extremely seriously. As I trudge up the front steps and covertly let myself into the hallway, I prepare to dodge the various array of buckets filled with water or sand that she has liberally distributed throughout the house for what she views as the inevitable night that a German airship will find the Stanley household. Mrs. Mitcham also heard that one wine dealer is letting out his cellars, and that people have furnished them and sleep in them fully clothed. Thus she has converted our tiny cellar for the same purpose. Various cushions and lamps keep disappearing from about the house. Nobody has stopped her. I think we are all too afraid of her, for though she is short, she has a violent temper that I have seen her take out on joints of meat with a rolling pin in the kitchen enough times to force my mouth shut.

I love London. I was born and raised in Wiltshire where the family seat, Mildenhall Manor, is located. But for all of its country air and vast grounds, it is apt to become extremely claustrophobic when one takes into account my mother, my four extremely overbearing sisters and then all of their tireless offspring of various shapes and sizes in the vicinity. London, for me, is more peaceful than the countryside. I tiptoe towards the stairs, narrowly avoiding spilling sand out of a tin vessel all over the landing, for my urban solitude is temporarily being usurped by my mother, who has stayed in town after visiting to coincide with my brother's Christmas leave. This morning she lambasted me for neglecting church, and so I try to make my presence as secretive as possible. I was feeling the effects of a heavy night of drinking with Bunny, and had not arrived home until daylight was breaking. I told her that I was engaged on special business. But she can normally tell when I am lying.

Having successfully evaded my mother and Mrs. Mitcham, I fall into bed in my uniform, making a ridiculous show of getting my shoes off and flinging them across the room. A yelp indicates that I have scored a direct hit on my brother's stupid Pomeranian. Perhaps with such skill I should fly Zeppelins, for presumably they would sell their mothers for that sort of aim. This is the last thought that enters my head, for since childhood I have been blessed with the ability to fall asleep almost as soon as my head touches the pillow. Then thunderstorm, riot, an apocalyptic barrage of German shells; nothing will disturb my slumber. The odd nightmare crept in last year, reliving sights, sounds, smells from the front; but they have gone away now. Aided by Bunny's champagne, I pass into unconsciousness, lulled to sleep by soothing, rhythmic ticking of the clock on the mantlepiece.

Tuesday, 9th March 1915

II.

My eyes fly open and I find myself in a state of utter confusion; sudden, frantic disorientation. I feel as if I have only been asleep for a matter of minutes as I am wrenched from my slumber. No light has yet begun to creep around the curtains drawn at the large sash windows of my bedroom. I am dimly aware of a presence trying to remove the covers from my bed. What is this nightmare? As I begin to regain a proper state of consciousness I hear voices growing louder in my ear. My wits are fully reinstated as I receive a stinging slap to the face.

"Get up, Will. Get up now." The flushed features of my godfather, General Nathaniel Marmaduke Phipps, and his enormous, grey moustache loom above me. Disturbingly, he is close enough for me to see little red veins on the end of his nose and to smell the gentle whiff of scotch on his breath. More commonly known by me as Pip, he is Adjutant-General. His administrative role, one that has to suffice as a Boer shot away half his knee-cap more than a decade ago and rendered him immobile in a fighting sense, is of huge importance to the army. He essentially oversees all matters of organising personnel at the highest level.

Pip's presence in my bedroom in the middle of the night cannot be good. John's ratty dog is snapping at my ear. The wretched little bundle of fur gets excitable over nothing at all and bounces about in a state of intense hysteria. But that is not what is disconcerting. When it wants something it assumes a bold, upright stance and a penetrating stare as it sits, menacing and unmoving with it's front paws dangling until you give it what it wants. Few words, and a monstrous amount of control over fellow beings that generates a sense of petrified awe. John named it Kitchener. I swipe at it a touch too hard and it flies away and rebounds off the wardrobe before scuttling under my dressing table to sulk, whining in high-pitched despair.

In the moment of distraction generated by this canine drama, my mother appears and shoves a thermometer into my mouth. My speech is distorted by its presence as I launch into a complaint about the scenario unfolding around me.

"Your mother says if your temperature is normal, then I may have you."

"Pip," I waffle incoherently. "There is nothing that you can say, after last week, that will impeach me to go anywhere near a boat in the immediate future; and as for an aeroplane, well if I live to be one hundred, I will never go near one of those damned things again. You can have me shot, for I shan't do it."

The General's response is to whip the covers brutally from on top of me, and then to purse his lips in disapproval when he sees that I went to bed fully dressed. "Look at me Will. The fact that I am here in the middle of the night, what does that say to you?" Sympathy was never my godfather's chief virtue. "Get up. Chill be damned, you reek of Champagne. You have had a few days of rest and I see that you have spent them well. Now it is time to return to work. I am speaking as your vastly superior officer at this moment, not a member of your family. Now get up." He smirks with approval as defeated, I dramatically swing my legs round to assume a seated position. "Besides, the business I am about does not require you to leave London."

Well, that is something at least.

I fumble with my shirt buttons in the bathroom. Pip nods and leaves me in peace, satisfied that I am not about to crawl into the bathtub and go back to sleep. It has been known. I cannot testify to being completely sober, but my faculties seem to be returning to me as I struggle into a new uniform after a perfunctory wash. I splash cold water on my face and check that there is nothing unseemly sticking out of my narrow, very straight nose. My opaline green eyes are understandably bloodshot and the skin over my high cheekbones is red on one side where my face has been stuck to a pillow for a mercilessly short period of time. My full lips are cracked on account of the extremely cold weather we have been experiencing of late and I waste several seconds picking dead skin from my mouth. Finally, I make a pig's ear of attempting to part my straight, dark brown hair on the side and fix it in place with oil. The end result looks rather like a duck that has been in a drunken pub brawl, but it is out of my eyes.

In a few minutes I have been bundled into the back of Pip's waiting motor car. "Have you got everything?" "Everything except my dignity," I snap as he shuts the door and slaps the side to indicate to the driver to move off. As I look back out of the window I see him standing on the pavement outside my house with a puzzled frown on his face.

As I ducked inside, I had felt the first few fat drops of water, and within a few moments I now hear heavy rain begin to drum on top of the closed passenger compartment. I begin to doze, but by the time the motor-car, after a length of time I could not even attempt to gauge, stops again and the engine is shut down, the downpour has stopped. We have pulled up on the edge of a vast, deserted junction on a city road. I am surrounded by darkened shop doorways, their colourful awnings pulled in. The main road lies in front of me, branching off in either direction, criss-crossed by empty tramlines that glisten in the moonlight. As I step down from the cab I thank the driver. "Where am I?" "Woolwich, Sir." As I walk into the road I hear him start the motor up again behind me and drive off. Superb.

To my right the wide, main road curves away from me and disappears into the night. Looming dead ahead is a capacious gatehouse of red brick. Atop the rather grand white stone pillars that frame it, it looks like a house, with neat windows and a pointed roof, offices perhaps. This top structure is flanked by two stout, ornamental cannon facing inward. Woolwich, cannon, high walls all about and sentries standing in the shadows cast by the thick, wrought iron barriers. The Royal Arsenal then, undoubtedly our most important establishment so far as the productions of munitions is concerned. There could scarcely be a more valuable complex than this one in the Empire at present.

Still, all appears to be quiet. I approach a very young-looking sentry standing stock still and keeping watch through thick-rimmed spectacles on the empty road ahead. "My name is Lieutenant Stanley, I've been sent here but I'm not sure why as yet." I yawn. "Most likely it would be because something awful has happened." The young man jerks his head almost imperceptibly, as if he is paying a game of statues, but then points to his right. 'Down there, Sir."

I cross slippery tram lines and begin to walk parallel to a high brick wall on my right that surrounds a secret city, a warren of workshops and warehouses hidden within the capital. The street lights are darkened, presumably to prevent any enemy craft from drifting haplessly toward this vital location. I suppress a shudder at the damp chill in the air.

I still cannot see what I am looking for. Behind and to my left on the corner is a public house which has closed its doors for the night and is now deserted, empty tobacco packets and spent matches lying sodden in the gutter along with the remains of a smashed glass. Then the street runs into houses that face the arsenal wall, fronted by small patches of grass hidden behind little hedges. All of the windows above are darkened. The only things breaking the silence for

the moment are my crisp footsteps clicking on the wet pavement, and the sound of the very recent rain still dripping from trees that line the civilian side of the street. Aside from those guarding the gates, I haven't yet seen another soul. Then, out of the emptiness in front of me emerge moving silhouettes, the dancing beams of electric torches being flicked about by their owners. They are still thirty or so feet distant, but the empty night air carries the gentle, muffled sounds of their voices back down the road. I shield my eyes at ten feet away as one of the shafts of obnoxious yellow light shines right into my eyes. "Who goes there?"
"Lieutenant Stanley, get that bloody thing off of my face." There is a muffled grunt and then the glare swings back to the floor. When my eyes readjust I see that it is being wielded by an angry looking police constable.
"We've been waiting for you," he says huffily.
 Beyond him, amongst a small group concentrated nearby, I can see a dumpy shadow with its arms stretched out. As I brush past the unwelcoming constable and approach it, the round-cheeked, cherub-faced being in front of me has his mouth wide open in an ungraceful yawn. "Hello Sir, you thawed out yet? You was blue this time last week."
"Crabtree. What are we doing here?"
He rubs his grey-blue eyes. Crabtree is about the same age as myself, and originally joined the East Surrey Regiment on the outbreak of war before answering a call for volunteers to join the Military Police. This decision was based entirely on his ambition to become a detective and follow in the footsteps of his great hero, Sherlock Holmes. "I'd quite like to know me'self," he says in insolent jest. "All I know, is that I've been turned out my bed after a full day separating out a drunken Jock battalion scrapping in Leicester Square, and helping frog march 'em back to their camp, and now I'm

on the wrong side of London, mindin' a dead bloke till you get here."

Which draws my attention to a mound in the middle of the road at our feet, concealed by a tarpaulin. As I light a cigarette, Crabtree hands me a torch and I move to stand next to him and get a better look. "They've got the arse 'cos we're here," he whispers, gesticulating to a total of four sour-faced constables loudly enough so that they might all hear him anyway. They exchange glances.

"This is our beat," one of them says. "The Metropolitan Police guard the arsenal, have done for years. It's why we have an office at the gate," he adds sarcastically.

I crouch down and pull back the waterproof sheet to reveal the body in question lying on its back underneath.

"We aren't in the arsenal," Crabtree yawns audibly.

"Fifteen miles." This comes from the original constable with the flashlight. "Fifteen miles radius around is ours."

"The relevant Act of Parliament," I say, holding my cigarette between my lips as I examine the corpse below me, "gives you fifteen miles jurisdiction on the condition that you only enact your powers in respect of property of the Crown or persons subject to the authority of the Navy or the Military." I gesture to them to shine their flashlights on the corpse. "As this appears to be a civilian, and as I have been sent here by the highest of said military authorities, I would suggest that you stop your complaining and illuminate this poor fellow so that I might get a proper look. Otherwise I shall see if we can't have you better employed directing motor cars at Piccadilly Circus."

Another member of this ghoulish coterie emerges from the shadows. He is in ordinary, smart attire as opposed to a uniform and, despite a round stomach bulging over his waistband and his age being somewhere north of sixty, he nimbly crouches down on the opposite side of

the body, stifling a smile at my remark, leaning into the stream of light now being obediently cast downward. "Scully," he puts out a podgy hand. The odd lighting makes him look slightly demonic, casting unflattering shadows on wide, black eyes behind little gold spectacles and a tiny, pointed nose. All of his features are pinched into the middle of his face. "Surgeon by trade. I work for the arsenal. They called me out to assist you. It is all most peculiar."
I shake his hand.
Crabtree crouches down beside me and inadvertently farts. Rather than sparing us all and pretending that it has not happened, he wafts his hand to and fro behind his backside melodramatically. "Scuse me," he breezes as if this is the most socially acceptable thing in the world.
I look at him, lost for words, and then turn back to the medical man in front of me. "Have you had a chance yet to examine the corpse?"
Scully nods enthusiastically, like a golden retriever, then composes himself as if this might be inappropriate. "It's all very curious!" Evidently his late night summons has caused him some excitement. He clears his throat seriously. "Obviously we have a male," he begins.
This much I had noticed, a slight man, dressed in ordinary working clothes. He possesses angular features dominated by a bushy, dark moustache, and startled, sightless dark eyes staring off to one side."A fit of apoplexy, perhaps?" I say.
Scully grimaces slightly. "I rather think there is a more sinister cause." The doctor mops his brow with a handkerchief. "Poor chap." He tips his head the other way to reveal two matching puncture marks on the dead man's neck, each surrounded by a little dark crust of drying blood. The corpse is wet from the recent downpour and I assume that any further evidence, such as blood, has been washed away.

"One of them's picked up his wallet," says Crabtree, waving a fart-covered hand at the police constables, who are standing together, glowering at us with torches in hand.

I hold out my hand without looking up, and one of them tuts as he slaps a battered, a leather item in my outstretched palm. "What brings him to Woolwich?" This last question is addressed to nobody in particular. "Begging your pardon, Sir, but he works in the arsenal." I look up to see a gangly, shabbily dressed man gripping a long-dead cigarette tightly in his shaking fingers. He is quite obviously petrified. He has been huddling behind the policemen and so his appearance is a surprise to me.

"And who might you be?"

"Stan Bailey, Sir. That's my mate, Fred."

I sit back on my heels. "And do you work inside too?" I gesture to the high wall in front of me.

"Yes, Sir."

"Would you like to tell me what happened?"

"We had a lock-in at Jim's." He gesticulates towards the pub at the end of the street. "We was both going home, the last ones out, but I forgot me cap. We barely got out the door, so I went back and he walked on. I said I'd catch him up."

I straighten my legs and stand up. "I'm very sorry for your loss," I make a point of looking at him directly, to show that I mean this and that it is not an empty platitude.

Poor Crabtree flails about trying to get off the floor and puts his hand in a puddle. He wipes it on his coat and then sniffs loudly as he takes a notebook out and begins to write things down on our behalf. This is how we work. I talk to the relevant parties and he records the conversation. I know that he doesn't appear at first glance to have brains enough to burden a flea, but Crabtree is well suited to this sort of work and quite sharp for all of his buffoonery.

"Did you find his body, Mr. Bailey?"
"Yes, Sir." Fred's colleague sounds as if he might break into tears.
"And he was already dead?"
He nods sorrowfully. "He's married to me sister. What will I say to 'er?"
"Don't worry about that now, Stan. I am sure one of these police constables will be happy to escort you home when the time comes and assist you in any way that they can." One of them nods graciously at him, but impressively he simultaneously manages to cast a disgusted look at me. Stan has walked around to place himself behind Crabtree and I. He is trying very hard not to look down. Not to acknowledge his relation lying dead on the floor. I turn my back on the body and gently guide Stan by the shoulder so that he might do the same. I offer him a new cigarette and he takes it with a shaking hand.
"Did you see who did this?" I ask. He shakes his head and shivers. His meagre coat is threadbare. I take off my greatcoat and put it around his shoulders with Crabtree's help. "You've had a nasty shock," I continue. 'But anything you can recall might lead us to explain what has happened here?" I am assuming that this is my purpose in being here in the middle of the night.
"He was already dead when I got to him."
"You didn't see anybody else in the vicinity?"
"The only other soul was an old woman. I smelled her before I saw her, she stank of piss; like she'd soiled herself, too. She was hobbling by on the other side of the road."
"Did she stop?"
"It's all a bit of a blur. She must have heard me, must have seen me rush to Fred and try to help him. I turned around and called out to her for help, but she was already gone. Then I ran down to the gate."
"How would you categorise your brother in law's health, Stan? We shall need his surname too."

"It's George, sir, Fred George. He was as fit as a fiddle. He's had a cold, but we've all had 'em, working in that draughty factory. Fred used to be a boxer. He looked after 'imself. We play football every Sunday afternoon." Played.
"So you can think of nothing that might have led him to expire so suddenly like this? He was not feeling ill when you left him to go back for your cap?"
"He was fine." Stan seems determined on this point. "He's got five nippers." He mutters this last statement, as if he is reminding himself.
"If you could provide your full name and address to Crabtree here, we will need to stay in touch for the time being, we may have more questions."
I take the money from Fred George's wallet. Theft was evidently not the motive for his sudden demise. "I must have everything else in case it is pertinent at present, but I think your sister will have use of this." Stan nods and puts the money in his pocket. I watch him quietly converse with Crabtree. Then I summon two of the police constables and instruct them to take him home and assist him in breaking the news to his family. Though they stare hard at me, they do as they have been told and I am satisfied that they are treating him with due courtesy after the shock he has endured. I have not noticed the approach of Dr. Scully and I jump as he coughs and I realise that he is at my left shoulder. He lifts his glasses and pinches the bridge of his nose between finger and thumb tiredly. "I will begin work first thing in the morning on an autopsy. If you were to come by shortly before lunch I should have some answers for you, I would have thought."

Crabtree and I watch in silence as Scully directs two remaining constables to either end of a stretcher. Carefully they place Fred George on top and recover him with his tarpaulin. They proceed back towards the main gate, Scully gripping a black instrument bag and waddling amiably along beside them. He barely reaches their shoulders. Left alone Crabtree and I crouch down to examine the spot where the body had so recently lay. My companion shines his flashlight up and down. There appears to be nothing for us to find.

"Do you think that Stan might have had something to do with his mate's death?" He asks.

"I highly doubt it. Fred George's body shows no outward signs of a struggle, and his reaction was one of complete shock. He ran for help. Additionally, do not forget that had he been the perpetrator, he would have willingly reduced his own sister to a widow with five children to feed. I would be very surprised if that turns out to be the case."

He nods in agreement. "What now?"

I pause to chew at my thumbnail for a moment or two. I look up and down the street, watch the last of the heavy downpour milling gently in the gutter as it tries to escape through a partially blocked drain "Where do you suppose the old woman that Stan called out to went? If she was hobbling, there is no junction or turnoff immediately nearby."

Crabtree shrugs. "Maybe she went in one of the houses?"

"And what was such a vulnerable person doing outside at such an hour?"

"Maybe she came out of the pub?" He is not being deliberately annoying. It is Crabtree's job to play devil's advocate.

"I would have thought that Stan would have mentioned if he had seen her previously in the pub, during the lock in?"

Crabtree nods and yawns at the same time. "Maybe she weren't drinking with them, maybe she weren't out for any length of time. Maybe she just came out of one house and then went into another, he said she was old, remember? Maybe she is mutton and didn't hear him shouting at 'er and she just went straight into another house?"

I smirk. Being from northeast Surrey, Crabtree is about as entitled by birth to speak in cockney rhyming slang as I am.

"What now Guv'nor?" He says with an impish grin on his face.

I yawn loudly and dramatically and turn towards the nearby entrance to the arsenal, which Scully thoughtfully informed us is called the Beresford Gate. "Well, even if we did know *where* she came from, or *why* she was out at such an hour, or *why* she chose not to respond to Stan's appeal for help, we can do little when we have no idea *who* she was. So I suppose the only thing left for us to do for now is to speak to the guards."

Walking back to the deserted junction at Beresford Square, the streets are just beginning to come alive, with the presence of the odd horse-drawn delivery wagon or lorry lumbering by. After confirming that no change in sentries has occurred since Stan went running to them with news of his brother in law's demise, Crabtree takes out his notebook again. Once more I lead the questioning. "Did you witness two men leave the public house across the street and walk in that direction?" I point towards where we have just come from.

"Oh yes sir," says the boy with the heavy looking glasses.

"The surviving man, Mr…" My tired brain is temporarily at a loss.

"Bailey," Crabtree interjects.

I nod thanks. "Mr. Bailey, he says that they stayed for a lock in?"

"Yes sir." This comes from the other sentry; another adolescent, this one with long, spindly limbs and an appalling collection of purple and red growths about his chin and face. "The main crowd turned out hours ago, then about half past two, the last few left."

The bespectacled soldier takes over again. "Three of them went that way," he points his rifle in the opposite direction, along the Plumstead Road. "Then one ducked back inside. His mate walked off up Warren Lane. Bailey? That is the one that came back shouting?" I nod. "Well he came back out the pub a minute later. He stood chatting with the landlord for a bit longer. Then he left too and followed his friend and Jim locked up. It can't have been more than five or ten minutes after the first bloke had left, that Bailey came running back down Warren Lane shouting that his mate was on the floor and he couldn't get him up."

All of this matches the version of events given to us by Stan. "The first man, his friend. How did he look to you?"

"Merry enough," says the taller guard. "But he was walking in a straight line. They have a late one every week on a Tuesday. I think they play darts after closing, but none of them leave blind drunk. They've all got work in the morning."

"He did not strike you as being ill at all?"

"No, sir." They both speak at the same time, Spotty and Spectacles. The latter takes up the story again. "Not at all, sir. Head up, whistling. *Tipperary*, I think."

I roll my eyes unconsciously. I hate that song.

Crabtree clears his throat. "Did you see anyone go up the road before them at all? Anyone who could have hung around and done him in? Did you run up when he raised the alarm? You might have seen an old woman?"

Spotty speaks. "I saw no one. We're not supposed to leave our posts, but anyway we didn't need to. Constable Morgan was only over by the pub on the far corner there. We shouted out and he was on his whistle and running off down the road with your man Bailey. Then the other Bluebottles turned up. We stayed out of it until they came and told us to ring the authorities. They must have rung up the doctor, because then he turned up. Then another half hour or so and you came." He nods towards Crabtree. "About fifteen minutes after that sir, your car brought you. It was a nice motor. Not as nice as that one though."

I look behind me and for the first time I notice a gleaming, blood red Daimler parked outside a deserted butcher's shop. I know who it belongs to immediately, thanks to the presence of a chauffeur in his late thirties who happens to be built like a heavyweight boxer; standing by the passenger door and holding it open for us. Half of his face is hidden by a great, fiery red beard and his bulbous features are, as usual, expressionless. "Hello, Gaylor, we must stop meeting like this," I say it in jest as I step past him, but I have long since ceased to expect to get anything resembling a smile out of the man that has been waiting for us.

"Where are we going?" Asks Crabtree, wide-eyed, as he joins me inside, looking in combined wonderment and terror at our giant of a driver.

"Down the rabbit hole again, I fear."

"Eh?" He sniffs.

I gesture towards our driver. "Wherever Mr. Gaylor wishes to take us, Crabtree. That is of course unless you wish to fight him."

III.

Dawn is breaking outside the motor car window. Cloudless grey gives way to a cold, icy blue hue, before a washed out, yellow winter glow begins to absorb the last of the night. The air outside is bracing, but I have the window pulled down as the ventilation serves to keep me awake. Crabtree is slumped against the side of our compartment, his limbs splayed as he snores his head off. But I have a suspicion of where we might be going, and I do not want to be half asleep when I get there.

Random thoughts mill about in my head. What ailment could possibly have struck Fred George down instantly after an innocent night of darts? If someone else is responsible, who? It would have been an odd location for a killer to wait for a potential victim, so could he have been singled out for death? If so why, and by whom? There is little point deliberating any of this until Dr. Scully conducts his examinations, or until someone actually informs me that I am to carry this investigation through. Something tells me I am about to find out what my rôle is to be.

We pull through a twisted , high black gate onto the edge of a large, deserted concourse. Our driver skirts the perimeter of it and passes beneath an embellished stone archway, pulling up in front of some steps. Here I am met by an acquaintance of my father; an officer named Wigram, and my suspicions are confirmed. Well, in part. I was under the impression that this is the man I would be here to see, but on enquiry he shakes his head, signalling that we can leave Crabtree dead to the world in the back of the motor for now. Instead of taking me inside, Wigram walks me around the side of the seemingly abandoned building into a rather magnificent garden. Next to the lawn, glistening with a thick layer of frost, paths lead off in different directions. After inquiring as to my father's health, and I after his wife, Wigram silently leads me to a point where one track winds out of sight into dense foliage. On it, two men in khaki have paused just under a canopy of trees on noticing our approach.

One of them is a broad shouldered individual in his sixties with his hands clasped in front of him. He towers above me. He is a little wide around the middle, but an imposing figure; strong. He has piercing, hooded blue eyes and a great cultivated, sweeping moustache, slightly grey. One that has spawned thousands in its

image. "I don't think we have met, Lieutenant" he says, glancing at the insignia on my shoulder and putting out a hand with a somewhat bemused look on his face at finding such an underling dumped in front of him. At least I am not the only one struggling to wrap my head around this strange situation. Salute? Don't salute? What am I to do? In the end I take his lead and simply shake the hand of the great Lord Kitchener.
"No, Sir, we have not," is all I can manage in a husky whisper.
"I have heard enough about you. Are you related to General John Stanley? From some where in the West Country, I think?"
"Yes, Sir, he is my father." He should know the divisional commanders, I suppose, but with the growth of the army of late, at his own instigation, one could hardly blame him for not keeping pace.
"And you have a brother in the Guards?" His questions are punctuated, quick, but this is hardly the barking spectacle I have been led to imagine by the world at large.
"Yes, a Grenadier, Sir." My brother, John, is even sadder in terms of importance and thus the Field Marshal's knowledge does impress me now. I think of John naming his noisy dog after the man in front of me and I feel guilty.

The great hero, seemingly satisfied with my lowly credentials, gives a curt nod and resumes his original stance with his hand clasped beneath his stomach. The second man is Kitchener's complete opposite, physically speaking. He is slight and three or four inches shorter than I. His neatly trimmed beard is flecked with white, and since I saw him last his large, watery, pale blue eyes now sit above dark circles. The lines on his face seem to me to have deepened in just a few weeks. As ever, though, he is immaculately dressed, despite the hour. He smells faintly of lavender.
"Have you no coat man?" he says by way of greeting.

His Majesty George V, King of Great Britain and her Dominions, Emperor of India, appears to be indignant at this fact. It is only then that I realise that my greatcoat is, in all probability, somewhere in Woolwich, draped across Stan Bailey's shoulders where I left it. I think of Stan going back for his cap and wonder, had he not gone back for his cap, would his brother in law's odd fate have been different? Which reminds me that my own is in the motor and I am bareheaded.

"I gave it to someone with greater need, Your Majesty." It feels like a mean excuse in front of a man known by all to be supremely fastidious in all matters concerning sartorial propriety. By his standards I might as well be half naked.

The King signals to a servant standing out of earshot and calls out to him. "See what you might find in the way of a suitable outer garment for the Lieutenant, would you?" The man disappears towards the vast interior of Buckingham Palace.

"The civilised world might be crumbling, Stanley, but we can at least uphold the small things. Perhaps you have need of a cap too." He is mocking me. It took me one or two supremely awkward conversations to gauge that our monarch has a very dry sense of humour and has retained a fondness for chaffing that he presumably developed in his naval days. I also know that he hates people who suck up to him, and that if he has deigned to have a conversation with you, he would have you speak to him, within obvious parameters, as you would any other man.

"It is in the car, Your Majesty."

"I think with the amount of articles you misplace, my boy, at the end of this war military outfitters will be sorry to see the back of you, if you decide to return to civilian life."

The fact that he is not angry with me is confirmed when he amiably changes the subject. "I finally recalled," he continues, "what it was that I read about your family. It was one of *your* servants that brought about the demise of Whitehall Palace in 1698. She started the fire, working for a Colonel Stanley."

"I hope Your Majesty will forgive us this this historical indiscretion." One of my family's embarrassing links to notoriety. Thank god he does not appear to be aware of our record during the Wars of the Roses.

His Majesty lets out a brief, loud exclamation of laughter. "Yes, quite, treasonous as it may have been, I think enough time has elapsed for us to put it to one side."

His servant returns bearing the precise style of coat I should be wearing and I pull it on gratefully.

"My sincere apologies, Your Majesty, I will return this as soon as is possible."

The King waves away the notion casually with his hand. "Consider it recompense for having been dragged out of bed in the middle of the night."

Literally.

"You would like to smoke, I think? Please do, and share if you can." It always rather astonishes me that a King should be so polite and so ordinary a man. One wouldn't be surprised if he were a raging megalomaniac, and yet on each of the few occasions that I have met our Sovereign, his consideration for others has struck me. That said, I have never met anyone quite so accomplished at swearing either. That is the navy for you. "Thank you, Your Majesty." I rapidly take out my case, offering them out. I try not to dwell on the fact that I am smoking in the gardens of Buckingham Palace at dawn with the King and the Secretary of State for War. The two most famous men in the Empire.

The King inhales deeply. "You must make a note of where you get these from for me." He examines the cigarette agreeably. 'You would probably quite like an explanation as to what you are doing here?'

Naturally, but diplomacy prevails in the presence of your Sovereign. "I had wondered why Your Majesty might be interested in a dead worker in the outer parts of London?"

"Ah," he says, raising a finger. "But what work did that man do, and precisely, where?"

Suddenly this bizarre interview begins to make a modicum of sense. "He was a munitions worker, at the Royal Arsenal."

There is a grim tone to the Sovereign's voice, suddenly. "Yes. It would be best, perhaps, if you were to begin by telling us what you have found at Woolwich?"

I describe the scene to them: the body, the circumstances of the man's death so far as I know, confirm who he was, what our solitary witness claims to have seen. "It seems quite possible that he did not die of natural causes, but I do not think that I believe that he just happened to have chanced upon someone waiting to do murder, either, in that location. So the question becomes, why was it necessary? What could the motive for taking this poor man's life possibly have been?" This by way of a summary to finish my speech.

Sovereign and makeshift politician exchange glances. They look as perplexed as I feel. The King speaks first. "Perhaps now, Lord K can explain a bit of the background as to the work that is being done at Woolwich. Then you will begin to understand why this seemingly benign incident might concern us so deeply." Kitchener looks at the King, who gives him a reassuring nod of encouragement. "Lieutenant Stanley has proved both his aptitude and his discretion on more than one occasion. You may speak with complete freedom."

There is a glint of surprise in those eyes, famous the world over. Then the Field Marshal nods his head in firm obedience and clears his throat. "We have been seriously hampered in our efforts to defeat the enemy by a lack of war supplies. At La Bassee, Armentieres, Messines and Ypres, since October last our lack of heavy artillery and ammunition for the guns has been apparent."

"We simply weren't prepared for war on this scale," the King interjects. Blowing smoke away across the perfect lawn, he gestures with his hands. "Now, by now means were the Germans either, you understand, but we do not think they were quite so far off the mark as ourselves and the French are no better. But if we do not catch them, and quickly, then we could lose this war."

That sentiment hangs in the air, along with each visible exhalation of breath in the frigid garden; the three of us letting that horrific eventually sink in. Lord Kitchener is the first to compose himself. "We have ordered what we shall need, but the country simply cannot produce it fast enough. We predict that soon we will not be receiving one quarter of what our troops want to launch at the enemy. Part of the problem involves technical considerations. For instance, Sir John French says that he requires 50% of his shells for France and Belgium to contain high explosive now. At the onset of the war, all that we provided were shells full of shrapnel. Now, he is not wrong, but this was unforeseen, and the machines that make such shells must be altered. This of course, takes time and slows down production."

This is turning out to be an utterly depressing conversation, especially when one hasn't yet so much as consumed a cup of tea so far this morning. "With regard to our future requirements," the King says, "in the next few days we hope that an amendment will have been agreed to the Defence of the Realm Act. In this way Lord K here will be able to compel manufacturers to take on Government work if they possess the necessary equipment, and when they do, to see that they regard it as of greater importance than their private contracts."

Well. At least there appears to be some way forward. "It may sound like a bold step," Kitchener continues, "and I fear putting these measures into practice may be immensely difficult. But regretfully no amount of cajoling, persuasion or even producing veiled threats on my part has had the desired effect with these people. Nor have the manufacturers, I rather feel, made enough effort to recruit the men that they should need to up their production for the country. They should be working around the clock, but they are not, they still have not the number of men to do it. Any problems that we had in terms of unemployment have gone into reverse. There are too many jobs that want doing and not enough men."

I can believe that. I well remember a short while ago, when heavy snowfall buried London and there were not the casual labourers to clear it. I had quite an amusing time wading through two feet of the stuff, but not so much fun listening to my mother complain about it. I am brought back to the present when the King speaks again. "We lack the requisite number of suitable buildings to a degree," he says. "But the more important issue is the employees. Many of those who are skilled have enlisted when we cannot do without them here at home."

Kitchener takes over again. The two great men in front of me are completely at ease in each others company, passing conversation back and forth. "As for those valuable men that have already joined the army or the navy, we are attempting to get them back again by way of an individual release system for particular workers who were engaged in munitions, and perhaps, too, there will be a bulk approach whereby we request back every man who is of a specific trade; explosives or metal working experts for instance." He waves his hand to suggest that such details have yet to be finalised. The King nods. "We are going to implement immediately, a system whereby skilled labourers who are needed at home are identifiable by badges, so that they are not taken for shirkers and may go about their business without reproach from these damned white feather pests. It is hoped that by taking this additional pressure of remaining here away from them, that they will keep to the work they are good at, instead of being pressured into joining the army."

I have no idea if it is appropriate for me to interrupt the course of their lecture, but I am tired and the words are out of my mouth before I can consider this point.

"Surely they need not all be skilled, Your Majesty? As an emergency measure can the proficient men be spread out to watch over those who have yet to learn?"

Until now, the great Kitchener, my boyhood idol, has done nothing to justify his fearsome public reputation. But when I say this he throws down the tail end of his cigarette and stamps on it. "The damned unions," he grunts. At least he is not angry with me for speaking up. He is at once calm again, though he clasps his hands in apparent frustration.

The King does not seem moved by the statesman's outburst. I presume he has seen such a thing before. "Lord K doesn't mean it in that way. I will attempt to explain." The Sovereign too throws his cigarette away and politely stifles a yawn behind the back of his hand. "The trades unions have worked to have many rules implemented for workers. These rules are having an impact on war production in several ways. For example, they prevent the idea of hiring a lesser skilled worker to do the work of a skilled one; they put limitations on output that prevents employers from taking advantage of their men, stops them employing women in place of those who have departed. There are safety rules too, and in a wartime climate, I am afraid that these restrictions rather hamper the employers from producing what we need, and the employees from facilitating our requests, even if they should want to."

"Yes, Your Majesty," I offer my cigarettes again. The King accepts. "I have heard from my mother about the amount of women that have tried to seek work and as yet have no jobs. One of her projects is the Work for Women Fund at Portland Place."

"Ah yes, of course," he says. "If she is anything like the Queen then it is quite difficult to keep up with her projects. They are quite relentless, our women. I think it is splendid."

I nod, but direct the conversation back to the shocking notion of running out of shells and bullets to loose at the Germans and the Turks. "Are there no ways in which this situation might be circumvented within the confines of these rules? A compromise for the duration of the war?"

"The rules are necessarily strict,' explains the King. "After all they prevent men from being exploited. As you say, you might think that some partially skilled men might work underneath a superintendent with all of the necessary qualifications and that would solve the problem. But that is forbidden and nobody will be the first to back down."

Kitchener, as he lights a fresh cigarette, seems to be at the end of his tether with the matter at hand. "The bastards will not relent, even temporarily. I have tried, the Government has tried as one formidable entity, representatives of the Board of Trade too. Nothing has moved them to see sense, the bloody fools. Men die in a real war because of these damned endless political battles and the vicious swine that propagate them."

The Sovereign sighs. "Their stance is understandable, to an extent, of course. But they must be flexible. We are supposed to be fighting the Germans, not each other! It is most frustrating for all involved and causes one great anxieties."

To an ignorant fool such as I, the situation appears utterly ridiculous. "I cannot accept that the unions will not entertain the notion of relinquishing that which they have achieved in terms of protecting their workers simply whilst it is necessary? Pardoning my language Your Majesty, Lord Kitchener, but it is damned unpatriotic if nothing else. Do they welcome the idea of the Hun landing upon our shores? Presumably the idea is that they believe that their workers will suffer a decrease in their conditions whilst their employers make piles of money from the manufacture of war material?"

Kitchener levels his conspicuous eyes slightly in my direction. "You are a very astute young man, Lieutenant Stanley. That, and the fact that they worry that they will have trouble seeing the restrictions brought back at the termination of the war; those are the two main points."

The King sighs. "The War Office needs to bend too, in terms of the safety and inspection requirements, but they must all meet somewhere in the middle. As it stands, we have to monitor the ammunition situation extremely carefully, and we shall have to continue to do so this year until we can increase production to anything like what will be needed. Everything that we produce at this juncture is precious, do you understand, Stanley? I hesitate to use the word crisis, but, well; it will dictate when and where we can fight. Not only that, but you understand that if this got out, the moral effect it could have on our soldiers and sailors; all of K's volunteers, it could be bloody catastrophic."

Lord Kitchener throws up his hands. "So, you see what I must deal with. Guns and artillery ammunition is only the beginning of it too, my boy. We are not manufacturing enough rifles; we have enlisted men in my new armies marching about the country pretending to hold them and waving sticks at each other. We have only produced approximately half of the machine guns we shall want; even small arms ammunition is a problem. Last summer, we had a stock of some 400 million rounds in the bank. We are down to less than 10 million now! And to maintain this we have to restrict the mens' firing in training! How are they supposed to do battle if we cannot teach them to shoot properly!"

My head is reeling. "It is a grievous state of affairs indeed, Sir. If I may, Your Majesty, what does this have to do with me? Or with the body I was sent to examine at the Royal Arsenal?" I realise that this could be taken for insolence immediately, but neither man seems in the slightest way annoyed. In fact, Lord Kitchener looks as if he appreciates a direct approach. I imagine there are never enough hours in his day for all that he must do, and I expect that he does not waste them willingly.

"We wanted you to know a little more of the general situation before we explained affairs at Woolwich," explains the King. "So that you might see just how crucial your intervention may be. If anything were to damage the balance of this already strained operation, we could lose the war. And Woolwich is the most vital site in respect of these problems."

My blank expression must be what swiftly prompts Lord Kitchener to expand upon this point. "This was not the first death to occur in the environs of the Royal Arsenal in the past week," he says. To the point.

The King nods. "The first was recorded as accidental, but now, given another death so quickly afterwards, and given that both have a rather strange aspect, we are not so sure."

"The fact that this second incident, too, could be an instance of foul play," explains Kitchener, "that is disturbing to say the least."

"Do you think perhaps that the two deaths are connected?" I ask.

"I am not sure that we quite know what to think at this stage," says Kitchener. "We don't want to jump the gun, so to speak, but given what we have just told you, we cannot be too careful where the Royal Arsenal is concerned at present."

"You wish me to investigate?"

The King nods firmly. "Yes, precisely. Firstly we want to know whether these two men were murdered, and then whether or not there is anything in common between the two cases. Lord K will make the necessary arrangements to ensure that you and your young friend, what is his name?"

"Crabtree, Your Majesty."

"Of course. He will make sure that you and Crabtree shall have unrestricted access at the site. Unless you would care to engage anyone else?"

"No, Your Majesty, I should be quite happy with him. I know that he can come across as a bumbling idiot at times, but he knows how I like to work and he has proved himself inordinately useful since I have known him."

Lord Kitchener seems satisfied. "Then you shall have him as long as you wish, along with any more men that you should have need of. You have only to ask, do you understand? But keep the circle as tight as possible, you are being trusted with the country's most sensitive information."

"Yes, Sir. Thank you, Sir. Crabtree will be quite enough for now." Thank you. It sounds ridiculous, but it is of course, polite.

"We will have Superintendent Gibbs at the arsenal informed that he is to assist you properly," says the King. "Perhaps you ought to get a few hours of sleep before you begin. You look rather... ragged. I am aware of your recent exertions. I trust all ended well?"

"Well enough, Your Majesty," I confirm. "For now at least."

"It did amuse me to think of the necessity of you riding in an aeroplane."

"Beastly things, Your Majesty," is all I can say in response.

He nods in agreement. "I would not be taken up in one, that is for certain."

"And where is this Crabtree?" A conversational diversion appears to be the last thing that the Secretary of State for War is prepared to stand about further in the cold for.

"Ah, I believe he is dribbling on the upholstery in the rear compartment of my motor car at present," says the King with a glint in his eye.

I cringe. "My apologies, Your Majesty, I shall move him immediately."

The King smiles and waves his hand. "You may keep the vehicle and Gaylor for the duration of your enquiries. I would rather that both are put to some war use if it is to keep drinking petrol that the army might have. He quite likes you, you know." This is surprising indeed, for I had taken Gaylor for a mute. Perhaps he wrote his sentiments down.

Kitchener sighs. "Of course, it would be a great relief to us if you were to find that these two deaths were most unfortunate and separate accidents, or put down to natural causes. But I would have someone I trust confirm this to me. Not least because, and this is extremely secret, Lieutenant, because the King and I are due to make a surprise visit Woolwich next week."

"It always gets out to some extent, of course," says His Majesty, "such is the way of these things, but officially it is to be sprung upon them."

I feel like I have been kicked in the chest. "Perhaps it might be pertinent to postpone your visit for the time being? Just to be on the safe side?" I stammer.

"Absolutely not." The King is as firm as I have ever heard him. "I am quite set on this point. The visit will go ahead."

Lord Kitchener seemingly agrees. Or has at least conceded defeat in the matter at some point previously. "His Majesty feels very strongly about doing his bit. He is quite adamant that we shall be present as planned."

The King sighs. "I can do little of physical use in this war. However, I am to embark on quite the tour of factories and shipyards, this being one of the first. I only hope that by shaking hands with the workers and meeting the manufacturers that I can help motivate them to give it their all, so to speak; show them how much their work is valued and how critical their part in the war is. I must start promoting unity for our cause and showing the people that victory in this cause will not come easily. I will not move on this point. If something is afoot, Lieutenant Stanley, you have a week to identify the perpetrators and to make sure that nothing untoward will happen when Lord K and I arrive in Woolwich. The fact that we plan to make this visit together, as a show of force, that should tell you something about how highly we value the contribution and the moral of those at the Royal Arsenal. That is my sad part in this war. I am putting my faith in you, my boy. Your part is to ensure that when I arrive on Wednesday next, that we are safe."

"Yes, Your Majesty. I will not let you down." Said with a lot more conviction than I feel at present, but when your Sovereign asks you to do something, it is the only line to take. A pantomime it is indeed. But who is cast as the villain?

IV.

I had never quite appreciated just how many people made their living at the Royal Arsenal. When Crabtree and I step out of the King's motor car into a seething swarm of workers in front of the Beresford Gate, the junction that was absolutely deserted just a few hours previously is unrecognisable. Tram after tram rolls into view, disgorging bustling, chattering men and plenty of women wrapped up against the brisk morning chill.

I have not bothered going back to sleep. I have been reading. The Borough of Woolwich, on the south bank of the Thames, lies a little under ten miles from the middle of London. It had a dockyard early in the sixteenth century, when the site had revolved around a Tudor mansion, a gun wharf and a large rabbit warren that bred meat for royal dinner tables. In the intervening four hundred years, the business of military destruction has gradually consumed the entire area. Depots were followed by foundries, which were joined by facilities making gunpowder and storehouses for keeping their weapons. By the latter part of the eighteenth century it was the home of the Royal Artillery, with barracks and workshops. Where Henry VIII would have seen greenery, bunnies and a pretty house as he sailed past on his way down river to his palace Greenwich, now the site is a sprawl of factories, test ranges, woodcutting shops, wheelwrights facilities, inspection sheds, "danger areas," warehouses, research laboratories, yards for storing guns, wharfs, piers, docks, houses, churches and offices that cover more than 1,300 acres.

The people that work here call the place, *'The Shop,'* and as they flood into the arsenal, Crabtree and I watch as each of them produce what looks to be some sort of pass at the gate from pockets and handbags. Of course we have no such thing, and so we give our names to an official at the entrance. He beckons with a finger to a young officer standing nearby. "The blokes you are waiting for," he says brusquely, by way of explanation. The officer is his opposite, smiling and amiable. "Lieutenant Stanley? Excellent. And this must be Private Crabtree? Very good."

He walks off and gestures for us to follow. "We've not far to go, just across here."

He guides us less than a hundred feet along a worn cobbled path to a ramshackle building nestled against the outer wall of the arsenal. At first it looks as if it lacks an entrance, but as we approach I can see that there is a wide arch filled with an old wooden door, painted green. It is so low that it is almost subterranean.

Dr. Scully is waiting for us just inside the arsenal's mortuary. It is tiny, and presumably little used, otherwise they would surely give him a better facility. Ageing white tiles cover the walls, lined with a dusting of black mould and on one of two white ceramic tables, stained, with a low dip in the middle, is Fred George's body. There is barely space for the three of us to stand. There is a dark wooden cupboard and a tiny sink, awash with blood up against the opposite wall. There is a damp chill in the air, along with the smell of mildew. The doctor is flushed and drying his hands on a blood stained apron. He gestures to the state of himself and the filthy mess on the floor all about him, bowls full of various entrails on the second table, by way of an explanation as to why he is not going to shake hands. Then he pulls back a bloodstained white sheet so that Fred George is visible from the neck up. The parallel little puncture wounds on his neck look blackish-purple, in contrast to the stark white of the corpse. "Two stab wounds, very clean, very deep and done at the same time. A very decisive wound. He would have died quickly. Though there was little external damage visible on discovery, an artery was pierced and he suffered massive bleeding."

I recall the rain the night before. That must account for the lack of blood at the scene. "I find it hard to believe that he would have stood still and allowed himself to be set upon," I muse.

"Ah." The doctor pulls the sheet away some more and turns the corpse slightly. "But he must have been set upon very swiftly. There is quite a bruise on his shoulder blade, see? As if we were struck from behind. And there is this." Carefully he reaches out to George's mouth and parts the mans lips with both hands. One of his front teeth has been shattered. It looks like a recent injury.

Crabtree is scribbling in his notebook. "We'll have to double check with Bailey, to make sure his tooth weren't damaged before."

I have taken up a stance leaning against a narrow, dark cupboard, my arms crossed and my hand rubbing at my face tiredly. "So, presuming that his tooth was indeed knocked out last night. In the space of a few moments, some unknown assailant has set upon a healthy, fit man, attacked him so violently that they have smashed his mouth, rammed a sharp object into his neck and he has dropped down dead on the floor. His clothes showed no sign that he had been in a fight, least of all rolling about on the floor."

My erstwhile companion yawns. "If this was a chance attack, then it's bonkers. Someone jumps upon a stranger on a deserted road and happens to be armed with… with what?"

"But if not," I nod, "then, presuming that they killer had motive to kill George, someone would have been lying in wait, knowing that they always had a lock in on Tuesday, and that he'd be hanging around for some time. If it was planned, I think the only person in the frame is Bailey at this stage. In which case, why would he run back for help at all?"

"To make himself look innocent?" Suggests Scully.

"We are to see him later," I say. "I think we shall ask Stanley Bailey to show us his knuckles, his arms. Whoever attacked George did so with enough force to break teeth, after all. I should think the culprit bears some evidence of this."

"So, if we think it probably weren't Bailey, we need to start looking at who he pissed off enough for them to want to bump him off?" Crabtree writes this thought down.

Dr. Scully is looking wistfully at the marks on Fred George's neck and rubbing the side of his nose with a finger. "I cannot account for all kinds of machinery and instruments that they must have inside the walls of the arsenal, things that might have made that mark on his neck, of course. But…"

He stops and I prod him. "Yes, doctor?"

"Well, it is just that, I wonder if it would be appropriate to look outside the box."

We stare at him blankly and he clears his throat. He is clearly embarrassed. "When I am not here I spend my time studying folklore; there are a handful of us in our little group. Folkologists, we call ourselves. Culturally all over the world people have sought for centuries to account for that which they cannot explain. This injury strikes me as perhaps a worthy candidate for one that might require a less traditional method of research."

"Such as?" I ask warily, looking at the parallel puncture marks on Fred George's neck I can see immediately where this might be going.

"Well, the marks, the force required, the way in which the culprit spirited himself away."

I hardly think in the guise of a bat, though. Bram Stoker's Dracula terrified me as a child, but I certainly don't believe that any of the book's contents represent fact. "Are we perhaps looking at an invasion of vampires?" I ask sardonically, unable to mask my disdain for such a suggestion. "Surely the rain washed away the blood from the scene? Was he bone dry inside?"

He straightens up defensively on the other side of the corpse. "No, well, no of course not. I mean, well, one ought to rule nothing out until one has solved the problem at hand."

Wide-eyed, Crabtree, unused to being the sensible one in the room, changes the subject swiftly. "What can you tell us about this first man, the one that met his end in front of a tram last week?"

"It happened last Friday evening, I can tell you that," says the doctor, apparently relieved to leave his nonsensical suggestion behind. "His name was Richard Carrick. I have made an exact copy of my findings for you to take away. Nothing seems out of place. All of the injuries that he bore were consistent with being struck by a tram. There was extensive bruising, two broken ribs. He was most unlucky, in fact. The tram was actually coming to a halt at the stop. If not for the fact that his head took the brunt of it and he suffered a fracture of the skull, he probably would have survived. It really wasn't going very fast."

"I am right in saying that he was also a worker here? That is what I have been told?"

"Well he worked here, yes. But he certainly wasn't the same sort of worker as Mr. George here. He was wearing smart clothes, tailored, and he had well kept hands and nails. I remember that. Of course the Superintendent will be able to furnish you with much better information, but I can always be reached if you think I can assist you." He hands me a card and a buff coloured folder which presumably contains the report that he has alluded to. I thank him for his thoroughness, which will make our lives just that bit easier in assessing the death of this doctor.

Outside Crabtree whistles. "Bit of a nutter, ain't he? Going on about bleedin' vampires?"

I'm not going to even entertain such a notion. "What has two identical points, Crabtree? And is sharp enough to puncture a man's carotid artery?"

"Big prong of some sort?"

"Yes. And I don't know of any man that carries one of those as a force of habit. And surely no elderly woman could have found the strength to puncture so solid a part of the anatomy as the neck to the extent required with such a thing? If hunched over she wouldn't be tall enough to straighten up and get such force behind the blow, though she remains our best lead at the moment with regard to her witnessing the attack.

Our guide leads us across the street to a grand building. It stands taller than anything else nearby: five storeys of brick with stone decoration on each corner and an elaborate stone facade that makes up the entrance in the middle; complete with carvings and coats of arms. There are flashes of grandeur within too; such as glazed green tiles on the wall, a coffered

ceiling with ornate marble columns. The staircase is finely crafted and adorned with decorative ironwork.
"You have come from the mortuary, I believe?" Says the Superintendent as we are shown into his office. I nod, shake his hand, and introduce myself as a representative of the War Office. "And what was the verdict?" He is a gruff man, gingery hairs as fine as a baby's are all that covers his otherwise bald, freckled scalp. He has more hair in his moustache, which is full and almost completely covers his mouth. His pale complexion is blotched with scarlet patches.
"Very much foul play, I am afraid." I explain the concept of the prong, or whatever it was.
He sighs dramatically, as though he was hoping that I was about to lift a great weight from his shoulders.
"Dr. Scully told us that the first man, the one that died last week, was named Richard Carrick?"
"Yes that's right." The man in charge of the Royal Gun and Carriage Factories sits down and gestures for us to do the same on the other side of the desk.
"I'd like to ask you some questions, if that is all right?" Crabtree is ready, pencil poised above notebook. Gibbs eyes him suspiciously. "Is it necessary for this fellow to be present?"
I nod firmly. "It is, Sir, yes. Private Crabtree has assisted me in a number of sensitive matters and is wholly trustworthy." I pray that the lump isn't about to do anything new to embarrass me in the immediate future.
The Superintendent and Crabtree stare at each other for a moment longer than is comfortable, the latter with a deliberately smug and annoying grin on his round face. Gibbs, defeated, breaks first and turns to face me.
"Richard Carrick was an eminent chemist. Manchester University," he says. "Although he excelled at other branches of science and research too. He volunteered his services free of charge by way of contributing to the war effort. He was lame and could not join the army, you see. He wanted to be of use. He had his own

laboratory here, and he reported to a higher authority than I."

"May I ask if you have any notion about what he was working on?"

"Well, it's hard to say. You see eminent does not in fact quite cover it. Carrick was an extremely odd fish, a complete loner, but quite brilliant. He worked inordinately long hours. So much so that we were looking at accommodating him inside the gates, but he rarely spoke to anybody."

"I suppose you left him to his own devices then? A man that clever, working for free."

"Well yes, of course. One doesn't begin annoying such a man by assigning him tasks that would be demeaning by his standards. But, I understood his work to be connected to chemical compounds. I had no interactions with him personally; unless he invented something he thought might be useful in my field. Crabtree is frantically scribbling all of this down. I expect to see steam coming from the end of his pencil at any moment. The Superintendent continues. "He had an assistant; someone he brought down from the university. I think he returned to the north immediately, but if you think it pertinent I can have someone motor up and fetch him, so that he may brief you as to the exact particulars of their projects."

"Perhaps that is not quite necessary at present, but I shall bear it in mind." I hated chemistry at school. If there is any way I can avoid being bored to distraction by someone who finds joy in fiddling with a Bunsen burner or a test tube, I will take it. "Was his work in any way connected with that which was carried out by Fred George, the man who died last night?" I ask.

"No. Not in the slightest. George was a skilled worker, but his job was purely mechanical. He was a foreman in A.25, it's a bullet factory. He had no hand in anything to do with research; nothing that would remotely overlap with the work being carried out by Dr. Carrick."

"It seems quite unlikely then that they should have been acquainted with one another?"

"Quite. I cannot think how, though it is not impossible of course. Have you reason to believe that they knew each other?"

"None at all. At present, the only thing that the two men have in common is that they are both dead. Dr. Scully tells us that Carrick fell in front of a tram, and that unfortunately it was going just fast enough to kill him?"

"Yes. A travesty. Scully thinks that if he had not gone head first he would not necessarily have suffered fatal injuries."

"Yes. He told us as much. Were there any witnesses?"

He clears his throat. "Hundreds. That was the problem. I take it you have seen how crowded it gets outside the gates?"

"Yes. So his death was purely accidental?"

"Well, I believe so. At least I did, completely, until this other man died and now you are sent here. Everyone who said they saw him fall claimed that he simply stumbled out into the path of the tram of his own accord."

"Was he walking at the time?"

"I beg your pardon?"

"Was he on his way somewhere at the time, was he moving when he tripped?"

"Well, no, I shouldn't think so. The impression I got was that he was going to board the tram and he was already at the stop. I should think he was stationary."

"And yet he stumbled?"

"Obviously."

"I should think then, that that would have required some secondary contact, jostling to get a better position at the tram stop, perhaps? I don't wish to jump to conclusions, but the fact remains that had he merely been standing still, and remained untouched, that it is highly unlikely he would have just elaborately fallen in front of a slowing tram. Is there any chance that he jumped?" The Superintendent has gone quiet. I prompt him. "Sir?"

"Well, I just thought, I thought absolutely everyone else was adamant that he fell over, and it was only one child that said anything different at all."

"Would you care to explain?"

"There is rather a sinister, but very stupid whisper doing the rounds within the arsenal gates. A boy, standing with his father just near the Beresford Gate. He is only small, we discounted what he said, because of his youth and because it did not fit with proper witness accounts, but he was absolutely certain that he had seen a woman behind Professor Carrick just before he fell in front of the tram. I am afraid that I cannot remember the details precisely, but it was absurd. He said that the woman spoke to Dr Carrick and that then he lurched forward."

Crabtree is now scribbling with a puzzled expression. "Do you know who this boy was?" I ask.

"Oh yes, I have a note of it. His father works here on our railway. He drives one of our engines about the site. We have our own railway, did you know? The densest railway Britain has ever, or will ever likely have."

I nod. "I have read of it. I'd like it very much if you could arrange for me to speak with him?"

The Superintendent calls out and a secretary of some kind breezes into the doorway; fresh faced with a great pile of dirty blond curls attempting to escape a careless bun at the back of her head. They are almost as distracting as her enormous bosom, which enters the room before the rest of her. I can see that Crabtree is immediately smitten by the fact that his jaw is slack and his pencil is suddenly limp in his hand. Gibbs mutters some instructions at her and watches intently, longingly, as she flounces out again.

Then he appears to exit his stupor as swiftly as he entered it. "I am sure you sensed that there is some friction between the army and the Metropolitan Police when it comes to who has jurisdiction in these parts. We had a complaint this morning about your intervention."

"Surprised it took the miserable gits that long to have a whinge," Crabtree quips, then looks mortified at having voiced this sentiment out loud and gazes straight down at his pad again.

The Superintendent does not seem bothered at all by his interruption or by the idea of police frustrations. "They have now been told under no uncertain terms that they are not to get in your way. Also that if you are to summon them to aid you, they are to render all possible assistance. You should have no trouble."

"I should think that went down well."

He shrugs. "The vagueness of the Defence of the Realm Act is perfect for situations such as this. I quite enjoyed it when Scotland Yard demanded to know on whose outrageous authority he was to tell his men that they were to subordinate to you. I told him that he might direct his complaints straight to Buckingham Palace and he blustered a great deal in getting off of the telephone."

His seemingly worldly assistant returns and he has a brief conversation with her chest, for it appears that he is unable to draw his eyes any higher. "Mr Noakes says he can bring the boy to the pub on the corner of Beresford Square where the victim was drinking tomorrow morning." She turns and stares straight at me. "I can be there too, if you like." She winks audaciously and prances out. I can feel my face growing red and Crabtree is stifling an attack of the giggles.

I try to ignore the diversion. "Did Mr. Bailey come to work today? I suspect not, after his shock last night. If that is the case, could you furnish me with his address please?"

Gibbs inspects a file in front of him and then speaks as he takes a piece of notepaper and begins to write, referring to papers on his desk. "I will make a note of Mr. George's address too. I was told this morning that they were in fact related by marriage, so you may well find him there, I suppose. I must also furnish you with the relevant documents so that you might move freely through the arsenal. I have been instructed to give you complete liberty, and so you will need these." He opens a drawer in his desk and produces two black cards. Each has a strip of white at the bottom for our names. He signs one and hands me his pen so that I might print my name. Then he does the same for Crabtree.
"These are not the ones that I saw workers providing on our arrival this morning?"
"No, these black ones are rare. They provide the bearer with unrestricted access to the arsenal"
My interest is sparked. "How many black passes are there?"
"Less than half a dozen for senior people. If others require wider access outside their usual jurisdiction, then I would just broaden their access with a temporary pass detailing the relevant buildings. Is this pertinent to the case?"
"Almost certainly not, I am just trying to acquaint myself with how the arsenal operates. So what would a man, or woman, usually have?"
He produces one from a drawer. "They would have a card with his or her name, and a large number stamped on it, on normal brown card. The number would correspond to the building that they have leave to enter to go about their work. All of the buildings have a designation, for instance, Fred George belonged to A. 25. Our security practices are not under investigation?"
"Oh no, not at all, Sir. Nothing untoward has happened within the walls of the arsenal, after all. My apologies, I was just wondering if they cards might have been some

kind of motivation for a killer, if he wanted to gain access to the site."

He opens his drawer again. "Fred George's was on his person. It was handed to me this morning and I destroyed it. And I have Mr Carrick's here." He brandishes it but still looks distrusting of me.

"All I have been instructed to do is to consider whether these two unfortunate deaths were accidental, or natural, or foul play, and to ascertain that there will be no danger to His Majesty or Lord Kitchener when they visit next week. You will understand our need to be thorough, but there is no insinuation that you or your people have done wrong, or that you have been negligent in any way. I have settled concerns such as this for the Home Office, the India Office, the War Office before, that is all."

He seems much relieved and hands us our passes. "I must urge you to treat them with extreme care. We cannot have them fall into the hands of the wrong person. Usually they would have a photograph attached, but we were short of time. I live on site, and there is a telephone in the house in case of emergencies, I have written the number on the back of this. I shall do all I can to help you."

Crabtree is so busy craning his neck to get a look at the Superintendent's assistant that he walks into the doorframe on the way out. "What an offer that was for you, Sir."

"She would eat me alive."

"And that'd be the fun of it, Sir. Cor' what I wouldn't give to have a play with those fun bags. It'd be glorious."

I look at him in disgust at his choice of vocabulary as he steps outside into the cold. "Fun bags? I am speechless."

"You know, Sir..." Crabtree cups both of his hands in a lewd gesture over his chest and jiggles them about.

"I know what they are, you idiot. Stop doing that." He has got rather carried away and is attempting to do a

55

seductive dance and I slap his hands back down by his sides.

After a fruitless trip to the Bailey household on the next street, a frail-looking woman opens the door just a touch at the George residence. She has black hair streaked with steel grey and pulled over her shoulder in a messy plait, and she is wracked with sobs and fiercely clutching a damp handkerchief to her face. "Mrs George?" I ask. She can do little better than a shuddering nod. "Is your brother here?"
Another nod. Stan Bailey appears at her side and opens the door fully. An elderly woman appears and guides away the widow in the direction of a kitchen at the end of the cramped hallway. Bailey shrugs by way of an explanation.
"Sorry, we don't know what to do with her."
"Is there somewhere we may speak?" He nods and extends his arm towards a doorway beside us. The house is tiny, busting at the seams I would imagine, with five children. Nothing is new and yet everything is neatly placed, immaculately clean and well cared for. Crabtree and I wedge ourselves onto a small settee and Stan Bailey perches on a green armchair opposite, the back draped with a piece of flowery embroidery.
"Stan," I begin. "I must ask you some uncomfortable questions. They may appear insulting but I need you to understand that at this point it is imperative that we are diligent in our work. Else we might miss something important."
"You want to make sure I didn't do it." It is a statement, not a question.
"Yes. Describe your relationship with Fred George for me please?" Crabtree is already scribbling away.
Bailey shrugs dejectedly. "We've been mates for years. I introduced him to me sister. I wouldn't have done that if I didn't think he was a good bloke. I've got no idea how I am going to feed 'er and the kids."

"And you have had no falling out of late? No disagreement?"

"No. None." This with a mournful shake of the head. The dire economic situation he now finds himself in with Fred's demise, married with his obvious grief, makes me think he would be fit for the stage if he had done anything to facilitate it. I can tell by a quick glance from Crabtree and an almost imperceptible shake of the head that he agrees.

"Stan, in what condition were Fred's teeth?"

"What do you mean?"

"Was he missing any?"

"I'm not sure. He had one pulled a couple of years ago, I think. It was giving him jip."

"His front teeth, they were all present?"

"Oh. Yeah. This one was right up the back. Moaned about it for weeks before Anne finally made him have it yanked out."

"Can I ask you to show us your hands please Stan?" He hesitates for a moment, as it must seem like a strange request, then holds his hands out, palms up. I exchange a quick glance with Crabtree. "And could you turn them over please?" He obliges. And now if you could roll up your sleeves as far as possible for us please?" Again, the confused man in front of us does as he is told. Crabtree nods at me. Relieved. There is not a mark on him. Certainly not one that would imply he had smashed his friend's mouth with enough force to break his tooth. "What does your work entail at the arsenal, Stan?"

"Same as Fred. We were both Foremen."

"If you could tell us the number of your building?" I want to have it examined it for any likely murder weapon that may match Fred George's wounds, in the interests of being thorough. "Could you arrange with the Superintendent to have that carried out, please Crabtree?"

Stan now looks utterly perplexed. "A.25. Is that it? Are you satisfied now?"

"Yes. Thank you. I am sorry that we had to do that." He didn't panic at all when I mentioned searching their building.

"It's all right. I think I'd rather you asked everything you could fink of and then still believed I couldn't 'ave done it. Because I didn't."

"I have a few more questions if you don't mind? About Fred now?" He nods tiredly and tries to light up a cigarette, his hands shaking. Crabtree has to strike the match for him. "Can you think of anyone with cause, or who might have believed that they had cause to hurt him?"

Stan shakes his head firmly and blows out smoke. "I've been up all night, trying to think of someone."

Crabtree clears his throat. "It's just that it don't really make sense mate, if this was a maniac that was hanging about waiting to jump on a stranger, why would he be waiting there? There was nobody around. He wasn't robbed. It makes it more likely that someone he knew did it."

"I know, but I just can't think of a single person who'd want to hurt him."

"Is there a chance that he might have been involved in something that you were not aware of?"

"I just can't see it. Me and 'im are together all day at work, we go for a drink after sometimes, but then if he ain't with me, he's with my sister and the kids. There ain't the time." I nod. At the door I press my card into Stan Bailey's hand and insist that he has all bills regarding the funeral of his brother in law and a headstone sent to me at the War Office.

"That was generous of you, Sir," Crabtree says on the way out.

"Not really," I say, as we make our way to the kerb where Gaylor is waiting for us with the door to the motor open. "I will give the bills to my mother and my sister. Their philanthropy knows no bounds and they will get them past my father will well-practised and skulduggerous ease."

V.

I dispense with Crabtree for the evening. There is nothing more we can do until we interview the Noakes child tomorrow and we are both badly in want of a decent sleep. Once almost home though, I realise that I am beyond tired now; my mind awash with disappearing old women and bizarre deaths. With the terrifyingly high stakes involved in being able to tell His Majesty that he will be safe on his visit next week. I turn away from the house and go in search of a stiff drink.

A private room in a club is far more a home of gossip than any lady's parlour. Men are terrible for it, and more so as they progress in years. Bunny and I have been joined by a selection of our society's members at his club after dinner and we have been exchanging the latest war gossip. I knew Simon Goffin many years ago at prep school. We call him Goff and when I ran into the tall, sandy haired, bespectacled fellow on the retreat it was the first time I had seen him since both of us were annoying, spoilt, lazy little boys at The Dragon in Oxford. His demeanour hasn't much changed in terms of his lack of energy, though thankfully he is without the monocle that he insisted on wearing in those days. He was wounded in the eye on the Marne and currently sports a patch, which gives him the air of a very slovenly, ineffectual pirate. The last of our number is an acquaintance of Bunny's a few years older than the rest of us, rotund with a florid complexion and thinning, middle brown hair. Horatio Nelson Keyes was, as one can tell by his name, born for a life in the Royal Navy. He is in intelligence as am I, but at the Admiralty. We have recently had cause to join forces, so that I have got to know him quite well. He is overly serious, but a good man in a tight spot, and I like him.

Bunny is reclining in his wingback chair so deeply that he is almost lying down. "Germany are under the cosh. Haven't you heard?" He blows cigarette smoke at the ceiling languidly. "Politically and economically they are about to collapse. They are close to starvation and on the verge of revolution."
Keyes snorts disdainfully. "Yes and I am sure that if you read the nonsensical drivel in their newspapers, you would find that that they are saying the same about us; that the price of bread is so high that calamitous, open rebellion is about to break out on the streets of Eastbourne."
"I don't fancy being in Berlin when the inevitable does happen and we show them what's what," says Goff. "I was there last spring, before everything went to pieces and the German socialist is getting far too big for his boots; too brash. He shows no fear, nor does he temper any of his outspoken opinions. This would not be so if their party did not have some measure of strength behind it, and should the old order crumble…"
Goff stops talking as a crumpled up ball of paper hits him square in the eye at my own hand. "Booooooo!" Bunny says gustily, as if Goff were a pantomime villain. He has encroached upon a condemned topic of conversation. Anything that might incite boredom is expressly not allowed within the sanctuary of the Society of Socrates and naturally all forms of socialism and its workings are utmost in this category. Discussing anything connected to Opera (that one was Bunny's addition) is also outlawed, as is anything that one has seen or heard about in the Daily Mail or indeed any of Lord Northcliffe's horrid publications. That was my contribution to the list. I have no remorse about making Goff's one good eye water, as I received much the same punishment from him last week for having the

cheek to mention and sympathise with the case for India's self-governance when Europe is at peace again; in recognition of her contribution to the Empire's war effort.

Keyes has already resumed trying to put the balance of the Empire's survival in the hands of the Navy, a favourite past-time of his. "I've said it from the beginning. Blockading the buggers is vital; starve the Hun into submission. Was it not one of the greatest of all Englishmen, Nelson no less, that said desperate affairs require equally desperate measures?"

I cannot help but make fun of him. "As desperate as the rumours doing the rounds of Whitehall? That we are to land on the coast at Zeebrugge and sweep the Germans away? Or better still that Fisher wants to claim the Baltic? If your beloved Nelson saw the decrepit fool at the head of his Royal Navy, he would rise from his elaborate grave in protest."

Keyes nods. Bunny laughs and anyone in earshot cringes. "Well my uncle..." (A Cabinet member no less, so well placed to hear the best gossip.) "My uncle says that at one point Lloyd George seriously asked someone if it would be possible to pick up the entire British Expeditionary Force and drop it somewhere new!"

There is raucous laughter at such a notion. "Pray, where would the Welsh gnome have them put? "Asks Goff drily.

"I bet it was the Austrians, he would have gone for the Austrians." This from Keyes. "Of course this is all based on the theory that they hate each other as much as they hate any common enemy, and assuming that the various ethnic factions under their yoke would be so busy squabbling that we could overrun them. But what does he think the Hun would do if he caught wind that we were marching from the Adriatic with Italy's cooperation, or moving on their positions through Salonika with the help of the Greeks? Because both of these possibilities, I would think, would require a nation declaring war upon Germany. Which I would think that the Hun would notice. Now would he idly stand by or reinforce his fractious ally before we were remotely within range of him?"

"We are desperate indeed, if that is the speculation that supposedly the greatest minds in the Empire are reduced to," I mutter.

"But of course," Goff chimes in, "things would not be so desperate if America should pull her finger out and do what is right!" He slaps the palm of his hand down on a side table to add gravity to his point. This is usually the manner in which he will clarify some opinion.

"Oh god!" Exclaims Bunny, "he is off again!" Goff is forever chastising the Americans for dodging the war. This topic is permitted because it is highly amusing to watch Goff turn bright red and foam at the mouth.

"Ah but Bunny, my dear, blasphemous fellow," I say. "Everything has changed with this threat the Germans have now made against all merchant shipping," Of course I am speaking about the Kaiser's unsavoury instruction to his submariners, which now threatens those who ply the seas with being sunk by a torpedo if they sail the waters about Britain. One always has to make things a little clearer for Bunny. "Goff is right is he not?" I continue. "Surely America cannot stay out of it now? It is only a matter of time before one of the neutral ships that is sunk is full of their own. I have to say I find it quite incredulous that a nation that is usually so quick to exclaim their opinions loudly and forcefully to all in earshot, should they want to hear them or not, should remain completely silent on this matter."

"Well what is it that they *have* said?' Goff is incredulous. "That if her ships were sunk then it would be an indefensible act against their rights as a neutral power? Surely that points to the idea that as and when it happens, which of course we all know is inevitable, they will want to come on board, so to speak?"

"The Hun certainly are increasingly bold," Keyes agrees. "They think that this mere announcement will have us all cowering from their submarines and that they will be celebrating victory as a mere formality in a few weeks' time. Do they not realise that even if this diabolical course does in fact work, it would take some time to strangle us in this manner!"

Bunny snorts. "More importantly, do they not realise how this makes them look to the world? Especially as Germany have as good as said that when they sink something flying the stars and stripes it will be America's own fault for not condemning Britain's use of neutral flags to evade her U-Boat menace? I read that in a proper paper," he adds proudly. "Not Northcliffe."

"Yes, you will have got it from the *Ladies' Field*," I joke. "But I am not sure, Bunny," I say. "I think you underestimate just how badly Wilson wants to keep them out of this mess. There is also a striking difference between the Yankees one meets over here and the vast, ignorant majority across the Atlantic who either have no interest in, or no knowledge of what is transpiring in Europe. They are like ostriches. But it is certainly true to say that Germany cannot help but harm her interests as far as all neutrals are concerned with such intolerable behaviour. It is remarkably offensive, even when you do consider that the Royal Navy have blockaded her ports."

"I read one glorious statement in the press," Goff tells us. "It said that Germany "*presents a strange psychological tragedy of over-excitement*" and that when inevitably their hopes are dashed and this campaign against merchant shipping does not crush us into submission, that the resulting melancholy will lose them the war." He gulps down more whiskey and then points knowingly at nobody in particular whilst suppressing a belch. "There is something in that, I think."

"I saw," Bunny is laughing ridiculously as he replies. "I saw a hilarious image in the pictorials this week. Some crew of some navy boat or another all wearing their life preservers with a chalked up sign in front of them that said *"still waiting."* What do you think of that? A wonderful example of British pluck I say. As if to say, *come and get us*, to the beastly Hun."

"They make a good point," I say. "When was the last time we heard reports of anything being sunk? Clearly their ploy to annihilate any craft on the seas about Britannia has yet to get off the mark!"

"Ha!" Goff exclaims a little too loudly. "Like you at prep school, Will! The starter gun went, everyone was off and you, fat as you were, you were still trying to get away!" He sees the scowl upon my face and stops laughing. He mumbles whilst looking at the floor. "You look spiffing now of course old man."

Bunny is still chuckling away like a rabid hyena. "I say Stanley, were you very grotesque?"

"I was somewhat rotund," I say huffily.

Goff has moved on. "Perhaps the Hun is inconsequential in this war? Did you think of that? Perhaps matters won't be decided by him? Perhaps everything that we are discussing will make no difference to the outcome of it at all!"

"Oh Christ!" Says Bunny. There is that laugh again. "Can we add Dardanelles and the Turks to the unsavoury subject list? Will, please! Vote with me? The rules say two of us must agree? Quick, let's get it on the list before he begins!"

Suddenly everyone is talking on top of one another. East versus west. The country is irrevocably divided between those who believe that the war can only be decided on the Western Front, and those that agree at least partially with the madness of Lloyd George. They are convinced to varying degrees, and with various solutions, that war in the west is at a standstill and that we ought to consider opportunities elsewhere, invariably eastward, to force it to a conclusion. Bunny is disinterested, and therefore abstinent; Keyes (when he not lauding the role of his Navy) and I are firmly of the belief that nothing conclusive will happen away from the western theatre but Goff is adamant that this is not the case.

"Well, I say..." he has to begin his statement two or three times to be heard. "I said, I SAY." He pauses for a moment to make sure that he has our attention. "Thank you, gentlemen." Goff steels himself with a drink and waves his empty glass in the air. "I say, that there is nothing whatsoever occurring in the West. The East presents a real prospect of turning the tide now that we have become completely tied down in France and Belgium."

"You are a fool," I tell him. Not least because my intelligence role means that I am aware that as we speak, Sir John French's force is hours away from undertaking his first wholly offensive effort of this war in an attempt to break the German Army in France; thereby reigniting the war on the Western Front. Keyes supports my statement, probably because he is privy to some of the information that I possess too, although of course we will not discuss it. "We have neither the men," he says, "nor the resources between us, Britain and France that is, to engage a second enemy on a second front to the necessary degree so as to be decisive."

Goff is beside himself. "What does Aubrey have to say?" Suddenly he turns to face me. "He is a ridiculously clever man. One does not get offered the throne of Albania multiple times if one is an imbecile. Surely he sees sense?"

Goff is referring to the Earl of Carnarvon's half-brother, Aubrey Herbert, whom my brother fagged for at Eton at some stage; who indeed could have been the King of

Albania if he had been stupid enough to accept the crown and incite probable hostilities of some description by accepting such a hilarious offer. Nobody should be king of anything when one of their middle names is Nigel. Half blind and having never soldiered a day in his life, he procured a uniform and slipped apparently unnoticed into a battalion of the Irish Guards to get to France last August as an intelligence officer. Wounded on the Retreat, he subsequently sailed East and is currently with the Arab Bureau in Egypt.

"Well!" Goff presses. "Have you heard from him man?"

"Yes," I yawn nonchalantly. "He said that the entire peerage and half the House of Commons seem to be littering Cairo at present." I pause to drink. "His wife has joined him and he is quite glad, but furious at how frivolous the place is; society carrying on as if there were not a war at all." I quieten my voice. "Understand that this is not official knowledge, simply his opinion… I think Aubrey is not against *any* kind of action in the east at all; but he thinks that attacking the Dardanelles is ludicrous, and he is certainly not alone."

"Ah so he is against the *Dardanelles*, not against pursuing a different course to victory in the East?" Goff gloats.

I sigh. "Nobody is going to start a new war anywhere, in terms of land forces, I would wager. Not in any large numbers anyway." It certainly didn't sound like it when I was in conversation with the two most well-placed men in the land just a short while ago. I came away from that encounter wondering how we were managing to function as a nation at war at all, never mind dreaming that we may be in a position to consider expanding our endeavours. What would we arm this new front with, water pistols? Schoolboys bearing slingshots? All I say is: "We will all be sick of the sight of the France years from now and it still wont be over. That is if we aren't all dead or maimed." I drink disconsolately.

"What would you know of it, Stanley?" Demands Goff. "You've not been within a hundred miles of the front in weeks. What would you know about anything? How do you get away with it? You seem fighting fit to me!"
I simply raise my glass in his direction. I can see on his face that his question was delivered half in jest and half in all seriousness, but I will not say a thing and he knows it.

Keyes has been swilling his whiskey around, staring at it and contemplating his reintroduction to the conversation. "Hang the Dardanelles. It is in the west that this ghastly war will be decided. Or in the waters about it. The German buggers are lurking like poisonous serpents in the Irish and North seas, threatening to torpedo every Tom, Dick and Harry approaching our fair isle. Did you know that Nelson regarded submarines as *sneak dodges down below*. Bulgarious, he called them. I agree wholeheartedly. It is a coward's method of warfare born out of the Hun navy's inferiority to our own. We shall send every single one of their cursed U-Boats to the bottom; hook, line and sinker."

I cannot help but snigger.

"You think the destruction of the British Empire is funny, Will?: He blazes. "The Admiral would turn in his grave."
"Not at all," I assure him, for he is a pompous and quite angry drunk, "but I was just wondering if you cared to cram any more tricolons into one tirade?"

"I'll conserve my favourite until we march into Berlin," Keyes snaps. Then, his rage seemingly subsiding, he raises his glass with mock solemnity. "Veni, Vidi, Vici."
The table collapses into fits of laughter. Except for Bunny; the singular individual amongst us who appears to have remained stubbornly impervious to any semblance of the classical education that he received, and likely has no comprehension of what a tricolon is. He is never bitter about it, but he does take on a quite amusing, doleful look until someone brings him up to

speed. "*I came, I saw, I conquered*," I tell him. Then: "Latin," I clarify when he still looks nonplussed. although it mortifies me that he might not have known that.

He grins broadly. "I'll drink to that!" Good old Bunny. He'll drink to anything. In the background, Keyes is once again pontificating about the virtues of Lord Nelson to a bleary (one) eyed Goff.

I attempt to rescue him. "Not everything that your hero said resonates still, Keyes. Don't forget that Nelson also said that we should hate every Frenchman as we hate the Devil," I add. "If he could see us now, eh?"

"Ah," says Keyes. "But in the same breath he also said that you must consider every man your enemy who speaks ill of your King, and that sentiment will never grow old."

"To Nelson!" Roars Bunny, who will probably amble through life not knowing that the hero of whom we speak and the one armed chap atop a column in Trafalgar Square are one and the same.

"To Lord Nelson!" We all holler.

"And to His Majesty The King!" Adds Goff, ever the most ardent patriot I have known. The rest of our coterie join this last toast. But not I, for the mention of His Majesty is instantly sobering to me, having stood in his presence but a few hours previously and seen the worry etched upon his narrow face. Not only that, but mortifying is his determination to visit Woolwich next week, having largely placed his safety at the mercy of my own ability to untangle the mysterious happenings at the Royal Arsenal. That is apt to suck the fun out of anyone's evening. Keyes notices my silence almost immediately. He leans across and speaks in a low voice.

"Trouble, again?" I simply nod.

"Well if you require naval assistance, you have only to ask." I touch my glass to his as a show of thanks and sink the contents of it in one. It is time that I called it a night.

Wednesday, 10th March 1915

VI.

My first thought is thunder. There is a low rumbling. But then it doesn't stop. And then an odd rhythm becomes definable. Rather than a natural roll that ebbs away, there is a constant, irregular staccato pounding. I open my eyes, thinking of shells, but as my senses return to me one by one I realise that I am lying in my bed, and that the thumping in my head is someone at my bedroom door.

My mother does not wait for me to invite her in. She bustles across to the end of my bed and perches on it. "Will, I have heard something." My head is too foggy with sleep to discern what she is talking about. I stare at her blankly. "I heard something that I shouldn't have, about the front, about things that are happening at the front," she continues.

I sigh. "Oh mother, you shouldn't be party to such gossip. And whoever started it should not be discussing things of military importance, if they truly do know anything."

"I know." She fiddles with her sleeve for a few moments. "Will John be in it? It's happening now, isn't it?"

"I honestly don't know," I lie. "And even if I did I should be breaking all manner of rules if I were to talk about it." I feel cruel and so I try and add something to put her at ease. "But if something were to happen, then it has been well thought out. Well planned."

"They will still be shooting at each other. I worry about him so, your brother."

I clasp her hand. "I know you do, Mother. But he is a good officer. Everyone says good things about him. I have to believe that when he is sent into a fight he will make a good account of himself."

"Do you know that Lady Bamburgh has *five* sons in the army? I have fallen to pieces with only two of you, and you have hardly been at the front at the same time. I thought I should go mad with worry when I received a telegram to tell me that you were wounded."

"A piece of shrapnel in my foot mother, a very small one. As a family we have been extremely fortunate."

"So far."

"Yes," I concede. "So far."

She holds my chin in her hand. "Oh but if I had had you both a few years later, you would be out of all this." She would have been too old by then, but I do not think that pointing that out will do any good, and so I say nothing. We sit still for a few moments. Then she pats my leg.

"Come, your breakfast will be getting cold. And Mrs Mitcham will make you eat it anyhow. You know she will."

Having escaped my mother's worried, maternal clutches, I finally prepare to enter the pub where Fred George spent his last night on earth. *The Pyrotechnists Arms*. Did you ever hear of such a name? It is apparently referred to as *The Pyro* by the locals, one of whom is sitting on the doorstep playing a mandolin and singing rude songs; making the most of the milder weather today. Having climbed over him with some effort, Crabtree and I find our witness waiting for us. The pub is dingy throughout, with small, old-fashioned mullioned windows the only source of grey light other than the dull bulbs overhead. The smell of stale beer is all but overwhelming and adds to the oppressive gloom. I have to strain my eyes to find a large, bulbous man whose clothes are bursting at the seams and an uncomfortable looking child. They are positioned in a dark corner, Mr. Noakes with a glass of bitter in front of him.

I hope we have not inconvenienced you," I breeze as we sit down, knowing that unfortunately we have.

"My manager said I 'ad to come with Frank. I'm missing half a day's work."

"I will reimburse you, if they will not," I say with a smile, trying to break the ice.

He seems satisfied, and the scowl on his face relaxes to more of a concerned grimace, but I am not interested in fostering a friendship with him. I slouch down into my seat. The less officious I look, the less terrified the boy will be. Crabtree takes out a notebook and a pencil and places them on the dirty table that separates us from the child, along with a crumpled paper bag. He prods the latter towards the boy. "Want a toffee?"

After eyeing them somewhat suspiciously, prompting Crabtree to nudge the bag closer to him with the end of his pencil. The small boy grabs two sweets and his freckled cheeks bulge as he shoves them both into his mouth before Crabtree can object. I can't help but smile. He is in his twenties but pulls this childish trick on me and my sweets all of the time. He seems not to mind.

"So tell me Frank," I begin. "What did this lady look like? The one that you say was beside Dr. Carrick?"

"Nobody believed me." His voice is barely a whisper, his hands are in his lap and he stares at them.

"Let's say that I do, and that there was a lady standing behind him when he went in front of the tram. What did she look like?"

"It was a tall lady what done it."

"Done what, Frank?"

For the first time he looks up. "Pushed him."

"Are you sure?"

"I don't know what you mean."

"Perhaps it was an accident and she fell, and somehow caused him to fall too?"

"No. She just talked in his ear. Went right up close to his ear and said something. Then she grabbed hold of him and he fell"

"And you are certain she didn't stumble, or perhaps even push him?"

"No. She stood very still after he fell and just watched him. She weren't falling over and her 'ands was behind 'er back."

I have already decided that to ridicule him will serve no purpose, no matter how silly his account might seem. I want him to be open with me. "Do you recall anything else about what the lady looked like?"

"Not really. She 'ad a shawl over her head."

"Will you do something for me Frank? Close your eyes for me, imagine the scene. Imagine you are watching the accident again, like a cinematograph, and picture her. Can you recall if she was fat or thin?"

He tentatively closes his eyes and thinks for at least half a minute. His father watches him sceptically. "She weren't fat, she was skinny. Scrawny like a witch. Maybe she don't eat nuffin', just drinks potions," he adds at the end with a flourish of imagination. He sounds like Scully with his vampires.

"Was she as tall as the doctor?" This time he screws his eyes shut of his own accord and thinks about it with a curious expression on his face.

"She come to his shoulder, I fink." This is something, as Carrick was said to be well over six feet. In that case she was indeed tall.

"Do you think she was old, or young?" I continue.

"I can't see her face. Her hair is in the way."

"Frank, what colour is her hair?" His eyes are still tightly closed.

He thinks hard about this for a moment. "I fink it's yella."

"Not grey? Or white?"

He opens his eyes. "Nah, it were yella. She weren't old, but she's got a bony nose."

I nod some encouragement. "Did you see where she went? I expect after the accident there was quite the commotion?"

"She vanished. I looked at me dad to see if he'd seen what happened. I said there was a woman what pushed him and he told me to point 'er out. But she were gone. That's what witches do. They can disappear."

His father rolls his eyes at me, as if to apologise. "I didn't see no woman. He's always 'ad a vivid imagination."

I produce a shiny coin from my pocket and hold it out towards him. "You have been most helpful, Frank. Take this and buy yourself some sweets. Mind you share them with your siblings though." The boy looks at his father eagerly, waiting for a nod to signify that he can accept his payment.

I climb into the motor, which Gaylor has parked a few streets away. As I do so he brandishes a small slip of paper for me, a telegram. I have no idea how he has obtained it. What he does when we leave him waiting for us it utterly unknown to me. He is truly an enigma. As Crabtree follows me in stepping into the cab, I notice a small gleam of silver dangling at his neck. "Are you wearing a *crucifix?*" He has no religious inclinations at all, and I am suddenly reminded of Scully and his vampire nonsense. I cannot help but laugh. "Really?" He tucks it back inside his collar and puffs his cheeks pompously. "Doesn't 'urt to be careful. Just in case."

"You are quite ridiculous," I scoff.

"Yes Sir, but I'd rather look ridiculous and know that whatever 'appens, I ain't going to get chomped on by Dracula." I shake my head. Crabtree still checks under his bed at night before he climbs into it, no matter where he is, lest there be something lurking there. Since Scully's suggestion of a vampire he will have been letting the concept of a blood-sucking fiend consume him, to the point where he has slept with a light on, and donned this crucifix, and probably has a vial of mountain ash and a bible stuffed into each of his pockets. I'm sure that Stoker wrote about his vampire holding more sway over those with mental deficiencies, which would explain a lot in Crabtree's case. There is no point debating something this ludicrous with him when he is in a mood like this, with his nose stuck snobbishly in the air in defiance, and so I begin to mull over the case as we trundle away from Woolwich.

At one scene we have a fair, tall woman with a large nose and a dark shawl concealing much of her head, who Noakes says pushed Carrick in front of a tram. At the other we appear to have a murder either committed by a ghost, or by an old lady who cannot even walk straight and smelled none too pleasant. "Sir?"
"Yes, Crabtree."
"An old woman is not an old woman where she is merely playing the part of an old woman. Call it an 'unch, but I don't fink that was no old woman."
I hold up the telegram. "The Bluebottles have been door to door. Not even the ones that were near the pub recognised the description."
"It means she buggered off at some speed. Too fast for an elderly person. And besides, I've read about a case where this 'appened."
"Whose case was it, Crabtree?" I know what is coming.
"I know, Sir, but it fits. It's in *A Study in Scarlet*. The killer is still there when they arrive, and so he staggers about and just pretends to be pissed. It works, nobody pays any attention to 'im."
As much as it pains me, his argument is not without merit. "Have you the description in your notebook that Stan Bailey gave us?"
Crabtree flicks through his notes. *"I smelled her before I saw her, she stank of piss. She was hobbling by on the other side of the road."*

I chew on my thumbnail, deep in thought. "I'll buy that this person might have hunched themselves over, and that she might have pretended to be a helpless old lady. But she stank of urine? It's a bit over the top? It would have been an elaborate disguise for attacking a factory worker on his way home from the pub. Maybe it is just an exceedingly unhygienic individual."

"What if the kid's witch bird did 'em both?" My assistant poses a surprising question.

"A female killer with multiple victims would be so very, very unusual." I muse.

Crabtree shrugs. "But then, there is nothing more deceptive than obvious fact." I eye him suspiciously, for this sounds like another Sherlock Holmes quote. He is defiant. "I make a point of never having any prejudices, and of following docilely wherever a fact may lead me."

"Shutup Crabtree."

"Yes sir."

His silence lasts for all of four seconds. "So what now?" He sighs dramatically.

"We try and identify either of these 'women.' Otherwise how can we help to make sense of what motive anyone had to have to want such vastly different men dead? I suppose the 'witch' that Frank Noakes saw with Carrick might use the tram regularly."

"Long shot."

"Yes, but I think we ought to see if we can get some of our friendly constables out at turning out time to see if they might spot someone matching her description at the tram stop, with the boy in tow."

"Rather than us wasting our time you mean?"

"Quite. It will be highly satisfactory if she were to turn up, but I just don't see it. With his exalted position at the arsenal, her presence would seem to me to have been specific to the doctor and he is no longer there. I'm so tired I cannot think. Go home and spend the afternoon with your mother Crabtree. She will be glad of your company. I'll have Pip arrange the police and then contact you in Sutton when I've had a few hours of sleep and decided how we might progress. But be prepared to be out all night."

"We're going to try and follow up the George killing then? The Bobbys take care of the witch and we get the vampire?"

I roll my eyes at him. "I'm not keen on our chances given the simplistic description we can furnish, but we must give it our best. This woman, and this other person that might be masquerading as an old woman are the only leads we have. What else can we do but amble about the vicinity asking patrons, "Excuse me, but do you known of a displeasingly fragrant septuagenarian who wanders the streets nearby?"

"You're going to have to word the question in proper English if you want a straight answer, sir."

We have reached Victoria Station and Gaylor swings the door on his side open. "Go away Crabtree, you impertinent swine."

"Yes, Sir. See you later, sir." I wave him away, he take five paces then runs back and shoves his face through my open window. "Oink oink, Sir." He snaffles like a rabid piglet.

Gaylor has climbed back behind the wheel. "Feel free to run this idiot over as we depart," I tell him.

VII.

If you had willow trees in your childhood you never lose your attachment to them. I have found a warm, sunny spot in my memory, dozing in Pip's chair in his lofty room at the War Office whilst I wait for him to return. My eyes are closed and I have managed to send my consciousness far from the incessant bustle of war-time Whitehall below, to a spot in the grounds of the family estate many years ago, where long, willow tree foliage hangs almost into my eyes from the branches above and I can hear my siblings laughing and talking nearby.

The house is just outside the village of Mildenhall, not far from Marlborough. The oldest parts were were built in the reign of Henry VIII, but that is nothing. In the grounds are the ruins of a much older monastery; among the willows and on either side of a gentle stream; one of the first that he had pulled down. There is a bizarre mix of architecture, built around the original Tudor courtyard. The rooms smell of highly polished wooden floors that echo your footsteps. There is the promise of a thousand and one stories of things that have taken place in aged interiors and secret passageways, the faces on myriad canvases gazing down knowingly, having seen them all. My favourite place is the Stuart orangery, which looks out on grounds designed by whoever constructed William III's Privy Garden at Hampton Court Palace. I have no doubt that it was our house that inspired my love of history.

My five siblings and I were all born there. John was the first. His is a Stanley family name that stretches back for countless generations. After that my father professed not to care what any further offspring might be called and my mother took him at his word. Four girls followed and she, who was named with her siblings for the three sisters in Sense and Sensibility, followed her own mother's mad example and stole their names from her favourite book, Pride and Prejudice. There is slender, pretty Jane who is style over substance personified, who glides instead of walking, who has always felt like a complete stranger to me. A stranger who was delighted by me when she could preen me and dress me up, and then lost interest in me when I grew bored of such things and began to fidget through those encounters and thanked her by hiding snakes in her bed and dirtying her things with my muddy boy hands. Then she went and made her own playthings, a never-ending procession of coiffed and obedient little people with manners that are unimpeachable and unnerving. Lizzie, my favourite sister; controversial, abrupt, opinionated and intellectual Lizzie, broad and unfussy. She professed to all that she wished to be a spinster. So she therefore stunned us all when she found a husband, but it was a perfect match, for he is meek, fascinated by her, and utterly devoted to doing her bidding. Mary is my least favourite sister. My father adores her, no doubt because she is the prettiest, but she is a vapid narcissist and cruel to boot. As my entire childhood bears witness, she cannot abide anyone preventing her from being the centre of attention. She started by pinching me hard to make me cry when I was a baby because our mother said that I was ugly when I bawled, and progressed to slapping me when our withered old crone of a nanny had her back turned. There was an interim period when I punched her in the face as a small boy and scared her off. Then I went off to boarding school. Now stony faced and reserved, she tries to wound with her words, but the fact that she is also the stupidest member of our family and has the wit of a vegetable means that most of the time she is left rather humbled. Kitty is the brain. Archaeology, so we have something to talk about at least. But she is currently weighed down by a set of triplets that mean she can't get anything useful done. When my mother fell pregnant a sixth time, so far as Jane Austen was concerned, I should have been a girl named Lydia. Instead, I am Fitzwilliam Darcy Stanley. Did you ever hear of something so ridiculous? Lydia, I remain to my teasing sisters. My mother is rather fond of me as the last of her babies, but my father had his heir, and had been exhausted by girls, and so I think he was little moved by my arrival.

Suddenly, I am torn from my daydreaming by the sound of the door opening. "For someone who is always complaining about being worked to death," I say, "you are never in your office when I need you." I am slumped low in Pip's chair, my shoes off and my feet, complete with a hole in the big toe region of one of my socks, crossed on top of a pile of inevitably important pile of papers. My hands are interlaced behind my head. And so when I open my eyes and see the immortal Lord Kitchener looking at me with those piercing, hooded eyes, one brow raised; instead of feeling the sensation of a warm Wiltshire sun on my face, I feel nothing but sheer, unadulterated terror. Then complete humiliation in my haste to sit up, as I fall off the chair onto the floor, bashing my head on the desk on my way down.

"Get up, Stanley."

"Yes, Sir."

"Follow me."

"Yes, Sir. I'll just put on my shoes and…"

"Leave them."

I look at him forlornly, but he is already out in the corridor. "Hurry up Stanley."

His own office is but a short distance away, but I feel like a fool padding half-dressed after the Secretary of State for War. His highly capable and friendly aide, Fitzgerald, who I have met once or twice before, nods at me, bemused at my state of undress as we pass his desk. He is an outrageously handsome man in his late thirties, with thick dark hair; who has always been happy to forsake his own advancement in favour of staying with his master. There is another, private secretary, George Arthur, but he is nowhere to be seen at present.

"Sit down Stanley." I do as I am told, and he positions himself on the other side of his desk, looking out of the window at Whitehall. "Have you solved this mystery?" He asks gruffly.

I have the distinct impression that I am in trouble. "No, Sir, it is a puzzle indeed. I came back to plead for General Phipps's assistance in marshalling some police officers to try and seek out a woman I need to speak to when the arsenal turns out this evening."

I am braced for an explosion, a surge of anger and profanity reminiscent of the destruction of Krakatoa, but there is only silence, and then suddenly Lord Kitchener's demeanour relaxes. He sighs wearily and sits heavily on his chair. "So you have made some progress at least? It is unfair of me to have expected this to be unravelled so soon, of course. You must forgive me, I have many frustrations and anxieties at present, but you are not the cause of them."

Once again I am surprised by the absence of the fearsome aura that along with everyone else, I have been brought up to believe veils this man. "It is only a little progress, I fear, Sir. We may well be looking at two murders, but the circumstances surrounding one are very odd indeed." I fill him in as to Frank Noakes's testimony.

"You shall of course have your policemen." He scribbles a note for Fitzgerald, calls him in and his secretary leaves to make the relevant telephone call. "Regarding the fair-haired woman, you may also have use of some files kept at the Home Office that I can think of. I will have them brought here for you." We pause our discussion as an office girl enters with sandwiches and a stern expression that tells the Secretary of State for War that he is required to take this sustenance without protestation. When she has departed he pushes the plate to the middle of the desk and indicates that I should help myself to them too. "So you plan to try and find the perpetrator, or both perpetrators," he says as he bites into his lunch. "I think I quite agree with your man's logic about the possibility of them being the same person. Have you considered, given the strength required to kill George, that it might even have been a man dressed as a woman?"

"Yes, Sir, I have thought about it. I think it matters little in the steps I plan to take next, so long as this is a regular disguise." I explain the course I wish to take regarding the tram stop using the borrowed policeman. "And Crabtree and I will, I suppose, lie in wait tonight in the vicinity of Warren Lane where Fred George was killed to try and find this person, man or woman. It is not a subtle approach, but we have no other alternative."

"Perhaps not, but your plan is not so absurd." He stops chewing, dabs his mouth with a napkin and thinks for a moment or two. "A woman only wanders about in the middle of the night in an area that she knows exceedingly well," he remarks slowly. "If indeed you are looking for a woman, to assume that she may return to the scene of the latter killing is not so far-fetched."

"And yet I think that it is more likely that the key to this affair lies with Carrick, as opposed to George. Of the two he is the key figure. Violent murder done by a female though, perhaps multiple victims. It is a very shocking concept, she may not do what we might expect."

"Yes, I thought that poison was the weapon of a woman so moved to take a life." He is right, of course. He resumes eating his sandwich. I have not been dismissed and so my eyes wander about the room. On his desk is a silver frame with a photo of an officer inside.

"Do you know Lord Desborough's sons?" It is a reasonable assumption to make given my university affiliations.

"I know of them. He's a little older than I," I gesture towards the photograph, "but we still were at Balliol at the same time, briefly."

"His mother is a great pal of mine. I think if I had had a son I should have liked him to be just like Juju, or Billy.

The latter has joined my new armies, of course." From what I can recall Julian Grenfell was already a soldier before the advent of war. Billy was not. I rowed with him at Oxford. He was much better at it than I was.

Lord Kitchener changes the subject. "Is there anything else I should know?"

I have become somewhat comfortable with my surroundings and I lift a triangle of sandwich and sit back in my chair as I tell him of Dr. Scully, his band of Folkologists and his absurd suggestion that we should not rule out necromancy and vampires from our inquiries.

The War Secretary guffaws with laughter, spraying the odd crumb from his mouth. "Where would he get such a ridiculous notion?"

"A little too much Bram Stoker, I fear."

"I have heard the name, an author?"

"Yes, Sir." I smile. Reading the book is a fond memory now. "He wrote a novel about twenty years ago featuring an abomination, a vampire by the name of Dracula. He came to England and commenced all kinds of evil doings. Including biting people and drinking their blood."

"It sounds fascinating. I think I should like to read that book. I am trying to broaden my literary horizons. I have spent my life reading military manuals and texts, and I rather think that it is time for me to experience something else."

"I am sure that my boyhood copy is in the nursery at our London house. I should bring it here for you."

"I think I would like that, thank you. It does me good to read a little before I go to sleep. These damned politicians keep me awake with their foolish webs and tangles of deceit and self-serving nonsense."

I do not envy him his position at all. "Did you know, Sir, I think that you are the first serving soldier to have a Cabinet post for generations?"

He laughs. "Yes. I can quite see why nobody else should have wanted to do it in the interim." He becomes more serious. "The fate of the nation simply doesn't occur to them, they are so busy clambering and crawling their way upwards with their own aspirations at the forefront of their minds. And their gossiping will be the downfall of us all. One cannot tell them anything without it getting out. Why, the Germans must know absolutely everything about the conduct of the war from our side. And just now it is important, more important than ever that we are prudent with regard to secrecy."

I cannot help but agree with him. "Just this morning my mother was concerned about something she has heard about events at the front. I have no idea where she would have got it from."

"I am sure that you know that the BEF went into action this morning. I am much preoccupied in waiting for news, but I fear we will not be as successful as we might have hoped. I can only have so much influence."

I know for a fact that he does not think much of Sir John French, who is commanding the British Expeditionary Force in France. His anxiety explains, at least in part ,why I am still in his office, discussing novels and the dastardly behaviour of politicians. He is at a loss until news arrives from the front.

"Might I ask if my brother is in it?" It is worth a try. "Grenadier Guards," I remind him. "First battalion."

"Not as yet," he sighs. "I shall keep you informed as to his safety if I can, but you must be extremely discreet."

"Of course, Sir." He nods, and there we sit in companionable silence, both eating sandwiches; both contemplating what might be happening at this very moment across the Channel. He begins an assault on the endless pile of files on his desk, and I glance at his newspapers until it is time for me to depart.

VIII.

One doesn't get an invitation to tea with Lizzie so much as a summons. She is a suffragette, but no nearly so militant as we, as in her brothers, had hoped. She has more brains than John and I combined. Therefore I don't have any objection to the idea of her having the vote. I daresay she would make better use of it than we two, and if anyone bellows about how preposterous and catastrophic it would be for the future of England if womankind was given a political voice, I could name a dozen or so very stupid men of my own personal acquaintance that shouldn't have one on that basis, and who are already Members of Parliament.

The tea-room is filled to capacity. To a large point it illustrates London's determination to at least try and go about their business as though there is no war. Those that inhabit the capital have ever been a stoic breed. My sister catches me looking at a young woman on the next table and rolls her eyes. I spend some time merely looking longingly at my scone, piled high with thick clotted cream and rich, glistening strawberry jam, knowing that the instant I put it in my mouth I will have to pay for it somehow. In the end I can stand it no longer and after a swig of tea I ram half of it into my face at once. "I was hoping that you might come and help me one afternoon this week."

There it is. Subtlety was never Lizzie's strong point. My sister operates a charitable endeavour that looks after the spawn of female factory workers and supports needy families; all through a church in Camberwell.

"Please god, not children. Anything but other peoples' children," I say with my mouth full.

She cringes at my blasphemy.

"You are enjoying yourself far too much Lydia, there is a war on you know."

"Don't call me that in public."

"I mean it, it isn't right. You have got to do your bit." Aware that I already look extremely undignified with my chin covered in cream, I stick my foot out from under the table and point to it whilst looking at her fiercely. She hands me a napkin. "Wipe your face your fool. And curse that stupid foot of yours, it doesn't stop you cadding about London since you got home from France." Cadding about. I certainly wouldn't call being chucked into the English Channel in the midst of winter cadding about. Obviously I cannot tell my elder sister this. She has assumed a highly irritating facial expression, her head cocked to one side, which regularly infuriates me. "I understand..." she says in a patronising manner.

"No, dear sister," I interrupt brusquely. "I don't think that you quite do. A bullet a foot or so higher, and I might have been one of these poor fellows waking up in one of these Lady Wotsit-so-and-so's homes for broken officers that have sprung up all over Mayfair with a stump where my leg ought to be. Or worse still, I might not be waking up at all. You can have no comprehension of what is happening over there, while you sit here rolling bandages. Now, that it isn't your fault, but damned if I am going to have you tell me what I should and shouldn't do. I escaped a slaughterhouse with my life, a place designed to chew men up and spit them out by every conceivable method of invention and I will, in all likelihood, be sent back there to meet my end at some point. And so as a consequence I intend to spend every moment of my existence possible, here in London, in the pursuit of nothing serious at all. I mean to enjoy every moment as if it is my last, because it could well be the case to some degree." Lizzie looks as if she might cry, and the two elderly ladies on the next table have stopped with their cake forks midway to their mouths to gawp at our little spectacle. I take her hand from the table in both of my own and try a more gentle approach. "I only mean that, I intend to make the most of whatever time I may have left. In case the worst happens. The world has changed, Lizzie. One doesn't know if one will be here in a year. Everything is here, everything is now, and we must live life to the full in case it is snatched away. Do you understand?"

She squeezes my hand. "You never had such a temper before you went over there."

This causes me to sigh. "I saw so much waste, and in truth I think we are in this for a bloody long time if we are to see it through to the finish. There is much more to come. I saw so many lives snuffed out last year, Liz, it *does* make one lose one's temper to think about all of those men never coming back from there. Many of them were my age, there is no reason why, when I go back, I shouldn't become one of them. And there isn't a damn thing I can do about it. It is out of my hands. Luck. That is all it will come down to."

"At least you are not with a fighting battalion." She must see the instant scowl upon my face. "I know it is an awful thing to say, because so many men must be, but, well. I will say it. If given the choice they can hang. I want my father, my husband, my brothers and the rest of the family; *my men*, to be safe."

"We all feel that way dear," interjects one of the women next to us as she reaches across pats my sister's free hand. "Sometimes it does one good to get it off one's chest."

At her church, Lizzie has me stacking boxes of donations in a dusty back office whilst she bludgeons me with unsolicited advice. "Ada Swinton would do well for you."

"Who?"

Finding me a bride is her favourite topic of conversation. She thinks a wife will improve my behaviour. My sister sighs. "You know, she is one of Martin's sisters, the youngest one."

"Isn't she twelve or thirteen at most?" I find that mockery is the best approach to fend off her advances.
"She's twenty one. And very pretty. She thinks highly of you."
"I don't think I have ever met her." This is not a joke.
"What does that matter? She has seen your portrait."
Which means she has been dishing it out again.
"Lizzie," I sigh, "I don't want a wife, not for at least two decades, if ever. And even if I decide then that I do, I would not want you shopping for one for me as if you were assaulting a catalogue from Fortnum and Mason."
She is unperturbed. "What about Beryl Farquhar?"
I cringe outwardly. "Absolutely not. She looks like that horrible squashed face little dog that she carries everywhere under her arm."
She is grinning, knowing that she is exasperating me. "But her family is fabulously wealthy, and she is very clever."
"Good. Your husband is ludicrously old. When he leaves you a widow you can have Beryl for yourself."
My sister uses a scarf in her hand to whip me with. "Don't be awful. You are out till all hours every night. I dread to think what you are up to and with whom."
"I can tell you if you like. I can drop a report onto the breakfast table along with your copy of *The Times*."
"Shut up. I would feel quite ill if I knew the details. But mind you don't do anything stupid. Father is dour at the best of times, I cannot imagine what he would do if you started presenting him with illegitimate grandchildren. Or doctors bills for cures for iffy diseases."
"Elizabeth, I am not an idiot." She has no idea how close to the mark she is.
She ruffles my hair. "Oh Lyddie, you are. But we love you for it. Now here, this box is heavy, take it down for me will you?"
I do as I am told. "What is all of this rubbish? Why on earth have you got boxes and boxes of old clothes?"

"Donations, dear. Yet another job. You can do it, they need sorting out. Some, I'm afraid just won't do." As I begin pulling out items of clothing an idea strikes me, and my sister will be just the person to help me bring my plan to fruition.

IX.

Instead of taking part in the operation to attempt to spot our murderous woman, 8 o'clock finds me sitting inside The Pyro with Stan Bailey, eating a stale ham roll and waiting for Crabtree, who is late. I am dressed in borrowed donations from my sister's charitable collections: itchy trousers, a scratchy, holey, olive green jumper over a grey, possibly once white, flannel shirt, open at the neck. She let me keep my own socks. I wouldn't have thought of shoes, but Lizzie did.

She had rather too much fun arranging my disguise and dressing me up, which brought back disturbing recollections of my youth; being forced to stand impeccably still while my sisters put me in their old dresses. Lizzie has taken my shoes and given them to a needy elderly gentleman, replacing them with a sensible, worn pair of workmanlike boots. As a final flourish, she bent my head over the sink, washed the oil out of my hair and jammed the towel dried, undressed result under a flat cap; ordering me not to neaten myself by tucking any ends up. "Do you assume that all working class people don't bother with their appearance?" I had asked.

"Of course not, you fool. But they cannot always afford luxuries like the three pints per day of the stuff you put in your hair. I have spent the last hour creating *a look* for you, and this finishes it off. I won't have you ruin it. And don't overdo the accent. You can fit in without doing a bad impersonation of a chimney sweep."

I think she was rather jealous of the evening's impending caper. "In actual fact," she carried on, "you look incredibly handsome in a dishevelled way. Like you earn a living with your hands instead of sitting on your velveteen arse at the War Office." She had suddenly grabbed my hands, looked at my palms, grubby from her boxes, and then turned them over. "Don't wash these. In fact you ought to try to keep them out of sight. It is obvious that you don't use them."
"I hardly think I am going to be scrutinised that closely in a smoke-filled pub," I had protested, but by that point she had already turned her back and gone back to stacking her boxes. When she wasn't looking I had slipped my revolver into the back of my waistband and commandeered an old, short jacket of faded navy blue to conceal it.

The constables were out earlier in the evening, in what turned out to be a futile attempt to watch thousands of arsenal workers dispersing at the end of their shifts and weeding any out that came close to fitting Frank Noakes's description of the woman that he claims shoved Dick Carrick in front of a tram. There are multiple entrances by which workers might gain entrance to the arsenal, and if she was about, she did not use the Beresford Gate by the tram stop. They pulled out eight women, but Frank, positioned with his father nearby, shook his head at all of them. I am not surprised, because for no reason that I can properly articulate, I don't think she works at The Shop. If this strange woman is indeed responsible for the death of Carrick, and even Fred George, then she would have had ample opportunity to attack both within the confines of the arsenal, rather than risk taking them on outside; where in one case there were hundreds of witnesses and in another where she risked finding no opportunity to seize her man at all.

Stan Bailey is present so that I can ask him some follow up questions, and quite frankly, so I can buy the poor man a drink. "Can you recall anything more about the woman on the other side of the street?" I ask.

"Like what?"

"Take me through it again." I dust off my hands. "Humour me. What made you think you were looking at an elderly woman?"

He looks as if he thinks I am mad. "It was obvious. She was wearing skirts, and she was all 'unched over, hobblin, like they do."

"But you don't recall seeing her face?" I persist.

Now he screws up his face. "Well, no. It was dark."

"I'm not saying that you didn't see what you claimed. Of course, we are acting quickly to see if we can locate this person, as they are at the very least a witness. But, well... Is there anything else that you saw or heard of her that would serve to back up your assumption that this person was old or female?"

His mouth is suddenly agape. "You think it was a bloke?"

"I am not ruling anything out at all at the moment," I say, impressed by his quick deduction.

"This get's more and more bonkers. So now, a younger person, a bloke even, wearing women's clothes, might 'ave murdered Fred?"

"With you having witnessed nobody else in the vicinity, it is a possibility, but equally, the killer could have just as easily jumped into a garden and made off around the back of one of the houses. As you say, it was dark. Even more so because the streetlights are dimmed round about the arsenal. And when you ran off to seek help they had plenty of time to accomplish this."

"I'm doubting every'fin I saw now."

"Please, Stan. do not chastise yourself. You were in shock, and if indeed this person you saw on the other side of the street was not what "she" seemed, they will have proven themselves to be a cunning actor." After this has sunk in somewhat, and Stan has taken a long swig of his Guinness, we begin a cursory discussion about what motive a man, or indeed a woman, might have in killing a munitions man. "Perhaps they're a pacifist?" I muse.

He nods but shrugs at the same time. "Would someone go from being unknown to you lot to doing murder?"

"Probably not." Again, his reasoning is sharp.

"I just mean that I would 'ave thought they'd be a protestor, or have opened their mouth before, or thrown red paint at someone in Traf'gar Square."

"Yes. You would expect the behaviour of someone like that to escalate gradually, though of course there is a lot of that about, they may well have simply eluded the authorities."

We ponder that for a moment. "Maybe it's a suffragette?" He says.

"But women are freely being employed now, and will continue to be so. And all militant activity is supposed to be suspended at least for the duration of the war."

"Maybe they're a pro? Maybe they've been paid by someone to do it?"

"We would be in very strange territory then. I suppose it is possible, though it would be the first instance of such a thing of which I have ever heard if it is a woman."

"You know what tho?" Stan takes a sip of his pint and places it back on the table, wipes his mouth with the back of his hand. "If you do sumfin' like that you're wanting to make a statement."

"Yes." I agree,

"Well then, why Fred? He was no-one really."

"Honestly?" I sigh. "I'd be very surprised if Fred was specifically targeted beforehand." I cannot tell him about Carrick and his eminent background of course, and that I believe his death may prove to be the key to this affair. "I am inclined to believe that Fred was simply in the wrong place at the wrong time. You are right, it would be a very odd statement to make. And unless he was involved in something terrible without your knowing, which seems improbable, to intentionally plot to kill him of all people, it seems bizarre. Not to mention the manner in which it was done would have been atrocious planning. It seems to be spur of the moment; a sudden necessity."

"The fact that he died when he'd done nuffin' wrong makes it worse." I can only nod my head in agreement. "There's more to this though. I know you ain't going to tell me what it is, but there ain't no way they send a special like you in to investigate the death of a fact'ry worker, no matter 'ow gruesome it is. One that's driven about in a posh car. Promise me one fing though? Lieutenant?"

I can't help but smile slightly at his continued astuteness. "Of course, if I can do so without compromising my duty."

"Promise me that whoever the bastard that did it is, that you'll catch 'em and make 'em pay. I don't care if it is a bird or not. I want them to pay for what they've done to my family."

"I have every intention of making them pay, Stan."

He raises his glass, it clinks against mine and then he drains the rest of its contents. "Thanks. I needed a bit of peace. It's bonkers trying to sort everyfin' out at home. You know where I'll be. If I can do anyfin' to help, whether it's official or under the table, like, just ask."

As he leaves, another, larger figure is on their way through the pub's narrow entrance. For a moment, I see nothing amiss, and then, as the colourful apparition begins to make its way towards me, the unbelievable realisation dawns. It is Crabtree. And he is dressed as a woman. "I don't know what is more disturbing, the fact that you stand before me wearing your mother's clothes, or the fact that you might actually pass as a female," I hiss in a loud whisper. Insults are the only weapon in my arsenal, for I cannot make a scene.

"It's my rosy red cheeks sir."

"Shut up, Crabtree."

"You said to wear a disguise," he says indignantly, in a foolish approximation of a feminine voice.

I told him to arrive looking nothing like an MP so we could quietly watch for the missing perpetrator/witness from Fred George's murder scene, not to put in a Widow Twanky inspired turn that will give me nightmares. "For goodness sake, just sit in the corner and at least try to look normal."

He flounces down into the seat opposite me. "Shall we 'old hands?"

"Not unless you want me to pull out my revolver and shoot you."

"I've got a gun too. He whispers loudly. It's in me knickers." I can only glare at him in horror.

"If your were my gentleman friend you would hold my 'and."

"If I was your gentleman friend, I would pull out my revolver and shoot myself." Determined not to indulge his nonsense, I get up, intent on our going for a walk outside to see if we can spot our mystery woman. That and the humiliation of anybody mistaking Crabtree for a conquest of mine in a lit room is more than I can bear. He makes to follow me. "Hold on sir. I mean… dear. These drawers don't 'alf leave everyfin' swinging about."

"Crabtree. Are you… are you wearing you *mother's underwear?*"

"Clean ones" he says indignantly, as if this were a reasonable thing. "She said I've got to burn 'em when I'm done."

A wiser woman there never was. Unfortunately for us, the female that we seek, or male; killer or witness, is nowhere to be seen, despite an evening of unceasing pain in having to sit on a low wall outside the pub with nothing like enough drink in my hand, listening to Crabtree as he smokes his way through all of my cigarettes daintily; chattering away about Sherlock Holmes and his skill in disguises in a voice that made him sound as if someone has inserted an army boot into his groin with no small force. He only stopped to flirt with any man that passed us. "I don't feel we can leave before we wait it out until the approximate time of the killing," I say miserably. "If 'she' passes regularly it might always be at that time."

"You go 'ome, Sir. I 'ad a kip this afternoon, I'm not tired. She probably ain't going to show anyway." Despite his terrible appearance, I could kiss him. "Stay on the main road, don't do anything stupid." I say as I give him money to buy some breakfast when his fruitless vigil is over. "Come and see me at the War Office tomorrow morning. Early."

"Yes, Sir," he says, giving me a flash of an ankle and a shimmy as I depart. I have no idea what he has got wedged into his blouse, but there is no cohesion as the twin objects fly heavily about in different directions and he grimaces in pain.

As I let myself into the house my mother startles me, for she has heard me unlocking the door and stepped out of her sitting room clad in a floor length dressing gown with her long, greying hair unpinned and plaited over her shoulder. "You are late," she whispers. She looks exhausted. I take off my cap and my greatcoat; hang them up and begin to climb the stairs. "Why are you dressed like that?"

"I have been working, mother." She probably assumes I have been off gallivanting with various girls. For once she is wrong.

"Yes, I know. I telephoned to the War Office and I was told that you were taking care of an important matter." I stop. "You needn't have waited up."

She is fiddling with her hands. "I couldn't sleep. Thinking about your brother."

As I move away she calls out behind me. "You had a caller this evening, a woman."

"A woman?" I am unable to curtail my panic. This is potentially very awkward. "What did she look like?" I am expecting a description of some theatre girl, a dancer or an usher that I half remember.

"I have no idea, I shall have to call Mrs. Mitcham." Shortly, our housekeeper shuffles through from the kitchen, which she was preparing to abandon for the night. I put the question about my visitor to her instead.

"You stink," she says.

"I still smell better than you," is my reply. Ours is a unique friendship.

She sighs as if bored. "Well she was tall, a lot taller than me." This is what happens when you give someone thirty years of leeway, but we wouldn't have her any other way. "Bony. Blonde. She had a great big, crooked nose. Doubt she was one of your good time girls, you mucky little bugger. Too ugly."

Mrs. Mitcham knows nothing specific about any dalliances, thought she is alarmingly accurate. But I have other concerns. "You did not let her into the house?"

"She was in the kitchen. Have I done something wrong?" She is alarmed more than defensive.

"What did she say, or do?" I run a hand back over my hair. "I'm going to telephone Scotland Yard and have someone posted outside should she return."

"Will, you are frightening us." My mother is genuine on this point.

I have descended the stairs again. "Mother, I'm sorry, but this woman is potentially very dangerous." She is responsible for the death of at least one man."

"That is absurd. And why would she come here?"

I take her by the shoulders. "I don't know, but if she comes here again, nobody is to so much as open the door to her, do you understand?" There is a pause. My mothers lips are pursed and her brow furrowed. Mrs Mitcham is perturbed.

Something else occurs to me. "Did she by chance smell terrible?"

"Of course not, I wouldn't have let her in otherwise." Our housekeeper looks at me as if I have lost my mind.

"I have been looking for this woman all day, is there anything you can tell me about her? Did she have an accent?"

"She was a London girl. East London, perhaps. Very 'cor blimey."

Girl. That means she thought her considerably younger than herself. "And can you remember anything else at all? Any other distinguishing features, the colour of her eyes?"

She shakes her head, any mockery in her face gone now. "I'm sorry, Will. I barely looked at her. I was in a hurry. I was busy in the basement." I'm probably going to go upstairs to find that she has moved my bed down there. "And I was looking for that book you wanted. It's on your night stand."

"Thank you, on both counts, but would you recognise her again?"

Mrs Mitcham shrugs. "I am not sure. I doubt it. I just remember thinking that she was very tall and that she had a very unfortunate nose. Oh. And a horrible complexion. Her face and hands are all flaky."

"What did she want?" The most obvious question, one which I have so far completely neglected.

"There's a box up on your night stand, too. She said it was connected to a case you were working on and that a gentleman she worked for wished you to have it."

It seems that while I froze outside The Pyro with Crabtree, a woman we desperately seek was standing in our kitchen. Distinctly disturbed about what awaits me upstairs and in a foul mood I make for the stairs, cursing as my foot slams into one of Mrs Mitcham's buckets of water and it sloshes all over my foot.

"Have you… is there any news?" I hear my mother call up after me nervously.

To my instant regret, I snap at her. "Mother I could tell you nothing of what is happening in France, even if I knew." I watch her face fall and feel awful. "I can tell you that as of this afternoon I was assured of John's safety. And that I have a promise of swift information should he go into battle, if it is forthcoming from the front."

She smooths her dressing gown with the palms of her hands. "Well, I suppose I cannot ask any more than that. It is a lot more than some people get."

I dash back down the stairs before departing to my room and kiss her cheek. "Yes mother, it is. Pray for him, and I will do all that I can to ascertain when he emerges unscathed for you."

In my bedroom, next to a tattered copy of Bram Stoker's *Dracula,* is an ordinary looking, brown cardboard box. It fits comfortably onto the palm of my hand as I eye it with suspicion. It weighs almost nothing, and the contents make just a little noise when I shake it gently. I am bewildered. What could she possibly have been doing in my home? And why? If she is responsible for any of the goings on at the arsenal why one earth would she seek me out instead of going to ground?

I take a deep breath and lift the lid off the box. To reveal cigarettes by Fribourg and Treyer on Haymarket; who have renamed themselves Evans and Evans since the onset of war. I sniff one. The exact concoction that I have rolled on a weekly basis. Lying on top of the cigarettes is a calling card and scrawled in expensive black ink on the exclusive stock, in tiny letters, is a note:

"Even if you find her, you're still terribly cold, Lieutenant. Welcome to The Game."

On the reverse of the card is a stamp: *Stangerson & Drebber - Salt Lake City.* Through a fog of stunned surprise, thoughts are now racing into my head. Never before have I been taunted by a criminal that I am trying to pursue. Criminals. The woman did not write the note herself. There is more than one. A gentleman she works for. Nothing that has been happening at Woolwich is in the slightest bit coincidental. And worse, they appear to think that all of this is fun.

Thursday, 11th March 1915

X.

Early next morning I am sitting at my desk at the War Office waiting for Dr. Carrick's assistant, a Mr. Giles, to come to the telephone. People are starting to filter into the building, tramping through the corridor outside and shaking rain from their umbrellas. The entire place is coated in a layer of dirty water, made worse by dripping overcoats and the smell of damp humanity. It gives off an unpleasant fug when combined with radiators on full blast.

After a lengthy period of rustling, the voice that arrives on the other end of the line is much higher than I'd expected, and well spoken. I begin by asking him for his version of events, which tallies with the official line.
"It was so terribly sad," he sighs. "And so unnecessary. Such a brilliant mind, just extinguished in a simple accident."
If that is what it was. "And you have returned to Manchester University?"
I drum my pencil on the desk. Another sigh. "Yes, there was nothing left for me in London. I could not carry on his work alone, I really was merely his assistant. So I came back to the university here, it really is a very progressive institution and I would like to stay if I can. Initially, of course, I escorted his body, so that his wife and daughter might bury him. I did return to London last week to collect my things from the office."
All perfectly plausible. "Did you remove everything?"
"No, everything else had to remain at the arsenal."
I write that down. "Did you know what it was that you were working on?"
He is understandably hesitant. "I can talk about chemical compounds, if I am given permission, and certainly about the experiments that we carried out. But if you were to ask me what the practical applications

were to be, I am afraid that I simply don't know. My speciality is chemistry and that is was I assisted him with, but Dr. Carrick was not merely a chemist, he was an excellent physicist too, a mathematician, he was well versed in lots of emerging technologies. He liked to keep things close to his chest and his work was highly confidential. As such he carried out much of it in private. When I think of what the country has lost with his death... He was quite brilliant. It is incredibly rare to find someone who is a genius in so many fields."

I'm tired, and I cannot be bothered to listening to his fawning. "Can you think of anyone with cause to hurt him? Either on account of his work for any personal reason?"

"No," he sounds very distressed. "None of them."

From a position of impending boredom I am suddenly alert. "I'm sorry, I do not follow." A face has appeared at the door, one dominated by that giant moustache. Lord Kitchener indicates that when I have finished my conversation I should find my way to his office. I nod my understanding.

"...And so nobody has seen anything of them since before the Professor's accident."

I've not been listening properly to the doctor's assistant. "Sorry, Mr. Giles, say that again for me, please?"

"I attempted to call on Mrs. Carrick myself immediately upon my return to the north, to impart the news of her husband's death in person, but I could not find her, or her daughter. Millicent is seven, so she must be with her mother, don't you agree? I have exhausted every lead I can think of, but cannot find a single trace of them. Yesterday I gave up and went to the police up here. Dr. Carrick was a devoted family man. He was very happy. I would be shocked if anything untoward emerged from investigations into his private life."

"And so far the police, they have turned up nothing?"

"It has only been twenty-four hours, but no. For all we know Dr. Carrick's family are not yet aware that he has died. They say that nobody knows of any trip they were to take. The authorities here are treating the matter with the utmost urgency."

"Good, that is good." I stifle a yawn. "Will you contact me at the War Office as and when you receive any news?"

"May I ask why?"

"I am afraid that is confidential."

"Do you suspect foul play? My goodness.. If…"

"I really cannot say."

He lets out yet another sigh. "I understand. I am well used to operating on these confidential lines. What did you say your name was?"

"Stanley, Lieutenant Stanley."

"I will telephone the instant I hear anything, Lieutenant, but in the meantime the man looking into the affair up here is a Detective Chantler, if you need to speak with him." But a brief call to the Manchester Police adds nothing new. Detective Chantler sounds younger than I would have expected, probably no older than myself. He has sent men out to speak with Mrs. Carrick's mother and a sister out in Cheshire, and explains that he has been laboriously telephoning or wiring every hotel in every seaside resort he can think of. The woman and her little girl seem to have vanished into thin air without telling anyone where they are going.

I stand up, straighten my uniform and make for Kitchener's office, still deep in thought. I place my copy of *Dracula* in front of him and drop down into the chair opposite the great man. "Where are we?" He asks as he signals his thanks for the book and puts a letter he is writing to one side. He leans forwards on his desk, his elbows resting on the surface and his hands clasped on top of a blotting pad. I lean back in the chair and cover my face with my hands. Then I let out a groan and begin. I describe Mrs. Mitcham's account of the woman who I think was present at Carrick's death

visiting our home. I take the cigarettes and the card from my pocket and hand them to him. He examines both, baffled, as I continue speaking, and then replaces them next to a pile of papers and clasps his hands again.
"Damned cheek of it. Does the front of the card mean anything to you?"
"I'm afraid not, Sir. I have never heard either name, and I am sure I could not even point at Salt Lake City on a map."
He calls Fitz through and instructs him to make some enquiries. Then I talk him through what I have just found out from Giles and Chantler in the northwest. He takes a deep breath. Then he picks up the cigarettes, shrugs and fishes one out, before throwing the box to me. Waste not, want not, I suppose. "What are your thoughts right now?" He says in the initial cloud of smoke emitted after he lights his.
I inhale from my own, tapping the box on the arm of the chair. "I'm angry, Sir. She has brought my family into this. Women, no less."
"Yes, I can well imagine your sentiment. The brashness of these people is infuriating, as well as worrisome."
However, a plan has already been forming in my mind. "We should forget Fred George. The investigation into his death is proving time consuming. We concentrate on Richard Carrick, because it all began with him. I feel sure that George was merely in the wrong place at the wrong time. Otherwise the perpetrator is an idiot. If we find those responsible for the doctor's murder, we stand a good chance of apprehending whoever it was that killed our machinist too, I am sure of it."
"Agreed. Have you still no idea why that *was* the wrong place? For George?"
I look about for an ashtray. "None, I'm afraid."
Kitchener takes an empty one from the windowsill and puts it between us. "What is the motivation of these people?"

"Surely whatever Carrick was working on."

"Again," he says, "agreed. The problem is that he worked in complete isolation, on the assumption that as and when he developed anything of military use, he would reveal it to the authorities. And thus far, he had done so. A number of projects are in progress that were the brainchild of the doctor. But his assistant was not exaggerating. The man was brilliant, he could have been working on something new in any number of fields, and we cannot even begin to assume who that might have offended, or who might have benefitted from stealing his work. The enemy, one presumes easily enough, but what they intend to do with it is a completely different prospect."

"If someone wanted access to what he was working on, why kill him? If it was something that he had completed then we should have known about it. We have no reason to believe that he kept anything from the authorities. Surely he was infinitely more valuable alive?"

"Presuming that having killed him, they have whatever it is, why were they still outside the arsenal? To be in such a position as to kill the other chap?"

Kitchener sighs. That question hangs in the air for a time. Because neither of us can answer it. The obvious connotation is that they are not finished at the site, that there is something else that they want. The War Secretary suggests that it is now necessary to increase security at the arsenal even further. To do so without effecting productivity may well prove problematic, but he is right of course, we have come to the point where he has little choice. He has Fitz come into the room and instructs him to make the appropriate telephone call. A girl enters with a tea tray and leaves again. As Kitchener begins to stir milk and sugar into his cup he tries a different thread. "What do you make of the missing wife and child?"

I shrug. "I have no idea at the moment. But my instinct is that it is sinister. A woman and her child do not simply vanish. And not at almost precisely the instant that the doctor tumbles in front of a tram."

"The young boy is right. It was definitely not an accident."

"No, I agree. Everything about his death is queer. The time and the place, the manner of it all smack of opportunism and a lack of access to him. Perhaps even a measure of desperation."

Kitchener nods. "Quite, someone was taking the best chance they had, and therefore I think they do not have access to the arsenal, which is good. It bodes well for His Majesty and I next week. So what do we do now?"

I sit up in the chair so that I can drink my tea without pouring it all over my uniform. "I am waiting for Crabtree. Then we will go to Woolwich and see what we can get our hands on in terms of Carrick's work. The assistant says he removed nothing, so with luck, we will be able to piece together exactly what he was working on and identify who might have an objection to it, who might wish to acquire the knowledge."

A different, pretty girl knocks on the open door. "Excuse me, Sir, but I've bought someone up, an odd little man wearing a skirt. He says he needs to see Lieutenant Stanley."

Kitchener raises an eyebrow. This should be highly amusing. I don't even bother to suppress a grin.

"Waste of time that was, Sir. Nothing to report, bugger all going on last night." Crabtree stretches dramatically as he barges into the office. "Urgh. I don't know how women walk about with these, they don't 'alf give you back ache." He hasn't even looked up to see where he is being directed by the female clerk.

"Them not sharing an approximate weight with root vegetables might lessen the feminine plight," I guess cheerfully, waiting for the penny to drop. For it has become obvious what is struggling to escape the confines of his mother's blouse.

"You ain't spending time with the right girls, Sir. Oooo," he says, eyeing the box of cigarettes in my hand. "Don't mind if I do." I hand the box to him. As he finishes lolloping into the room a turnip falls out of his blouse and rolls across the floor, hitting the desk.

Then he looks up. I wish, with all of my heart, that I could capture the look on his face when he sees whose desk he is looming over in all of his lopsided womanly glory. He looks like a startled pheasant who has realised that it is about to be shot. He stands to attention and salutes, causing the other turnip to come flying out and land on his foot, and ends up saluting while hopping up and down.

"At ease, Private." Kitchener appears unperturbed, but I think he is trying not to laugh. "Sit down." Crabtree flings himself obediently into the nearest chair, sitting bolt upright. "You are the chap who suggested in the first place that the woman at the second murder scene might not be all that she seemed?"

He nods, his mouth still agape. "I know I'm right."

"Even a stopped clock is right twice a day Crabtree." I look up and he is crestfallen. "I am sure you are right" I concede. "Well done. He got it from Sherlock Holmes, Sir," I say by way of explanation to Lord Kitchener.

"Good work, Private, excellent application of knowledge. This is what I was talking about, Stanley, broadening our horizons has value. Now, where were we? You saw nothing at all overnight?" This is directed at Crabtree.

"Nn-n-o, Sir," he stammers.

"Smoke a cigarette, Crabtree," I say. He is all over the place. His hands are still shaking. I turn back to Kitchener. "Sir. I propose that Crabtree and I will go to Woolwich and sift through what we can find of Carrick's belongings there; try and find some sort of motive for killing him."

The War Secretary nods. I look across and Crabtree is jigging about in his chair, his face flushed, as if he will burst if he does not get to say something on the tip of his tongue. "Spit it out, Private Crabtree." Kitchener looks bemused.

My lunatic assistant, in helping himself to a cigarette, has also picked up the calling card delivered with them. "Sir. It's a piss take. Sorry, a joke."

Kitchener frowns. "Explain it to us."

"Yes, Sir. The names, Stangerson and Drebber, and the location, Salt Lake City. It's from a Sherlock Holmes story." Of course it is.

"A Study in Scarlet, the same one that gave me the idea about the killer disguising themselves at the scene."

Which would mean that not only does the comedian with the cards and the cigarette know intimately about me, but they are well versed when it comes to the bizarre world of Crabtree too. And that if the connection to the same story is not coincidental, and I am sure it isn't, that they have knowledge of our investigation. That, considering the tight lid on it, is concerning indeed.

"Crabtree, go and get changed," I order, standing up. "I will meet you back here in an hour and a half. I will make sure that Gaylor is waiting for us. We need to start going through Carrick's things as soon as possible." He scampers out.

"God speed, Stanley," says the great man as I follow him.

XI.

I kill the time waiting for Crabtree to return to a normal, somewhat masculine appearance by wandering up to The *Criterion* at Piccadilly. In search of coffee to bring my senses back to some sort of alertness. I have always liked the ridiculous opulence of the place; the

Neo-Byzantine grandeur with its arches and columns. But in the midst of the war, the presence of so much oblivious chatter and inane activity seems somewhat wrong.

However, it is usually a good spot to run into one of the Socrates chaps at any given time, and indeed Horatio Keyes is there, in the East Room, surrounded by lady shoppers and staring into an early drink. His brow is furrowed and lined with a light sheen of sweat, his complexion even more flushed than usual. He looks up and beckons me to sit with him at his table. "What are you so depressed about?" I ask.

"The bloody Dardanelles. You?"

"The end of the world as we know it."

"Again? Right. Well we'll need a bottle of something then." He signals to a waiter, and my intention to stick to coffee goes flying out of the elaborate window next to him, past Eros into the middle of the usual chaos outside on the way down.

"Care to talk about it?" I ask.

He sighs and leans over to whisper to me. "We are about to become embroiled in an absolute mess now in the Dardanelles. I am sure of it. Nothing is going as it should. We will have troops on the ground there before you know it, you mark my words."

"What will they be armed with? Potato guns?"

"This is not a laughing matter, Stanley." He lowers his voice even further. "We have troops in Egypt waiting to occupy Constantinople, but at this rate, they will all be walking there from Europe."

"No go then?" All that I know, is that for the last month or so, the Government, led by Churchill, have had some nonsensical idea that they can begin to threaten the Ottoman capital by forcing the Dardanelles Straits using an array of battleships, minesweepers and submarines, with more craft kicked in by the French, and a lowly contribution by the Russians, who got us into this secondary mess when we cannot even address the one we've made for ourselves in France and Belgium. Then they were supposed to burst into the Black Sea and charge up to Constantinople. "I thought they had sent the *Queen Elizabeth*?" This, I am aware, is a shiny new ship of some sort. I have no idea what it does.

Keyes eyes me with suspicion accordingly. He takes a deep breath and I know that he is about to launch into naval strategy. At least I've got a drink in hand. "Before the war," he says, after clearing his throat, "they had fortresses, yes, There were also some mines stretching from the European side to the Asian. Then there were a string of additional defences going all the way up to the narrows, which is of course the fundamental point that they do not want us to pass. A lot of their guns were obsolete, and they lacked ammunition. And it was just the bloody Turk, not the Hun. Now of course it is a very different prospect. They've upped their game and reinforced themselves with Germans who know what they are doing. They've overhauled their weapons, and they are armed by creditable soldiers. Not to mention they have dropped mines everywhere. A dozen lines of the little buggers, probably. And there are searchlights. Still, they cannot have made them impenetrable in that time. We should be able to get through. We started well, in November, but then they dug in their heels. A few days ago we sent four battleships in, but there are still bloody mines everywhere. My cousin commanded the sweepers. If you can call them that. Bloody trawlers with civilian crews. Didn't like enemy fire, if you can believe it. Since then we've lost a batch of marines too. Yes the Queen Elizabeth is there, but thus far her involvement has not remotely swung it in our favour."

I yawn unashamedly. "So what now?"

"We go again." He thumps the table lightly. "In the next day or so. We must clear these bloody mines if we are to get through, though I think not even the crews believe that it is going to happen now. Like I said, we'll end up throwing a land force in. Which was exactly what we did not want in the first place." He takes a long drink. "How goes things at your end?"

"The usual mayhem. And John is probably in action by now. Though I know practically nothing about that."

Keyes empties his glass. "You've been seen, well, hob-nobbing, for want of a better expression, with greatness. Are you working directly for the man himself?"

"Yes, but I cannot say more."

"Understood." He pauses to replenish his glass. "How did you get so high up so quickly? I won't lie, it drives me mad trying to think of what you might have done to get there. Unwittingly of course, you are not a wretched crawler, we all know that."

"You can have it all if you want it. I'll go back to my motorcycle in France." I empty my glass and put my hand over it when he moves to refill it. "Off in a minute, must have a clear head."

He shrugs. He is by nature a sulker, but he is in a particularly melancholic mood this morning. "That mad old dog Fisher is hardly Kitchener's equal at the Admiralty. He won't last much longer, with luck. Can you send your man over to us?"

"I fear he is at the end of his tether with just the army to look after."

"Shame. We want one just like him. Fisher has been rendered worthless with age. I hear you're going about in a fine motor too."

I cannot help but laugh. "Do you chaps in naval intelligence have nothing better to do than watch me?"

"The King's car, Will? His chauffeur is hardly inconspicuous."

I merely smile. "Look," he says. "I know you cannot talk, but my offer stands. You know where to find me. If there is anything we navy boys can do, we could do with some action."

"You have my word," I promise him, standing up to leave. "If there is any way the army can entertain the Royal Navy while we are doing all the work, we will do our best." He thumps me jovially in the arm. "And cheer up, H," this as I get up. "This war will drive you mad if you let it."

I have not even made it up the steps to the main entrance of the War Office when the same tea girl that introduced Crabtree in all of his mother's finery earlier comes flying towards me. "What on earth is happening?" I am forced to catch her by the arms to prevent her from falling onto the pavement.
"Another one, Sir, whatever that means." She sighs breathlessly and then whispers in my ear. I can feel her breath on my face and smell her light perfume. "Your car is waiting. Lord Kitchener says you are to hurry to your destination now, and that events have made a turn for the worse. Your soldier is in the car. He has the pertinent information."
Crabtree is waiting impatiently for me on Horse Guards Avenue. "Well?" I bark at him. Gaylor springs into action and His Majesty's car lurches forward towards Whitehall Gardens and the Embankment, pointing its nose eastward.
"They are inside the arsenal, Sir. This one is particularly gruesome, Sir. Lord Kitchener has ordered that nobody touch anything until you arrive." This game of theirs has escalated, and my assumption that it had nothing to do with what transpires inside the arsenal has been blown away in a matter of hours. They are inside the walls, and they are not going away. Worse, for me, whatever they are doing there, they have no desire to cover up their presence. The King is due to visit in less than a week, and they are killing anyone who crosses their path. Which cannot be good. Truly reckless behaviour like this, It would be foolish, futile, unless they were planning something truly, horribly awful.

XII.

Nothing appears untoward as we climb out of the car at the Beresford Gate in Woolwich. The sun has broken through what has, for weeks, been an impenetrable and featureless pale grey sky, dumping endless sleet on the capital at various intervals. Crabtree and I add our footprints to thousands in the ageing slush that blankets the cobbled street just inside the Royal Arsenal as finally, spring appears to have arrived.
 Waiting for us after we have shown our passes is a rather relaxed looking soldier. He is lounging on a lamppost just inside the gate and chewing on a grime-laden fingernail. He is exceedingly scruffy, his shirt half untucked, his boots covered in muck, a shoelace dangling in a puddle. His curly dark hair is streaked with grey, far too long and sticking out from under his cap. He is short, his nose is running and he has a bit of a belly poking out of a gap in his shirt where a button should be. It all conspires to give him the air of a mischievous schoolboy in his early forties. He seems to be oblivious to any offence this might cause an officer. He wipes his nose with the back of his hand, uses the same hand to shake Crabtree's jovially, and tips his cap at me. "A'right Sir?" No effort at a salute. He intrigues me already. Not the man you'd expect sent out to escort you at a highly secretive murder scene.
"Oh!" He produces an envelope, evidently reading my mind. "Supposed to give you this." He passes it to me and I open it.

This is Williams. He looks terrible, but he's incredibly useful. Knows every inch of the arsenal. He is up to speed, and bears the same pass as you, so can be trusted. He is at your disposal for as long as you need him, Superintendent Gibbs."

"All right, Private Williams, lead the way," I say, folding up the note and shoving it in my pocket. Chirpily he sets off, rabbiting away to Crabtree, as I remain several paces behind. We turn right and pass Dr. Scully's dank little mortuary and the surgery that he has next door. It is all shut up and he is nowhere in sight as, with some trepidation, we begin to penetrate further into the maze of the arsenal than Crabtree and I have yet ventured. It transpires that we are on Avenue H, for the powers that be have shown little imagination when it comes to labelling this venerable and historical site. More buildings are huddled like Scully's up against the boundary wall, protecting us from the bustle and the prying eyes of the Plumstead Road. Passing a low, brick building with a rambling frontage that constitutes lodging for some of the single men who serve as arsenal policemen, we turn left onto Street No.6. Williams is, indeed, like a rat in its favourite sewer, shaking hands, calling out greetings. I make a mental note to ask him what it is that he actually does here, other than spread joy and a liberal helping of body odour. He smells worse than some of the men did on the great retreat last year. And yet he bears a venerable black pass. Interesting.

For the first time I can see the real business of munitions and it is bewildering and alien. Most buildings are labelled, but some only sport numerical designations. The engine rooms and forges I understand, but a turnery, and the random distribution of cranes and machinery sitting in the open are a mystery to me. The vast infrastructure shouldn't surprise me given the size of the place, but there is even a sawmill as we turn onto Avenue E, accompanied by a smell of freshly cut wood and a cloud of related dust that I can feel entering my nasal cavity.

Immediately on our right is a gargantuan building labelled D.78. It is all brick for the first ten feet or so and then gives way to a towering edifice piled on top, made out of a combination of iron girders, glass plates and metalwork. Williams comes to an abrupt halt outside a doorway cut into the corner. An arsenal policemen is standing outside, and Williams produces his pass to get inside. Crabtree and I copy the gesture and one by one we step over the threshold and past the sentry into an office of sorts. What it really is, is simply a corner of the building that has been enclosed by wooden panels that only stand about eight feet high, so that above it is open to all that is happening elsewhere inside. Worktops have been affixed to two sides, and they bend under the weight of piles of drawings, loose tools, ledgers, buckets. There is even a ladder on one of them. Rather than a functioning administrative space, it looks like a dumping ground for inconvenient paperwork and any other object that various owners whose passes bear the D.78 designation have become tired of looking at. The one thing that it does lack, however, is a corpse, and so Williams quickly leads us through a cutting in the panel wall and out into the workshop.

"Mate, what happens in here?" Crabtree asks.
"Boring," Williams calls behind him. Crabtree shrugs and follows him.

There are no workers inside. They were sent away as soon as the first of them discovered the body that we are about to intercept. Beyond the wall, the size of the place defies comprehension, an endless hangar towering above us, with vast windows set high up, grimy with dust and letting in nothing more than a pale yellow light from outside. A naval gun looks impressive attached to the front of a battleship, but a factory filled with dozens of them is a stunning sight. In the centre of the vast room there are two long rows of guns, each some fifty feet long each, laid in cradles end to end. "12 inch guns. These beauties are destined for Dreadnoughts. 60 odd tons each, they weigh, when they're done." Williams waves a hand at one as we pass. "Each shell weighs as much as three men." "What's the range?" I am genuinely interested by such a monstrous weapon.

"A little under fifteen miles," he says proudly. Staggering. And this is a failing effort at arming Britain for war? Standing at my full height of about 5'10, I am barely taller than the base of the contraptions holding them in place. Huge, circular wooden wheels support them at one end, a complex arrangement of gears and mechanisms at the other. Williams was answering Crabtree's question, not passing judgement. Here they are boring out the barrel of new guns with finite precision to make sure that they will accurately spin projectiles on a path of destruction toward the enemy.

In addition to the mammoth guns in the cradles, the vast floorspace is filled with more, piled up like matchsticks and pinned back. There are smaller guns of all different sizes waiting to be worked on. Huge chains lace their way across the floor. Together Crabtree and I would not be able to lift a single link. Underneath there are what look like tramlines crisscrossing back and forth, there to facilitate trolleys which will move out guns that have been dealt with onto the next part of their construction elsewhere. A great gantry is affixed overhead, strung with more thick chains and devilish looking hooks spaced all the way down the hangar. One gun hangs from the ceiling, waiting for a place on the ground, suspended in a dubious looking pulley system. It unnerves me that something so monstrous could be dangling so carelessly above our heads.

Williams has walked on up the hangar, and having taken all of this in, Crabtree and I hurry to catch up. Our guide waits for us to draw level, then points forward to a gap between guns where I can already see Dr. Scully bent on the other side of one of the monstrous weapons. "I'll wait over here." Williams takes ten paces, turns the other way, and considerately waits out of earshot. He may look and smell revolting, but I'm already starting to like him in spite of myself.

Scully is standing with two voluntary policemen. Both are past recruitment age for the army, just, it seems. One is quite bald, the other, taller, with straw coloured hair, has been using his cap as a sick bucket. They nod grimly. "A'right, Crabtree," one of them says to my assistant.

"Watcha, Dave," he says to the bald man. Crabtree seems to know every cherry knob in town.

"He's one of ours," Dave volunteers sadly to my assistant.

Despite the fact that it is no warmer in the hangar than it is outside, I take off my cumbersome greatcoat and sling it over the nearest gun. "Well, then," I say, "let's have a look at him then."

There is not much left. Now we are up close, I can see that a pile of guns has rolled apart, leaving a line of them in disarray all the way back to where they were stacked against a wall some fifteen feet away. They are dwarfed by the giants, but still more than twenty feet long each. The first gun has stopped up against a cradle opposite us, a second has rolled into it and stayed there, whilst the others have backed up behind them with some force. Our victim is sandwiched in between these first two pieces of ordnance. Only his head, shoulders and upper arms, grubby with coal dust, remain intact. There appears to be a partial black handprint on the side of his face. It appears that he was lifted upwards on impact and slung back slightly so that his face is raised toward the ceiling. He might have been a handsome man, he has quite smooth features. He looks to have been about thirty. His hair is white blond, and his pale, blue eyes bulge uncomfortably out of his skull in a terrified, cruel look of surprise. Blood trails from one corner of his mouth. From the middle of his chest down, he has been half spread along the surface of the two guns almost like a paste by several unforgiving tons of metal. I wonder if it was a quick death. I hope it was a quick death. Blood has pooled next to a drain in the floor underneath this horrific spectre, and what is not congealing is dripping thickly out of sight below ground. A few lightly bloody footprints surround the mess and then lead way from the scene of the crime.

Dave's companion has begun retching into his cap again. "What happened?" Crabtree whispers at my shoulder.

"Physics," I reply. "Who was he?"

"Remington. Mordecai Remington," says Dave, spitting on the floor.

"What do you know?" This to either of the policemen, but the other still looks decidedly green and simply bends over and holds onto his knees, breathing deeply. Dave appears to have come to terms with the horror on display more readily than his cohort, but he is avoiding any glance in Remington's direction.

"We were all on our normal watch last night, patrolling D Section. We'd stopped to have a cup of Bovril in the scaffold store across the way, use the latrines. Remington was convinced that he heard something."

"What time was this?"

"Two-ish. We break at two on the dot every night for fifteen minutes."

"And what did he hear?"

"He called it a 'muffled bang'. We laughed at him. He spooks easily. We said he should go and investigate. He did. And well, he never came back, We assumed he'd gone on with his walk. We didn't realise he was missing until this morning when we all came back together at the end of our watch and he never turned up. Then we came looking for him."

"Did you see anything suspicious on your rounds? Hear anything?"

"Nothing at all, Sir. Nowhere in our section at all. Whoever did it, they got away without us even clocking they'd been here."

"Would there have been any lighting in here?"

"No," Dave informs me. "All the lights go off at night in here."

"But you carry lanterns?"

"Yes, Sir."

I am trying to paint a picture in my head of what Remington walked into. Almost complete darkness, it seems. Suddenly I can hear a cacophony of chewing in the region of my right ear. Crabtree is eating a corned beef sandwich as he looks over the body intently. I feel my stomach lurch. He catches my horrified look.

"What?" He whispers indignantly. "I went home to get a uniform and me mum didn't want me to go 'ungry." He looks a little sheepish. "She sent a ham one for you too…" He moves his hand towards his pocket ever so slightly, then sees that my expression has not softened and thinks better of it.

"Do you know him?" I ask coldly.

"Nope." As I step as close as I dare and examine the mechanics of what has befallen Mordecai Remington, Crabtree resumes alternating between chewing his foul smelling sandwich loudly and smacking his lips. Just when I feel ready to throttle the life out of him with my bare hands, possibly shoving the thing down his gullet until he chokes on it; he swallows dramatically and lets out a small belch that he at least has the good grace to stifle with his fist. "Sir?"

"What, Crabtree?"

He points to the floor. "The footprints."

"What about them?"

"Well…"

"Spit it out."

"The height of a man can be told in nine cases out of ten by the length of his stride."

I give him my plagiarising disapproval look, but it is a bloody good point. The strides are long, surely too long for a woman, even a tall one. "Conan Doyle?"

"Yes, Sir." He goes back to his sandwich. How he can eat the thing whilst observing in minute detail the former shape of a human being who now closely resembles its filling is mortifying. He wanders off on the trail of the footprints and I leave him to it. Confiscating the damned thing will make no difference. He is useless when he is hungry. Scully is on tiptoes gazing at the remains of Remington, trying to decide how to begin having him scraped off the gun and removed to the mortuary.

"Williams?"

"Sir? " Our guide obediently steps to my side and pushes his messy hair out of his eyes and back under the peak of his cap.

"Talk to me about how this happened."

"If you'll follow me, Sir." He walks off towards where the incriminating guns were originally piled up. As I pursue him, we are obliged to duck under one of the cradles and step around the others that have toppled all over the floor like lethal ninepins. He shows me, using a nearby stack, how they are assembled, using hooks, into an uncovered frame and pinned back by a system of heavy bars and a lever at each end that prevents them from rolling out onto the floor.

"What would it take to bring one of these piles down?" I ask him.

He clears his throat. "Well, Sir. Most importantly for you, it would take two people. You couldn't have let them go from one end. Both ends of the frame would have to be opened up at the same time. Secondly, the frames are not designed to be released like that, least of all by human hands. They've had to break those pins to do it. Two very strong blokes did this, probably wielding metal bars or something similar that they picked up." They've snapped the pins at both ends, simultaneously, otherwise the guns wouldn't have rolled the way they have."

I note the improbability of our mystery woman's involvement in this murder. But then killing Fred George took some effort, and she might have been responsible for that. On the way back I use a flashlight to look around and about as many of the guns as I can get between, but find no more clues. The foreman of this particular workshop has arrived and is waiting by the office. All I can do is leave instructions to have them retain anything they find when they clear up this mess, and contact me immediately; for it will take hours, and I have work to do. As soon as I return to the vicinity of Remington's demise, to fetch Crabtree, I hear his voice. "Sir?" I cannot see him, until he pops his head up and waves a hand at me. He appears to have walked around the immense cradle and is on the other side of the behemoth sitting in it. I join him and my gaze follows his extended arm. Now I feel anger in the pit of my stomach as well as bile. As if we needed any more evidence, the fact that someone appears to have dipped their hand in Remington's blood to slather the words: *'Still cold, Will,'* on the front gun rules out any possibility of this being an unfortunate and very gruesome accident. I ask Scully to send my a copy of his autopsy report, not that I expect it to add anything new at all. The manner of Remington's fate leaves nothing to the imagination. A look around the rest of the hangar yields no clues, including an inspection of a latrine in the far corner which contains nothing more than the stench of stale urine.

Crabtree has been taking notes, and now we step outside for a look about the area. He starts to draw a little map of our surroundings, but everything seems innocuous. I cannot see why anyone would want to kill a man in this spot. Surely there are more useful areas inside the arsenal than this, if one has mischief in mind. One cannot steal a 12 inch naval gun. Nearby there is a small shop that deals with fashioning sighting machinery, a coal bunker, a boiler house, a little place that tempers metal, another that produces hammers, and a dirty little pond. "Williams, exactly how far are we from Carrick's domain?"

He puts his hands on his hips and sticks his stomach out; screwing up his face as he turns to face the direction in which I suppose Carrick's work was carried out. "A mile?"

"That much?"

"Wrong place, wrong time," Crabtree mutters.

"Surely it has to be? If Carrick is the key to this insanity, then what on earth makes this boring facility the *right* place for these maniacs? Two men now perhaps. To add to the woman, and to the author of the smug note, if he is not one of the former. Not to mention whoever might have killed Fred George if none of them were the perpetrator." My head is swimming. They have access to the arsenal, at least they did last night. How? And why? Perhaps they are still looking for something that belonged to Carrick. Or perhaps they need *something;* equipment, materials, to put one of his inventions into action. Williams confirms that he is taking us to the deceased doctor's office next. We have already begun to stride away from the murder scene, and what remains of Mordecai Remington, when I realise that Dr. Scully is breathlessly waddling behind, trying to catch up with us. Without exchanging a word, Crabtree and I have begun to pick up speed; the same escape in mind. "I, say, I say Lieutenant Stanley. Have you heard of the concept of telekinesis?" I ignore him. "When you have eliminated the impossible, whatever remains, no

matter how improbable, must be the truth." Is that not right? Private Crabtree?"
I stop and turn abruptly, so much so that he walks straight into me. I grab him by the collar and lift him up so that we are eye to eye "What did you say?" He panics, his feet are flapping about trying to connect with the floor again. "How did you know to say that?"
"We've talked about Sherlock Holmes, I've heard the two of you joking about it too!"
Crabtree puts a hand on my upper arm. "Sir, people are looking"
I let the infuriating little man go and he straightens his tie. I have not finished with him yet though.
"Telekinesis? Good grief man, you are a medical professional, will you not act like it?"
"How else do you explain a naval gun moving itself?" He snaps.
"Well, obviously it didn't."
"And it could not have been your suspicious old woman? Men of exceptional strength at the very least would have been required to orchestrate that accident, and nobody saw anything of the sort." Through gritted teeth I apologise for my rough treatment of him, but I do not acknowledge his last statement. Crabtree, Williams and I continue walking away. He has to have the last word before he stomps off in the direction of his mortuary. "Any truth is better than indefinite doubt."
Curse Arthur Conan Doyle. And a bloody pox on Sherlock Holmes.

XIII.

Williams flags down a passing car and simply commandeers it using his pass. As we set off east, Crabtree goes through his notebook pointing out all of the reasons why the idea of Scully being involved in this deteriorating situation in a sinister way is laughable in his eyes. He has always been better at seeing the bigger picture, whereas I have more of an eye for detail, but I don't really believe that the doctor has anything to do with it. He just happened to open his mouth at the wrong time with his folkology nonsense and irritate me. Williams merely sits and picks his nose with one hand and tries to examine the contents whilst driving with the other, which does not inspire me with confidence given the speed at which we are going.

We barrel for some time through a winding labyrinth of roads and impossible shortcuts that seem dead ends until Williams suddenly makes one last turn and we spring out onto a proper street and continue on our way. Soon we break free of the oldest part of the Royal Arsenal, where workshops and stores sit haphazardly, crammed together, and thousands upon thousands of people work on top of each other. Buildings become newer, more spaced out; and a lot of them look of dubious, hasty construction. They all have an 'E' designation now, and Williams informs us that where we are going, the facilities are off limits to almost everyone. "This here is my domain. You have to have a damned good purpose to be hanging round," he says. And yet we are not looking at anything impressive, architecturally speaking; scattered and vaguely labelled little buildings, some of them no more than sheds. One is surrounded by hazard warnings. I see a small workshop, something called a nitrating house, a 'doubtful cartridges hut,' which is worrying, and a disturbingly named 'acid plant.' All of them have a decent amount of empty space around them. "What exactly is your job, Williams?" I ask

"Bit of this, bit of that, Sir," he breezes as he pulls the car up alongside what looks like a pair of boring, suburban, semi-detached houses in the middle of yet more empty space and opens my door for me. One is locked up and looks disused. "Been here since I was a kid. Mostly, I like to make things go boom." The grin that accompanies that statement is disconcerting. I let the subject go for now.

We are met at the door to the laboratory by another officer, a Captain with a long, sad, pasty face; exacerbated by dark, gloomy features that include lank hair, a protruding chin, a mouth turned down at the corners and droopy eyes. I'd wager he looked exactly like this before the war, but they certainly won't be putting his face in any of the inspirational pictorials promising victory any time soon. He professes to have been waiting for us, but not so as it sounds like he is complaining. Even his handshake is limp. "Ingalls," he informs me.

"Stanley," I nod politely. He is senior to me, after all, despite that handshake.

The entire ground floor of the laboratory has been knocked through to form one large work space. I stand at the door initially, trying to take it all in. Benches line all four walls. Dozens of shelves have been put up above them, and cabinets pack out the spaces below. Every conceivable bit of surface space has been accounted for by instruments, books, paperwork, diagrams and other scientific ephemera. It is going to prove an investigative nightmare trying to dig out one piece of pertinent information to explain either Carrick's death, or what is happening at the arsenal. "As you can see," Ingalls says in a lacklustre, droning voice, "we haven't even made a start yet."

Something is bothering me. "Where are all the compounds? The Bunsen burners and such? He was primarily a chemist was he not?"

Ingalls shrugs. "We were told to give him anything he wanted, of late he'd been working more in line with other things, judging by the lists I was given. He used a bigger testing facility on occasion, but not recently."

"Did you know him well?"

"No, not really," sighs Ingalls. He is leaning on a workbench like he would collapse out of sheer inertia if it wasn't there to prop him up. "I have enough of my own work on, but I was assigned to make sure he got what he wanted. He'd send requests up to me in my office and I'd requisition materials for him. I only met him once or twice. He was always courteous. A quiet chap, introverted I'd say, not one to brag about what he was capable of, or what he was doing."

That is interesting. I hadn't thought of that. I suppose it lessens the possibility that he was talking carelessly about his work, and that the wrong people overheard. "Do you recall anything out of the ordinary about these lists? Types of things he asked for, any larger quantities of chemicals?"

"I'm afraid not, in fact, he hadn't asked for much of late. He was a bit all over the place though, jumped from one thing to another judging by how unpredictable his lists were. I suppose that comes with being a genius."

I nod. I am relieved. In my mind a nightmare scenario has been forming in which these scoundrels have obtained the recipe for some disastrous explosive compound, but with everything Ingalls says this might be receding as a possibility. "We can look upstairs too? I don't think he carried out actual experiments up there but he kept important papers up there. There is a safe," he sighs.

Perfect. With luck we can disregard the chaos of the ground floor as not being of significant enough interest to warrant killing the man and find what we need upstairs. The staircase is dilapidated and narrow, and we trudge up one by one. Crabtree has surmised that I am not interested in his mother's ham sandwich and has begun eating it. At the top of the stairs, two rooms are wide open and simply filled to bursting point with equipment that I presume Carrick had lost interest in. The third is secured with two padlocks. Ingalls looks puzzled and simply stares at them.

"I don't have the keys." Williams is outside with the car and I call him in. "Is picking locks in your repertoire?"

"Certainly is, Sir" he says from the staircase.
"Then up you come." He removes a set of metal instruments from his pocket, as if this is a problem he deals with on a daily basis, and in less than a minute both padlocks have been sprung and are on the floor.
"Anything else, Sir?"
"No, but just wait outside here." I have a suspicion that the most valuable of Carrick's documents might be under lock and key.

Sure enough, as soon as we enter the tiny room above the entrance to the house my eye is drawn to solid-looking, dark green safe. In fact there is nothing else of interest. It appears that the doctor only used this strong room to lock away his more dangerous secrets. There is no space for anything else. "I need to get at what is in there as soon as possible. It is a matter of the utmost urgency. Can we open this?"

I have tried to be forceful, to press Ingalls along, but his doleful response is predictable. "I'm afraid I don't know the combination," he even yawns.

Is he joking? I've driven past enough explosives at Woolwich today to light up the entire south of England, and it hasn't occurred to this scientist how he might take the door off a safe? God Help him if he ever has to command troops. More appropriately, god help the troops. Then I remember Williams's vague job description. "Williams!" I shout.

"Sir?" His dirty head appears round the doorframe.
"Do you want to make something go boom?" His face lights up like a child's at Christmas.

Ingalls clearly does not approve at all, but I am banking on his being too flaccid to order me to stop what I am doing. It works, for he simply scratches his head as Crabtree and Williams drag the safe onto some kind of trolley that they have located in one of the store rooms and hump it down the stairs, swearing plentifully.

"Where now?" I ask when they have manoeuvred it over the doorstep and outside.

"There's a range nearby that will do," grins Williams. Ingalls nods wearily, and Williams jumps behind the wheel of the car. "Back in a jiffy!"

And off he rumbles. In the meantime, Ingalls gesticulates vaguely that we should follow him. Crabtree has a good handle on the trolley now it is outside, but I steady the safe with my hand as he comically pushes it along to avoid mishap. There is another security gate for us to negotiate, and the guards eyebrows arch when they see our black passes. The ground becomes spongy, for we are getting out towards Plumstead Marshes now, I think. Crabtree now pulls at the trolley whilst I shove at it from behind. Much of the space is open, but we pass, of all things, a little pavilion and then some soldiers huts and a 'splinter proof shelter' that doesn't look like it would shelter one from the tamest of hailstones, let alone shrapnel or high explosives. Speaking of which, there is a hell of a noise coming from just to the north, where Ingalls informs us that there is a high explosives range, for a start, as well as other testing ranges, butts etc. Added to that, there are nearby magazines storing dangerous concoctions and an 'experimental explosives magazine' that he informs us Carrick had used earlier in the war, but not of late. And there is a 'bursting chamber,' which sounds particularly unhealthy.

The sound of a motor car causes us all to look up and see Williams returning at breakneck speed. He screeches to a halt, almost taking off our toes, and jumps down from the car. After a few moments digging about on the back seat he emerges with a worrying combination of wire, pliers and explosives. He begins whistling a cheerful tune. Bloody *Tipperary*. "Might want to to put some distance in between you and this, Sir."

Crabtree, Ingalls and I take his advice, leaving him crouched down and affixing some arrangement to the

front of the safe. We stop ten feet away, but Williams looks up, chuckles and waves the pliers. "More than that!" Ingalls looks flat out disturbed now, presumably worried about how big this unscheduled explosion is going to be. Williams finishes what he is doing and then saunters back, lighting a cigarette. The safe sits some thirty feet away. "Are you a good shot? Sir?"
"Reasonable."
"Care to do the honours?"
I take out my revolver. It's been a couple of weeks since I fired it.
"Just aim for the packet on the door." I do just that. The explosion is much bigger than anticipated. The safe jumps some ten feet off the floor, before landing on its side, but the door cannons towards us at high speed. Ingalls makes a show of ducking, but it sails way over our heads and lands another ten feet behind, smoking.
"BOOM!" Says Williams enthusiastically.
"Boom," says Crabtree.
"Boom indeed," I reply.
Ingalls simply lets out a little groan, as if the explosion has dislodged something painful in his gut.
"Fun, ain't it?" Williams breezes as we walk towards the remains of Carrick's safe.
More than I care to admit. A few papers have come out, some deeds and bonds are charred, but Carrick appears to have meticulously bound his paperwork into categories, whatever they may be, and these merely lie cluttered sideways now on one of two shelves.
However, before I can approach them, Ingalls puts out a hand to stop me in my tracks. It is the first convincing gesture I've seen him make. "Not so fast, Lieutenant. Proper channels must be observed."
"I am here on the highest authority…"
"I know exactly whose authority you are here on. Nonetheless. I will remove these documents, box them and they will be delivered securely to the War Office later on today. You are welcome to observe them being

packed, so as to be sure you have everything, but then the seal cannot be broken until they have reached Whitehall. I am afraid that I really must insist."
Frustrating, but I can see his point. It's the kind of thing Kitchener would insist upon himself, and who knows what pivotal information concerning the war effort is contained in this safe. Ingalls does not know me from Adam. Crabtree and I can do little but get back into the car with he and Williams, who takes us all back towards the Beresford Gate and Building 22. Crabtree remains outside with him while I laboriously witness the Captain count and roughly catalogue everything from the safe, record it going into a large cardboard box and then painfully slowly, secure it with tape and a seal. Then he writes a veritable essay on the side.

The light has begun to fade outside by the time I finally get out of there, having signed documents as to the shipment of the box to the War Office by a messenger. It is turning out time at the arsenal, and I walk into a thick crowd of workers. Williams is leaning on a lamppost outside, but there is no sign of Crabtree.
"Said he was starving, Sir. He went for something to eat about ten minutes ago. He said he'd meet you outside The Pyro when you're ready. I believe your car is waiting for you there."
"All right," I say, "Thank you for your help today Williams."
"Just doing my duty," he grins, before turning on his heel.
"Williams?" I cannot let it go."
"Sir?"
"What *is* your official role here?" He simply chuckles again. "Boom," I reply.
"Boom, Sir," he laughs before he strides off whistling again. Still no salute.
Outside the gate is a sea of humanity heading off in all different directions. I am forced to press my way across

the busy junction to get through to the car, which Gaylor has parked just by The Pyro. He is standing guard over the vehicle and watching people pass by from underneath his scowling, bushy red eyebrows as if he doesn't trust anyone not to attack the King's Daimler. There is no sign of Crabtree, however. "Have you seen him?"
One, almost imperceptible shake of the head. I'll take that as a no. My temper flares. I wait for fifteen minutes, checking my watch repeatedly and muttering obscenities under my breath. The crowd begins to thin, and still there is no sign of my assistant. It is most unlike him to drag his heels like this. And he knows how urgent the job we have on is. I check inside the pub. He is not there. Finally, I decide that he can make his own way back to the War Office, then when he sheepishly appears at the door to my office I can conveniently take something from my desk and bowl it at his head.

XIV.

So much has happened today, that I deliver myself straight to Lord Kitchener to fill him in on both the murder of Mordecai Remington and the impending arrival of the contents of Dr. Carrick's safe. Lord Kitchener's immediate response to all that I tell him is to remove a bottle of brandy and a glass from the windowsill and put both in front of me. "Have at it," he says. "It sounds like you need it." I gratefully pour a large measure and sit back in my chair.
"And to cap it all off, Crabtree has bloody disappeared just as I need him to sit down with me and go through these papers."
"Has he done that before?" Kitchener looks concerned.
I must admit that my anger gave way to worry the nearer I got to the War Office. "Never. But it was very

crowded. The meeting place was clear, but he may have got distracted."

"We will give it a few more hours and then review the situation if we have not heard from him." He does, however, call Fitz through and ask him to speak with the Superintendent's office to see if they have seen him. "Don't worry about notifying Remington's family," he adds. "I will have it done by the arsenal."

"Thank you. I could do without that." Nursing my brandy, I admit to the War Secretary that I nearly struck Dr. Scully silly, lest it get back to him anyway.

He is sympathetic. "You should try and get your head down for a few hours of proper rest tonight. It will do us no good if you are exhausted."

I cannot help but smile. "I'll strike a deal with you, Sir," I say. "I'll heed that advice if you do too."

"Ha," he laughs, as he takes another glass from the windowsill and pours himself a drink. He takes a sip and then goes back to annotating a typed document in front of him. For want of anything else to do while I finish my brandy, or until Carrick's paperwork turns up, I pick up a file that is one of many almost ready to topple off the desktop under their own weight and open it. We sit quietly for twenty minutes or so before his concentration is broken for a moment and he sees that I am reading. "What is that? I am trusting that you will put back anything particularly sensitive."

"No, Sir."

He leans back and stretches in his chair. "If you have time though, you might brief me on some of the more routine ones. On any points you think require my attention. So much of it is fluff, and Fitz is doing his best out there, but the stream is relentless."

I show him the front page. "This is simply a report on safety conditions in munitions factories. The perils of working constantly with certain chemicals and so forth."

There is a knock at the door and Fitz appears holding a pile of buff coloured folders, some thicker than others. "From the Home Office, Sir."
"Ah, yes," Kitchener gesticulates at me. "They are for Will. I mentioned them before," he says. They are referred to as the Dangerous Women Files. Anyone on the Government's list for reasons of criminal activity, vandalism, endangering the public, suffrage nonsense like chaining themselves to things, etc. I asked for blonde women aged 25-45, who are thin."
"There are twenty or so," Fitz informs me as he puts them on my lap.
This is a potentially exciting development. "If you'll excuse me, Sir?" The War Secretary waves his hand. Outside his office I have a thought that might grease the wheels of the particular approach I have in mind. "Fitz, will you do me a favour?"
He nods. "Of course."
"Will you telephone my house and order the housekeeper up here, a Mrs. Mitcham? She saw this woman."
"Yes of course, but…"
"She's liable to tell me to sod off. She washed my nappies, and, well, you know."
He laughs as I recite the number for him. "Understood. You want her here now?"
"Yes please, as soon as possible. And lay it on thick won't you? Put the wind up her." I am chuckling as I descend the stairs back to my office.
 She arrives inside half an hour looking extremely flustered, her hat on wonky and her coat undone. She gives me a look of complete thunder when she is shown into my office and realises that it is merely I who has summoned her. "Ooh you little bugger! I ought to clip your ear! In the middle of getting dinner ready I was, when I get an urgent call from the War Office. I thought I was in trouble. Or that someone had died!"

"Of course not, you old goat. Did you bring me anything?"

She takes her gloves off and hits me with them. "Less of the old."

"Here, sit down. And calm yourself woman. I need your help." I pull a chair out for her and she plonks herself down, her anger subsiding. "The woman, who came to the house. I need you to look at these and tell me if you see her face. Remember, anything in them is confidential."

She looks at me as if I am teaching her how to suck an egg and opens the first folder. She discards it to one side and opens the second. "Was it really Lord Kitchener's office what called?"

"Yes, his secretary, Fitzgerald."

"Nice gentleman he was," she goes for the third folder. "Not like you."

"And here I was about to have you a cup of tea brought up. You can poke it now."

"Liar, you're not that considerate."

I pour her a scotch from a bottle in my cupboard. "You thieving little git, this is your father's!" She exclaims. It doesn't stop her drinking it though. But her visit is in vain, for eventually she claims that no woman in the ranks of these vandals, arsonists, murderers and so forth looks remotely like the one that came to our door with the box of cigarettes.

"Then I am sorry to have troubled you," I say genuinely.

"It's important, isn't it?"

"The problem is that I don't think that murder is the end of it."

"What is worse than murder?"

"That is what I'm trying to establish. Don't tell mother." She nods. I scribble a note for her. "There is a red car outside. A great redhead brute waiting with it. Give him this and he will drive you home."

"You'd put me in a car with such a man?"

I shrug. "I'm not that fond of you." When she scowls I have to laugh. "The car belongs to the King himself, Mrs. Mitcham, and the man is his personal chauffeur." Rarely do I see her speechless. She puts her gloves back on. "I'll leave some dinner out for you," she says by way of a thanks. It is a significant concession, for if you miss dinner in our house you go without. I flag a clerk down outside the office and ask him to take her downstairs to Gaylor.

She has barely disappeared down the corridor when Lord Kitchener approaches from the other direction, cap and greatcoat on. "Get your coat."

"Where are we going?" I ask, already obeying his order.

"To the palace. I've told Fitz to ring us up there immediately should Private Crabtree show his face. I'm starting to worry that he may have fallen foul of these people."

"Yes, Sir," I say as I follow him down the stairs. "The longer he is missing, the more unlike him it is."

We walk from Whitehall. St. James's Park is a bleak spectre. The lake has been drained lest its reflection at night guide any these phantom Zeppelin men towards the palace. There are few people about, for the temperature has dropped well below freezing with the coming of darkness. In the gutter at the end of The Mall though, a woman is howling and clutching her ankle as a bewildered looking taxi driver stands over her, his hands open in a pleading gesture. He says he didn't see her. Some London Members of Parliament are demanding a relaxation in the restriction of lighting, so dramatically have the number of traffic incidents risen. The King's secretary awaits us in his room. Lord Stamfordham has a military bearing, thanks to his years as an artillery officer. He is tall and thin, with a large, bald forehead. His remaining hair is neat and dark, and he has sharp, keen eyes. "His Majesty has just returned from Aldershot. He has been watching some of your New Army troops," he explains to Kitchener. "He has asked me to check in with you." He gestures to two chairs and we sit down. Then he searches for a notepad on his desk and pulls it toward him with a pen. "The King is fairly well up to speed, thanks to Lord K here, but if you will just break it down for me into the simplest of terms."

"Yes," I take a deep breath. "I now believe that all of the deaths in the vicinity of the arsenal are connected. The first, that of Dr. Carrick, I believe to be the key. My theory at the moment is that he was working on something confidential and that a group have killed him to get at it. His wife and daughter are currently missing, but I am struggling to believe that he was involved in anything untoward. Police in Manchester are currently investigating their whereabouts. All of his most secretive papers are now on their way to me at the War Office where I will consult them and try to establish exactly what it is they were after." He nods as he finishes writing that down, and I continue. "It does not seem that killing Dr. Carrick got them what they wanted, because they are still in the vicinity of the arsenal. There have been two more deaths. Neither of these took place in a location pertinent to Dr. Carrick or his work, and so I have to believe that the two unfortunate gentlemen; a factory foreman and an arsenal policeman, were in the wrong place at the wrong time, and were just unlucky enough to come across them."

He underlines something on his pad. "And what makes you think it is a group, as opposed to an individual?"

I clear my throat. "They have made contact with me."

Lord Stamfordham stops writing. "Really? How astonishing. With what aim?"

"To mock me, Sir." I feel pathetic admitting it. "The woman witnessed at Carrick's death delivered a package to my house by hand. A very specific brand of cigarettes that I smoke. And there was a note making fun of me for not having found her."

The King's private secretary leans back in his chair and makes a steeple with his fingers. "Then they are watching you. The note was from someone else?"

I nod. "She mentioned that she worked for a gentleman when she spoke to our housekeeper. And the death of Mordecai Remington, the policeman. It required two people, two strong men. The footprints at the scene appear to be male. So I believe there to be at least three of them, four if the author of the note was not one of those responsible for that death last night. Possibly even five if someone else altogether killed Fred George."

"And we know nothing about them?" This Stamfordham directs to Lord Kitchener, who shakes his head firmly.

"Sir," I continue. "The third death, it occurred within the walls of the arsenal. They have access to the site, which I believe may be a new development. If not, then why take such a risk with the death of Carrick? In a crowded public space? Whilst he was on his way home? I suspect they may be after equipment and materials to facilitate this invention of his."

Stamfordham nods in agreement. "We don't know how?" Kitchener shakes his head again. "What was he working on?"

"I have been able to ascertain that of late he was gravitating away from chemical experiments and working more along a mechanical line, but I'm afraid that it means little. I hope that his papers will shed light on this question. I do, however, think that whatever they want, it was incomplete, or it was a plan of sorts and they need to assemble it."

"Do you agree?" Stamfordham asks Kitchener.

One more nod. "I do. Carrick was very proper. When he had something ready for development, or ready to be of practical use, he delivered it to the authorities promptly."

"What was the last thing he reported?"

"Just refining processes that already exist. In terms of explosives production, and five weeks ago. Nothing worth killing for."

"Any thoughts, Stanley, on the type of perpetrator we are looking for?"

I'm afraid not, Sir. So far 'the enemy' is the logical deduction."

"Yes, naturally. K, will you talk to someone at SSB? Find out if they have anyone that they are looking at with scientific links. Or if they have heard any chatter about something new and effective that the Germans are interested in?" Stamfordham is talking about the Secret Service Bureau.

"Naval intelligence too," says Kitchener. "You never know. Stanley, do you have anyone that you can trust to keep a lid on a discreet enquiry, so that I don't have to bring in that gasbag, Churchill? That man expels more gas than a Zeppelin with a puncture."

"I do, yes Sir." Keyes.

"Approach them," says Stamfordham. "That covers people of German and Austrian origin. We can't put all of our eggs in one basket though. I will reach out to some of my civilian contacts regarding problematic groups on our own shores; pacifists, suffragettes, socialists. Any other suggestions?"

I shake my head. "The doctor at the arsenal thinks that a race of vampires with telekinetic powers are responsible."

"His Majesty has a sense of humour," Stamfordham grins, "but if I tell him London is awash with bloodsucking fiends and people shifting things about with the power of their mind, I fear I might be on the wrong end of one of his tempers. Anything else to report?"

"My assistant is missing," I admit.

"The chubby little fellow?"

"Yes, sir. I have not seen him since I left the arsenal. I am hoping he will turn up this evening, but…"

"Of course, you are thinking the worst. After all they have made it clear that they are keeping an eye on you. Well, here's hoping that he turns up without any fuss."

"I'm sorry sir," I say. I'm not quite sure where that comes from.

"You've accomplished a fair bit so far, Stanley. And there is time yet before His Majesty is to pay his visit next week. Let us hope that these papers turn up something. If you'll wait outside I'll just finish up with Lord K and then you can go back and await them."

Lord Kitchener tells me that I did well in my interview as we walk briskly back to the War Office, but I feel like a failure. Realistically I have no idea who is responsible for the crimes perpetrated at the arsenal, why they have carried them out, and what they intend to do next. When we arrive at Whitehall there is still no sign of Crabtree, and nobody at Woolwich recalls seeing him. Williams has even been on a drive about the site and just outside and turned up nothing. My concern for the little idiot deepens. He has never done anything like this. He's too fearful of my temper, which in truth has completely dissipated now with regard to his absence, I just want him to be safe.

If his whereabouts is a mystery, though, the Carrick box is diligently waiting for me on my desk, guarded by a humourless messenger from Woolwich who wants to go home for the evening. I sign for it, check the seals are still intact and get rid of him. I hardly know where to start. I try to put Crabtree out of my mind as I begin pulling the paperwork out and laying it on my desk.

Piles are tied up with string, and in case I stump myself by meddling with Carrick's filing system, I am careful to keep them separate. That said, schematics and diagrams are the first thing I go for, to see if anything leaps out at me. They are all for components though, as opposed to a finished plan for something that could turn the tide of the war or at least spark the interest of the enemy. No wonder scientists are dull in social settings, if this is what they spend all day concocting. Still frustrated, I turn to a pile of diaries and another of notebooks. I suppose I am hoping that at some point he confessed in writing that he had thought of something exceptional, but a quick glance at the last three months of 1914 merely shows appointments, reminders to submit lists to Ingalls, and dull information like the date of his wife's birthday.

I turn to the notebooks, and suddenly I have too many possible motivations to steal the product of the man's enormous brain. Jules Verne could have got several novels out of the stuff that is in them. There are great land ships, propelled on metal tracks and impervious to bullets and shells, and for the navy he has sketched special bombs that might be dropped from the deck of a ship, and timed to explode at a certain depth to wreak havoc on enemy submarines. He seems to have had a field day with aerial matters, for I suppose with such a new technology there is huge scope for development. He has devised machine guns that can be mounted on the front of aeroplanes and fired without shooting off the propellors. Any German agent worth his salt would kill to get his hands on any of this. Perhaps it is not one particular invention that interests our criminals at all, but the full scope of his designs.

I have almost given up for the night when I notice that in the last, unfinished notebook, several pages have been hastily torn out at once. The scraps left near the margin indicate that they contained full pages of notes. I almost throw the thing across the room, until I realise that the professor was in the habit of putting the date at the top of each page. The last date before the missing pages is 15th January 1915, and in a feat of remarkable common sense, I decide to cross reference the date with the relevant diary, just in case. As soon as I open the 1915 diary I notice that there are heftier entries than in the one Carrick was using before

Christmas. He was not exactly verbose, but at least there is more than the occasional boring appointment recorded. Going forward from 15th January, I look for something, anything that might hint at what the man was up to. On 19th, I find the only possibility that week.

"M14 - Do not pursue."

The first part, I think I can fathom. Somewhere I have seen a master list of what he was working on. Things for the army begin with an A prefix, then it is N for the navy and F for flying. M is miscellaneous, which he seems to have applied to ideas that might be used across the board. When I find the list, my frustration is palpable. It finishes at M13. Having turned through everything else, I can recall no reference in any diagram or plan to an M14. My eyes are closing, the clock has struck three. I have had enough. Making a mental note to begin again first thing in the morning, and to scrutinise minutely everything I have. I also intend to put in a call to Williams to see if he has heard of M14. I pick up my coat, mindful of Kitchener's instruction to get some proper rest. In ordinary circumstances, I would put a fresh set of eyes to the task. Crabtree's. But on even further enquiry at the front desk there has still been no sign of him.

In a foul mood, I wrap my coat around myself and begin stomping up Whitehall towards The Mall. The streets are deserted as I cut up Marlborough Road, St, James's Street and Albermarle on my way up to Green Park. I can take any number of turns on my right, off Piccadilly, to get myself home. Tonight I pick Half Moon Street. More fool me. It is not a long road, terminating when another street cuts across it at the far end, but it is quiet, and dark, and I am only a third of the way along when my thoughts of the case are disturbed by the sound of footsteps getting louder. At least two sets are picking up pace behind me. Rather than reach for my revolver. I decide to stay calm and try and get to the end of the street, where there are at least a few people, and it is better lit, even in these gloomy times. It is the wrong choice, because before I know it, the footsteps are running. The first blow comes from the left, someone grabbing my arm and yanking me downwards. Then another comes from behind. It feels like a foot slamming into the small of my back. Another arm comes from the right and pins me to the ground by my neck. Then they begin to kick and punch me. There are a few stamps thrown in for good measure too. My body begins to numb with every blow. With about the third or fourth to the head, my brain begins to go foggy. I am dimly aware of grunting and heavy breathing, but they say nothing. When they are done I hear them walk away, not run. They are even talking and laughing amongst themselves. London accents. I hear one voice above the rest: *"Next time, it'll be lights out for good, if you don't mind your own business."* The street lamp nearest to me begins flicker, and everything goes black.

Friday, 12th March 1915

XV.

It is daylight again and somehow I am in my own bed. As I open one eye, painfully, and then the other, it becomes apparent that I am not alone. Crabtree is sitting on the edge of my bed sporting a purpler shiner himself. He also has marmalade dripping from his chin as he crams toast into his face with an obvious expression of delight and enjoyment, shedding crumbs all over my bedspread. Mrs. Mitcham never misses an opportunity to feed someone so appreciative of her efforts. And I think he reminds her of her own son, who is in the Army Service Corps somewhere in France.
"You seem to have fared a lot better than me," I groan.
"They clumped me." He licks his fingers. "Three of 'em there was. But then I escaped."
"And how did you manage that?" My companion is not known for his speed.
I wish I hadn't asked, for I am then subjected to a five minute tale of classic Crabtree buffoonery, that in no way explains why he disappeared at the arsenal. He jumps straight to the previous night and recalls hurrying through Trafalgar Square, fantasising about something to eat, tripping over the kerb as he turned on to Whitehall out of sheer excitement about what he had to tell me and ruining the knee of his trousers. On he goes to describe scrambling to his feet, putting his hand in a pile of horse shit in the process, before arriving back at the War Office to find that he had just missed me. It may be the beating I have taken, but I feel like my ears are bleeding; like my brain is leaking out of my ears. After a description of all of the places he thought he may find food at that time, not to mention a pointless explanation of stopping to give someone directions to the Café de Paris, he finally begins ambling towards the point. Having decided to wander up to Victoria

Station and the soldiers canteen, he had the expedient idea of taking a shortcut through St. James's Park in the middle of the night. I resist the urge to point out that he is an idiot as he describes nearly tripping over a large bird, he thinks a swan, that subsequently chased him towards Buckingham Palace. By the time he gets to the part when, as he rounded the bend in the path towards the barracks on Birdcage Walk, his assailants leapt out, I am contemplating blackening his other eye. Judging by his approximation of time, they cannot be the same men that saw fit to batter me. With complete honesty he then describes screeching like a girl and tearing out of the park, to find two Special Constables sharing a smoke and staring at him in complete bewilderment. "They must have thought I was barmy." I can only imagine. However, the men flagged down a cab for him and sent him up to my house, which he deemed as the closest possible refuge, where he found two gentlemen outside delivering my semi-conscious form home, having discovered me and rifled through my pockets to find out who I was, and where I lived.
"You look bloody terrible, Sir. I'll be the good looking one for once. Don't worry, I'll send a couple of girls your way."

My head is pounding. This must be hell

"What happened to you then Sir?"

"Much the same, they got me on my way home."

"What did you do?"

"I killed them with a stroke special to those versed in the Japanese art of Ju-Jitsu using just my thumb and my forefinger."

"Really?"

"Of course not you fool," I sigh. "Look at the state of me. Clearly I lay on the floor and let them beat me. Where or earth did you get to yesterday, you imbecile?"

He dusts the breadcrumbs from his lap, jumps up, pulls a chair opposite the bed uncomfortably close to my face and sits in it. "Well, Sir, that's what I was so excited about. You know how they say that nothing is a detective's friend during an investigation so much as luck? Well we finally got some. I was coming out of the arsenal to get something to eat and I caught a swish of skirts and blonde hair coming out of a shop. Dunno what made me, but I thought I'd follow the woman for a bit. Well then, I saw her whopping great big nose and her bony face and thought, bugger me, that's the bird we are looking for! It's uncanny, how close the kid's description is."

"You are sure?"

"Not exactly, but wait 'till I tell you what this woman was up to. It ain't right."

I sit up suddenly. It hurts. I could kiss him. "What was she doing?"

"Walking away from the arsenal. Looking shifty."

I am wary of giving him license to waffle again, so I keep my questions to the point. "Where did she go?"

"Up onto Plumstead High Street and onto a tram. I carried on following her."

"To?"

"Into town. All over the place we went before we ended up at Charing Cross Road. Then she walked through to Trafalgar Square and all round the back just to end up where the shipping offices are. Took forever."

I have to lean back on a pile of pillows. "You think she knew she was being followed?"

"Wouldn't surprise me," he shrugs. "The route she took, either she's paranoid, 'specially careful, or she was trying to shake me."

"And you ended up where, Cockspur Street?"

"Yep."

I am at a loss, unless she wanted to buy a ticket to flee the country. "What did she do there?"

"What's the line, the German one that's all boarded up?"

"Norddeutscher Lloyd?" I answer immediately.

Germany's answer to the likes of Cunard and White

Star, a big passenger line. Obviously it is doing no business in London at the moment.

Crabtree nods. "Yeah, the front's all covered in recruitment stuff, ironic ain't it?" I expect that was the point. "She had a good look about and then went and wrote on the posters. Then she was off again so I carried on after her, all the way to bloody Norwood."

"To a house?" I have no other earthly idea what else one might find in Norwood.

"No, you'll love this," he leans forward. "A bloody home for nutters. I asked a bloke outside a pub nearby what it was. And she didn't go in through the front door, nei'ver."

I shrug. "How else would she get in?"

"Window round the back," he whispers conspiratorially. As if anyone can hear us apart from my brother's dog. Kitch is sitting up ons his back legs at the end of my bed and glaring at us. He looks ridiculous.

That does it. I drag my legs out of bed and put my feet onto the floor. I feel like my head is in a vice, but I am utterly determined to pick up where Crabtree left off and determine if this is the woman that we have been looking for. She certainly wasn't behaving normally. I send him downstairs to wait for me. My hands are shaking as I do up my buttons, I nearly keel over as I attempt to put on my shoes and tying my laces is a feat of endurance. Unsurprisingly, as I descend the stairs, kicking another infernal bucket full of sand and swearing, I find my mother barring my progress to the front door. "You will have to strike me down dead and climb over my lifeless body to get out of this house," she declares; all five feet of her.

"Mother, there is no need to be quite so dramatic." I try and sound lighthearted, but it is hard when you are wincing in agony.

She folds her arms. "I have mad women delivering mystery packages, policemen outside my house, and now someone tries to kill my son. No, Will. No."

"If they wanted me dead they had every opportunity to murder me last night. They didn't take it." This is evidently a little too light hearted, because she politely requests that Crabtree wait in the parlour for a moment. Then she explodes. I withstand a torrent of parental despair until there is a quiet knock on the front door. I have never seen my mother speechless. Nor Mrs. Mitcham. The fact that they are both silent when the latter opens it speaks volumes.

"Good morning, Lady Stanley." Kitchener of Khartoum's large frame moves inside the house. He removes his cap and nods politely. "I wonder if might speak to Will in private? War business, I am sure you will understand." All anger instantly forgotten, she nods. "Of course." She ushers him into my father's study. "Mrs. Mitcham, fetch some tea, would you?" As we await a tray, which I sincerely hope includes some form of sustenance as well as tea, John's dog emerges and sits up again, front paws hanging limp, and commences staring at the great war lord as if he were some sort of menacing intruder.

"Does it have a name?" He asks.

"Lloyd George." A reasonable lie on the spur of the moment.

"Well, it does look rather sordid. And it is small."

Tea in hand, he gets down to business. "You are not badly hurt?"

"No, Sir," I say, painfully attempting to manipulate a teacake into my broken face.

"Did you recognise them?"

"I couldn't even see them."

"Damned fiends. Must have been our friends from the arsenal."

"Crabtree was worked over too." I tell him about the warning.

"Is he all right? Where is he? He apparently turned up at the War Office looking for you, but you had already left."

"Yes, he's here. In the parlour. Eating, probably. Which suggests that he'll live. He looks better than I do."

"We will call him in in a moment. But before we do, your brother went into action yesterday morning. I know very little thus far. It is most frustrating all round. It is times like this I wish I were on the field of battle, commanding myself, rather than waiting for news in an office."

"Well, thank you, Sir." There doesn't seem a lot else to say at this juncture. My brother may be dead, alive, wounded, anything. "Without meaning to push my luck," I continue, "is the battle proving satisfactory?" Perhaps this will at least confirm that my brother is not fleeing from the German hordes across the north of France.

He sighs deeply. "It is difficult to say at present. As soon as I can confirm that he has emerged safely back out of it, I shall."

"I am most grateful to you, Sir. I appreciate that you have far more pressing concerns than the fate of one junior officer."

"Nonsense," he assures me. "I am glad to be in a position to put the mind of one mother at least at rest. You should not say anything to her at present though, I think." No. She is worried enough, imagining the worst as events play themselves out.

Unsurprisingly, when Crabtree joins us he has cake on his face.

"It's time to get organised." The War Secretary unfolds a map the size of four sheets of paper that diligently represents the arsenal and its environs. Each building has been drawn on and labelled, and coloured green dots represent the sites of the murders. Red dots mark where each victim worked. "Now, I can see no pattern emerging, other than the fact that all of the deaths have occurred at the western end of the site, where there is the most going on. Considering that this is a long way removed from where Carrick worked, I think it is safe to say that they have been unable to penetrate further into the arsenal. They would have to come further into the open, and they haven't dared. So far. Perhaps adding all of the information we have to this plan as we continue might help us to see something we are missing."

"There will be more deaths." Of this I am absolutely sure.

"Yes. I find it is always better to be prepared for the worst," agrees Kitchener. "Though of course we must hope that nobody else stumbles into their way in the course of whatever it is that they are doing."

Crabtree barely suppresses a snigger, and when I look at him he attempts to covertly point to a label on the map. *Erection shop.* Kitchener has not noticed, so I glare at him with enough venom and for long enough that his face falls like a kicked mutt.

"Crabtree may have successfully tailed our mystery woman last night," I say to make him feel better. "We are about to go to Norwood to investigate."

"That is excellent news. How did you find her? Where is she?"

"Sheer, clueless luck," I admit. Emphasis on the clueless. "She is in an asylum of some sort, it seems. The last Crabtree saw of her last night, she was climbing in through the window there."

"Interesting." Kitchener folds up the map and hands it to me. "Yes, you must go and investigate one way or another. If we have found one of them it will perhaps open this whole case up for you. Are you well enough to go?"

"I'll manage, Sir," I say bravely. Wishing that I could go back to bed. "That is, providing that I can get past my mother."

"I shall speak with her on your behalf, I am sure we can make her see the sense of it." This will require more bravery than I possess.

I nod. "I wonder, Sir, if I might ask for some assistance with something?"

"Name it."

"Locked in the cupboard in my office are the papers we removed from Dr. Carrick's safe. They need to be examined forensically, looking for any reference at all to a creation known as M14."

He nods. "I shall have Fitz do it immediately."

"But I fear there is another task that requires our attention that is far more labour intensive."

"Explain it to me?"

I take a deep breath. "We need to establish whether anything is going missing from the arsenal. They are lingering on the site with Carrick gone for a reason. I fear that auditing the entire place will be a nightmare, but it is the only way I can think of, to try and account for what they are doing. Something is keeping them there. If I may, I suggest that we begin with departments that deal with dangerous materials?"

"Let me think for a moment." The sound of the clock is all that marks our presence in the study as Kitchener sips his tea, concentrating hard. "How far back?"

I shrug. "We don't know how far back this goes. August 1914, I am afraid, when Carrick arrived. We cannot rule anything out yet."

A few more sips of tea, and the War Secretary puts his empty cup down. "You are right. To audit every workshop, every department, is going to require a lot work. But we will begin as you suggest. The most expedient thing to do, I think, is to order a clerk from every applicable outfit to be put onto an audit of all materials and equipment that have come in and out in their domain since the beginning of the war. I will put the order out in my name and make sure that everyone understands that I want these figures as quickly as possible. I will say it is in the act of investigating production so far, and how it may be improved henceforth."

It is a brave concept, and one that will land Kitchener in hot water. "Surely your Cabinet colleagues will have something to say about such a sudden and lofty undertaking?"

"Oh yes, I expect they will. Churchill and that infernal Lloyd George for certain. But that is for me to worry about. The alternative is to tell them that we have a huge security concern at the arsenal, and I don't trust any of the wittering fools to keep quiet about such a thing. They can't limit what comes out of their mouths any better than they can limit their alcohol intake, or the amount of time they spend fawning over women who are not their own wives. They are not straightforward like you or I, Stanley. They are never what they seem. Do not forget that."

We leave Kitchener placating my mother. Crabtree and I walk as swiftly as I am able down to Trafalgar Square. I am drawing surprised and distasteful looks all the way along Piccadilly. The brief look I got of myself in the mirror as I fixed my hair into place was not pleasant. One green eye is tainted with red where a blood vessel appears to have burst, and it is encircled by a bruise of various shades of purple and black, which spreads down my jaw and meets another large bruise on my neck where someone appears to have put their hands around my throat and half throttled me. One of my assailants took great pleasure in repeatedly stamping on my abdomen and kicking my chest, meaning that I am struggling to walk upright or to breath properly. I am clutching at my side with a hand that bears at least one broken finger, and quite understandably all manner of people appear to be drawing the swift conclusion that I have been scrapping in a manner unbecoming of one of the King's officers. Pulling my cap down over my eyes spares me a modicum of attention, but I feel rather conspicuous as we approach Cockspur Street behind the Union Club; the enclave for the likes of the White Star Line and Canadian Pacific.

Norddeutscher Lloyd is dragging the ambience created by the presence of these giants down somewhat. All of the windows were swiftly covered up to protect them against patriotic vandals last August, but the boards are invisible now. There are recruitment posters in abundance; Lord K's face looking stern as he points a finger outward. Someone has drawn a pair of spectacles on him in one instance, but mostly, renditions of his face are small oases in amongst a mess of graffiti. *"Hun go home"* is a common theme, *"death to the Kaiser;"* and a multitude of lewd cartoons involving pickelhaube helmets and German sausage.
"Where did she write?"
Crabtree takes two steps backwards. "This side."
He stares at the wall. "Look up," I suggest. "She's more my height."
"Of course! Sherlock Holmes says people write at their eye-line!" I resist the urge to slap the back of his head as he takes a good look. "See, Sir! It really is useful! There. In pencil, really feint."
Two clubs. As one would see in a pack of cards. And perhaps a Dolphin, though anatomically it is not the best rendition. At a push it could be a lizard.
"What does it mean?"
"I suspect one club for you, and one for me, judging by last night." He looks confused. "To call clubs was an old rallying cry among apprentices in London. It is how they would summon their kind to help them, I believe."
"So she called for some heavies and we got done over. What a cow. What about the fish?"
"No idea. I think perhaps that appeals to a particular individual?"
"Might be a signature, for her?" He suggests.
I shrug. "Perhaps we can go and ask her?"

XVI.

Our route to Norwood includes a lengthy diversion out to Woolwich to collect Frank Noakes, the only person who might definitely be able to identify the woman in this asylum as our suspect. We might have telephoned ahead to verify that a woman matching her description is at the place, but I don't want to take the chance that someone might tip off this nurse, inmate, whatever she may be, about our arrival. Frank is thrilled about the idea of a clandestine journey across London in a posh motor car, especially when Crabtree produces a paper bag full of treacle toffee. His mother leans in through the window one last time to tell him to mind his manners and do as he is told, but he is too excited to pay much attention to her. He and Crabtree chatter away inanely as we make our way west, whilst I prop my aching head against the side of the cab to try and alleviate the dizziness.

Dr. Waller's Residential Home for the Mentally Impaired does not look as entirely hopeless as one might expect of such an institution. Though the large detached house is fashioned from dark grey stone, they are making a decent fist of the large garden at the front, which gives the place a homely feel even this early in spring. Near the door a stocky young man who looks to be a victim of mongolism is happily turning over an empty flower bed with a little trowel. He waves at us with a big smile and we return the greeting. Closer to us, a man in neat grey trousers and a white tailored jacket, rather like a ship's steward's, is on his knees pulling at weeds along the front path. "Bloody 'ell. You two look like you've been in the ring with Jack Johnson," he says as we approach.

"You should see what he looks like this morning," I say sarcastically. I am already bored of being reminded that I look terrible. "Might we see Dr. Waller?"

He is friendly enough as he continues to pull at his weeds. "Afraid he's not here."

"May I ask who you are, then?"

He sits back on his heels and extends a gloved hand. "Church. Vernon Church. Head Porter. I live here, and I'm in charge when none the medical staff are about."

"Your garden is impressive."

"Got all the help I need with the residents. They love it out here, especially my friend here." He raises a trowel to the man at the door. "Isn't that right Tom? "

Tom nods enthusiastically and Church groans as he climbs to his feet. He must be in his middle fifties, and a little round. He is evidently a bit stiff from his time spent on the floor. "It's not a hospital," he continues. "It's a private residential home for those who can't live on their own."

Tom has spotted Crabtree ferreting about in his toffee bag and asks bravely if he might have some. "Of course you can mate, here, keep the bag."

Church smiles. "Tom has a sweet tooth. He's been with us eight years now, haven't you?" Tom's mouth is glued together with sugary confectionery and he is unable to answer, but he nods happily before he wanders off.

"They're not locked in, unless it's necessary, he continues. "The doctor pops in for a couple of hours each day to see everyone, and there's a nurse here overnight, in case anyone needs her. Other than that it's me and I've got two men and my wife working under me. That about does it for the dozen or so we usually have. It ain't the poshest, but our rooms are clean and comfortable. Can I do anything to help you?"

I nod. I am conscious that we can be seen from the windows and I want to get back to the car. "We are here on urgent War Office business. In fact, a matter requiring some discretion. Might you have a woman here; tall, fair-haired, with a large nose. She's very thin."

"Yes, a resident. Is she in some sort of trouble?"

"Possibly." I briefly explain to Church what it is I'd like him to do, and how important it is that this woman is not alerted as to any presence that is out of the ordinary. A few minutes later, holding Frank Noakes's hand he disappears inside. Less than a minute later, they reemerge and Noakes bounds up to Crabtree, who squats down on his haunches nimbly.

"Well? Little man?"

"It's 'er."

"How sure are you?"

He nods with vigour. "Really sure."

Crabtree ruffles his hair. "Well done, now do us a favour and wait safely in the car for a bit. I'll be in in a minute."

"Can we be seen here?" I ask.

"No, she is in her room and it faces the back."

"Is there any way for us to see her without entering the room?"

"Yes," he puts his hands in his pockets. "Each room has a glass window in the door so that we might do rounds and check on people without going into each and every room."

"Can you take us inside?"

Church nods. "Of course."

The room in question is on the ground floor and it takes us no time to reach it. Silently. Crabtree and I each take a quick look inside. The woman's features are exactly as Noakes originally described to us. She is picking at the wall, but rather than looking at the extent of the minor damage she is causing to the floral wallpaper, I am looking at her hands. I can see the flakey skin mentioned by Mrs. Mitcham, and I have spotted a nasty scab on the right one; a gash across her knuckles that could quite feasibly been caused by punching Fred George hard enough in the mouth to break teeth.

Crabtree has seen it too. "Nasty scrape, Sir," he whispers. "Let's get in there and 'ave 'er for the two murders."

"No," I whisper, leading him away to the end of the corridor. "She's a small fish. We will make her pay for what she has done, Crabtree, but before that, I want her to lead us to the others, to the men who killed Remington and more importantly, the man they all answer to."

He nods firmly. "The one sending you cigarettes?"

"That's the one." Church reappears drying his freshly washed hands on a tea towel. "How long has she been here?" I ask.

He doesn't have to think about it. "Since mid-January. She's not so much as made eye contact with one of us in all that time."

"And she isn't locked in?" I have noticed that a bolt on the outside of her door bears no padlock.

"Nope. Never made any attempt to leave her room without being pressed. Let alone the building. I think you'd have to drag her out screaming."

"You don't lock them in at night?"

"Not into their individual rooms; but the front and back doors are bolted shut."

Crabtree flashes me a cynical glance. "What is the cause of her sickness?" I continue.

"Bereavement, we were told, but like I said, we can't get nothing out of her. Just sits there all day and all night. Barely eats. Vicious, though. Try and make her take something, or get too close and she'll go at you like an alley cat. I've had the scratches to prove it." He rolls up his sleeves to display some old, long scabs on his inner arm.

I change my line of questioning. "I take it someone is paying for her stay?"

"Of course, couldn't tell you who though. The doctor would have all that in his office."

"That's a very Germanic sounding name." I point towards the chalkboard nailed to the wall by her door. I have noted that it reads *'L. Hahn'* and has a date of birth underneath of sometime in the middle of 1880.

Church shakes his head. "She's as English as they come, name's Lynette. She was married, so it must be his name. It's him that died."
"When was this?" Crabtree pipes up as he scribbles notes.
"Just before Christmas. It wasn't long before she wound up here. That's all I know, I'm afraid."
"I need to see the doctor's notes on her, along with details of who is funding her accommodation."
"That's not proper. I should wait till the doctor comes. But that won't be till tomorrow now."
"You can confirm my investigative authority with the War Office, I am operating under the Defence of the Realm Act."
He smiles wryly. "Useful one DORA, isn't she? Gives His Majesty's Government license to do and say what it wants. By all means, take it, so long as you leave a note of explanation for Dr. Waller, explaining why it's gone and where to, otherwise he'll have my guts for garters." He is already walking away down the corridor, pulling a large bunch of keys out of his pocket and beckoning us to follow. He opens the door to the doctor's office and points at a cabinet.
"In there. You'll probably have to jemmy the lock, but I must check on Tom. He likes to wander."
He makes to leave, but I have one more question for him. "Does she have any visitors?"
He turns back. "Just one. Her brother comes, once a week give or take."
"Could you describe him for me?"
"Um... Big bloke, wide and tall. Curly dark hair, bit of grey. Looks like his nose has been broken a few times."
"Does he give a name?"
"Not that I've heard. Probably be in the file. The visitor book is on the doctor's desk, have a look. Everyone has to sign it, no exceptions." With that he doffs an imaginary cap and walks off to find his fellow gardener.

While Crabtree is picking at the lock on the cabinet with an unwound paper clip, I pick up the telephone and put a call through to Fitz, asking him to arrange for MPs to watch the home at all hours of the day and night, lest Lynette Hahn decide to leave again. I am sure that she will. Despite the interesting act she has put up for Dr. Waller, Mr. Church and the staff here, she is clearly coherent and comes and goes as she pleases. We agree to stay put until they arrive and then I ring off as the doctor's filing cabinet pops open.

I light a cigarette and ease myself gingerly into the doctor's chair, drop Lynette Hahn's file on the desktop and open it to the first of only two sheets of paper. Crabtree leans over my shoulder. "Looks like bugger all there. Born in Romford but living in the East End. Look at that address though, nobody living in a place like that can afford to stay in any residential home."

"Quite," I agree. "Married to one Wilhelm Hahn. Deceased." Crabtree is taking notes in his little book. "Anyfin' else we can use?"

"Under children we have a daughter Sophie and a son Henry. Both deceased, but no details."

"Gawd. Explains the miserable face on 'er." The second sheet is merely a receipt for her stay, paid up to the end of the month.

"Who's funding all this?" He asks.

I sigh. "A firm of solicitors."

"Shall I write the name down?

"You can, for what it is worth," I say dejectedly. He looks at me questioningly. "Stangerson and Drebber."

I have noted something else regarding her family too. "You can write this down, though. According to this file, Lynette Hahn doesn't have a brother." I lean across the desk and open the visitor book to the last page with any writing on it.

"Here," Crabtree points to the penultimate line. "She had a visitor two days ago." I trace the line with my finger to reach the name, sit back for a moment, then launch the infernal book across the room. The man who came to see her signed his name as Lieutenant The Hon. Fitzwilliam Stanley.

XVII.

Crabtree and I find Horatio Keyes in one of his usual haunts on Pall Mall, deserted at the moment, nursing a drink at the bar and looking morose. I limp onto the stool next to him without waiting to be invited, grateful to be sitting down in my discombobulated state. Then I lean forward onto the bar top on my elbows. "Cheer up, old man, it can't be that bad. You could look like me." I order a scotch.
I only warrant a brief look. "Did you make fun of Lizzie?" He says drily before taking a sip of his drink.
I ignore him. "What do you want to drink, Crabtree?"
"Whiskey an' water please, Sir."
His usual tipple is half a pint of shandy lest he get stupidly drunk. "Are we playing the part of Holmes or Watson?" He was merely trying to appear sophisticated and I feel bad when he looks hurt. I pull out the chair on the other side of me and place a menu in front of it. "Sit down, and order yourself some lunch too.'
His good humour returns instantly. He scrambles into his chair and I turn back to Keyes, who is still staring at the bottom of his glass. "Do you know the disadvantage of being on the same corridor as the First Sea Lord at the Admiralty?" He says.
"Is it the snoring?" I joke. "I hear that Fisher spends most of his time asleep."
"Nice try," he whispers back, "but no. The snoring I can live with. It's him and Churchill bawling at each other. I wonder why we bother with Room 40 when the Germans could just stand under the window and hear

them tearing each other to shreds. It's a wonder there is a secret left in the Royal Navy."

Room 40 is some sort of codebreaking outfit for the boat people, as Crabtree refers to them. Keyes was recruited to it last November due to the fact that he is a remarkable mathematician. His occupation is the precise reason I want to speak to him. "Have you had any chatter come through from the Hun in the past couple of weeks, about a new weapon?"

"No. Why?"

"Nothing about a new type of ammunition, perhaps, any sort of invention that is exciting them? It would be scientific in nature, and probably quite brilliant."

He is genuinely interested. "Such as what?"

"I don't know, that's the problem. They'd be stealing it, something new fashioned by us. They've made headway, too. Of course we suspect the Hun, but are looking into other scoundrels closer to home."

"You really are up to your neck in it, aren't you?" He leans back.

"Drowning, H. All of this is as hush as it comes."

"Naturally. Well, no, nothing at all like that has come through. Do you want me to make it official?"

"No, not my call. Lord K wants a lid on it."

"Lord K? Chums now then? You are running with the big nobs now aren't you?"

"He really is decent. But a touch paranoid. Mind you I would be too sitting in the Cabinet Room with the likes of Churchill and the Welsh Imp."

Keyes shrugs. "Well, it doesn't matter. Something like that, anyone listening in Room 40 would jump on it, even if they did not know the context. And the job I am on, it would then come past me. Either directly or I'd be briefed on it swiftly enough. I can let you know if anything comes up."

"Thanks. If you get anything, and you cannot get me, go straight through to Fitzgerald at the War Office, he's Kitchener's secretary. He knows all."

He lifts his glass as if to say cheers ."Right-o. Remember us little people when you are knighted."

I leave Crabtree stuffing a gargantuan sandwich for the time being, discussing, of all things, naval architecture, and head back towards Whitehall. My destination is not the War Office, but the ridiculous Home Office building next to Downing Street. It is not particularly over the top from the outside, despite elaborate sculptures by Armstead and Philip. However, once I enter in search of whoever has had the misfortune to be placed in charge of dealing with enemy aliens since the outbreak of war, I find myself trudging through Italianate grandeur; up a luxurious staircase, under ornate chandeliers and painted ceilings, past priceless art on the walls. It is a far cry from the corner of the War Office building that I have been wedged into, with its chipped, cheap furniture and grim decor.

Firstly I am directed upstairs to a small room that has had four desks crammed into it. Despite the valuable furnishings and adornments, there are chaotic piles of paper everywhere, spilling from one surface to another. I can see two arms flailing about whilst their owner bellows down a telephone. "I'm telling you, I don't KNOW! I appreciate that your Chief Inspector wants an address, but short of me spouting another pair of arms, he isn't getting one today. If this is unsatisfactory then I suggest he comes down here from Gallowgate and digs for it himself. Tell him to bring a shovel!" From the other side of a tower of paper I hear the banging down of the receiver, and then a head appears. I don't think the smirk on my face does the situation any good. "What?" The clerk is small and dark, his face flushed and beads of perspiration stuck to his forehead. "Oh! What happened to your face?"
I ignore him. "I'm told you might be the man to speak to about registration of an enemy alien."

"A fortnight I've had this job. The four chaps before me gave up the ghost and ran away after less than a week. Somebody should have stopped the fools arresting everyone with a foreign accent and throwing all of their paperwork in here with no regard to cataloguing it. Look at this mess!" There is a pause whilst I wait to see if he is going to address my query or if I need to repeat it. Then he sighs heavily. "Do you have any idea when they were registered?"

"No. But he's been dead since before Christmas."

"Excellent. Well, not for him obviously. But you might be in luck. If you can get over to the window there's a cabinet with the early ones on index cards."

"And if not?"

"Then it is somewhere in all of this shit." By way of a final flourish he throws up the papers he is holding and they come back down in a state of disarray that is hardly noticeable when added to the rest of his domain. With not a small amount of discomfort, I climb over two desktops using my one good hand, trying to cause minimal damage to the piles of paper perched precariously on them, and manage to get one foot down on the floor near the window where the aforementioned cabinet is standing. "All done by county and then sorted alphabetically," he says without looking up. "In theory, London is supposed to be in the top drawer."

I pull said drawer open and look inside. It looks reasonably organised, though someone has been lately throwing papers in on top of the index cards. That and the unwanted crusts from their sandwiches by the looks of it. Wilhelm Hahn's card is coated with a grease spot and the remnants of some sort of fishy spread which smells unhealthy. There is only one word underneath his name and address, which corresponds with the that on Lynette's file at Dr. Waller's. "Where are the documents if it says *interred*?"

"Not here, luckily for you." He still hasn't looked up. "They should be in the basement with the interred alien people."
"Let me guess, theoretically?"
"You've made out better than anyone else so far, so don't complain;" he snaps. "I've got a Glaswegian policeman hollering down the phone at me every day, convinced that he's part of the plot for a Le Queux novel. If you've finished bothering me, I've got work to do." As I leave, I make sure I nudge a particular wobbly pile of papers sitting on the nearest desk. I can hear the gradual slide turning into a floor-bound avalanche before I have limped out of the room. As I head for the basement I can hear a string of obscenities coming out into the corridor behind me, only slightly muffled by the sound of my own evil sniggers.

Once I have managed to gingerly make my way down the stairs and follow yet more directions, things are much calmer in the basement, where three clerks have been squashed into a corner alongside some dripping pipes. This constitutes the 'office' that deals with the internment of enemy aliens. After a brief greeting which involves me once again listening to an exclamation about how awful I look, they appear willing to help.
"We're actually releasing lots now," one of them explains; a tall and exceedingly thin youth in office clothes that look like he inherited them from someone half a foot shorter. "Local authorities were a bit over exuberant last August. Now there actually has to be some justified suspicion attached to the alien in order for them to be arrested."
"So the chap I am looking for might not have done anything untoward?"
"It's quite likely he didn't," says a fair haired young man with a significantly receding hairline. "What is his name?"

"Wilhelm Hahn. He lived in East London. He's dead, I don't know if that makes a difference as to where you keep his paperwork."

A third clerk shakes his head and gets up. He looks like he might be Italian or Spanish in origin. He leans over to a cabinet behind him and opens a drawer, rifles through part of it, withdraws a thin brown document and opens it. "This will be him. Oh."

"Oh, what?"

"The *Saxon*." He says this knowingly to his colleagues, who look none too comfortable at that piece of information.

"What does that mean?" I have no idea.

He is flicking through the document as he is talking to me. "A few thousand enemy aliens have been rounded up and put on ships at Southend, near the pier. The *Ivernia* is full of soldiers from the front. The *Royal Edward* is not so bad, civilians, and they can purchase cabins for a set amount and live more comfortably if they have the means. Your chap was on the *Saxon*, which is another story. There's about two and a half thousand of those unfortunate enough to be here last August when war was declared; crammed into close quarters. None of whom have got the money to buy themselves out of it. It's not too unsanitary now, but it was worse before Christmas. They had an outbreak of fever which killed more than a few unfortunate souls. Looks like this fellow Hahn was one of them. Signed his name as William though."

"May I?" I hold out my hand.

"Of course," he gives up the file.

"So, what happened to the families of these men? Were they interred with them?"

"His wife was English, so no. The odd woman willingly went into internment with her husband, but it was rare." The file says that Hahn was a dockyard worker. "So his job paid a minimal amount, it is unlikely that there were

savings in this case. If his income suddenly vanished, what provision was made for the family?"
"None."
I find it all rather hard to believe. I sit on the edge of one of their desks and begin to flick back and forth. "So, if I am right, this man, William Hahn, as he was known, came here at the age of two with his widowed father, back in the 1880s. His father was a German merchant and took a second wife, a widowed Englishwoman, within a year. The father then died in 1888. This means that William was raised in England, by an English stepmother with his English stepsisters. He claimed during an interview that he did not read, write, understand or speak German. There is no record of his having a passport, and therefore of ever setting foot back in Germany. He married an Englishwoman and they have two English children. Then last August, war was declared. The Government rounded him up, put him on a fetid old ship as an enemy alien, where he died for want of proper care. According to this, in the meantime, his wife was left to fend for herself and both of her children then took ill and died. One of them on Christmas Day. Is that about the size of it?"
The nearest clerk shrugs. He takes the file back. "It's not even the worst case we've come across. But yes, that seems to be a succinct interpretation of this one"
The blond one leans forward. "Why is she of interest to the army?"
I am not about to answer that. "I'm going to take the file with me."
"On whose authority? I'm not trying to be difficult, but, well…"
"You may verify my right to do so with General Phipps at the War Office." Best not to mention Kitchener. "It's just a missing persons case that the army have got unwittingly wrapped up in. I've had it shoved onto my desk." I stand up and am forced to rest back down immediately, for my head is spinning and I cannot keep

my balance. I feel distinctly nauseous. One of the clerks dashes to my side to take my arm.
"Are you all right?"
"I will be, I have only to get to the War Office."
"Here," he says, picking up his coat and the file. "I'll walk with you. I was going to go and fetch some lunch anyway."

It is all I can do to struggle across the street and up Whitehall, and when I try to mount the steps to the War Office, I find Gaylor behind me. He nods a thanks to the Home Office clerk and firmly takes my arm like one of the brutes that mans the stage door at the Palladium. None of them like me. "I've orders to take you home, mate. His Lordship has apparently said you can call him up from there on the telephone, but you're done for the day. Something about a promise to your mother." The man is twice my size and has a vice-like grip. Unsurprisingly, I surrender. From the house I explain to Lord Kitchener, who it transpires promised that he would send me home as soon as possible, everything that I have found out about Lynette Hahn, everything that explains so clearly why she might have a vendetta against the British war effort. He tells me that the Secret Service Bureau, much like Room 40, have heard nothing untoward about a new weapon or piece of equipment. Lord Stamfordham's enquiries suggest that no group of suffragists, socialists, anarchists, or any other type of "ist" is currently thought to be anywhere near contemplating military sabotage, but he is still digging among his contacts for information. A watch on the residential home is to be maintained, subtly by police constables in civilian clothes, should Lynette Hahn leave again and for now, all is quiet at the arsenal, where security has been increased and where clerks are busily auditing their departments to account for any missing materials or equipment. Williams has never heard of anything called M14. With nothing to do but await new developments, having had a brief chat about his progress with *Dracula,* at Lord Kitchener's insistence, I climb into bed and sink into oblivion for the rest of the day.

Saturday, 13th March 1915

XVIII.

Since three o'clock in the morning I have been waiting for dawn. Partly through worry, but also because I had slept for twelve hours, and my brain needed no more rest, even if my body was still screaming out in pain. For that reason I continued to lay there, contemplating what might have become of my brother. He has fought. I know that much. He might still be fighting. It has been 48 hours, give or take, since the Grenadiers went into action. Trying to ascertain the fate of one man in the midst of a large-scale battle in that space of time is a ludicrous expectation. Kitchener does not yet even have a proper grasp on how the whole battle has progressed, and to what exact degree it has succeeded or failed. I remember the retreat; how it took days, weeks even after Mons, last August, for things to settle down and for stragglers to finish wandering in and rejoining their units. Not to mention the droves of them that turned up in various hospitals and dressing stations having been wounded or having collapsed from exhaustion. Some of my classmates from Eton and Oxford are still missing after later fighting on the Aisne and at Ypres before Christmas. It is unbearable for the families. The idea that their loved ones, sometimes two or more brothers at a time, have succumbed in such numbers that one cannot even tell if an *officer* is dead or alive. It is incomprehensible in this modern age, and the aristocracy in particular has never endured such a wartime concept with such alarming constancy. How long will they wait and hope? I do not think that I could face it; months of uncertainty and not knowing what has become of my brother.

John might be dead, but I feel like I would know if this was the case. What might I have been doing if he is? Speeding about the arsenal with Williams at the wheel?

Lying prone on a London street having been beaten senseless? Sitting in my office? Death could have come in any number of ways. I have seen enough of this war to know that. It could have been a rifle round. He could have been picked off for looking like an officer; an oft used tactic for causing confusion and disarray amongst the men. He could have been torn apart indiscriminately by a shell, or wounded fatally so that he bled to death as they rushed him to the nearest dressing station. Of course he might be hurt and still alive. He might at this very moment be suffering untold agonies as doctors struggle to save his life. He might be waiting for someone to find him, alone and abandoned. He might have a minor wound and be on his way home to some grand house where like-wounded officers are convalescing before being sent back to the front. He might have been taken prisoner. There are terrible rumours about London concerning the treatment of British captives by the Germans. Apparently they are singled out above the French for all kinds of foul tortures. John might equally have not a scratch on him, and be with what is left of his unit. He might be clapped out in a farmhouse, encrusted in mud and snoring his head off. I can see all of these possibilities vividly in my aching head. I become annoyed at myself for not having any comprehension of the probabilities and statistics that would enable me to reason for myself the most plausible scenario. And I still can't tell my mother. Everything could be all right. I could worry her for nothing. For now I will shoulder the anxiety on my own.

Having exhausted all possible eventualities so far as my brother is concerned, as I listen to the house coming to life downstairs my mind drifts back to the arsenal. I'd like to say that it is diligence. But in reality it is that I refuse to believe that a group that is utilising someone as volatile as the grieving, angry wife of a dockworker as their main weapon can have accomplished all that they have without making one single mistake. I refuse to believe that she has outwitted me, that all of them have. Something is gnawing away at the back of my brain and my ego is not going to let go of it until I put my finger on what *it* is. Somewhere there is some fact, some statement, some piece of evidence that doesn't fit.

And so I begin to reason through the arsenal case meticulously in my head in search of answers. Lynette Hahn has been identified by Frank Noakes as the woman standing next to Dr. Carrick when he met his end. Frank is a child, but he has never wavered in his version of events, despite constant opposition. He has been completely assured of what and who he saw. He is a bright child, and I believe him. Hahn also bears physical evidence that means I am convinced, that despite the force it would have apparently taken, that she also broke Fred George's tooth in the act of killing him. This means that she then pretended to be an old woman when Stan Bailey arrived at the scene in order to get away. Having investigated her background, her motive for criminal activity somehow directed against her country is obvious.

But then there is the ghastly death of Mordecai Remington. Having seen what It would have taken to pull off the crime, despite her strength in attacking Fred George, I do not believe that Lynette Hahn can have been responsible for playing a part in releasing the guns in question. An entirely new level of brute force would have been required. That means there are two men involved in this mess who are willing to kill too. It could be one of them who is watching me intently enough to know my name, my rank, where I live, and where to have me beaten unconscious on my way home. Watching me intently enough to mock my lack of progress in stopping them at whatever it is they are about, and intently enough to be able to replenish my unique cigarettes. This person also knows enough to make fun of Crabtree's obsession with Sherlock Holmes, so they are watching him too. But somehow, just from my minimal contact with him, I wonder if he would dirty his own hands with such a thing. I sense a pomposity about him.

Add to that the fact that I was attacked by three male assailants. At the same time two men tried to accost Crabtree. So there are more of them willing to participate in at least thuggery in the name of their ambiguous cause, if not murder. It is becoming quite the crowd. I have a description of a man who claimed to be Lynette Hahn's brother, yet signed my name in Dr. Waller's visitor book. For now I suppose that who he is is irrelevant. There are some half a dozen individuals or more, bent on stealing, or at least utilising M14, whatever it is, to their own ends. I rule out that their motivation is simply to derail it. Because not even Kitchener can claim to know what *it* is. If nobody is working on it now that Carrick is dead, and I would know by now if they were, they would be wasting their time. My sense of urgency is acute, because any secret invention by a genius, undertaken at the most important munitions site in the whole of the Empire, is going to be something that you don't want an enemy of Britain to have.

After a period of lambasting myself as to my inability to fathom what is going on at the arsenal, my brain starts to tire, I feel my eyes closing again. But then I suddenly realise that in all of this mess it is one, possibly two members of this abominable party in particular that constitute a threat bigger than even those willing to kill. Someone has access to me. To the War Office, to the nature of what I do, and for whom, and with respect to the task that I have been assigned in order to root out the cause of these disturbing goings on at Woolwich. Someone also had access to Carrick, to his work, to his secret projects. And it is then that I realise what I have been missing. Reluctantly, and yet determinedly I drag myself out of bed, hellbent on going to work.

XIX.

It is nearly lunchtime by the time I arrive at the War Office. I can walk with far more ease this morning, and my head has ceased pounding, but my chest hurts. I still feel like my aching ribs are spearing my insides as I mount the stairs to my office, and I am suffering the after effects of one side of my face being ground into the pavement. I barely take my greatcoat off before I find out that I am wanted by Lord Kitchener and have to negotiate a path to him, too. "Duty calls I'm afraid, Will." He is already getting up and putting his coat on. "The King wants to see us, at the palace." He eyes my grazed face and my slightly hunched posture. "I'm awfully sorry to do this to you, given your condition. But we will not walk through the park, we will hang the petrol expenditure and have Gaylor drive us."

After passing through the stone arch to the garden entrance at Buckingham Palace for the second time in a week, I have to negotiate more stairs, before we spend fifteen minutes waiting to be admitted to see the King. Next to a huge window, Kitchener stands sentinel-like, observing some ceremonial troops practicing some flag thing below with his hands clasped in front of him in what I have noticed is a default, public pose. I, on the other hand, without the pressure to look like a national hero at all hours of the day and night, lean on the wall and try to concentrate on not collapsing into a heap. The door to one of the King's private rooms finally opens and a General emerges. He is of a similar build to His Majesty, though slightly taller. His hair is mostly dark, but heavily interspersed with grey; and a big dome of a forehead is emerging from underneath it as it recedes backwards across his skull.

He has a large moustache, equally speckled with grey, and a fixed, aloof-ish expression. He looks primed to pass judgement, as my vastly superior officer, with regard to my terrible appearance. But then he glances at Kitchener and thinks better of it. He salutes the Field Marshal instead. "Stanley, do you know General Sir Ian Hamilton?" The War Secretary says officially.
"No, Sir, I have never had the pleasure." I lie as I salute him.
He looks like he has something distasteful on his tongue. I am too polite to publicly remind him of the only other time our paths have crossed during this war. It is not likely that he will have forgotten. "My father, perhaps?" I suggest. "He is General Lord Stanley." That he might not have known. He gives a slightly discernible raise of the eyebrows. "I thought there was just the one boy in the Grenadiers." I am hardly about to deny my existence, and he cannot do that whilst I am stood in front of him, or go so far as to begin questioning my parentage, again, so it is a moot observation and one that seems to irritate Kitchener because there is no point to it. He steers me past this military underling of his with a curt nod, wishing him good luck and leads me into the room beyond. Hamilton sees a bit put out that the he has nothing to say to him about why he is at the palace, but there is no time for the younger man to comment upon it. I'll wager that he's about to leave for the Dardanelles to command the land force there. I cannot put my finger on it, but Kitchener does not seem entirely comfortable with that fact.

My uniform is looking slightly shabby and dishevelled after our recent mayhem, but for once I am sure that it is not my sartorial impropriety that makes the King's jaw drop. "Good grief, my boy, what have you been doing?" He says the instant that he sees my face, which though I have been attempting to hide it with my cap in the street, is on full display at the palace as soon as I remove it in His Majesty's presence.

I fumble over an answer and so Kitchener interjects. "Our friends at Woolwich, so I would hope that means he has them worried."

"How awful." Platitudes aside, the King never can resist a good adventure yarn, "Did you get a few good punches in at least?"

"I fear not, Your Majesty. I was too busy flapping about on the floor."

"Oh, well. Perhaps you will have another opportunity before this matter is brought to a conclusion. Give them a good biffing."

"I will do my very best, Your Majesty."

He sighs and drops down into a chair. "You saw Hamilton, I take it?" This is to the War Secretary. Kitchener nods. "It is as I said Your Majesty, I fear he is the best we could do. His ties to politicians concern me, more than anything."

"I fear we will suffer more anxieties over this Gallipoli affair," says the King. I see a look pass between them. "He is a good man, K."

"Yes, Your Majesty." He's not having it at all.

"Go on, get it off your chest you ornery bugger." Kitchener clears his throat. "Will has just been telling me in the car, he needs to place an urgent telephone call. Perhaps if he goes to do that then we might discuss those developments? Then when he returns we can move on to matters at the arsenal."

I am grateful to get out of the room. I have had heard enough about bloody Gallipoli from Horatio Keyes in the past weeks. I have no desire to learn anymore about a campaign that I am sure from my lowly and ill-educated position listening to the whispers in the intelligence community of those who know better, is a complete waste of time and limited British resources. I place my call outside in the same ante-room from which I have just entered the King's presence, and then I wait. I get half a verse into humming *Tipperary* before I realise what I am doing. Thankfully there is nobody nearby to hear me. The voice that appears on the other end of the line sports its strange accent, and my comprehension is rendered more complicated this time, because it is all that I can do to focus on my own conversation as the two eminent voices in the next room get louder and angrier. I disconnect, and wait uncomfortably until Stamfordham appears with notepaper and his pen. At the sound of shouting he rolls his eyes towards the ceiling as we make eye contact and then raps loudly on the door.

The King is flushed red and a vein in Kitchener's temple is pulsating, but His Majesty's Private Secretary does exactly what any courtier should in such a situation and breezes past the obvious tension in the room discreetly, as if he hasn't seen it. He gestures for me to sit down and I do so, taking the same line. "Was everything to your satisfaction?" Asks Kitchener.

"Yes, Sir. I spoke to Detective Chantler. They are mounting an immediate search for Dr. Carrick's assistant."

He gestures for me to explain to His Majesty and Lord Stamfordham. Kitchener has been making sure that someone in proximity to the King has been updating him constantly as to our progress, but these sit downs appear to clarify things for the palace.

"Someone has to be feeding our culprits information. They had to have known what Carrick was working on in order to know that it was worth stealing. Now, his assistant told me that he was merely a chemist and that if Carrick was working on something in a different vein, he would be ignorant of it." I pause to take a mouthful of tea from a tray that has appeared and then Kitchener rolls his hand, encouraging me to go on. "It took a good few kicks to the head for me to put it together, but Carrick has not been working on anything of a chemical nature for some time. All of the relevant equipment I saw was not in use, not a bunsen burner in sight, and this was clarified by Ingalls, who dealt with all of their equipment and supply requirements. And yet Giles was still gainfully employed. Every day. I have had Williams check his comings and goings. So if he was in the building what was he doing if not helping Carrick? This is reinforced by my second point, which is that Giles also claimed that the doctor carried on numerous private experiments upstairs at their facility to which he was not privy. I have seen the place. There is not enough room to swing a dead cat upstairs. The safe in the office that contained the confidential papers barely fits in there. Crabtree and Williams could not both get in there at the same time when they took it out. There is no room to keep anything, monitor anything, so no experiments could have been carried out behind closed doors in that room. The only other room up there has been used as a rubbish dump for quite some time, judging by the piles of stuff in there, since long before the doctor arrived. Which leaves only downstairs, one large room full of equipment and ongoing work. And if Giles was downstairs in that open plan room, then he would have been able to see exactly what Carrick was doing. He was there and he saw what was going on. So he has lied twice already. You don't lie unless you've got something to hide. The relevant pages concerning M14 that have been ripped from his notebooks. I don't think he destroyed them, I think this man *stole* them, in my opinion. And then finally, and this really irritates me the more that I think about it, Carrick dies; a sudden, awful death. As far as Giles is concerned, he says he goes straight to Manchester with his body, to deal with the wife, distraught as he is at the loss of his friend and employer. He finds her missing. A mother and her young daughter, gone from their home with no explanation in the middle of a war when her husband has just died under suspicious and unnatural circumstances, and he waits days to tell anyone. Something about this man stinks, and the more I think about it, the more I believe that he is a spy. What became of the body? That he is the one that has revealed to a group of saboteurs what they could hope to gain by pilfering Carrick's work from the arsenal."

"Good work Stanley." Kitchener nods encouragingly.

I feel a substantial glow of pride. He let me say all of that in front of the Sovereign, no less, without vetting the goings on in my head himself, first.

"You should get kicked in the head more often," the King guffaws.

"But what does this mean, Your Majesty? That is what is important," Stamfordham reminds us all.

"Yes, quite." The King sobers up quickly. "Well, if the Manchester police can round up this scoundrel and Stanley is right, then of course we might hope to find out what it is he told them about, whether or not they have the wherewithal to use it, and what for. That, I should say, would be case closed once we employ that information to stop them."

"Has there been any more progress on who they are?" Asks Stamfordham.

I recite to the King and his secretary the ambiguous description of the man who visited Lynette Hahn, claiming to be her brother, furnished by Mr. Church at Dr. Waller's, and tell them that she doesn't have one.

"Did he leave a name?" The secretary enquires.

"Yes sir, mine."

"Cheeky bugger," interjects the King. "Perhaps she has a brother in law?"

"Her husband had two stepsisters, but neither were married."

Kitchener sighs. "But even if we do not know who they are, we have surrounded Section E, of course, on the chance that any of them try to go there. Though I rather think they have everything they need from Carrick directly. Fitz has found nothing in a second going over of Carrick's papers with regard to M14, but the arsenal are still working on discrepancies in stocks. They have three dozen people working on it, and in fact, Fitz should have the first submissions soon."

Stamfordham nods and then fixes a serious stare on me. "But now I have to ask, what is the likelihood that anything they are up to has to do with the joint visit next week?"

I have been considering this. "May I ask, on what date was it decided that both His Majesty and Lord Kitchener would go together to the arsenal?"

The King's secretary looks through his notes. "K decided he would go on 6th. But it was not until the 7th that His Majesty decided that he would accompany him."

I breathe a slight sigh of relief. "Then Carrick was already dead. Whatever it is they are planning, and the concept still terrifies me, it did not originate with the royal visit to Woolwich in mind. If these reports being generated at the arsenal show items being removed from the site, whatever they may be, then I will feel even more comfortable about the motivation for their activity having nothing to do with the presence of His Majesty or Lord Kitchener." Stamfordham writes this down, seemingly as pleased with it as I am.

There is a soft knock as the door and Clive Wigram appears. He is brandishing a piece of notepaper and a grim expression. "What is it?" The King asks ominously. He hands the note to Stamfordham. "The woman under surveillance."

"Hahn?" Confirms Kitchener.

"Yes, Sir. She's gone. Dropped out of a back window, so says one of the idiot constables supposed to be watching the building."

"The same window that she likely left by every other time," I say to nobody in particular.

The silence is broken by one single word from the Sovereign. "Bollocks," he says.

Sunday, 14th March 1915

XX.

Mrs Mitcham comes crashing through my bedroom door at seven o'clock with a tea tray. I spent much of last night racing about the streets of Norwood looking for Lynette Hahn, with no faith that she would be within a mile of the place. The woman is a ghost. I have only been asleep for three hours, and so I resist the urge to throw my brother's dog, which is snoring at my feet, at our housekeeper's face. "Go away woman," I snap as I put a pillow over my head.
"You're wanted at the War Office. Fitz-Something or other called, the polite one, and said hurry up."
"What have I done now?" I ask as she slams my tea down next to my bed.
"Humph." Is all she says in response as she flounces out. As I am dressing I walk over to the window. In the midst of doing up my shirt buttons I think I realise what her irksome behaviour is all about. There are two military policeman flanking either side of the steps leading to our front door; fully equipped with rifles and standing as still as statues in a light London fog.
Downstairs my mother is sipping at a cup of tea as she reads the newspaper, a plate of untouched toast beside her on the table. "They are stationed at the back of the house too, Will," she says without looking up. "And at either end of the street. Mrs Mitcham interrogated the poor chap outside the kitchen. He said they were ordered here at five o'clock this morning and that's all they know, and that there will be a constant vigil here until further notice."
"He'd stand more chance being interrogated by the Germans," I mutter. I say nothing about their presence.
"Is it that woman?" My mother persists. "I am scared, Will." She slides her newspaper across the table and

points to a small advertisement box near the bottom of the page. "What *have* you got yourself into?"

'The Game is Afoot
Lieutenant Stanley is still terribly cold.
He appears to have lost his edge.
Please return c/o The War Office, Whitehall,
so that he might stand a fighting chance.'

I resist the urge to beat the table with *The Times*. I sit down and take my mother's hand in mine. "Perhaps you should go back to the country," I say in as calm a voice as possible. "Shut up the house and take the old crone with you." This last bit is for Mrs. Mitcham's benefit, as I can feel her lurking menacingly behind me in the doorway, as if the possible reappearance of a madwoman in her kitchen is my fault.
But my mother is adamant. "No. I must be close to things. I cannot leave town until we hear from John. You don't tell me anything, but I know there is fighting, I cannot go anywhere until I know that my boy is safe." It doesn't matter that he is in his thirties. He will ever be referred to as *her boy*. There is no point arguing with her. Not when it comes to her children. There is little left for me to do but assure her that I am taking every precaution possible as I attempt to put a stop to this threat, and promise to tell her if I hear anything about the Grenadier Guards when I get to the office.

Speaking of which, on my arrival at Whitehall, I do not even get a chance to approach the question of where on earth Lynette Hahn has got to before I am called to the telephone by Crabtree, who has clearly spent the night in my room. His uniform is askew, his hair is sticking up all over the place and he has some form of carpet burn on one side of his face. Waiting for me on the other end of the line is Detective Chantler. He gets straight to the point: "Bad news I'm afraid," he begins in his thick northern accent.

"It always is," I say glumly.

He sounds as if he is holding back a wealth of anger and perhaps even tears. "We've found the Carrick girl. Dumped in the River Croal at Nob End, which is Bolton way. Seven years old. It's hit my men hard, I can tell you. It looks like she had weights tied to her ankles, but for whatever reason they 'aven't 'eld and she came t'surface. Cause of death is drowning." He lets that sink in.

"So whoever is responsible flung her into the water when she was still alive and left her to die?" I feel sick.

"Looks so. Though she'd had a hard blow to the head, so with luck she was unconscious, poor thing. The wife is still missing but we are dragging the water nearby, we expect she's down there." I cannot conceive of why such a monstrous crime was necessary, but Chantler keeps talking and things start to make sense. "It looks like there was a scuffle at the house. After we found the body we kicked the door in. The place was ransacked, there was a pool of blood on the floor."

"Someone was looking for something," I say absent mindedly. Something to do with M14, surely.

"And they killed a woman and a child merely to get them out of the way?" Chantler is incredulous. "Or to protect themselves? Just *who* are you dealing with?"

"People who don't leave loose ends," whispers Crabtree in my ear, for he has been listening in by way of leaning as close to the telephone as he can. His morning breath smells and I bat him away with my cap. Chantler has composed himself somewhat. "I take it the discovery of the daughter should be confidential?"

"Please."

"We've had no luck on your man, Giles. Seems he's cleared out. All of his clothes are gone from the rooms he occupies near the university. How aggressively should we be searching? Is he responsible for this?"

"I expect so, at least to some degree. As aggressively as you can. I can get you more men, if you need them."
"We've got the men. And if we find him?"
I sigh. "I need him in London as soon as is conceivably possible. We can arrange that at this end, I am sure."
The detective clears his throat. "No need. After what we've seen this morning, if he's had anything to do with killing that little girl we'll gladly truss him up and drag him there ourselves."

As if my morning could get any worse, I laboriously climb the stairs and enter Kitchener's office just in time to dodge a miniature bust of the Duke of Wellington that comes flying at the wall next to my head. It is robust, for it bounces off the wall and then the carpet and lands by the door relatively unscathed. Which is more than can be said for the wall, which bears several dents of this nature. "I have sent police to you and down to your man's house in Sutton too," he thunders. Though last I heard he was snoring in your office. I will not have any more victims due to a want of diligence on our part." I take it for granted that there is still no sign of Hahn, for the War Secretary is still ranting. "Damned, useless police. I should never have agreed to use them in the first place. Should have just told Scotland Yard to bugger off out of it." I can see he has a copy of *The Times* on his desk too, open to the page with the advertisement mocking me. Kitchener sits up in his chair and I look about to see if there are any more busts nearby. But the fight has gone out of him now. He leans forwards and clasps his hands together. "Fitz has those lists for us, from Woolwich, but first, Will, sit down."

I am perplexed, for I cannot think of any glaring transgression on my part that would warrant a telling off. But then I notice that his face has assumed a sympathetic expression and I start to panic. He produces a slip of paper and slides it across the table, in doing so turning it around so that it is the right way up for me.

"A return for the first battalion of the Grenadier Guards. The adjutant has listed your brother as missing."

I have no idea what to say. "Since when?" Is eventually all that comes out.

"They came out of the line on 12th and he was not with them then. The battle began on 10th, as you know. Your brother's battalion carried out an attack the following day. They were under heavy fire and did not get far, however in that time, half of their officers had been put out of action. Most lamentable. Things, I fear, have not gone nearly as well as we would have hoped at Neuve Chapelle, in trying to dislodge the enemy."

I cannot form words at all. I know there are a dozen questions I should ask, but not one of them occurs to me. All I can think of is what this news will do to my mother.

"Your father is on Salisbury Plain, is he not?" Kitchener says gently.

I nod. "Yes, Sir."

"I can delay this news getting to him perhaps by 48 hours. It would give you time to break it to your mother here in town as gently as possible, and in person. And perhaps in that time your brother might even be located. Then I must have a telegram sent to him, before it appears in the newspapers, you understand?"

Still speechless, I take the piece of paper in my hands:

1GG: 4 officers killed, 6 wounded. JOHN STANLEY MISSING. No more now.

"Did you make this enquiry especially, Sir?"

I am sure of it, but Lord K skips over the question. "You understand at this point he could be a prisoner, he could simply be mixed up with another unit, he might wander in at any moment. He may be in hospital…"

"And he may be dead," I say quietly.

He sighs. "Yes. He may be dead."

XXI.

Fitz has appeared at the door holding a pile of papers from the arsenal, but it is evident that he was aware of my bad news already, for he too has an air of quiet concern about him. We three sit down together, me with a glass of brandy in my shaking hand. Fitz has spent the last twenty-four hours arduously pulling out the relevant information from our hurriedly compiled departmental returns from Woolwich. Kitchener is impatient. He folds his hands across his stomach. "Boil it down for for me, Fitz." His aide begins laying paper down on the desktop. "I started by going over the top sheets for establishments inside the arsenal that have anything to do with dangerous materials: filling sites, cordite stores, naval quick firing ammunition stores, shell stores, magazines out on the marshes. And I am sure I've found what we are looking for."

"Which is?" Asks the War Secretary.

"Well, firstly, there is a missing consignment of 56 empty shell cases. Big ones for Howitzers. That may or may not have something to do with this. More importantly, negligible amounts of TNT have disappearing from across the arsenal, since November. Almost exclusively from the outskirts of the research department. It seems that there is a lapse in security procedure that has allowed for the stuff to simply vanish in between delivery and when it is taken by any number of people who need it from the same store. All I did was reconcile what arrived with how much various departments had used; then I found the discrepancy."

Kitchener swears. "How much?"

Fitz turns his papers around for us to see. "Burn that," says the War Secretary. Nobody else must find out about that number.

My head was reeling enough already, from the news about my brother; without this new information. "TNT is very easy to move. And safe," I mutter. "On its own you could do little damage to yourself smuggling it about." "Quite," agrees Fitz. "It appears to have been a very drawn out, slow, process. Patient. Hence it was never enough to raise much attention. But if you add it all up across our timeframe, it is a substantial amount of explosives."

Kitchener clears his throat and makes a steeple out of his fingers. "56 Howitzer shell cases would be hard to move covertly. And it may simply be an administrative error. I will have the Superintendent follow it up, Will, but let us put that to one side for now." I nod. "Fitz, with regard to the TNT, none of it is turning up on other people's balances?"

"No, Sir."

"So it is no longer on site?"

"Not so far as I can make out. I have instituted a thorough search, under Ingalls officially, but on your orders I've told him to leave it to Williams; to see if we can locate it stockpiled anywhere at the arsenal, just in case. If this pile of TNT is still at Woolwich he will find it. He has started at the High Explosives Research Department where most has disappeared from, and is having the search radiate from there.

"Is anything else missing?"

"Unfortunately, Sir, yes. Tetryl. Disappearing in the same manner."

"You need one to make the other explode," I say numbly. Doubtless they both know that already.

Fitz is exasperated. "Perhaps we could simply be looking at a black market in materials being siphoned off at the arsenal?"

Sheer wishful thinking, but it has to be raised as a possibility and discounted. I get up and move to the other end of the desk. "Sir, are these the same reports that were here at the beginning of the week?"

"Fitz?" Kitchener looks to his secretary for the answer.
"Yes, they should be, but why…"
"It is them, I am sure of it." I begin dropping files onto the floor until I find what I am looking for. I go back to my seat, open the buff coloured folder and begin scanning it. "Our witnesses have made comments about Hahn; about her complexion, and Mrs. Mitcham mentioned that the skin was flaking off of her hands. Here."

I find the relevant page. "This is the report I was reading a few days ago. It is all about the effects of prolonged exposure to explosives on munition workers." I put the file in front Kitchener and point. "TNT poisoning. Jaundiced effect on the skin, flakey skin." He leans forward to read what I am showing him. "Just what one might expect from a woman who has been handling the stuff since, say, Christmas? Well done, Will."

I've already begun chewing on my lower lip. "But one thing bothers me, Sir. If it was just explosives, why Woolwich? There are sites far more prevalent with TNT. It isn't manufactured there, and they'd arguably have been easier to get into and would have had more of the stuff. And the concept of how to make TNT go bang does not require any specialist access or knowledge. And yet they have gone out of their way to obtain this M14. They've killed a child, almost certainly, to get at it."

"Yes. I am convinced, not to mention concerned. What more can this invention do to augment the effect of all of this TNT? Hahn's symptoms. She has no history of working genuinely in munitions?"

"No, Sir."

"So it is them. They intend to blow something up. But what?" Asks Fitz.

"We must cast a wide net, run a thorough search in, around, under and on top of every major war site we can think of," replies Kitchener. "Williams is taking care of the arsenal, though it looks as if both the TNT and the tetryl have been removed from Woolwich. If, however, it is merely well hidden, then I am confident he will find it. Fitz, we will need to pull in every Special Constable we have. Bugger it, get on to Baden Powell too. He's itching to get involved in some war work. Have him round up his boy scouts for the more menial checks. Nothing too risky."

"Perhaps if we tell them all it is a drill?" I suggest. "What about invasion protocol, training should we ever suspect any of these sites have been comprised?"

"Yes, that's plausible. Use that, Fitz. But no mention of explosives, imagine a different scenario."

Fitz has seized a notebook. "The War Office, the Admiralty, Downing Street, Westminster - both the Lords and the Commons, obviously." Kitchener looks as if he is going to make a comment about the possibility of letting someone annihilate the House of Commons with every politician in it, but thinks better of it. He lets Fitz continue. "Essentially, the whole of Whitehall to be safe."

"All the London railway depots," I add. "The network is vital. And major stations that deal with troops such as Victoria, Waterloo, Charing Cross."

Fitz is talking to himself as he scribbles things down. "Then we ought to throw in Euston and King's Cross, bringing men down from the north."

"The Royal Gunpowder Factory at Waltham Abbey," adds Kitchener. "The small arms places at Enfield and Birmingham, they're obvious ones. Then there is Oldbury, and the chemical works we've commandeered at Rainham. Fitz, you will have to obtain a list of magazines across the country."

"Their reach certainly extends as far as Manchester, as we have seen," I say. "We cannot take for granted the fact that the stuff is still in London."

Kitchener agrees. "Troop movements. Get on to local rail and shipping authorities at Southampton, Bristol,

Portsmouth, Dover. Feed them the same twaddle. I'm sure you'll find plenty of bureaucratic officials willing to leap into action for the thought of this game." He sighs deeply. "I'll go and see Churchill. I'm going to have to let him in on this so we can ensure that the naval bases: Scapa, Rosyth, Harwich, all of them, are safe. They can take care of that themselves."

"Perhaps we should also put the navy onto shipbuilding centres such as the Clyde and the Tyne?" I ask.

"Yes, you're right, I'm sure he will be amenable to that if I give him enough information," says the War Secretary.

"Goodness," mutters Fitz. "This is going to be like looking for a needle in a haystack."

I already have an idea which site I will be put on to.

"Will, you know what to do?"

"Yes, Sir."

"Take Crabtree. And Gaylor. Get him out of the car. The bugger is huge and you may well have need of the weight he can throw around. Any sign of the TNT, call in Williams, if not, get back here so we can plan our next move."

I have Gaylor park at the house, for I do not want any of the attention drawn to us that comes with the King's Daimler. Our destination is Seaford House, or more precisely, 37 Belgrave Square; which is no more than a five minute walk from my own home. It is a grand abode perched on the corner of the square, four floors of opulence painted in magnolia; fashioned in the early Victorian period. It belongs to Lord Howard de Walden, until three years ago the richest bachelor in the country, or so it was said. He was at Eton with my brother, and still cuts a rather dashing figure with immaculately fashioned dark hair swept to the side; where mine would never stay without a bucket of oil, and a pointy chin. He competed in powerboat racing at the London Olympics.

He comes out to greet us in his officer's uniform, for having served in South Africa with John when they were two very lowly and stupid subalterns, he had since left. Now, of course, he has gone back into the army for the duration of the war. His bachelor status is a thing of the recent past, and he has been busy; for there is the sound of a multitude of infants bawling coming down the ornate, rounded staircase into the entrance hall to where we stand on polished black and white, geometric tiles. He must see me glance up.
"Twins not yet three, and a new baby. My apologies."
I wave my hand to signify he has no need to offer them. "Congratulations."
He really is very nice, thought he must be wondering what I want. "I say, you aren't related to John Stanley are you? You look awfully like him."
"He's my brother."
"Then you must be little Fitzwilliam! I'm not nearly so observant usually, but we did chum round Africa together and there is a strong similarity. How is he?"
"At the front," I say. It does not even occur to me to tell him that John is currently unaccounted for.
"Well next time you see him, tell him that Tommy sends his regards. I should like to try and catch up with him some time." I nod uncomfortably. "What can I do for you?" He asks, still smiling.
I launch into a prepared code. "I've heard that you have quite the collection of books in your library, and that it included a rare copy of More's Utopia with an inscription?" A book I wouldn't touch lest I needed something with which to fuel a fire to keep my arse warm in France.
"Oh gosh," he flusters. For I doubt he was expecting that. I can see that he is fumbling for his response in the script, having never expected to use it.
"Let us go and have look," he says. That is close enough. He marches us along the corridor to his ornate and newly refurbished library, lets us in and then moves

to shut both doors behind us. His butler is behind us, presumably ready to make some polite offer of tea, perhaps something stronger. "That will be all thank you Gerald." He locks us in. "Can I do anything to help?" He asks breathlessly.

"Thank you." I have no idea what we might find. I'd appreciate another set of hands, and he has proved he can keep a secret. He walks over to the desk under the window and removes a revolver from a locked drawer, checks that it is loaded. He also retrieves four torches and distributes them. "Shall we, gentlemen?"

He strides over to the floor to ceiling bookshelf closest to the window and scans it until he finds Utopia. Then he pulls it towards us from the top corner and there is a loud click as the bookshelf slides impossibly backwards, then sideways, halfway behind its neighbour; to unveil the entrance to a stone staircase hidden behind the wall.

"Gaylor, what you about to see, you never breathe a word of it. Do you understand?" He merely narrows his eyes at me as if this were an insult. "You too, Crabtree". He merely nods, wide-eyed and takes out his revolver. "If you'll bring up the rear?" I say to my brother's friend. He nods firmly and gestures for everyone else to pass in front of him.

You are in no fit state, says Gaylor. As he firmly pushes me to one side with the back of his hand to take the lead. "How far?" I think it's the first time I've heard him speak in months, and I am not about to argue with him. My whole body still aches from the beating I took earlier in the week.

"Half a mile." Kitchener was right about how useful he might be. From somewhere he has donned brass knuckle dusters on each fist.

The overwhelming smell of damp has erupted from down below, filling the library. As soon as I follow Gaylor in putting my foot on the top step it slips slightly on the wet staircase. There is an old wooden bannister and it is necessary to try and grip the rotting wood in order to steady ourselves on the way down. At the bottom there is nothing but the sound of dripping water to fill the black void in front of us. "Bloody 'ell." Crabtree whispers. "Where are we, Sir?"

"At one end of the only underground access route to Buckingham Palace," I say quietly as I begin to edge along the passage behind Gaylor, making a point of shining my torch in the opposite direction to his, so that we might have maximum visibility.

"How long has it been 'ere?"

"Since my house was built in the early 1840s," responds our aristocratic host. "At the time Queen Victoria had not long made Buckingham Palace the official London residence of the Sovereign, and given the state of things, it was thought prudent that she be able to make a swift exit if necessary."

"So it's a royal escape tunnel?" Crabtree doesn't seem able to grasp the concept.

"Yes," I confirm. "Running just under the surface. It goes along Chapel Street and under the palace gardens."

"Who'd 'ave thought it?"

"Only sensible," mutters Gaylor.

"'Ardly gonna save Their Majesties from a Zeppelin, is it?"

I wish he'd shut up. If there is anyone down here they are going to hear us chattering away. "Well, the world was simpler in the 1840s," I hiss. "I am sure there are new protocols for such things." I glance at Gaylor, who, as the King's personal chauffeur, might know, but his face is completely impassive.

Thankfully we fall into silence. As we tiptoe on, the sound of dripping water gets louder. I suppose on account of our proximity to the *Thames,* or the Serpentine, or some other famous wet London landmark. There is the odd alcove along our path, but they are for the most part empty save for a few rotten crates. I can't imagine this passageway, which resembles one of London's sewer tunnels in its constriction, is conducive for storing anything. Not to mention that you wouldn't want anything in your way if you were trying to speed the Royal Family along it for the sake of their immediate safety. We can see the far wall looming in front of us, along with another staircase, and thus far there is no conceivable place where a pile of explosives could have been hidden. Nor sign of any intrusion. The relief amongst our little party is palpable.

The silence is broken by the sound of something hollow and metal as it goes flying across the passageway in front of us. Gaylor waves a hand as he stops to investigate with his torch. A spinning top. In front of us is the entrance to a small recess on our left, and just inside is scattered a lot of childlike debris. Some old tin soldiers, some exercise books that are sopping wet. I open the cover of one gingerly. A place for the King's late father to come and hide as a boy, it would seem. We are about to ascend the staircase at the other end when the door above opens and a shaft of bleak natural light floods down to meet us. Into the gap appears the face of Major Clive Wigram, who beckons for us to come and join him. He is flanked by Superintendent Quinn, of Scotland Yard, who often takes responsibility for His Majesty's personal safety when he is out and about.

It is glorious to breathe fresh air again. The staircase turns out into the Queen's dining room, which is rather cluttered, as seems to be the fashion. Not only by her mania for this painted furniture being produced in London at the moment that my mother, too, has been buying in piles; but with her knick knacks, photographs and collectible items. We have emerged from the one thing that looks out of place in the corner. A Queen Anne cabinet that stands taller than I am. There is nothing in it, save for a panel which Wigram has

evidently removed to allow us up. "Kitchener called ahead," he says. "Anything?"
"No. Nothing that's been moved since the King's grandmother was on the throne. Consider it cleared."
"Well thank goodness for that," says Quinn. Though of course I will be checking it repeatedly whilst this is ongoing. Heads have rolled since those constables let your woman get away. I will be overseeing any police involvement in this case myself, henceforth."
"I will take extra precautions at my end too," says Lord Howard de Walden, and Wigram nods thanks to both.

XXII.

Come evening, I find myself automatically heading for Kitchener's office. He has his chair turned towards the window and he is reading *Dracula*. "Ah, Will," he spins around to face me. "I have some information for you." My heart is in my throat, and it must be written on my face. "No, no. Good god not that. I'm sorry. No, there is an officer on his way to London. He has been slightly wounded in the attack. He is in your brother's battalion. Not the same company, but he may know something. You ought to be able to go and see him tomorrow."
"Thank you, Sir."
He nods. "Make some time in the morning." He passes me a note. "Here. His name is Cruyff. He is being sent to Princess Beatrice's little recovery place tonight. Do you know where that is, I can have Fitz enquire?"
"No, thank you sir. I know it. Hill Street." Not far from my mother's similar establishment.

He sighs deeply. "What is this M14, Will? What hypothetical invention can have such power for these people?"
"Perhaps it is not hypothetical anymore, Sir." I yawn. "*Frankenstein* would be a good one for your reading list. You see it is not just about a monster. It covers

another theme of ours. The quest for knowledge that these people have undertaken. Shelley examines how a ruthless pursuit of knowledge above all else can be destructive. It's product is the monster, the modern Prometheus."

"It sounds fascinating, Perhaps you can lend it to me when I have finished with Stoker. But who is our Frankenstein, Will? That is the question? And what is his Prometheus?"

A tall, broad young woman intervenes with a fresh bottle of brandy on a tray. Annie gives me a wink as she leaves again and I try desperately not to make eye contact with her.

Her charms have not been lost on Kitchener, either. "A fine looking one, that one." I nod in vague agreement. "This war has done wonders for our young women. It is as if they are birds let out of a cage, with all of this newfound independence. Though of course some of their behaviour leaves much to be desired. That is not to say, of course, that our young men are not equally to blame." I can only smile. Annie went to an exceptionally good school. And she is the worst of the lot. So much for dancers, her father is a Marquis or something and she is the worst behaved girl in London. Kitchener leans forward conspiratorially. "One ought not to gossip, it might harm her reputation, but… well I hear the most shocking things about that young woman." Her reputation is already shot to pieces. My mind is filled with a flash of her curly, voluminous, jet-coloured tresses being tossed over her naked shoulders. Everyone at the War Office calls her Black Maria because she has the velocity of a high explosive shell.

"Really?" Is all I can muster by way of response. I cannot look at him, a fact which I am sure gives me away.

Kitchener tosses the file he has been reading in front of me. "Venereal disease, my boy. And other such horrors. It's rife in the army. Society appears to have lost its head since the beginning of the war." His expression softens. "Our young men ought to be careful. War makes one do all sorts of abnormal things, but being militarily ineffective owing to this sort of illness would be damned unpatriotic." This as he swings his chin around to look out of the window again.

This sentiment is all well and good, but so far as Annie is concerned it is a moot point. She suffers from a common new affliction called *Khaki Fever*. Once a young man in in uniform is within her clutches, he might as well be captured by the Germans. The girl is insatiable. Two hundred years ago she might have modelled for Rubens. In my own experience one has simply to give up and lie on one's back, clamped between her thick thighs while she writhes like an Amazonian on her knees with one's hands forcibly attacked to her magnificent breasts until she has extracted her full dose of pleasure and collapses in a panting heap. If a man survives a couple of rounds of this, he might be allowed to escape with his life.

Kitchener has been talking, but I have lost the thread of his relaxed diatribe.

"Of course, I am getting old. It rather alarms me." He sighs heavily. "I wish I was young again, Will. There is so much I still want to do. Not in that vein, useful things. But I feel so tired and old." Then he fixes me with a pointed, penetrating look. "I suppose if he is careful a young man of your age might have a fine time with all of this wanton sexual abandon."

"Yes, sir," is my pathetic, meek reply.

"If, he is careful."

Then he lets out a laugh at the sight of my discomfort. "I've heard things about you too. Be off with you, Stanley. Get yourself to bed."

"Yes, Sir."

"Alone."

XXIII.

Before I can go home, however, I have a visit to pay. Kitchener is right, to a degree. There is a certain amount of moral abandonment going on in war time, but as a member of the Society of Socrates I am fully determined to engage in it as much as possible. As I have told my sister, we all might be dead soon. Ironically, the killjoys have never had so much fun either. Any piece of escapism they can attack, they do. If it isn't football, it is the immorality of the music halls. They are apparently trying to get London County Council to refrain from renewing their licenses. I wonder they have time to even think about the war, they have such a gleeful time judging other people. I doubt they spend much time considering how important it is that people have some little piece of enjoyment to cling to through this trial.

I have a standing appointment at the Duke of York's Theatre on a Sunday. There is no show tonight, and the lights outside are mostly switched off. The foyers are gloomy and dark, and the few performers that have wandered in to rehearse, along with the relevant staff, seem to be there to sit at the bar and gossip about the war. I enter through the stage door and go straight upstairs to the dressing room reserved for the chorus girls. There is only one inside, and she turns towards me, her long blond curls pulled over her shoulder, and narrows her hazel brown eyes, frowning. "You're late today. I've missed you." She gasps. "What happened to your lovely face?"

"I'd have been here on time, but there is a lot of work on. The alarming kind." She has already approached me to kiss my cheek, and now she rubs my crotch. It is supposed to be a mischievous gesture but she is a nice girl, and it comes off as shy instead. She does, however, sport a wolfish grin, and there are things that she can do with her mouth that no reputable girl should know.

"Well, I've missed parts of you, anyway."

I drop down onto the chaise lounge under the window. "You should save your affection for someone more worthy, Lucy. Somewhere out there is a nice boy that will treat you like a princess. I am awful."

"You do look after me, you're not all bad. I know I'm not your only girl, though," she says wistfully. I don't answer, because I don't want to lie to her, or upset her, and after a moments silence she sits on my lap and begins to undo my belt and my trousers.

"Poor darling, you look exhausted" She kisses my bruised cheek. "I'll be gentle with you, I promise."

A short while later she has lit a cigarette and is tidying up her clothes. "Do you have everything you need?" I ask, as I look around for my Sam Browne belt.

She sighs and sits down. "They've halved our salaries. It is the only way they can keep the doors open."

"Make me a list." She hesitates as she pulls a scrap of note paper from underneath a pile of cosmetics. Potatoes. Vegetables. Bread. She comes from a large family and her father is a cripple. She is the only one bringing home any money. I'd buy it for her even without our arrangement. "Nothing for yourself?"

"No, thank you." She is fixing my belt for me. "Is everything all right? You're not yourself, Will."

I sigh and take her hands, lead her to sit next to me, for I know this will not be easy for her. "My brother is missing."

Her hand flies to her mouth, open in surprise. "Oh god. Have you told Agnes?"

I shake my head sadly. "I haven't told anybody. I'm going to have to break this to my mother. There is still a chance he will come in right as rain."

"And if he doesn't?"

"Then he is probably dead."

"I can come with you, to see Agnes."

I kiss her forehead. "Thank you. I may need you. I do not know her and I doubt I will be a comfort to her." She pulls my head towards her shoulder and hugs me tightly. "There is still hope though?"
"For now. I could not be better informed, either."
"Well, then we will hope."

Monday, 15th March 1915

XXIV.

It is past midnight and somehow I just don't feel like going home. It might be the idea of telling my mother about John, which I feel completely unable to face after the day that I have had, it might be the tense atmosphere that surrounds the place now that it is under armed guard. It might be the fact that to move from my chair at the War Office causes me pain, or it may be the fact that I cannot bear to see my brother's stupid dog staring at me, wondering where its master is. Most likely it is a combination of all four. "Is everything all right, Sir?"
"What?" I have forgotten that Crabtree is in the room. He is slurping a cup of tea loudly. Some of it is dribbling down his boyishly smooth chin. "I've been talking to you for five minutes and you haven't insulted me once."
"Were you saying anything interesting?" I yawn. We sit in silence for a moment.
"Something is wrong, though, isn't it, Sir?"
"My brother is missing. After an attack."
"Bloody 'ell."
"Do not breathe a word of that to anybody. My mother does not know yet. I am going to have to be the one to tell her if he doesn't turn up in the next day or so."
"Course not."
"Crabtree, you can go home. Be back early tomorrow. I will have considered by then what we should do next."
"What are you going to do? Are you going to go home too?"
"No. I'm going to have Gaylor take me down to Woolwich. I'll have Williams meet me and we can patrol, see if we can catch these people at anything."
"I'll come with you, Sir."

"You should get some rest. Tomorrow will likely be another long day."
"Still, cant have you going off on an adventure without me, in'it?" I don't really know what to say at this little show of solidarity as we put on our coats and get ready to leave. "Sir," he says with a face full of some treat his mother has given him.
"Yes, Crabtree?"
He offers an open handkerchief with some crumbling brown substance on it. "Do you want some of my bread pudding?"

Gaylor drives us through the Beresford Gate and brings the King's car to a neat stop outside the main office block where Williams is waiting for us, rubbing his hands together to keep them warm. He nods to Crabtree. Still no salute for me.
"Anything doing?" My assistant asks him.
"All quiet for now."
I pull on a pair of leather gloves and then open my cigarette case and offer it to both of them.
Williams clears his throat and spits the contents to one side. "How do you want to play this?"
I have only the vaguest idea. "I want to have a look about. Get a feel for the place at night. Then perhaps we can revisit the scenes where George and Remington were killed and look about the vicinity, see if anything stands out in terms of how they got in and out without being seen. I just don't think it is possible to gauge in daylight when the place is full of people."
Once we are equipped with something to smoke and a torch each, we set off. Of course, the arsenal is necessarily dark on account of the non-existent zeppelin menace, not a street lamp illuminated. Who knows when they might finally discover the way to London. I hope it will not be tonight. A frost is forming on the cobbles underneath our feet, a stiff breeze is coming off of the river and making our eyes water, and

every warm exhalation meets with the cold and forms a fog in front of us, even after our cigarettes have been extinguished.

The whole site is eerie when all but shut down. Silent buildings loom on either side of us, not a good thought for our artillerymen in France counting out their last shells. Most of the gargantuan machinery lies ominously at rest. In a few hours it will all be brought properly to life again and set to work; producing the means of absolute destruction for use at the front. As far as the King and Lord Kitchener are concerned, it is not enough. To even be in with a chance of winning this war these machines need to run day and night. The arsenal must not be allowed to sleep like this.

"Gives me the bloody willies, this does." As ever Crabtree finds a unique way to articulate the mood.

"Not surprising," Williams says as we continue to stroll up toward the river.

"Eh?" Crabtree has located a ripped paper bag of rhubarb and custard sweets in his pocket and is offering them round. It is necessary to pick lint off of them, but needs must, and I am hungry.

Williams lets our a loud yawn and then lowers his voice to a sinister tone. "Full of ghosts. Probably the most haunted place in London."

"More than the Tower?" Crabtree scoffs.

"Course. Far more dangerous being here, look around you. Fire and brimstone. Hell on earth. But they get all the famous ghouls at the Tower." He grins, enjoying the effect that this is having on my assistant. "See over there?" He points to Brass Foundry; a neat little brick building with a decorative finish and a neat cupola. "Couple of hundred years old, that building is," Williams whispers. Makes sense. Nowadays they'd just shove up a brick square. "At the back of the building, they had a big pit in the floor. What they used to do, was make a mould out of clay. Then they'd stick the thing in the pit and pour boiling hot, liquid bronze in it.

Once they had let it go cold and harden, they'd break the clay off and hopefully they'd have a shiny new gun to go and bore out and get ready to fire at some Froggies." Crabtree is wide-eyed, transfixed on William's tale. Especially since he has brought his torch to his chin and pointed it upwards to create a sordid mask of light on his face. "Well, the story goes, that one day they were pouring bronze. Was as dangerous at sounds. No rules about having kids around then, either. What happened was, that something went wrong when they were about to fill the mould, and they shouted for this boy worker to dash in and fix it. But he didn't get out in time. Like lava the bronze was. It hit his hand, started running down his arm and slowly swallowed him up. Cast in bronze he was. Walk past that building at the right time of night and you can hear the poor little beggar scream." Crabtree trots a little faster away towards the river after the conclusion of that anecdote. I find myself thinking about whether or not the boy's body would have maintained its integrity and formed a cast, as opposed to just melting. This is what happens when you spend most of your time with dead people.

Williams comes to a halt by two octagonal little guard huts set up against the river wall. They are labelled A.41 and A.42. He nods to a sentry outside the former. "Now, you wouldn't know it, but this little guardhouse once housed a prince. I am dubious. The building is uninviting; squat, dingy. I find it hard to believe that it was ever more appealing than any one of London's innumerable hotel rooms. "Of course, he was dead at the time." Well, that explains it.

"Prince Louis Napoleon. He was only 23. Mullered by Zulus he was. Stabbed him nearly twenty times. Apparently his eyeball exploded. His old girl, the Empress, still lives down in Surrey. They brought him back to her. God knows what state he was in by the time he got here, long voyage like that, no refrigeration then, of course. But he stayed in that hut overnight."

"If the wind's blowing the right way, you can still smell him," interjects the sentry with a wink. Crabtree looks horrified.

"Anyway, they had a big procession down to Farnborough. Queen Victoria was there too. His mum's had a big Imperial crypt built down there and shoved him in it with his dad."

I vaguely remember a story about this being how Lord Stamfordham became known to the old Queen. He'd known the Prince in Africa.

"Here," Williams beckons to Crabtree to join him at the river wall. "Come and have a look." I follow. The view is of the Thames, looking off towards Gallions Reach. Directly in front of us is an immense t-shaped pier, equipped with massive cranes for the loading and unloading of guns and materials at the arsenal. "Smell anything?" Williams asks. Crabtree looks baffled.

"Garlic, perhaps?" Now I am baffled. "That stretch of water was a prison a hundred years ago. We rounded up so many Frenchies during the wars with the original Napoleon that we housed them on two old navy ships out there. Didn't end well for them though, poor, smelly bastards.

I try and conjure the scene in my mind. Two Nelsonian ships: masts bare of sails, yards creaking as they rocked back and forth on the *Thames*, the decks illuminated here and there by the odd bobbing lantern. The gun ports would have been open, and through them the sound of chatter, perhaps even French voices singing, would have carried to where we stand on the shore. And the smell. You would have been able to smell them. Not garlic, but unwashed bodies. Once, when Nelson sailed the *Agamemnon* into Portsmouth after a prolonged cruise, the stench of several hundred filthy men crammed into such close quarters was said to be so bad, that people on the shore could smell the ship when it was still out of sight on the other side of the Isle of Wight. I think of Lynette Hahn's unfortunate husband. Squashed into such unsanitary conditions on the *Saxon.* "What happened?" I ask.

Williams shakes his head a little too sadly for me to take him seriously. "They were stuffed in there so that they were overflowing, and orders came down to the Royal Marine officer in charge that he needed to get rid of some of them. Now, the authorities meant move them on, find somewhere else to put them. But the officer had a more literal interpretation. He had a couple of hundred of them lined up, attached weights to their ankles and sent them over the edge. Plopped in and died, all of them."

"Like walking the plank?" Crabtree gasps.

"Exactly like that."

"Never!" Declares my assistant.

Williams shrugs nonchalantly, as if it makes no odds if Crabtree believes him. "You're looking at a mass grave. Sometimes when you look out at night you can see the ships' lanterns shining up and down, hear the splashes one by one as they hit the water. Hear them scream as they hit the water." He sighs. "That and their bones have washed up over the years, bits of French uniform, personal effects. We collect it all up."

I push myself off from the wall. "Come on. Enough tall tales. Let's get inside and have a cup of tea. Then we'll go land have a look at our murder scenes."

We are completing a circuit by walking south down Street No.4 towards Building 22 again, having seen or heard nothing untoward. The only people that have crossed our paths are arsenal policemen and perhaps Williams's ghosts. As we approach the office block Williams starts up again. "One that makes my skin crawl is in here, though. On the back staircase. I've heard it myself. There was a murder here a few years ago. Artillery officer was stabbed, and they never found out who did it. All sorts of nonsense with loud banging, lights flickering on and off, screaming. Nobody wants to be in here alone at night."

We jump as the door swings open and a worried looking MP sticks his head out. "Where have you been?" He chastises Williams. "We've been looking everywhere for you!"

"Didn't look that bloody hard, did you? We were only up at the river."

"What is it?" I ask, the MP, trying to sound authoritative.

It is only then that I realise that he is actually shaking; convulsing almost. "It's bad. Really fucking bad. Sir."

XXV.

We do not have to walk far. Building A.73 is but a few steps away, a huge round construction just northwest of where Mordecai Remington was found crushed between two guns; in between avenues C and E. It resembles a giant aviary on the inside. The whole interior is illuminated by shafts of perfectly straight, stark moonlight, that highlights piles of heavy artillery pieces and equipment. At the room's centre stands a massive radial crane, nearly 80 feet tall. It looks like the inside of some great clock, with all of its wheels and dials, supported by a framework of huge metal shafts angled inwards like an industrial teepee. "You should see her in action," whispers Williams, as we all set out towards where two torch beams are fixed on the floor. "Swings sixty tons of gun in a circle around the room like it was a pencil."

Strung upside down on the immense framework, lashed to a large cog, is what remains of a human being. I am glad that my stomach is presently lined with no more than a furry rhubarb and custard sweet. One look and Crabtree is in the corner, painting the floor with regurgitated bread and butter pudding. Williams stands in a relaxed pose with his hands in his pockets, hips thrust forwards. His face, however, wears a grimace. "Not the worst I've seen, what with accidental explosions and shit. But bloody gruesome."

I shake my head. "Do we know who it is?"

"Not yet. Told them not to touch nuffin' till you got here." He nods his head towards two men who are staring at us from across the room, their torches shaking in their hands, trying not to look at the scene in front of them. One of them is an arsenal policeman, the other wears civilian clothes but a Special Constable's armband and looks like he has just come off the battlefield. He has either tried to cut down the victim, or at the very least slipped and fell into the blood on the floor in the act of finding him. His eyes are wide and primal.

"No missing persons at present?"

"No. But this looks fresh. Doubt there's been enough time for someone to think about raising the alarm."

We are interrupted by the sound of the patter of small feet on flagstones and I look up to see Scully coming towards us like a penguin with a respiratory problem. "Oh dear god," are the only words he can muster when he lays eyes on the remains of the sight in front of us.

"Right." I take a deep breath and step around a substantial puddle of blood, avoiding that which is still dripping from the corpse above. "Let's get this over with."

I've seen people blown up, shot, torn by shrapnel, but I've never seen a person that has been the subject of some rudimentary experiment in flaying. "He was alive when they did this to him." My first supposition is based on the sheer amount of carnage on display. Blood was obviously still being pumped around his body. The second is based on what remains of masculine genitalia dangling from the body. It isn't only blood pooling on the floor, because the man's bowels and bladder have quite naturally voided onto the floor too. Faeces, blood, urine and whatever else can possibly leak out of a recently deceased man now creates a trail running slightly downhill toward a manhole cover in the floor. Not only has our victim been scalped, but his face has been half taken down over his skull, peeled or ripped off; revealing muscle, bone, sinew, and causing one eyeball to hang out of the socket. It is pointed unfortunately towards us. The rest of his naked body has been slashed to such an event that skin hangs off in flaps, revealing a morbid, gruesome study in anatomy below. Quite simply, this poor fellow has been savaged. As I try to survey the whole scene, I keep going back to that face. That eye. His mouth gaping open with an old rag stuffed inside. How can someone with no face we such an expression of such sheer terror?

"Sir? You might want to have a look at this." Crabtree has straightened up and in doing so has been shining his torch on the wall next to his ungracious pile of sick. Four words have been smeared just above his eye level:

Getting warmer.
Beware Cerberus.

"What does that mean?" Asks Williams.
"Cerberus was a three headed dog in Greek Mythology," I say, chewing my thumbnail. "The Hound of Hades. It guarded the underworld."
"You have to go to posh school to learn shit like that," Crabtree whispers to Williams with a sense of pride at my education, mixed with a patronising air that leaves Williams bemused.
"And of course…" chimes in Scully, who has crept up behind us. Here we go again. "This has evolved into folklore and mythology surrounding hell hounds."
Williams looks at the doctor as if he is mad. "You been sniffin' something in your lab?" He asks irreverently. I mentally applaud his irreverence on this occasion.

References to nonsense like this? Surely the only explanation is that these people have overheard Scully wittering on about his folklore.

"Nobody's saying nothin' about dogs being seen or heard round 'ere," Crabtree points out.

"Ah, but you wouldn't," Scully replies smugly. "You wouldn't, unless you were close to death, or unless you have looked death in the face. Then a person can see a hell hound. They are commanded by demons, and they send them to drag evil souls to hell. With a glowing red light emanating from their eyes and mouths." He adds that last bit as if such a pointed detail will convince us all.

I've had enough of this nonsense. "Dr. Scully? I presume it falls on you to have the remains cut down and moved to your mortuary and to instruct men on cleaning this up when you have finished collecting your evidence?" He can have the dirty work. I turn to face Crabtree and Williams. "There is a wealth of machinery within the arsenal walls that could have a catastrophic impact on the human body before we start suspecting fictitious dogs. More important, I think, apart from identifying him of course, is the fact that this, to me, is a staged presentation, for us. A show. A sick performance on their part. Essentially, as far as our criminals are concerned, I think it is a sordid progression from the cigarettes, and the assaults, and the stupid newspaper advertisement designed to capture our attention or put us off. The explosives appear to be gone. All of the TNT on site is now under additional guard. Carrick is gone, it looks as if they have their hands on his invention. So what is this? Are they trying to keep our attention here now? Presumably so that we do not divert it elsewhere? If so does this horrid killing have any bearing at all on what they are trying to achieve? Or is it a classic case of misdirection?" The more I think about it, the more I am convinced that this dramatic and hideous performance is irrelevant in the scheme of things. It feels all wrong. But how can we not investigate it? Even if we are on to this ruse, if it is a part of their hideous game, might it not be better to persist with letting them believe that they have duped us? My head hurts.

I turn to question the two policemen and find that the one dripping with blood has wandered off. "Where is the other fellow?" I ask a sickened looking youth. I think it is Spotty, the boy who was at the Beresford Gate on the night of Fred George's murder.

"He just went out," he says quietly.

"But you were told to stay here, and await questioning?"

He nods. "Sorry, yes, Sir."

The hairs on the back of my neck bristle. "They why did he leave?"

"I don't know. I wasn't walking with him. He's new. One of the additional Special Constables down here at the moment since all this funny stuff started happening. He raised the alarm and called me in as I was going back to the office for a tea. When I got here he was trying to cut the body down."

"Which way did he go?" He points a shaking hand towards an exit, and I am already on my way. "And you never saw him before? Never?"

"No, sir."

"Williams?"

"Didn't even give him a proper look," he is jogging to catch up with me, but I have already flown out of the door.

"Crabtree, get to the main gate, and Gaylor. Do not let anyone through it," I scream as I disappear outside. I see the Special pacing quickly away from A.73. "Hey! You. Stop!" I call. He looks back over his shoulder, an alarmed expression on his face, and then he begins sprinting away.

XXVI.

I like to think that it was my ready wit and charming intellect, but sometimes I think that my godfather only recruited me for my job because I was a runner at Eton. Every task that comes my way involves me running. Usually after someone whose life depends on getting away, or after someone who would gleefully kill me without a second thought. Every exhausted muscle, not to mention every bruised rib, is screaming as I set off in pursuit of the man I am sure has just carried out a hideous murder. He has dashed south and across Avenue E and into the nearest large building. I know that if I lose sight of him, I will never find him in the maze that constitutes the arsenal and so I force myself to push through the open doors after him. Already straining to breathe, I immediately inhale a face full of fine wood dust and realise that we are in one of the arsenal's saw mills.

The floor is slippery with debris and we are funnelled into running in one straight line by freshly cut planks of timber stacked at shoulder height either side, along the entire length of the shed. Trying to run whilst coughing on sawdust is bad enough, but as he reaches the end of the hangar, the killer kicks over a huge basket filled with sweepings to slow me down. Through a blizzard of wood shavings, I just about see him push his way through a door in the end of the building. Sliding over what must be a track for one of the arsenal's locomotives, I arrive outside just in time to see him vanish into the next structure along.

The heat hits me in the face as soon as I follow him inside. It is like a vision of hell. Sparks flying, glowing embers. At one point a luminous stream of molten metal is being poured from a chute coming down from above, men on a gantry above watch it intently. They hardly look up. At one point our killer stumbles towards a furnace, and I almost expect him to catch light, he arches so close to the flames. But he swerves in time, and through several interlocking buildings I have to follow him further and further into this flaming underworld. We reach a large blacksmith's shop, with small gauge tracks running right through the one end of the open hangar and out the other. There are piles of coal everywhere, and a change in atmosphere is immediate discernible. I can taste the filthy dust in my mouth and at the back of my throat as I try to gulp in air to keep running. Smoke hangs in the air, and a criss-cross pattern of metal bars supporting the glass ceiling above our heads casts a bizarre pattern of moonlight up the walls. The odd worker, there to stoke the furnaces overnight and keep them going for the next working day, looks up in surprise as we stagger past, one after the other.

He can't be very fit, because I can barely keep up a jog, and yet he is not pulling away. Either that or his clothes are so covered in his victim's stiffening blood that it is making it difficult for him to move. Through a huge workshop he goes, past vast machinery, the purpose of which is completely alien to me. Presses, rollers, smouldering furnaces, workbenches, cutting machines, huge sheets of metal. I can feel myself gaining on him as he searches for a path through all of this. I reach out to grab him by the tunic, and I feel a handful of it within my crippled fingers, but then my foot runs hard, and yelping in pain as I collide with the base of a hand press of some kind, I loosen my grip and he twists free and bursts out onto Avenue E. I can barely walk now, and with my foot throbbing I limp out into the open in time to see him trying to break a lock on a large structure at the juncture with Street No.2; next to the main office building. He looks utterly spent, unable to run anymore, desperate to find somewhere to hide, to wait it out until we give up and abandon the chase. He is not stupid enough to make for the main gate, apparently; or in the direction of anybody who I might call to my aid.

Finally the lone padlock gives and he disappears inside. By this time Williams has made up the distance between he and I, huffing and puffing. He puts a finger to his lips to indicate that we should be silent, and beckons for me to follow him. Instead of directly following our killer, we edge up along the side of the hangar, which is labelled as a carriage inspection store, drawing our revolvers and making sure to stay as quiet as possible. I am convinced that my heavy breathing will give us away as Williams lifts a loose panel in the corrugated metal wall and leads me inside, signalling that we should keep as low as possible.

The interior of the store is pitch black at floor level, though above our heads moonlight is filtering in a little through neglected, dirty windows. As my eyes adjust, I can see that in lines on the floor are immaculate rows of gun carriages; the wooden frames with huge wheels on which innumerable eighteen pounders will be mounted so that they can be dragged back and forth across the front. Williams and I stop. It seems odd that such care would be taken to make them look so nice, when the fate for many of them will be to end up smashed to bits by weaponry mounted on their German counterparts. I find myself holding my breath in order to try and get some kind of audible indication of where our killer may be. I can hear nothing but the pounding of my own blood in my ears; my heart thumping. My ribs hurt so much that I have tears in my eyes. Williams must be faring better at listening, because he uses standard military hand signals to guide me forwards, past two rows of carriages to where the floor plan opens up to accommodate some work benches laden with carpentry tools for making final adjustments.

Suddenly I see something move out of the corner of my eye. Williams has seen it too, and he darts off in pursuit as the chase begins again. The killer opts for the next hangar along, and Williams and I pause briefly. "Is there another exit to that one?" I pant. "Can we head him off?" He nods. "Go there."

The fittings in this place are far less obstructive than in the last building and I can see our prey making his way off towards the far end. All of the machinery is low to the ground. To me it looks like dozens and dozens of industrial spinning wheels facing each other in two double rows down the centre of the room. At the culmination of both aisles are huge buckets full of empty bullet casings waiting to be taken off and filled. It occurs to me as I stagger past, that I cannot believe the effort that goes into the fashioning of something so seemingly simple as a bullet for a rifle; something that every Tommy needs in vast handfuls to stay alive. I've always just taken them for granted. I've never had any appreciation for just how difficult it is to keep an ever-burgeoning army firing at the enemy.

Back outside we go again and I recognise Street No.1. He races across it towards a jumble of buildings and I falter slightly. I am startled to see a steam engine coming towards me, of all things. It is in miniature form, of course, making its way to the gate, I presume, ready to ferry workers about come morning; but still, I am lucky to dart across its path just in time; for miniature or not, I cannot imagine being run over by it would be comfortable. The driver leans out of his tiny cab and calls me a pillock.

The killer has disappeared somewhere into the abyss of ramshackle buildings. They look like sundry establishments that support the main work of the arsenal. One has paint pots stacked outside, one is labelled as a tool store. I can no longer see our quarry, but I can hear his heavy footsteps lumbering away from me. He appears to have kicked a latrine bucket into my path for good measure. Lord knows where Williams has got to, but in fairness I no longer have any idea where I am, either. I have no way at all in such a built up area, cluttered with equipment, to get a bearing on where we have ended up; although at one point I think I see the exterior wall of the arsenal flash by ahead of me. I am distracted, however, by the banging of a screen door as I pursue the killer into yet another hangar. Standing up on tables are thousands of identical shell casings, each a foot or so high, with their pointed caps off, waiting patiently to be filled. There is a crash as he knocks a number of them down like skittles on his way back out into the open.

Now I know exactly where I am, because I can see the little guard house that sheltered a dead French prince mutilated by Zulu tribesmen. I can see the West Wharf with its cranes looming over the water beyond the river wall out towards Gallions Reach. I can see two alarmed sentries watching two beleaguered and determined runners coming towards them. I cannot go any further. I feel myself involuntarily slowing down. My prey might be marginally too heavy and unfit, but he's not broken and sleep deprived. My heart feels like it is going to explode out of my chest, my breath is ragged, my lower back feels like someone is sitting on it. My vision has started to blur, so much so that although I hear the sound of a car screeching to a halt and see the flash of twin headlights spinning across the road ahead I have no comprehension of what is happening until it is almost over.

I stagger to a halt, lean forward and hold onto my knees, just in time to see the door of the King's car come flying open into the path of our fleeing killer. He tumbles face first into it and knocks himself out, then collapses into a heap on the cobblestones just as Gaylor steps down from the driver's seat. Shortly afterwards Crabtree jumps out too and laughs. "Where did you come from?" I wheeze as I approach the car and give the unconscious man a prod with my newly bruised foot to make sure he really is unconscious.

"Gaylor thought he saw you from down by the gate, 'eard you shout out to Williams. So we raced up here." Williams has arrived by now too, and I motion for the two of them to get the unconscious lump into the car. I raise an eyebrow at Gaylor, who still bears no discernible facial expression. Then I think there is the faintest smirk on his face. "His Majesty said to me last week;" he explains. "You can't even dress yourself properly and that I should keep an eye on you." By now I am hanging onto the river wall. Regardless of whether this particular stretch of the Thames is a resting place for several hundred unfortunate Frenchmen who walked the plank, I cannot resist the impulse to vomit straight into it as our captive is heaved into the back of the Daimler, with Williams giving him a final kick up the arse before slamming the door shut.

XXVII.

As soon as the hour is sociable, from the War Office I make my way along Whitehall to Birdcage Walk, cut across Green Park, past Piccadilly and continue painfully in the direction of Grosvenor Square until I reach Hill Street, at which point this relatively minor excursion has almost finished me off. The building that I am looking for is a pretty, brick townhouse; with a large black front door, flanked by two rounded, white stone columns. Princess Beatrice has secured use of it from one of her friends and turned it into a 'hospital.' In reality, these small establishments springing up in private houses all over Mayfair are convalescent homes, and don't deal with serious cases, but nonetheless they are doing a roaring trade in looking after officers with light wounds who have been sent home from the front. One or two are standing outside enjoying a cigarette; arms in slings, or heads swathed in bandages, and as I mount the stone steps to get inside they nod acknowledgement.

Inside the house is immaculate; shiny white flooring and leafy green plants; like a Parisian cafe. I look for some sort of desk, or reception area, but there is none. I am merely standing in someone's home. Eventually, the smokers from outside come back in and I stop one; a tall man of about my age who appears to have broken all of his fingers. "Sorry, I wonder if you might help me? I'm looking for a patient here. A new arrival. His name is…" I realise I've forgotten it and start fumbling around in my coat pockets for Kitchener's note.

"He's upstairs. Foreign sounding name? Croff? Or something? There's only eight of us here, it's not too difficult to keep track. Follow me." I express my appreciation and follow him up the main staircase; a grand, square effort, with alcoves here and there housing expensive looking Chinese vases.

My guide stops and points for me. "Down the hall, all the way to the end, door on your right." I follow his instructions, check the note in my pocket and then knock lightly on a freshly painted white door. From within, a small voice invites me to enter.

Second Lieutenant David Cruyff, Grenadier Guards, is a slight boy of about nineteen or twenty with a protruding lower lip, wispy blond curls and a worried expression. He is sitting on the edge of his bed in a neat set of pyjamas, holding an unlit cigarette nervously. Crabtree had offered to carry out this interview for me, being less personally invested in its outcome, but it was something that I felt I had to do myself; alone. "Are you Stanley's brother?" He all but whispers. "You look like him. They said you might come."

"Yes. John is my brother. I was hoping to ask you about the battle, to try and get some idea of what happened to him."

"I don't remember a lot. It was… I don't know. It wasn't like I expected it would be. The battle, that is."
"Don't be afraid. It isn't a test. It doesn't matter if you cannot answer me. You don't need to tell me what you think I want to hear, either. If you know nothing, then that is all right."
He seems to relax at this. "He hasn't turned up then?"
"No, he hasn't."
I allow the conversation to lapse into silence. I find it is better, that you get more out of a friendly witness if you let them approach it in their own way, in their own time. Especially if they've seen something awful. Eventually, Cruyff takes a deep breath. "There were so many shells," he says. "We could hear them on the day the battle started. We were sat at Estaires, if you've heard of it. To be honest I think we were glad we were out of it. But then we were called to go forward. We spent that night somewhere closer to the battle, I forget where."
"You were in No. 2 Company, is that right?"
"Yes. I'm sure the King's, that's you brother's company, isn't it?" I nod. "Well I'm sure it was the King's that were ordered to attack with us."
"Would you like me to light that for you?" I gesture towards his cigarette.
"I'm not sure if I'm allowed to smoke in here?"
"I'm afraid I don't know. But I am sure they will tell you if they don't like it."
He relaxes when he has a cigarette in his mouth. "It wasnt even morning when they sent us off to get ready. The first German trenches we saw had already been captured, so we walked right over them and formed the company up. It was odd. Seeing all their things. They must have left in a hurry. Anyway, then it all started to go wrong. The rifle fire hit us as soon as we went on. They were on us from all sides. As far as we were concerned, we were coming up behind some of the Northamptons sitting in a trench in front of us.

The Germans were supposed to be about 150 yards in front of that. But we couldn't go anywhere. We were stuck. Brigade Headquarters just told us to hang on, so we did. There was really an awful lot of shelling. Anyway, when it got dark, they pulled us back again and that was that. Nothing doing really, but we lost a lot of officers, I think."

"When did you last see my brother?" I ask, I am terrified of what I might be about to hear.

"I suppose I last saw Captain Stanley advancing with his men into a cloud of smoke. I'm almost certain it was him."

Which tells me nothing at all. "Did you see, well, to your knowledge, did anyone at all see him killed?"

"No, but then I was out of it quite quickly. I certainly heard nobody say anything about him being dead."

"Did you see any of the dead officers?"

"No, I was shot in the wrist, you see, and well, it was damned painful. After that I suppose you can say I was rather self-involved. I wasn't really thinking about anybody else." I sigh. We sit for a while in silence. "I'm sorry I can't tell you anymore," he says awkwardly.

I stand up. "It's not your fault. I'd rather you told me nothing than you make something up that you didn't really see. Thank you for your time. I hope your wrist feels better soon."

He nods as I make for the door. "I don't think I acquitted myself very well," he says softly as I open the door.

"I am sure you did very well. Battle is confusing, and it was your first go at it," I say as if I really have any idea at all.

XXVIII.

I spend half an hour or so sitting in Trafalgar Square after meeting with Cruyff, trying to establish if I have learned anything at all. Just that John led his company into battle. And that he survived at least the opening moments. I suppose it is more than I knew before, but it is of little consolation. I am starting to realise that doing nothing and hoping that he will turn up and solve all of my problems, as he has always done, is not a viable course of action. Surely the battle has petered out now, which means that things should be clearer. And yet they are not. As a Captain, surely, if he was in a British hospital, or his body had been recovered, they would know who they had. It is an odd frame of mind to be in, to be praying wholeheartedly in that case that the Germans have got him, and that in due course we will receive word from a prison somewhere that he is at the very least alive. Because the alternative is that he is still there, lying on the battlefield. Dead and forgotten.

I walk slowly across the front of the National Gallery and cut up St. Martin's Lane to the Duke of York's Theatre, where on making an enquiry at the stage door, I am told to stay exactly where I am, and that Lucy will be down shortly. The dragon manning the entrance doesn't like me, and there is no chance I will get by her. After five minutes Lucy appears wearing a heavy overcoat and pulling a hat down firmly over her fair hair, before she begins pulling on a pair of gloves. "Any more news?" She frowns.

I shake my head. "I've spoken to one of his fellow officers, but nothing."

"So we must go ahead with this?"

I nod. "I think so. It is unfair not to tell her."

"Well then," she says firmly. "Follow me."

I am extremely grateful that she seems ready to take the lead, for I have never met the woman we are on our way to see, and I have to give her terrible news. Lucy strides purposefully up the road, turning right onto Long Acre, left onto Mercer Street and setting her sights on Seven Dials, where she lives with her own family. It isn't the nicest part of London by a long way, but when we reach Shorts Gardens, Lucy turns just off the main road and up a neat staircase to a selection of flats that overlook an attractive array of window boxes in the yard and face away from the bustle of the road. "Agnes?" She calls as she knocks on the door briskly. "It's Lucy. Can I come in?"

There is no answer. "When was the last time anyone saw her?"

Lucy shrugs. "I could ask around..."

I try the door and the handle turns. "Here," she says, "let me go first, a familiar face. Agnes?" She calls again. "Are you here?"

I do not hear any response, but I can hear a light banging sound coming from somewhere down the hall. Lucy pushes the door to a sitting room open gently and her eyes widen at the state of the room. There are clothes everywhere, plates with the remnants of sandwiches, cosmetics. A slight figure appears in the doorway to what must be the kitchen, for the girl is drying a plate with a cloth.

"Did you not hear me knocking?" Lucy rushes forward and puts her arms around the surprised looking resident. You could not call her a woman. If she is twenty I will be surprised. She is staring at me, at first I think because of the bruises on my face; but then I realise, it must be because I look like my brother.

"Are you Will?" She asks boldly.

I nod. She turns and goes back into the kitchen, leaving us to follow her. Like her sitting room, it is a mess, though she appears to be in the middle of making some attempt to clean it up. She has for now, however, sat down at a kitchen table and folded her hands on top of a bread board. I gesture for Lucy to take the second chair. "You're here to say he's dead, aren't you?" Agnes's tone is odd; petulant.

"No, darlin' we're not." Lucy reaches out and takes her hands. She looks at me pleadingly.

Officiousness takes over. "I'm sorry to have to tell you that he is missing. Since earlier this week. I thought you should know, but of course I will tell you more as soon as I know myself. I am hoping that he is merely a prisoner."

"How do you know about me?" She asks.

"My brother told me before he left last autumn. In case anything happened to him. He has left things in order, well, should the worst happen. He wanted you to be safe." No response. "Both of you," I add.

The banging in the flat grows louder and a toddler appears in the doorway. I have never laid eyes on my niece until now. Her dress is a little grubby, and I may be biased, but her dishevelled appearance does nothing to detract from her beauty. She has a mass of dark curls, one of which hangs down over her forehead and into her opaline green eyes; the same shade as my brother's. And mine.

"Hello Josephine!" Lucy holds out her arms and the child waddles over to her and climbs into her lap, still clutching a small xylophone which appears to have been the source of the noise on our arrival. Lucy smothers her with kisses, to the child's obvious delight. "I hate this war," says Agnes. I find her stroppy, childish. I am struggling to recognise what my brother sees in her. I suspect that if not for the baby, who during my limited and secretive conversations with him it was evident that he adored, he would have let her go swiftly. "I saw little enough of John before," she complains. "Now he is gone and I am all alone."

She gets up and leaves the room. It is unclear whether she will be coming back. She was a dancer, like Lucy, that much I know. Lucy puts the little girl down and stands up to whisper in my ear. "This is the worst I've seen the flat. She has more than enough money, but she just doesn't seem to have the will to look after herself or little Jossy. Thats what we all call her; your brother too. It's how she says her own name."

The child is pulling at my trouser leg, and against my better judgement, for I cannot stand small children, I bend down and pick her up. "Does she have any family?" I ask as Jossy begins hitting me with her xylophone stick.
"None that know she's had a child."
"Where is she from?"
"Somewhere in Bedfordshire, I think."
We are abruptly interrupted when Agnes reappears carrying a pile of dirty plates. "What will happen to me?" She asks. No mention of the baby
"I have everything I need from John to ensure that both of you are still provided for. Nothing will change in that respect."
She simply turns and walks out of the room again. Lucy puts a hand on my arm and squeezes it gently. "Look, Will. Go. I know you've got something big on. I'll stay here with her, help her clean this place up and make sure that she is all right; do any shopping, give Jossy a bath. Agnes has taken his leaving for war very hard. She really was lovely, so bright and full of fun. And very pretty, before all this."
"I'll take your word for it," I say grimly.
"But she's always expected too much of your brother." Lucy lowers her voice even further. "She thought he'd marry her one day. This isn't the life she anticipated." I cannot think of a more unlikely scenario than the future Lord Stanley marrying a dancer. It is an awkward subject given the regularity of my liaisons with the dancer standing in front of me, but Lucy hits me in the chest playfully. "Oh don't worry, you rat bag. I've got no expectations of you walking me down the aisle."
The best I can manage in response to that is a stupid, awkward grin. "Will you make sure that she has everything that she needs to be able to contact me in an emergency? Tell her I will be back as soon as I know anything more." She nods, leans up and gives

me a quick kiss, before shooing me back outside and onto the stairs.

XXIX.

As soon as I arrive back at the War Office I stop in to see Fitz. "Has he come round yet?"
"About twenty minutes ago."
"Has anyone been in yet?"
"No, K said to leave him for you."
"Where is he?"
"Room X," he says without looking up from his papers.
Room X is the polite designation for where I am going. It doesn't officially exist. If one were to look at a plan of the War Office building, there is a basement and that is as subterranean as it goes. In reality, there is a small staircase if one knows where to look, and it leads further down to a single cell. More colloquially Room X is known as *The Oubliette,* though it is not quite that sinister. In that there is at least an electric light and a toilet. But as soon as I step down into the room my shoe lands in half an inch of water. *"We're rather close to the river. This happens sometimes;" I say in a manner that makes it clear I am not at all sorry for any inconvenience he has suffered.*
"You can't keep me down here," our captive grumbles. I laugh. "The army is thoroughly capable of sending thousands of boys who have done nothing to offend us over to France to get blown up. What makes you think that Lord Kitchener will have any issue at all with leaving a cold blooded killer and a saboteur down here to rot?" And rot he would, eventually. Room X is damp, sweaty and airless. Water seeps through mouldy white tiles that cover the walls from floor to ceiling, and more drips from above. More tiles cover the floor, but have collected so much stagnant liquid over the years that they are no longer white at all. The atmosphere is

stifling. Someone well-travelled once made the remark that it was like sitting in some South American rainforest without the pleasure of insects, snakes and cannibals. Because down here there is nothing. Incarcerated down here, with nothing but a low slung military camp bed and a single blanket, a dim lightbulb that is only illuminated for an hour at a time, and if necessary no contact with any human being for days on end, a man is completely alone.

One has to have done something pretty diabolical to find himself down here, and being the only captive we currently hold that has ties to a group willing to perhaps destroy the British war effort, the British *Empire;* this man surely qualifies. He sits on a metal chair in front of a small table. At once I am reminded of the description of Lynette Hahn's 'brother.' He is a large man, wide and tall. His hair is curly, dark and overly long, with streaks of grey. He looks like he has been in many a fight, judging by the amount of dents in his nose. Looking at his hands, which he has placed on the table, I can see that skin is flaking off the back of them. The light may be terrible, and I may be exhausted but I am convinced too that if I stare at him hard enough, I can see a yellowish tint to his face. I drop a file on the table. It is full of scrap paper, but he is not to know that. I launch straight into my interrogation and sit down opposite him. "Who are you?" Nothing. "What is your nationality?" Still nothing. "Apparently you've been bellowing in a cockney accent. What about your parents, your spouse?"

"Fuck off," he says. Definitely a Londoner.

"Who do you work for?"

"Someone who's going to be on the winning side come the end of this bloody war."

"How did you know my name? I know that you signed in at Dr. Waller's using it."

"We knew they'd put you onto us."

"How?"

This time he merely smirks.
"What is M14?" On that he is silent, but his eyes are furtive. "Where is the TNT? And the tetryl?"
"Don't know what you are talking about," he says smugly.
"Your hands and your complexion say different. You are suffering from symptoms that come with too much exposure to explosives. What is your target? When do you intend to strike?"
Now he laughs at me. "You're not in a fit state to get nothin out of me, sweet'eart. We worked you over good. Talk is all you've got. And I don't feel like chatting." This is true. And in addition to my sorry physical condition, I was given a rude awakening by Crabtree upstairs as he slurped a cup of tea with approximately eight sugars in it: *"Problem is you ain't ugly enough, Sir. You're that bloody 'andsome nobody is scared of you. We need a terrifying bastard in there."*
And so I have one ready. I knock on the inside of the door and on my signal, Gaylor enters with his knuckle dusters on. He puts a revolver on a side table and sits in my chair. "You might have worked him over, sweet'eart, but I'm fighting fit. And let me be absolutely clear. I know what your lot did to that poor little girl. I've got a little girl myself. Nobody knows you are here. I could shoot you in the face right now and the only inconvenience we'd have would be wiping your brain off the walls. Nobody would ever find out what happened to you. Nobody would lose sleep over you."
Nothing.
"How many people have died down here?" I ask Gaylor, my arms crossed in a thoughtful pose.
"Hard to say. Don't think they've ever bothered with marked graves for 'em."
"Who are you?" I ask again. "
"Fuck you both."
"What is your nationality? What ties do you have to Germany?"

"The Kaiser's my dad."
"Who do you work for? Where is Lynette Hahn?" He flinches at her name, a flash of anger, perhaps, but he says nothing.
"You don't know, do you? You're as clueless about her whereabouts as we are?"
"I always knew she'd be weak. Never send a woman to do a man's job."
"Odd, she's killed two people that we know of. One of them in brutal fashion. They didn't see fit to send you, did they? And she didn't get caught. So maybe your superior sees *you* as weak." He bites his lip. I am getting to him. "Where are the explosives and what do you intend to do with them?"
"You'll see."

He has hardened up again, the shutter has come back down and any vulnerability I thought I saw is gone for now. I try to coax it out again by changing my approach. "You know, telling us what we want to know now may mean the difference between a capital punishment and prison for you." Not if he played any part in harming Carrick's family. But I don't need to mention that. "If you help us prevent whatever it is your group is planning, there can be some leniency in your sentence."

He leans forward as if to say something, then pauses. Finally, he smirks: "Look, pretty boy. You can hang me, shoot me, you can leave me here to catch pneumonia. You can leave me down 'ere to die of old age. I'll just be another casualty of this war that Britain has forced on everyone. I knew that could happen when I signed up for this. But if you take me out, you still won't stop us. We're going to leave a mark, whether I am alive to see it or not. You think just because you've got me here it won't happen? Think again." Content with his little speech, he sits back on his chair and folds his arms defiantly.

Tuesday, 16th March 1915

XXX.

Two more rounds of questioning go nowhere. We leave him down below the basement overnight to contemplate his fate, but my instincts tell me that he is immoveable. You never know, with Room X. Long enough in the dark and a man may react in a number of different ways, but for now, sitting with our prisoner whilst he insults me and provides us with no information is a waste of my time. Lord Kitchener has a number of different men he might send in with a different approach to mine, and should the prisoner suddenly become talkative, I can be contacted with any pertinent information.

After four hours sleep it is my intention to wash, dress, and leave for the War Office; but I find myself standing at the door to John's room in my pyjamas. He has long since ceased to live here regularly, but he stayed just after Christmas, when he was home on leave. He'd survived the horror of Ypres, the terror of his battalion being completely exposed and overrun by the enemy on the Menin Road. In front of my mother, he was much the same; cheeky, playing up to her as she worshipped his every move. But at night he would take a bottle of my father's scotch to bed with him. We talked about what he'd seen, what he'd done. The thing that really choked him, the thing he could not get over, was the expression on a young German officer's face when he shot him point blank in the jaw with his revolver. He had no choice. It was kill or be killed, but he said that as the boy fell to the floor, as he realised he was dying, he wore an expression of complete hurt and surprise that made John feel so overwhelmingly guilty that he just couldn't put it out of his head.

I enter the room and go straight to my brother's chest of drawers, by the window. Dropping to my knees, I feel underneath it and locate a thin cardboard box. When I was very small I remember that he told me that this was his place; the place where he put all of his secrets so that our mother, our evil nanny, or Mrs. Mitcham couldn't find them. I so wanted to be like him that I have always used exactly the same place in my own room. Not that any of my secrets are as alarming as my brother's. I draw out the box and taking it over to his bed I sit down. I feel an overwhelming need to protect him; to save him any embarrassment. And to protect my mother too, if the worst has happened. I lift the lid. Much of the top layer of paper and card is a selection of pornographic postcards, but on top sits a sheet of notepaper with a message:

"Thanks, Will, you always were the best of little brothers."

He knew I would come for his box if he didn't come home. He knows me better than anyone, I think. The gap in our ages was such that we did not grow up together, so to speak. By the time I formed any memories of my childhood he was off at Eton, but I remembered that I longed for him to come home for holidays, and that when he did he taught me how to bowl a cricket ball, how to ride my pony. He took me hunting for insects in the grounds of our house in Wiltshire. In London he took me to plays and pantomimes and museums. He never made me feel stupid, or annoying. He, Lizzie and I formed a little triumvirate and they doted on me.

His stupid Pomeranian has followed me into his room excitedly. He must think John is coming home, for nobody has been in here since he left after Christmas. It begins grabbing at my feet. It's not engineered properly so as to jump on the bed, but it continues to paw at me, so I lift it up and place it next to me. It climbs into my lap and against my better judgement I give it a pat on the head. "Afraid not, Kitch. He's not coming home just yet."

"What are you doing?" Mrs. Mitcham has appeared in the doorway, I suppose having just taken a tray to my mother. I put a finger to my lips to shut her up, and she steps inside the room and closes the door softly behind her.

"What are you doing?" She repeats in a whisper. Then she spies the postcards and things appear to drop into place. "Why are you cleaning up his smutty postcards? What has happened?"

The fact that she knows immediately what is in it hints that she has probably had knowledge of our hiding places for some time. I slap the lid back on the box, lest she see anything else incriminating, like photographs of Josephine. I realise I am going to have to tell Mrs. Mitcham something. "He is not dead, at least, we don't know that he is dead." Her hand flies to her mouth and she gasps.

"Sssh!" I tell her. "Look. He is missing, but he may turn up. He may be a prisoner, we just don't know at the moment. I just didn't want there to be anything embarrassing here if, well, if…"

"When are you going to tell your mother?"

"Today. At least, I have someone to go and see, a soldier. After that I may know more. You are not to say a word until then, do you understand?"

"Of course I won't you cheeky beggar. What do you take me for?" She stands looking at the cards. "Give me those. I'll get rid of them. Put the rest of that box away with your things. We don't need to do that. Not yet."

"All right." I nod, gather up my brother's things and prepare to go back to my room. If it makes her feel better, I will do as she wishes. But a growing sense of dread is taking hold of me. This doesn't feel like John's room anymore. I cannot see him in it, not again. It feels like any part of him that was here is gone. It's just an empty room. And I realise with a breaking heart that I am convincing myself that my brother is dead.

Victoria street is a flurry of colour; red, black, yellow, blue and white. Allied flags hang from every shop window, every doorway, from peoples' top pockets instead of handkerchiefs and some girls have them tied in their hair. They flutter as vehicles drive past with yet more of them affixed to their redundant headlamps. A procession of recruits is marching through, some in full uniform. But others still sport their own hats. A scruffy little urchin has turned a pail over and is beating a rhythm out for them on its upturned end with a stick. I stop in at the Army and Navy stores and arrange for Lucy's list to be sent to her home. I add a bottle of French perfume that I am almost certain she will give to her mother instead of keeping it for herself. My ribs are hurting, and so I decide to go back and take the Tube to Charing Cross. The weather has continued to improve, significantly, and it appears to have drawn all of London's lunatics out into the open to take advantage of the beginning of spring. I have hardly any change, and purchase a lower class ticket. In the carriage, a batty old lady has positioned herself at one end, one hand clinging to the rail overhead and the other clutched to her breast as she warbles out a dubious version of *Land of Hope and Glory*. At least it's not *Tipperary.* However, Clara Butt, she is not.
As I reach The Strand I see that two policemen have stopped the traffic passing at the end of the road. A large white flag emblazoned with a red cross flaps lightly in the breeze, and a snapping sound emanates from a long banner pulled across the wide thoroughfare in front of the Charing Cross Hospital. *'Quiet for the Wounded.'* Outside the gates a large crowd has converged in silence to watch a stream of ambulances lately arrived from some terminus discharge their pitiful cargo of broken men. They make

not a sound. They think there are here to show their respect, but all they want is to gaze upon the wounded out of morbid curiosity. I find myself disgusted.

One of the men recently offloaded and taken inside with a bullet in his thigh is Thomas Kelly, a Guardsmen who serves as John's soldier servant. He is a regular, so I am hoping that his experience puts him in a better position to have taken in all that was happening around them at Neuve Chapelle. Perhaps he withstood it all a little better than poor David Cruyff. I find him in a ward on the top floor, sandwiched in between two elderly gentlemen. It looks as if the hospital has had to utilise every available bed to accommodate the wounded arriving from the front. He is sitting up in bed, looking about. He seems bored. At first glance he doesn't appear to have any magazines, books, cigarettes, treats, anything to entertain him. He is a big, solid man, with a ruddy complexion and thinning brown hair. He must be about thirty. He looks up at me, and I see the usual momentary surprise at the state of my face, followed by the recognition. Another person who sees the family resemblance.
"I thought yous would come," he says wearily, in a thick Glaswegian accent.
"I'm sorry to have to jump on you as soon as you arrive."
"No, no of course you'd wannae know what happened to Captain Stanley."
"Can you tell me anything?" I ask, taking my coat off and sitting down next to his bed.
"I couldnae tell you what the point was." He says it with a bitter laugh. A private soldier rarely can. Their job is to follow orders; nobody sees fit to explain to them why, or what for. Then it is time to eat, sleep, and ready themselves for the next go. Come to think of it, it isn't much different for a junior officer; and even as a Captain, John wouldn't have had much of an idea of

what the grand purpose was at Neuve Chapelle, when he set out towards the Germans.

"I've been unable to find out much so far, so if you can tell me anything at all about my brother, it would be much appreciated." He is staring at his hands, and so I try and help him along a little. "I know you were ordered to go forward."

To my surprise he has tears in his eyes. I know that he has been with my brother for a number of years, but evidently John means a lot to this man. "I was advancin' behind the Captain when a shell burst." I feel instantly nauseous, but he then says that although his eyes were watering from the smoke, he saw John throw himself into a small crater.

"Was he hurt?"

He sighs heavily. "I've been running this again and again in ma heed and I just dinnae know. He's next to me, and then we go forward, and he edges just ahead of me. Then there are bullets flying, an' shells whistling. Then there's one big shell, and one big bang, and smoke. I stumbled, and he rolled into this hole, and I lost sight o' him. A shell burst in the middle of us and I had tae go the other way. I just keep reassuring myself that I didnae see him deed."

He asks if I will come and tell him if I hear anything more. Of course I agree. "Do you need anything?" With that accent I wonder if he can hope for any visitors at this end of the country.

"I could murder some cigarettes, ma sister will try and get down by the end o' the week, but it isnae certain." I give him the entire contents of my case on the way out and make a mental note to get Lizzie to have a care package made up. The women in my family will look after him. After I have given them the news.

The lack of definitive information is beginning to drive me mad. Nobody saw *enough.* What I feel in my gut is irrelevant. I feel like my brother no longer exists, but I cannot articulate why. I certainly cannot say that to my mother. I am going to have to stay positive, for all of their sakes. He *could* be a prisoner of war. That is the avenue we will explore next. I have friends doing it; writing endless letters to anyone they can think of and just hoping that by some miracle, their loved one will turn up safe and well in a new world where thousands of men a week are chewed up and spat out by a war that doesn't give two shits who cares about them at home.

Being a coward, I debate whether or not to stop by the War Office, as it is such a short distance away, before going home to talk to my mother. But in the end I realise that it would be unacceptable. The idea that she might be doing something so perfectly ordinary as organising her needlework guild, or seeing the officers in her little hospital whilst her own son lies dead on the battlefield, because I lack the courage to tell her, is more than I can bear.

XXXI.

But I fail to get any further than my front steps before the door is thrown open and she stands there looking flustered. For a moment I think Mrs. Mitcham has betrayed me, that she has told her about John. For an instant I am even relieved that this might be the case; that it might not fall to me to break her heart. But then she blurts out: "Will, you have to go to Whitehall. Lord Kitchener himself telephoned for you."

For a moment I simply stare at her, dumbfounded. "But mother, I…"

Mrs. Mitcham is at the door behind her and she gives one, almost imperceptible nod of the head as if to say *"It is all right. Go."*

"That woman," my mother continues as she rushes down the steps so as to be able to lower her voice so that nobody else can hear. *"The woman that came here. She is at the War Office and she will speak to nobody but you."* Now I realise the urgency, that I must go, and that our own potential family tragedy will have to wait.

Gaylor is at the War Office, where I left him, because I wanted privacy to go off and visit Thomas Kelly. Gauging that I would be no better off by the time I get to the Underground, wrestle the crowds down, wait for a train, make the journey and then wrestle the crowds back up at Westminster before racing up Whitehall; I take off my great coat, fling it at my mother and start to run. Again. I regret my decision before I reach the next street. By the time I reach Grosvenor Place and the back wall of the palace gardens, my chest is burning. As I crash through some hapless Canadian troops walking wide-eyed along Buckingham Palace Road I can no longer breathe. By the time I am level with the Royal Mews I am doubled over and the colonials are laughing at my expense.

At the sight of King's car barrelling down Birdcage Walk I have to laugh. Gaylor may be ornery, terrifying and sultry beyond belief, but as he pulls up alongside me and leans over to open the car door I could kiss the red-haired bugger. "Thought you could do with a lift," he says as I throw myself in, slam the door and give the Canadians two fingers. The gesture makes them hurt, but it is worth the effort it takes to straighten them. "She's jumpy, they don't know how long they can keep her without slapping handcuffs on her." He performs what I am sure is an illegal turn in the middle of the road, at the expense of every other vehicle in it. Other drivers begin shouting and grabbing at their horns.
"I'd rather we didn't. The last thing we need is another non-compliant witness sitting under the basement."
"Hmmm. She is a murderer, though," he says, and then he swears loudly as he realises that Birdcage Walk is now blocked by scores of Guards recruits coming out of Wellington Barracks for a route march.

"Tell me at least that they've locked the bloody door, wherever she is?" I cling to the side of the chassis as he banks hard, causing the car to jump onto the pavement. Then we begin careening down a small, steep hill into St. James's Park; towards a large group of shocked looking tourists.

At least one of them bashes the side of the King's car with his umbrella in disgust as we rattle past; after we nearly run over the woman I presume is his wife. We cause more than a bit of a stir as Gaylor screeches around the narrow, top end of the empty lake. Then it is onto a footpath, me clinging to the car lest I go flying out of the open window, more pedestrians scattering in all directions, him hollering out of the window for everyone to get out of his way. He turns sharply left in the direction of The Mall on the other side of the park; sending empty deck chairs flying. I wonder how many people in this vicinity might recognise the Daimler and assume that the King had lost his mind and taken up a new career as a racing driver; using the streets about Buckingham Palace as his very own royal Brooklands.

The car spins out onto The Mall and looking off to the right causes another stream of obscenities to come flooding out of the chauffeur's mouth. There appears to be some sort of recruitment demonstration occurring; women wearing brilliant white sashes and waving banners in protest against cowards as they ponder their way infuriatingly slowly away from the Victoria Memorial, down to Trafalgar Square. "I'd run them over; judgemental harpies," I say breathlessly, but instead of tackling them, Gaylor has shot left, across The Mall and down Stable Yard; where Clarence House flashes past on our right. Some surprised guards recognise the car, but not its behaviour, and can only watch in amazement as he swings onto the wrong side of the road to avoid oncoming traffic and barrels round onto Cleveland Row and along the back of St. James's Palace.

At least there are less tourists back here. But as we hurtle along Pall Mall, past numerous members clubs and bewildered shoppers, we attract plenty more criticism before Gaylor flings the car right onto Marlborough Road, left again and pops back out on The Mall behind the white feather brigade. Up we go, along the dead straight thoroughfare running through the middle of London like a Roman road. Gaylor has got no intention, however, of joining the usual complicated throng of traffic milling around the effigy of Lord Nelson down at Trafalgar Square, and so he swerves right onto Horse Guards Road and thunders along parallel to Whitehall. I assume he's going to cannon all the way down to Parliament Square and then ricochet back up to the War Office, because that is our only option, but the madman has other ideas. As we draw level with Horse Guards Parade, he suddenly throws the wheel over and begins to drive across it, repeatedly honking his horn to warn everyone milling about and hovering around several recruitment tents. Then it is through the arch, past two shocked Household Cavalry troopers. Until then the most interesting thing to occur on their mounted watch was the challenge of trying not to react to silly tourist ploys to make them move. The War Office is right in front of us, and I can see Crabtree waiting on the steps as Gaylor brings us to a screeching halt below him. Despite his exertions to deliver me to Whitehall, he is laughing his head off. "Well that was fun!" He says, hitting the steering wheel in delight.
Who knew the man had such animation in him?
"Lunatic!" I say breathlessly as I throw myself out onto the pavement.

"Where is she?" I ask my assistant; still trying to catch my breath.
"Shut up safely in a disused office at the back of the building. The ceiling leaks. Door's locked, man outside.

Took one of the men we had guarding him below the basement."

Fitz meets us at the bottom of the stairs. "What has she said?" I ask.

"Nothing; walked in, not a pretty sight I can tell you; ragged. And needs a wash. Eyes like a frightened rabbit; says she is here to talk to you and nobody else. We didn't cuff her, because she seems resigned to being caught, and we didn't want to scare her silent." A sound plan as far as I am concerned, but Lynette Hahn is proving to be slippery, to say the least, and I want to lay eyes on her as soon as possible. I march along the corridor, Fitz at my side, with Crabtree scurrying to keep up on his shorter legs. "Just around this corner," Fitz says.

However when we get there, the office is empty, unguarded and the door is wide open. Crabtree races off down the corridor and hails a languid MP who is leaning against a radiator examining what has become trapped under his fingernails. "Hey, mate? Where is she?" Crabtree sounds furious. In any normal circumstance this would be hilarious. His faces grows red instantly.

The MP shrugs and pants to the door to the ladies facilities in front of him. "Toilet."

"And you left her unguarded, you twat?"

His opposite number scoffs: "We're on the first floor, in case you hadn't noticed."

"How long has she been in there?" I demand.

"No more than ten minutes, she said she was desperate."

"Ten minutes?" Crabtree is indignant.

"I assumed she was taking a dump," he says indignantly. "I wasnt going to go in there and confirm that with her while she was in the act, was I?"

His flippancy is irritating me. "Is anyone else in there?" He shakes his head. He is standing up straight now, finally looking worried.

"What did you say to her?" I snap.

"Nothing!" But he sounds nervous.

"Nothing at all?" I don't believe him.

"Well," he has become positively sheepish. "Just that we already had one of her mates, so she better be the first to start talking."

I resist the urge to fling him out of the window, push in front of the impertinent fool and put a finger to my lips to silence the others as I gently press down the handle and slowly push the door to the ladies lavatory open. There are three cubicles and I immediately drop to my knee to see if I can see feet underneath them. There are none. For good measure, I push each door open to ensure that nobody is hiding inside; but I am already on my way to the open window. The bathroom is empty. Lynette Hahn is gone. As I was running into the building she must have been sliding down the damned drainpipe. A cursory lean out of the window reveals that there is one conveniently placed for her to have swung herself outside and then lowered herself gently down, via several wide windowsills into the relative solitude of Whitehall Court below.

She has a headstart, and so I push back past Crabtree, Fitz and the inept MP and bolt down the main staircase at the end of the corridor. I can only think of one place that she might have gone. I sprint up Whitehall, around to Cockspur Street and the abandoned offices of Norddeutscher Lloyd. She is nowhere to be seen, but I am sure if she had something to say to me, she would have come here. I scan the graffiti covered recruitment posters and find where she scribbled her clubs and her deformed dolphin. It dawns on me. The dolphin is the symbol of Vulcan, the Roman god of fire. In pencil she has scrawled: "I'm sorry, LH."

She may not have got far. I push my way through the lunchtime crowds into Trafalgar Square. The infernal white feather women have arrived; and their numbers have swollen exponentially as they have reached the end of The Mall. They are now a seething mass of angry femininity; hurling abuse at any man older than a child or younger than a grandfather that they see walking about the square. One of them has acquired a megaphone and is pouring additional scorn onto any gentleman she feels should be on his way to a recruitment office. The scene is becoming increasingly chaotic, some of the men have begun to answer their accusers in loud voices. After all, they may have perfectly sound reasons for not being in uniform, and who are these women to call them out when they have merely stepped out of their offices to find a sandwich? I push my way through to the fountains. They were only put here to leave less space for rioters and public disturbances, but today it is in vein. Several girls are now paddling about in them, still waving their banners and shouting their slogans. I've never seen so many women in one place; and their presence has destroyed any chance I might have had of spotting Lynette Hahn making a getaway. Looking around, all I can see are clouds of white feathers. In vain I climb up onto the base of Nelson's Column and then scramble onto the back of one of Landseer's lions. On shaky legs I manage to stand upright and scan the crowd, but all I can see is an endless crowd of women, masking the one that I need to find.

XXXII.

The Duke of Wellington bust is back on Kitchener's desk. I wonder for how long. The nose on the ornament is even more misshapen than the original is said to have been in life; presumably from being repeatedly flung across the room. The War Secretary's face is almost purple and he catches me eyeing his ornament.
"What?"

"I was just admiring it, Sir." He raises an eyebrow.
"Looks heavy, though." Fitz suppresses a smile.
"I don't follow?" Kitchener says.
"Please don't throw it at me," I say.
Fitz is trying not to giggle now, but there is no room for humour in the War Secretary's office this afternoon.
"So she has turned?" He says to both of us without further reference to the Duke.
"She is at the very least remorseful, but yes; I believe she may have."
"So talk to me about where we might find her," he barks.
I clear my throat. "She's not going to go back to Norwood, I am sure of it, but Keyes has taken half a dozen men there just in case. All Room 40. So discreet. They are pretending to measure the place for some new furniture. And none of them have shown their faces there before; in the event the place is being watched."
"Good."
"I cannot believe that they would find her at the arsenal," Fitz interjects, "but their police are seizing any woman with the misfortune to look like her at the gate. Crabtree has gone there to meet Williams, they are competent enough to oversee that. Ingalls is nominally in charge but he won't interfere."
"No. He had better not. That boy is wetter than a dead cod," sighs Kitchener. "And our friend downstairs?"
"The man you asked for," Fitz replies. "The intelligence chap from South Africa that you remembered. He's in there with him now."
"And nobody has found this pile of TNT?"
"No, Sir."
"Thank you Fitz. Would you excuse Stanley and I?" His loyal assistant nods and backs out of the room, closing the doors behind him. "You can join your man at Woolwich when you have taken care of your affairs,

unless you can think of anywhere else we might find this damned woman."

I nod. "Yes, Sir." He clearly suspects that I have not told my mother about John.

His tone has softened noticeably, and as he reaches for his desk drawer and takes out a tiny red envelope. A telegram. The kind of telegram that not a single person in Britain wants to receive. I feel dizzy, like I might actually faint on his office floor. "This is a copy of a telegram that is due to go to your father this evening," he says gently. "Still only missing, but it is official now. He has not turned up in any of our hospitals.

My hand is shaking as I reach out to take it. "We have lost thousands of men. Go home and deliver this to your mother. She should be told properly. Don't let a stranger put one of these in her hand. There will be a comfort in that, however small." I nod sadly, descend the stairs and depart the War Office. I manage to find a rare taxi to take me home. I have had enough of running about like a madman.

I find my mother reading in the parlour; some ladies magazine. It will be something practical. She does not waste her time on frivolous material; never has.

"Hello, darling," she says looking up. "Is it over? Please tell me that we can dispense with the guards outside the house. People will think I have been placed under house arrest."

I try to smile. "Soon, I hope."

I want to be sick. I love my mother more than anyone else on the face of god's earth, and I am about to hurt her more than she has ever been hurt in her life. I am about to rob her of her first born. I am about to threaten her hopes and dreams for my brother, put a potential full stop at the end of his narrative that would render years of dotage, education, preparation and most importantly, love, on her part, irrelevant. What has it all been for, and how can it be taken away like this? I'm about to tear an irreparable hole in her existence that, if John does not eventually turn up, will never, ever heal. In short, at best I am about to cause her a huge amount of pain. At worst, I am about to ruin her life. And yet if I don't, the blow will come from a stranger on the doorstep, or on the telephone, from my father. He has never been particularly emotive. I doubt his ability to soften the impact of the news that my brother has vanished on the battlefield.

I can feel my eyes filling with tears that will give me away. She closes her magazine, neatly marking her place, and puts it on the table next to her. "Shall we have some tea? And you must eat. You have scarcely eaten a thing the last few days, have you?" I can't answer her. I can hear her words, but I cannot form any myself. I am holding the little red envelope clenched in my fist, and I can see that she slowly starts to realise that something is wrong. "Will, what is it? Is it this woman?" I shake my head. She looks to my hand as I open it, and she sees the flash of red. She sits up straight, surprised. "No." She says firmly. "Not us."
For a moment we face each other in silence. I try to speak. "Mother, he's missing…"

"NO!" She barks at me. My mother never raises her voice. What am I to do? She continues to repeat the words: *"No. No, Not us."* I cannot put it away and forget about it. I am lost. Every step I take towards her prompts the pitch of her voice to rise.

Luckily, Mrs Mitcham is in the room as soon as she hears the noise and at my mothers side in an instant, ready for when the dam breaks. *"Not my boy!"* She lets out an ear-piercing sound as she collapses into herself and explodes into floods of tears. I cannot articulate the noise that emanates from her. It is not a scream, not a wail, but some visceral, terrifying combination of the two as she ululates back and forth. There is no other way to describe it, but my mother sounds like a wounded animal crying out in agony. Her body looks so small folded into our housekeeper's arms, and Mrs Mitcham, who can empathise so much better because she has a son of her own in France, holds my mother's head to her shoulder and attempts to comfort her. I pull up a stool, and she clings fiercely to my wrist. "I would know if he was dead," she says between sobs. "He is my baby."

"He's not dead," says Mrs Mitcham. "I refuse to believe it. He's just lost, that's all." I can feel tears rolling down my own cheeks.

"I need Lizzie, I need my Lizzie." The practical daughter, the one that will understand best, for she and John have always been as inseparable as a set of twins.

"We will get her for you, mother."

"I have to see it!" She is grabbing for the telegram, and I do not stop her. She rips it from my hands in a frenzy and tears away the envelope. She scans the simple text: *'Regret to inform Captain J. Stanley reported missing does not necessarily mean dead.'* She reads it over and over again, as if she has misunderstood it and is searching for an interpretation that absolves her of this agony. Then she gives up and as she grasps my wrist again it crumples in her fist.

We sit for what feels like an age as she cries away every tear that her body has to offer, clinging to us both. Every now and again she lets out a low, painful moan, as if someone is slowly, painfully cutting the bonds that tie my brother to her. We help her properly into her chair again and Mrs Mitcham departs to telephone my sister. She returns to the room with the largest glass of my father's scotch that I have ever seen her pour for anyone. Then, gasping to regulate her breathing again, my mother allows it to be raised to her lips so that she might sip it. "Start at the beginning, darling," Mrs Mitcham says gently, as she reaches out with one of her cloths and wipes the tears from my cheeks. "So that we understand."

My mother will not let go of my hand. One of her sons is slipping away from her and she is refusing to let the other go. In the other she grasps a handkerchief, and as I speak she wipes at her eyes and her nose.

My voice doesn't sound right. It is shaky and uncertain. "I've interviewed two people who were there already, but they have been unable to tell me much. The first was an officer. He told me that his company went into action alongside John's. They went off when it was still dark, so it is complicated to try and place his movements. They crossed a German trench that had already been captured, and then they were advancing up to where some of the Northamptons needed help." Now I need to spare her the graphic reality of shot and shell. "It was hot, where they were." That will do. I do not want to construct terrifying, bloody images in her head. The more sterile my description remains, the better. "The Grenadiers were held up. They hung on till nightfall, and then they were pulled back to the beginning again, but John was not with the others. They've lost a number of officers. The last this chap saw of John, he thinks he was still advancing with his men, but there was a lot of smoke and he lost sight of him. To his knowledge, nobody saw John killed, nobody talked about him being killed."

"Well, that is good?" My mother is looking for my validation.

"It is certainly not bad news," I reply carefully.

She sniffs loudly and wipes her nose again. "You said you spoke to two people?"

"Yes, I did. Kelly is at Charing Cross."

My mother gasps. "We must go to him," she says to Mrs. Mitcham. "He has no people down here."

Our housekeeper pats her hand. "We will, soon."

"What did he say?" My mother knows of this man, she trusts him. It gives her comfort to know he was at my brother's side.

"He says he advanced alongside John, but that a shell exploded nearby. The smoke was making his eyes water, but he is sure that he saw John throw himself into a crater to protect himself. He does not know if he was injured at this time. He tried to follow, but there were more shells, and he went into a different hole. He didn't see him again. But he says, too, that nobody claimed to have seen John killed, or to have seen his body."

"What do we do, Will?"

"Lord Kitchener is making appeals for information when he can. I believe the ordinary course of events for us would be writing to agencies, in addition to the Government, anyone that might have details of prisoners of war. The Americans sometimes make enquires with the Germans as a neutral party, or the Swiss, or the Dutch. And then there is the Red Cross. Anyone you can think of that is running a hospital out there, working at the front, and politicians. We must leave no stone unturned, but I'm afraid that it is going to be largely a game of waiting to see if, well, I mean to say, waiting for him to turn up."

God bless my mother. Give her direction, a task to undertake, a practical approach to a problem, and she will galvanise herself. Already she is wiping the tears from her face and attempting to get up. There will be empty hours of misery, of waiting, of praying, but the rest she will fill in doing everything in her power to try and locate her son.

Mrs. Mitcham is making a disturbing motion with her head, some kind of spasm. I realise eventually that she is beckoning me outside. "A pretty girl towing a baby left you this at the kitchen door," she hisses. Good lord. "What have you done?" She hisses.

"Mind your own business, woman" I snap. She stares at my face for a moment, like she is probing my expression for some tell. Then she nods. Which is surprising. She still has one eye on my mother through the crack in the door.

The note is brief. Lucy went to the flat this morning and found Josephine. Agnes was gone along with most of her belongings. The pitiful explanation that she left on the kitchen table is enclosed.

"I dident meen to leaf her but I carnt do it no moor."

XXXIII.

My sister Lizzie lives in an elegant white townhouse at Rutland Gate, a quiet street which forms a ring around a pretty communal garden a stone's throw from Harrods. When I knock on her front door, it is opened nervously by a bewildered looking maid. I imagine all hell has broken loose since Mrs. Mitcham's telephone call.

Lizzie's eyes are red, her cheeks tear stained. "Oh, Will!" She cries and throws herself into my arms in the hallway. It still looks as if a bachelor lives here; with all of the dark furniture and shipping themed paraphernalia. To be fair, it is how her husband made his money. It is all I can do not to begin crying again.

"How bad is it?" She asks.

"Bad, but not the worst. There is still a chance that he is alive."

She pushes me away and wipes her tears with the back of her hand. She is clearly preparing to leave for the house. "I am going to mother."

"Of course, she needs you. She is asking for you, but Liz, first we need to talk."

"I should be with mother," She has begun fastening on a hat. I turn her around and press her into the modern dining room that has been graced with my sister's touch; light, spacious and uncluttered.

"It is important," I whisper. "It's about John." And yet I have no idea where to begin. "You've never had children," I blurt out in the end.

"We've tried. What does that have to do with anything?"

I see no way to sugar-coat it. "He has a daughter."

"Good Lord." Her hand flies to her mouth. "Who is the mother?"

"A dancer." No response. Nothing. Rarely do I see my sister lost for words. She is the most sensible of all of us, but I fear I may have broken her. "I know this is a lot to take at once," I say gently. "But someone is going to have to step in and look after her. The baby. Agnes has never been what you might consider practical. I don't think he is in love with her, I don't think he ever was, really. He does right by her, but since we gave her the news she has run off and left the child. Whether she intends to come back, I don't know. Whether she doesn't, but she will see that she must eventually, I don't know. She's barely more than a child herself."

"And what am I to do, surely you do not propose that I take the child?"

"Perhaps you could say that the little girl was a waif from one of your churches? Mother need never know the truth. It won't be permanent."

"Well, what if the mother comes back for her child next week, screaming about who the father is?"

"Then I will fix it, I promise. I'm just trying to do the best for everyone, including our niece."

"You don't think she is coming back, do you? I can tell."

"I'm trying not to let my general dislike of the girl colour my opinion, but honestly? No, I would not be surprised if she has abandoned her child."

"Oh, John. Will, I could thump him."

"Join the club."

"You know that it is always going to be a possibility that she may return. Never underestimate the pull a mother feels towards her children. I may not have first hand experience, but that much I know. She will always feel bound to them, need to be close to them."
We stand awkwardly for what seems like an age. Then Lizzie claps her hands together, as she usually does when she has made up her mind about something.
"How old is she?"
"Almost two."
"What is her name?"
"Josephine."
"For Grandmother?"
"Yes. Liz. I know it isn't ideal, how she came to be here, but his daughter is his world. He sends his letters to her through me."
"So you know this dancer?"
"Agnes. I have only ever met her briefly. I pass everything through a… well… a friend of mine."
"Friend indeed. You men will never learn. I cannot believe that we are talking about John, that the most important thing in his life was a complete secret from us. We who love him more than anyone. How long have you known?"
"Only since the declaration of war. He told me before his battalion left. He wanted them to be known to at least one of us if anything happened to him. It was a toss up between you and I, but you were in the country. And now I need to pass it on, in case, well, you know, but also because I don't know what to do."
"Nothing is going to happen to you. What would I have to do? Where is she?"
"With my friend, Lucy. You must go to the stage door at the Duke of York's Theatre this afternoon and ask for her. The girls there are all looking out for her until something can be arranged. They didn't want the authorities to become involved. You can discuss with

her what story you will tell everyone. You women are much better at that sort of thing."
"More clever you mean?"
I was going to go with conniving and manipulative." I smile. I always know when I have successfully got around my sister. "But if you like." She thumps me in the arm. "Is that a yes?"
"She is our blood. Of course it is a yes. This Lucy and I will have to come up with a plausible version of events."
'There's a song. Lucy says it stops her from bawling. John sings it to her."
"Come Josephine in my Flying Machine?"
"How did you know?'
"The idiot has a thing about that song. Said it reminded him of Grandmother."
I kiss her cheek. "I'm sorry, but I have to go."
"You are an absolute state, Lyd, must it be you?"
"I'm afraid so."
She continues to talk, but gradually I hear her voice moving further and further away from me, as if she is receding into the distance. I have become fixated on something the the she has said and the cogs in my mind have begun to whirl. I grab her by the shoulders and kiss her on the cheek. "Liz, I really do have to go. I will at least try to telephone you later on. I need you to telephone the War Office and leave an urgent message with Captain Oswald Fitzgerald, do you understand?"
She nods. "Is it about what is happening at the house? The military policemen?"
"Yes, it is," I say breathlessly. I hold out my hands and she pulls open a drawer and lays a notebook and a pencil into them. As I race out of my sister's front door she is holding a scrap of paper with a short message on it.

URGENT. Have Gaylor meet me at Mile End Station immediately.

XXXIV.

The District Railway is already crowded when I climb into a first class compartment at South Kensington. I end up holding bags and boxes for an elderly passenger struggling to stay on her feet as we rattle east. Nobody has got up to offer her a seat. As I brace myself against the side of the carriage, I keep running Lizzie's statement in my head. My sister's words hit me like a thunderbolt in her dining room: *"Never underestimate the pull a mother feels towards her children... She will always feel bound to them, need to be close to them."* I think I know where Lynette Hahn might be, in theory at least. I need more information to be able to prove myself right, and perhaps catch up with her.

Half an hour of being thrown back and forth, then a slight altercation with a large gentleman who had remained sitting at my old lady's expense; and helping her to alight at St. James's Park. Finally we are barreling into London's East End. It is not an area I know well, and as I left Lizzie's house, I took advantage of her husband's mania for maps, old and new, and kidnapped a copy of an Ordnance Survey effort dealing with East London. I found a seat as the number of passengers thinned out at Aldgate East, and I prepared myself for another dash with Gaylor at the wheel by opening it up to the relevant section; for I doubt he has any clue in which direction we must go either.

He is waiting for me as I surface at Mile End; leaning protectively on His Majesty's car; for this is not his usual area of operations, and his appearance has attracted wide-eyed locals, especially young boys who all want to touch, or worse, climb on such an attractive plaything as a Daimler. He unceremoniously dishes out thick ears to any young ruffian who has the cheek to try and get a foothold on the chassis. "Hate the bloody

East End," he says gruffly. "Hurry up and get in the car." Several brats try to knock off my cap as I do so, but a backhander aimed at the ringleader sends them scampering off laughing. "Where are we going?" This should be fun. I hold the map up. "You're joking," he says. Gripping the wheel in complete disdain. "What? I hate the bloody East End too. Besides, I'm an officer in His Majesty's army. I am sure I wont have any trouble with a London street map. Just shut up, go straight on and take a right hand turn down South Grove." This much we achieve without incident, swerving to avoid pedestrians as the Whitechapel workhouse looms by on our left hand side, a grim four storey edifice of institutionalised red brick with several people milling about outside.

Then without such an obvious marker, as we plunge into the realms of almshouses and rows and rows of identical little terraced houses; a giant gasworks, it transpires that my map-reading skills leave much to be desired. After twenty-five minutes of looping back and forth, shouting obscenities at each other; and at one point Gaylor stopping the car and attempting to order me out onto the street, we finally condescend to ask a local for directions. He stares at the motor car in awe as he obliges, and a few minutes later we finally arrive at Walker Street. "Number thirty-two," I say, giving Gaylor the address of the Hahn family home, until last August at least.

I get out of the car and go straight to the house next door, bang loudly on the peeling red paint. A large, flustered looking, but handsome woman with a wild nest of auburn hair and red cheeks answers, balancing a baby on each hip. "Oh Jesus!" She cries with a hint of an Irish accent, obviously assuming that I am about to tell her that a loved one has come to grief on the battlefield. I have to help her support one of the infants as she regathers herself.

"No Madam, I apologise, I'm not here for that. I'm here on an investigative matter…" She uses her free hand to whip me repeatedly with a tea towel that had been tucked into the broad waistband of her skirt. "You bugger!" She cries. "Don't you scare me like that! I've got a husband in the army!"
I continue to apologise profusely, my hands raised in a gesture of surrender. "I am merely here to ask after your former neighbour, Mrs. Hahn?"
"She was married to a kraut. You lot locked him up."
"Yes, I know, but I wanted to enquire about what happened afterwards, when her children died."
"Aye, that wasn't nice." The woman has finally stopped beating me with her cloth.
"Did you go the funeral?"
"Did I… No. Did I buggery. Moody cow. Her across the road, staring out from behind her door," she raises her voice so that the woman in question can clearly her her. "She went." I thank her, give her her child back and glance up long enough as I cross the street to observe Gaylor in a fit of laughter at having watched me attacked by a housewife.

The woman at number 27 opens her door shyly as I approach. She is a fraction of the size of my attacker opposite, with lank mousy hair and very bad teeth.
"It's all right," I assure her. "Nobody is in trouble." She nods, checking behind her. "My husband is home. He wouldn't want me talking to the army. He's been out protesting the war."
"That's fine. I'm not interested in that. I'm told that when they buried Lynette Hahn's children, you went to the funeral?"
She nods. "And her husband. Me and Lynette was friends. We looked after each others kids."
"Where were they buried?" I ask gently.
"The big one over that way," she points.
"How big?"

"Massive."
I recall seeing it on my brother-in-law's map. "Can you tell me whereabouts they are?"
She shakes her head. "I don't know exactly."
I sigh. "Can you remember anything? Anything you could see from the graves?"
"Oh yeah. You could see the mortuary chapel. It was right nearby."
I am already running back towards the car. "Thank you! You have been a great help," I say as I grab the map and Gaylor sets back off down the street.

Daylight is fading as we approach the cemetery. It is that large that not even we could fail to find it, and as we enter the gates I have Gaylor slow down. To my surprise, much of it is in a state of disrepair, clearly unkempt. The mortuary chapel lies on the opposite side and we wind our way past endless rows of headstones and elaborate funerary monuments. As soon as the hexagonal building comes into view, I have him stop the car and I get out. I want nothing at all to frighten Lynette Hahn if she is where I believe she is.
 I scan the cemetery on either side of the little chapel, but see nobody. I deduce that there would have been no money to provide an elaborate marker, and indeed, no time thus far, and so I turn in the direction of a large expanse facing the other way; which I assume by a lack of headstones, is where paupers are buried. Lynette Hahn is sitting obscured, up against a tree with her back to me. Her shoulders rise and fall irregularly, which I put down to the likelihood that she is crying. I am careful not to make any sudden movements as I approach her, and indeed, when I am still fifteen to twenty paces away I call out as gently as I can: "Mrs. Hahn. Is that you?"
 She is beside herself. She barely turns to look at me, but I know that she knows who I am. "I knew if I sat 'ere long enough you'd come."

"May I?" I gesture at the ground next to her. I have so many questions. She looks surprised that I would extend her any courtesy. It is odd, but knowing what has happened to her, I find that I do not look at her as the cold blooded killer that she is. She has robbed Fred George's children of their father. I don't think she has been in Manchester, but she is certainly responsible for Dr. Carrick falling in front of a tram. And yet she is so pitiful, I cannot feel angry towards her. I have her. She will pay for her crimes, but oddly I do not hate her in spite of all that she has done. "You came to see me?" It seems as good a place to start as any.

She looks out across the large plot. She has taken off her coat and has it slung on her lap. You can see there are graves from the undulations in the grass, but that is the only thing that reveals that this is the final resting place of those who cannot afford anything more in death. "I can't even remember exactly where they are."

"Your husband? Your children?"

She nods. Her face is soaking wet and there is a trail of snot hanging from her nose. I give her my handkerchief, more so that I don't have to look at it myself than any concession for her dignity. "I was so angry. I wanted someone to pay for what 'appened to my 'usband." She pauses and I let the silence pass. She has more to say, I don't need to push her. "At first it was just to 'elp Germany win the war. I wanted to do that, after what this country did to me. But then it changed."

"What changed, Lynette?"

She finally wipes her nose. "They found out summin."

"The King's visit?"

"Yes, and they said Kitch'ner too. A couple of weeks ago."

That disturbs me, for that means a leak at the War Office or the Palace. "Do you know who gave them the information?"

She shakes her head miserably. "No. I did their dirty work for 'em. They didn't tell me anything like that."
"And what has changed?"
"I didn't mean to kill anyone. The doctor bloke was an accident, I was after his keys, and the other man, he just came from nowhere and he'd seen me, and I couldn't let 'im tell anyone. It was over so quickly. And 'e was just lying dead on the floor. I feel sick every time I fink about it. What was 'e doing? Walking about at that time?"
"What did you stab him with, Lynette?" This should be one in the eye for Scully and his vampire.
"An old fork from the fire place at the 'ome. Snapped right off, the end fit in my pocket."
"They are going to blow up the arsenal tomorrow, aren't they?"
She nods with such sorrow I almost feel sorry for her.
"I didn't want to 'elp them kill the King. Or Kitch'ner. I'm still angry, I 'ate this country, but that; It's just... *wrong.*"
"Tell me exactly what it is that they plan to do and I can stop it."
She is going to tell me. I can feel it. I leave her to spit it out in her own time. Part of me is terrified about what their plan entails, and the other part is jubilant that finally I am getting to the bottom of this.

Then Lynette Hahn jolts upright, as if she has seen something that alarms her. I hear a loud pop and look out in front and see nothing but a dissipating cloud of smoke and rustling in some undergrowth off to our right. Then I hear it, a terrible gurgling sound, and I look back at her. She has slumped against the side of the tree, her throat torn open. I throw myself on the ground, lest the sniper aim at a second target. But no bullet comes. I sit up and grab her coat, pressing it to her wound. Her eyes are fixed on mine. They are full of tears. "Lynette, who was paying your board at Dr. Wallers? What is it that they are going to do, tomorrow? Please!" There is silence save for the sound of air hissing from her throat and the gurgling as it fills up with blood. I scream for Gaylor, who comes running, but it is too late. The damage is catastrophic, and the moment between life and death is so clear to me, for I watch her leave her body. One minute there is panic and despair in her dull blue eyes, and the next: nothing. "Stay low!" I shout at Gaylor as he drops to his knees behind a headstone nearby.

"What happened?" He asks, gasping for breath.

"Sniper." I say, cradling Lynette Hahn's head in my hands and then pointing to the bushes behind him.

"Is she dead?" He shouts.

"Yes." I sink back onto my heels and let her go. The King visits the arsenal in a matter of hours, Kitchener in tow. And I am nowhere.

<u>Wednesday, 17th March 1915</u>

XXXV.

Buckingham Palace sits in almost total darkness as Gaylor turns in near the Royal Mews. I am escorted past a special detachment of volunteer guards, inside and upstairs, to a little reception room off of the King's bedroom. The aide, I am not sure who it is, but he is clad in an army uniform, takes a deep, dramatic breath, knocks lightly on the adjoining double doors and warily opens them; disappearing out of sight. The terror I feel at raising the King from his bed before dawn is acute, as is the fact that when he appears, tying up a dressing gown of some oriental design, he is unescorted. From my recollection, this is the first time I have ever been alone with the Sovereign. "What time is it?" He asks, yawning and then resuming what, from my observations, is now a permanent expression of war-time concern.

I stammer slightly. "Quarter to five, Your, Your Majesty."
"Has something happened?"
"Not yet, but it will, today at the arsenal. If you proceed with your visit, that is. I've come to urge you not to go. I'm sorry, Your Majesty. But I've failed you."
He signals to one of two wingback chairs by the large window, facing The Mall. I sit down on one. He occupies the other, facing me. "Tell me what you know."
I explain my meeting with Lynette Hahn, and her subsequent death, before she could give me precise details as to the change in her group's plan. "It is regrettable," the King sighs, "what happened to her; her husband's death. People lost their heads last August. I urged the Government to proceed carefully with enemy aliens, but they did not listen. That is no excuse for her behaviour, though, of course. More than anything I want to be able to hold my head up and say that I behaved with dignity, even if there is scant evidence of

such a thing in this damned war. I want my subjects to be able to hold their heads up at the end of it too. We are on the right side of this mess, and there is thus a reason to conduct ourselves as gentlemen." I nod in agreement. Though I'm not sure that there is anything gentlemanly about the effects of an artillery shell packed with high explosives, I can see the principle of what he is getting at. Inflicting death on civilians is quite another matter entirely.

"Have you identified the poor chap on the crane?"

"Yes, Your Majesty. A Special Constable named David Palmer. He was on duty that evening. It appears that he was paired up with our killer."

"The bugger you are holding at the War Office? You have had no joy with him?"

"I'm afraid not," I admit. "He is resigned to his fate and says he doesn't care what punishment we dole out."

"Did he have a family? Palmer?"

"He was a widower in his fifties. He had a married daughter; was a stockbroker by day. They are not going to tell her what happened to him. Merely that there was some sort of industrial accident."

"The poor, poor fellow. I will send a letter to his daughter from the Queen and I." The King sighs and folds his hands in his lap and says nothing. I consider pleading with him some more, but he appears to be deep in thought, watching the clock behind me as it ticks slowly on. Then he asks if I have any of my cigarettes about my person. He lights one and I watch the smoke curl gently towards the ceiling as he continues to mull things over. "Stanley, what was my Daimler doing thundering about the streets of London yesterday? Ponsonby is being threatened with a bill for eleven deck chairs. And a perambulator."

I cringe. "Your Majesty, it was…" I want to finish that sentence with "all Gaylor's fault," but I stop myself from regressing back to my fat little prep school self.

"Yes?" He is smirking. I think he just wants to see what I will come up with. I'm almost as scared of Fritz Ponsonby, the Keeper of the Privy Purse, as I am of upsetting the King. That particular courtier is formidable and possesses a tempter quicker than my own.

"It was… extremely regrettable and I am sincerely appalled that you should have been inconvenienced by the complaints. Of course I will pay any bill."

"Spoilsport," the King waves away the suggestion and laughs. "Never mind. Fritz likes a good row. And never mind the bill. He will give them hell until he tires of the game and then pay up, as usual. Just don't tell the Queen. She is very big on war economy and it will hardly have been a necessary expense. You can donate something to her needlework guild by way of compensation." He stubs out his cigarette with a cheeky grin.

"We nearly ran over some crones wielding white feathers at every passing man," I say, knowing he will enjoy that."

He suppresses a laugh. "Excellent. That nobody was injured, I mean, of course."

I nod. "Indeed."

Then suddenly his face is serious again. "You believe this woman when she says that they intend to light up the arsenal today?"

I tell him that I believe she was sincere at the last; that I have spent all night at Woolwich. Together with just Ingalls, Williams, Gaylor and Crabtree; as well as Superintendent Gibbs himself. We continued to search for the lost explosives; not wanting to include anyone with prolonged connections to the arsenal. There may be thousands of respectable workers and volunteers in the place, but at least one was a murderer in disguise, and surely his friends could be using the same ruse. We do not have the time to assess and trust any one of them today, after so recently catching our most latest murderer wearing a Special Constable's armband. "But we have just run out of time," I tell His Majesty finally: "The place is just too damned big. I cannot guarantee your safety. There is always the chance that if anything goes wrong, they may just try and assassinate you both as some sort of contingency. It's what I'd do."

I say that and then hope he didn't take it the wrong way, but he merely smiles drily. "Inspector Quinn, the Special Branch; other regular parties are all exceedingly good at providing me with security. Our personal protection will not be your job this morning."

"What is it that you would like me to do, Your Majesty?" I am dreading the answer to this. Even if he tells me to go home, I will do nothing but sit there and wait for a loud bang to come from somewhere to the east.

But I am not so lucky. "If their aim is not to try to directly assassinate myself, or Lord K, or both of us at once with their own hands, what do you think it might be?"

I answer in an instant. "A large-scale explosion, using all of the stolen materials at once. Why would they have come up with a whole new plan now? Why start from scratch at short notice? They have simply brought forward their intention to sabotage the British war effort because they thought they could suddenly get close to you both; make an even even bigger statement."

"As I thought. Then your job is to stop the explosion. My usual people will take care of the direct threat to us, and you will find the TNT and make sure that it does not go off."

"I fear you have rather too much faith in my abilities," I say quietly. It is not merely the question of His Majesty's safety that is at stake, or Lord Kitchener's; but potentially every soul at the Royal Arsenal today, including myself.

"My wife does not wish me to leave the palace," the King continues. "There are some, such as Stamfordham, that wish me to go to Sandringham for my own safety." There is no question, so I say nothing. "Do you know what I think, Stanley?"

I brace myself. "No, Your Majesty?"

"I think that if I were to cower, or run from danger when so many of my subjects face it daily in my name, when I urge them to do so; that I would not be a very good King."

I cannot help but smile. I realise that it is the exact sentiment that I should want to hear from him in any other scenario where his safety was not dependent on my own ability to find a smoking needle in an extremely flammable haystack. I sigh. "I don't suppose that I can ask Lord Kitchener to try and change your mind?"

"You can try," he says confidently. "But Lord Kitchener has never backed away from a fight in his life. In fact, I think the mischievous bugger is rather apt to go looking for trouble."

I smile. But then I realise it is the King's intention to try to help draw our enemies out. That is enough to kill any expression of happiness on my face. I offer him another cigarette and he smokes it standing by the window. A searchlight is sweeping London outside the palace window; illuminating his drawn face and then letting it fall back into shade. "Your Majesty, I feel that I have to say this very plainly. You are effectively offering yourself as bait. The very nature of your visit means that you must let people get close to you, that you must put yourself at risk."

Now he sighs. "You are good at what you do, Will. I will put my faith in you, Quinn, Superintendent Gibbs; all of you. Lord Kitchener and I will proceed with our visit to the Royal Arsenal this morning, though I will have our itinerary amended just enough to throw them off; and I will consent to put it back by half an hour, to upset any plans that these impertinent bastards may have to cause us harm. Beyond that, I am quite determined. I do believe that my presence there will help matters in terms of the war effort. It is help that is much needed as present. Besides, how would it look if someone five minutes older than my son managed to talk me out of showing my face in public?" He smiles drily. "I don't think I could live with myself. This is as close as I will ever come to marching into battle, Stanley, and I don't mean to desert now." If I admired my King before this conference, I feel now, at this moment, as if I would walk into fire for him. The trouble is that I may well have to before the day is out.

XXXVI.

Crabtree looks like a frightful character from a Grimm fairytale, designed to scare small children before bedtime. His uniform is crumpled, his face is unshaven and his eyes are bloodshot, rimmed with dark circles. He has been shovelling Forced March cocaine tablets into his mouth all night, and his expression is startled and jittery. His curly hair sits on top of his head like a birds nest that has been kicked to pieces by an errant schoolboy. Next to him, Williams doesn't look any worse than usual, but every now and again I will look at him and he will be swaying gently as he stands with his eyes shut. As for me, I am starting to smell like a badger, and although the bruising on my face and my side has begun to fade, my body still aches. Where I stubbed my toes, I am still limping slightly. Most of my fingers on my left hand are taped to their neighbours now in a rudimentary attempt to address the fact that they are likely broken. Any use of my trigger finger on the other causes me untold pain. Add that to the consistent throbbing behind my eyes, due to a complete lack of sleep, and none of us are at our best.

We have temporarily occupied a room in Building 22; a small office belonging to a junior ammunition inspector who is currently at the front. With us is Horatio Keyes, as well as Stan Bailey. He is aware that the woman who killed his brother in law is dead, but that there are associates of hers that need bagging. Urgently. His knowledge of the arsenal could be of great use to us. He has also brought a friend, Bill, at my request. He works down near the Plumstead Gate as a carpenter, has been at the arsenal in excess of twenty years and Stan says that he trusts him with his life. And then there is Gaylor. I suggested that he stay in the car, but I've already learned the hard way that to argue with him when he is excising his patriotic devotion to King George V is asking for a punch in the face, and so here he is. They are chatting amongst themselves as I sort out various plans of sections in the arsenal that I have obtained from Superintendent Gibbs. Outside fifteen men sent by Lord Kitchener are awaiting instructions. I can see them from the window and a more motley crew you could not imagine. Which I think is in our favour. All are military men, but they are dressed in shabby work clothes in an attempt to blend in. They range greatly in age, and appearance, and I think will succeed in this quite nicely. They are currently eyeballing half a dozen, younger naval men in similar attire suspiciously, men that H has brought with him. Although an army man has just offered a boat person a cigarette and so the ice appears to be breaking.

"The King will be arriving half an hour later than originally planned, at half past ten this morning." That seems as good a place for me to start as any. The room is immediately brought to order. "This is a precaution in case their itinerary has fallen into the wrong hands, and was the best that we could do without disrupting the visit entirely. The items on their schedule have also been shuffled as much as possible."

"There is no question of cancelling the visit, then?" This from H.

"None," I admit. "Now. We are not responsible for the safety of the His Majesty's person, or Lord Kitchener's.

A number of the usual precautions have been taken to prevent any direct attack on them. There are the usual aides, who will be briefed, and Superintendent Quinn of Scotland Yard will have his experienced men with him. Special Branch will be in attendance, too. They will be dressed up as workers, but there are not too many. We don't want it too be obvious. We're trying to strike equally between safety and successfully smoking them out."

"But none of them know the arsenal, these bastards do." Stan Bailey is rolling a spent cigarette end in between his fingertips nervously.

"We can but do as we have been told," I say, but I look at Stan in a way that makes it quite obvious that I have had no problem overstepping my boundaries on that score. He nods knowingly.

"He's right, Sir." Crabtree, exhausted and oblivious, probably hungry. He has missed the look.

Gaylor wouldn't have given a damn about the look. "I'm not interested in anything *but* the King's personal safety."

"Relax, big boy." I glance at Williams. "I have one or two contingencies up my sleeve." He winks at me and gives me a thumbs up to signify that everything is ready on that score.

"So, more importantly," Keyes interjects. "What *are* we to do this morning."

I might as well just spit it out. "We are to find the TNT that our saboteurs have been siphoning out of the Royal Arsenal, that they intend to use to cause an explosion here today, whilst His Majesty and Lord Kitchener are present. By being here you are in danger, I will not deny that. Stan, you do not wear a uniform, you are free to go. You too, Gaylor. I urge you both to, in fact."

"Bugger that," says Stan. "Nobody's going to blow up my factory." Gaylor merely gives me a look of contempt that I would even suggest he abandon our mission.

"What sort of damage can an explosion do?" Asks Keyes, for he is last to the party and still catching up. "There is precedent." I read about two explosions in a history of the arsenal a week ago. "1864?" I turn to Williams.

He nods. "'It happened early one Saturday morning. Two gunpowder magazines went up. There was panic for miles, could feel it throughout London. Even up at Cambridge and out at Windsor and Guildford. It obliterated the buildings concerned, tore apart barges on the river so that all what was left were splinters."

"Fatalities were few, owing to the fact that it was the weekend," I add. "Though, I remember that there were all sorts of bizarre animal deaths. People's pets dropped dead in the vicinity. There was another accident a few years ago, which you all might remember."

"1907," says Williams. "I was already working here, was on duty, too. Luckily it 'appened in the middle of the night. It was cordite this time; out at the Chemical Research Department on the marshes." He sighs at the memory. "Lit up the sky and blew a 15 metre crater; shook the ground like an earthquake. Tipped me right over it did. The roar was t'rific; like fifty trains rushing past at once. And you could feel the concussion; the air moved. Shattered quite a few buildings, it did; ripped the back off one of the stands at the Arsenal football ground, and they had a collapsed roof. We found massive bits of masonry and iron girders that had been blown half a mile. The blast ripped into the gas mains and we had a whoppin' big leak. It was bloody lucky nobody died, as if it had been a work day there would have been 400-odd workers about; but lots of people were in shock. I should say. 30,000 windows panes blown out, they added up; all the way up the High Street and the Plumstead Road. Ceilings, roofs, walls, buggered. Whole area was full of people running about 'alf dressed in a panic, screaming and hollering. Glass was crashing everywhere, every dog this side of London was barking. And all at half past three in the morning. It felt like we were on a battlefield. They say that the concussion rang the church bells all the way out at Wanstead and Woodford. People were writing letters complaining about broken plates and windows in Romford, Leyton; and apparently the ground shook at Bishop's Stortford, up in Hertfordshire."

"Comparatively speaking," Keyes says, "with 1907, I mean; how much fire power do our bastards have?"

"More." That much I will admit. "And what with the war, the expansion in operations, what they set light to isn't our only concern; it's what might be nearby when it goes up and how that may add to the disaster."

Gaylor's eyes widen, but only momentarily. Crabtree is wearing a beleaguered expression and Williams is as placid as ever. Stan Bailey is still wearing a determined grimace. Bill looks like he is wondering how on earth he ended up dragged into this. "Right," Keyes says. "Then let's get to work. Where do we stand on the search?"

"Williams, here, began with the location on the edge of the research department," I tell him. "Up by the canal where the majority of the TNT disappeared from. He's also conducted searches in the area surrounding the store where much of the tetryl was stolen from. So far, he has found nothing. My plan is to relocate our search; to concentrate on the route that the King and Lord Kitchener will be taking later this morning." I take one of the plans from Gibbs and spread it on the table. "As you can see, they are coming in from the Beresford Gate and proceeding on a loop. They will pass along Avenue E past this building, then deep into the Royal Gun Factory area, close to the river and then back west along Avenue A in line with the river. Then they will turn back south, along Street No.1. Some of this journey is to be covered by the arsenal trains, and the whole visit will account for some two hours before they are due to arrive back at the gate and depart." I say that in the knowledge that this is in doubt. But I must put such thoughts aside. "Now, unfortunately for us, this is the precise place in which both Remington and Palmer were found, where we captured one of their number. The route for the royal visit coincides completely with their area of operations as we know it."

"Do we have physical descriptions of any of them?" Asks H.

"No."

"Do we know anything at all about their access to the site?"

"No." Keyes looks distinctly unimpressed. I would be in his shoes, but I am too tired to care. "Well," I expand upon my answer, "one was most certainly pretending to be a Special Constable, though this was a new development. He pretended to be part of a fresh detachment sent to augment the night watch after this mess began. It would be wrong, I think, to assume that this was always the manner in which they accessed the site. They've been in and out since November."

"What should we be looking for?" This from Gaylor.

"Anything unusual, anyone behaving suspiciously, anywhere big enough to hide such a quantity of explosives. Williams here has a sample of TNT that you can look at." I point to an ignominious looking, yellowish block on the table next to him.

"Have you considered that they might have bits of it all over the place, and people ready to make it go up simultaneously." H's brain never stops. Never misses a trick.

"Only briefly," I admit. "Partly because in that case we would need a month to search the place, but mainly it is too complicated. That and it is a gut feeling that I have. The man orchestrating this, he is a show off. He likes to do things with flare; the public provocation, the manner in which he has tried to misdirect us with the depravity of David Palmer's death. He'd go big. One large explosion. A spectacle nobody would forget." I take out the rest of my plans and hand them out. "We will be dividing into three groups, each led by someone who is an expert on the arsenal. Stan will take, you, H, and your men, from the Beresford Gate and then north towards the river, keeping west of Street No.2. That is the area he knows best. Williams has by far the best knowledge so he will take most of Kitchener's men and cover everything between Street No.2 and Street No.7. Bill works to the east, and knows that area back to front; so he will take Crabtree, Gaylor and I, along with five of Lord K's men, down to the Plumstead Gate. We will remain west of the canal, and search everything between Street No.7 and Street No.10. If you find the explosives, or anything suspicious, raise the alarm. Don't be shy. I would rather we have some egg on our face through being overly cautious than disregard something important."

Gaylor puffs out his cheeks. 'There is no way we can cover this in time."

He is right, of course, but we cannot give up and go home. All I can do is hope that we get lucky. I hand out cards to all present, for not only them, but their entire group. "What do these do?" Asks Keyes.

Williams clears his throat. I had assumed that he was asleep, for he was leaning back in his chair with his arms crossed and his eyes closed. "They are a special kind of pass issued with the Superintendent's signature. With that you will be able to commandeer any vehicle, stop any train and board it, direct it; anything you need to make your way about the arsenal in a hurry."

"What if people refuse?" This is the first time that Bill has spoken.

"Nut 'em," says Crabtree. "Then drive yourself."

"Right," I say, "any other questions?"

Stan raises his hand as if he is at school. "What do we do if we catch any of them?"

"Of course, sorry." I signal to Williams who begins to drag a large locked box across the table towards himself. "If you locate someone in the act of sabotage, you have authority from Lord Kitchener himself to use whatever force you deem necessary, including killing them. Though if you can take them alive I would welcome the opportunity to interrogate them later on. Is everyone armed?" This question is mainly aimed at our civilians. Williams's box contains a selection of revolvers and he offers one to Gaylor, who accepts it and begins loading it with bullets handed to him by Crabtree. The ease with which he does this makes me suspect he has some military service in his background. He shoves some extra bullets in his pocket for luck.

Stan shakes his head. "Wouldn't know what to do with one of those." He reaches into his jacket and produces a lethal looking flick knife. "This will see me all right."

I turn my attention to Bill, who has produced something even more threatening; two sticks joined together by a chain which he demonstrates by way of swinging them about. "Served in China," he says by way of explanation.

"All right," I say, rather pleased that Bill is to come with us now. "We'll converge outside Building 22 in five minutes."

As they leave one by one, until it is just myself and my assistant left, I feel an overwhelming wave of guilt pass over me, for they have no idea of the scale of the explosion we might be facing. I cannot bear it.

"Crabtree," I say, "go home."

"What?" His startled expression is almost comedic.

"Go home, that is an order."

I make to walk away, but he grabs me by the sleeve. He is a clown, but he isn't stupid. I watch his mind puzzle out what he is hearing. "How much TNT have they got?" He asks finally, in a harsh whisper. Damn him. I refuse to answer. "Does the King know? And

Lord Kitchener?" His eyes widen even more as I nod my head once. "And they ain't cancelling?"

"No."

"They want us to catch them. If they cancel they might not turn up. They're going to be bait!" I nod again. Said out loud it is nothing short of ludicrous. "How bad? No. I don't wanna know. Don't tell me, because I ain't leaving."

"Don't be a fool Crabtree. Think of your mother."

"That's bloody rich. What about you? For all you know your bloody brother died last week. Your mum's probably sitting at home sobbing 'er heart out and here you are chasing about after a big pile of explosives. What do you think it's going to do to 'er to hear a bloody great boom and then get the bits of you back in a shoebox? If you're goin' in, so am I. If you think I'm going to bugger off out to Sutton and wait to 'ear if everyone's dead or not, instead of stayin' to 'elp, well, respectfully, Sir; you can piss off." He folds his arms in defiance.

"Have you quite finished?" I fume. Of course I have thought of what my death would mean to my mother.

"I reckon so," he says belligerently.

"Right, then."

"Right."

It looks like I'm stuck with him. He reaches into his pocket, pulls out a huge wedge of his mother's bread pudding and begins cramming the lot of it into his mouth at once. "What are you doing?"

"You've tasted 'er bread pudding. To get blown to bits with that in my pocket, without eating it. That really would be a fucking tragedy, Sir. And if I'm dying, I ain't dying 'ungry."

He hands me the last piece and likewise, I eat in all in one go. After all, if the worst occurs there will be a giant crater where the Royal Arsenal was, the war will be over; and the two men that the country looks to first for strength, and for assurance, will be liberally spread throughout the capital. The country will be crowning King Edward VIII. I've met him, this is not a good prospect. That is if they are lucky. If not, the Kaiser will be stomping his way across the Channel. Crabtree and I will be well out of it, but everyone that we leave behind will be speaking German henceforth.

XXXVII.

It is ten past six when our three groups disperse in front of Building 22. Light is just beginning to creep skyward, a promise of bright sunshine and a clear spring morning. But there is still enough sharpness in the air to cause little puffs of breath to form every time that I exhale. The walk to the Plumstead Gate is simple enough and allows us to take a cursory look at the arsenal this morning. We go east along Avenue E and then south along Street No.10. It is a far less ostentatious effort than the big entrance at Beresford Square; simply a break in the main brick wall surrounding the arsenal marked by two pillars of the same brick, one of which is mounted by a small clock. It is just wide enough for foot traffic and one motor vehicle to pass through at a time. Workers are already beginning to arrive, clad in flat caps, short jackets; the women wrapped in long coats against the chill. A lone soldier on a motorbike attempts to wind his way through them all. Amongst us all are feelings of fear mingled with excitement, anticipation, and yet we must move slowly and conscientiously. If we do find our saboteurs, they could unleash terror on the arsenal if they think that this game of theirs is up. We do not want to scare them into setting something off, regardless of whether or not the King has yet arrived.

It becomes apparent at our first stop, an engine house, that the rumour mill is in full operation so far as the visit is concerned, though most seem to think it is just Lord

Kitchener who is about to descend upon them. This works in our favour, because as we start poking around, all of the workers present at this hour assume that their building might be 'on his list' and that we are simply making sure of the War Secretary's safety before he arrives. We find nothing there, nor in the following two establishments: a small set of office buildings and a rather dirty, disused urinal. I shepherd everybody into a busy dining room to conduct our next search, convinced that it will yield nothing. Other than a few surprised people who can't understand why we might be looking in the larder, there is nothing. Nothing apart from a few jokes about the likelihood of Lord Kitchener being pelted with flour by anarchists.

We cross Street No.10 to look in buildings C.62 and C.65, both wheel factories. I cannot see anywhere that could be used as a hiding place for a pile of explosives. Both are vast open spaces, filled end to end with carpentry benches and tools, planes, saws. The wheels themselves take up much of the space. Each is nearly as tall as Williams, perfectly crafted in the image of its neighbour and waiting to be painted, finished and attached to a new gun carriage. We are going to find nothing here.

I step outside feeling like this entire search is futile. No matter how big the pile of TNT might be, in a place so vast as the Royal Arsenal, finding it is nigh on impossible. I sincerely hope that Williams and Stan Bailey are having more luck than we are, and that they are moving more quickly, for at this rate we stand little chance of tracking anything down. Sleep deprivation, pain, the stress of the past nine days. I cannot focus on anything. Perhaps everything will be all right. Perhaps they will grow scared and their 'plan' for today will simply involve someone attempting to run at the King with a handheld bomb, in which case he will be flattened by a member of Special Branch and all of this running about in a daze is for nothing. But then there is what if. What if they do intend something bigger. What if the explosives are in the next building. Or the one after that.

We have reached a long brick structure that accommodates part of the Royal Arsenal's fire brigade. Whilst Crabtree and Bill, whose full name I have not even thought to ask, lead the rest inside, I stand in the emerging sunlight conversing with two men who are washing down their fire truck. I light a cigarette and ask if either of them have seen anything out of the ordinary; dealt with any odd occurrences in the last few weeks. They cannot think of anything, and carry on scrubbing at their truck, a long vehicle painted in glossy red with a large, collapsible ladder mounted at an angle on top. Both men look hardy. I suppose you'd have to be to do the job. Some of them are both police and firemen, depending on the emergency at hand, and the whole operation is completely independent; contained within the arsenal walls. They have section houses for single men, accommodation for families. Something Crabtree is always quoting from Sherlock Holmes has been playing on my mind. *There is nothing new under the sun. It has all been done before.* I feel like something is staring me in the face and I have just failed to notice it. Think. Think. It brings to mind another Conan Doyle statement, I think from *A Scandal in Bohemia*. It always occurs to me in a tight spot, not that I would never admit that to my assistant. *"You see, but you do not observe. The distinction is clear."*

One of the burly firemen is wiping down the truck's leather upholstery. I briefly consider how much need there will be for him and his proudly maintained vehicle a little later on. How many do they have? They are going about their business in a completely normal fashion and yet by sundown, they might be imbedded in a tragedy of unthinkable proportions. His cohort is leaning over and polishing the side of the running board. Then he sloshes water in a huge bucket and throws it at the spokes of the wheel to displace a thin layer of mud. He begins scrubbing at the them as the water splashes onto the floor and then trickles off down a nearby drain. And then suddenly I can see it all laid out before me.The grate underneath Remington's remains, his congealed blood dripping out of sight; a similar site underneath the ravaged body of David Palmer; rain running down the gutter next to Fred George's body. Lynette Hahn smelt of piss and shit. It was the first thing Stan told us when we interviewed him. *Because she was in a sewer.*

Crabtree emerges from the fire station as I begin flagging down an open army truck making for the gate and the Plumstead Road. "I know how they are getting in and out." I cry. In response, he looks ever so slightly more baffled than usual.

The driver of the truck is reluctant to stop, to say the least, so I simply stand in the middle of the road and block his path. When I show my pass, he rolls his eyes. "Can I at least drive you? So I can go about my business when I've taken you where you want to go?"
"Of course." Neither of us can drive anyway. Well, Crabtree thinks that he can, but the experience is near lethal. I climb into the back and then help drag the idiot in behind me. "Show me your notebook," I say to him when he has stopped scrabbling about and got his bearings by plonking his behind on a case of ammunition. I snatch it from him when it emerges from his pocket and flick through and find the little plan that he drew when we were exploring the area around Remington's murder scene.

"Remington, what was left of him, he was marked with coal dust."

"I don't get it?"

"They have been underground. Here." I jab my finger at a large coal bunker. "Remington and Palmer. Both just happened to be killed for being in the wrong place at the wrong time. Look at the location. Both the boring mill and the radial crane are close to this, D.75. It's a large coal bunker."

"You think they've been living in the coal bunker?" He looks incredulous now, though to be fair my explanation is patchy, so far, to say the least.

"No, you fool. I think they are getting in and out *underground*."

He appears to think that I have finally lost my mind; I can see him wrestling between making a case for this and being too tired to put up any opposition. When he does speak his tone is like a patient adult trying to explain something to a small, stupid child. "Sir, digging their way in like that, it's too big a job. They would have had to tunnel under a massive section of the arsenal in four months. They can't possibly have…"

"The tunnels are already there," I cut him off as I spy one of Kitchener's men emerging out onto Avenue E. I hit the side of the truck to get the driver to stop and jump down. "Where is Williams?" He points to the building behind him. As I run inside, I see Crabtree sitting in the truck shrugging at the man with a resigned look on his face.

The interior houses a small forge, though there is no fire for now. Williams is checking inside a collection of huge, empty shell casings, minus their pointed caps. There must be two dozen of them lined up, standing as high as my waist and waiting to go somewhere else. I explain my theory to him in as few words as possible, and he is off towards the door like a shot, ordering his team to continue concentrating on the block of buildings they are examining up as far as Avenue C. He beckons for me to get into the truck quickly behind him. We make a brief stop at Building 22, where Williams sprints up the steps and emerges within two minutes, carrying torches, and then we cross Street No.1 and swing diagonally up towards the river. In response to Crabtree's continued expression of confusion, I explain to him what I know: "When I was reading about the history of the arsenal last week, I saw something. There are innumerable tunnels and cellars under this part of the arsenal, going all the way back to Tudor times. I don't suppose that they ever formed one big, cohesive system, or that it was intentionally built up; but they are there, nonetheless. Our saboteurs would only have had to gain access to one part of it, I presume, to fashion a way in that was far less trouble than digging tunnels for themselves; hence why Lynette Hahn stank to high heaven. It must involve the sewers."

Williams is pragmatic, but not dismissive. "It's going to tough to investigate. We have no complete plans. As you say, some of the subterranean tunnelling is hundreds of years old. Somewhere near where the original house was, Tower Place, there's a huge wine cellar from the time of Henry VIII, when this was a warren breeding rabbits for food; but nobody knows exactly where. Everyone jokes about digging for it and nicking the wine. Then there are various underground storage places, escape tunnels too, I suppose. It's because all of them have been bricked up over the years, some of them generations ago; they've just been forgotten about. This cellar shouldn't go more than a few dozen feet, where we are going, but it's the only old one I know how to get into."

"The tunnels have gradually been bricked up, but not filled in," I point out. "That would have been a monumental endeavour. Humour me, if only for a quarter of an hour." He nods, and directs the driver further down the road, to where we pull over on a paved square. Williams paces quickly towards an antique building facing southeast, flipping through a set of keys he probably seized on our stop. It must be at least two hundred years old. It is a beautiful structure; functional, but not without style. It is constructed of red brick, with elongated arched windows on the ground floor and small circular ones above them. The black double doors are flanked by square brick plinths jutting out, supporting an elaborate lintel that holds up white statutes; a unicorn and a lion. Atop it all is a clock and a matching compass; black with gold adornments. I ran through the open square outside and right past it the other night in pursuit of our prisoner at the War Office, but I didn't give it a second look.

Williams lets us in to a large entrance hall with a slate floor that bears off in opposite directions. "This is the old Royal Military Academy. At one point you had that on the left and a board room for the Ordnance Board on the right side of the building," he explains. "But it's been an age since those days. Now you've got a Mess on one side and a Model Room on the other. There have been a lot of changes over the years. There was even a chapel here at one point. Shouldn't be anyone here at this time." We follow him as he descends a damp stone staircase and then begins edging into darkness. We have arrived in a grim corridor, untouched for god only knows how long. There is an icy chill in the air. Water seeps through the whitewashed brick walls and runs down over dark green slime; and the ceiling is rounded and low enough that I have to stoop slightly. We pass one alcove, but it is empty. I am sure that we are retracing our steps, walking out under the square we have just traversed to reach the old academy building.

"Williams?" Crabtree whispers loudly. Our guide grunts acknowledgment from up in front. "The prostitute?"
"What?"
"The ghost story about the prostitute in the cellar. You never told us. Was that here?"

Williams flashes the beam of his torch at a locked door on our right, still some distance away.

"That used to be a wine cellar. Back in Wellington's time, apparently ol' big nose was due to come and stay here. I dunno what happened, but one of the officers who was also visiting, he was already upstairs with a prostitute, and there was a faff about hiding her. Apparently the Duke wasn't keen on that sort of thing and they panicked. Now, a junior artillery officer came up with a plan. He rushed her down here and locked her in. Don't worry love, he says. As soon as he's gone, I'll come down and fetch you. Only he didn't."

Crabtree gasps. "What happened?"

"She starved to death I suppose. Or froze, maybe. Who knows? They found her years later, just meaty looking bones. Damp and a body. It's not good."

"That is bloody terrible!" Crabtree is horrified.

"That ain't the worst of it."

"Eh?"

"She's still here. And she's angry."

"Fuck off." Crabtree's mouth is wide open. I would laugh at my assistant, but I'm almost as disturbed as he is.

Williams shakes his head firmly. "No lie. Junior artillery officers can't enter this building without stuff flying about, things crashing off the walls. Terrified of her, they are. I've seen it myself. And if they come down here, she's got a thing about trousers. She undoes 'em. Seen that as well. Can hear her laughing. Sometimes she screams, really high pitched. You can joke about the ghost stories here at the arsenal, but her? She's as real as you and me. Raving mad she is." I don't blame her. I'd be fuming too. I suppress a shudder as we pass the doorway, and try to imagine what it must have been like to die down here, terrified, starving and alone.

Ahead, Williams has stopped. We have reached a dead end, for there is a wall of white brick in front of us. "What do you think?" I ask Williams. "This is as far as this has ever gone down here, and it's undamaged." With my good foot, I give the lower part of the wall a good kick. Nothing moves. Williams edges past me and tests the integrity of the wall in a few different spots. "This hasn't been bricked up. Look." He points off to the

right, where the tunnel makes a turn, runs on a little way and then abruptly ends. "That's where it went. You can see the shoddy building work where they blocked the way."
"What is on the other side of this?" I ask, returning my attention to the wall in front of us.
"No idea," he replies.
"It doesn't feel particularly thick. I can feel some give in it. It doesn't sound like hard packed dirt is behind it. Let's find out, shall we?"
He nods and disappears back up the tunnel. In less than ten minutes he has returned carrying two big sledgehammers. With my useless hand, I can do little to help and so I get out of the way. I'm not convinced that Crabtree will even be able to lift the thing, but he manages well enough. Together they take alternative swings at the wall; and thanks to the damp it is not long before a hole appears. Williams kicks away the surrounding bricks and we end up with a three foot high hole; big enough to crouch down and climb through.
It is already evident what is on the other side, from the stench now wafting into the tunnel. I shine my torch through the opening to confirm. "Sewer," I state, not without some pride. Williams is apparently unaffected by the stench. I simply hold my sleeve up to my nose and mouth, but Crabtree looks distinctly green. "What's the matter?" I ask, as I duck through the hole and balance on a ledge about six inches wide to avoid wading into anything unseemly; then shuffle along to make space for him. "Not hungry again? Are you?" His response is to stick his fingers up at me as he follows. In doing so he loses concentration and staggers slightly. For one awful moment I think he is about to fall face first into the sludge below; but then he recovers himself. I pull my compass out of my pocket as Williams joins us and shine my torch onto the face. "If we go left from here, that is north. That's the river and they don't sail in. They'd have been caught; the amount

of people watching it. Especially rowing about with blocks of TNT. So we will go right. That way the tunnel is bearing off to the southwest and the arsenal's boundary wall. How far, Williams?"

He hardly thinks about it at all. "A hundred yards, at most."

We are on to something, I can feel it. The smell is indescribable as we creep along the ledge. Thankfully, after ten yards or so it widens out and we can walk normally, if not carefully; and angle ourselves slightly away from the river of filth at our feet. All three of us try to concentrate on the job at hand as we shine our torches back and forth in silence, crossing them over in wide arcs; checking, double checking every inch of the sewer tunnel. There is no marker that might signify when we pass underneath the arsenal wall, but just as I estimate we must have travelled Williams's one hundred yards, perhaps a little more; there is a slimy metal ladder rising upwards. "Come on then mate," Williams invites Crabtree to follow him. Together they apply their shoulders to the manhole cover above. Suddenly there is a rush of air as they manage to dislodge it and slide it to one side. Above us, someone swears and a cart rattles by, presumably surprised to see people emerging up onto a road. Crabtree tentatively sticks his head out.

"Well?" I ask.

"It's Warren Lane," he proclaims, amazed. Williams drops down the ladder and I take his place. I poke my head up too, to find that we are less than a yard away from where Fred George fell dead to the ground.

XXXVIII.

It is quarter to eight, and we have a little over two and a half hours until the King and Lord Kitchener arrive at the Royal Arsenal. Crabtree and I descend back down the ladder to meet Williams at the bottom. "This is without a doubt how they have been getting in and out of the Arsenal."

Crabtree nods. "Fred George must have witnessed Lynette Hahn climbing out of the sewers."

"Yes." I recall Hahn's words to me just before someone put a rifle round through her neck. *"He just came from nowhere and he'd seen me, and I couldn't let him tell anyone."*

"We should move everyone below ground and map out what they've done. It will narrow the search by miles." This from Williams.

"It will," I agree. "But let's have a cursory look up the other way first so we know exactly what we are looking at." We retrace our steps back towards the gap we have fashioned in the cellar wall under the old military academy. Then we carry on. The going is much, much less favourable. The tunnel grows narrow and lower and more disgusting. I can feel slime moving beneath my feet, and the ledge narrows so much that we struggle to balance. After thirty or so feet I signal for the others to stop. We have reached a large pile of bricks that have been used to build up a platform in the sewage to stand on. In their place there is a significant hole in the wall that undoubtedly leads on under the Arsenal.

"That's got to be a continuation of what we saw blocked up from the other side," says Williams, looking back down the sewer. "But on the other side of the barrier." One by one we quietly slip into the tunnel, revolvers at the ready. We now find ourselves thankfully away from a river of effluence and other unthinkable things, in a damp, black tunnel about three feet wide and five feet high. As I shine my torch up and down, the brickwork looks ancient. It was probably tall enough for a man to stand upright when it was hewn out. I would think it is hundreds of years old, which is interesting. Expensive building materials for a cellar. Whoever built it was not short of money.

"If it is here, the TNT is below ground," I whisper firmly. "It never left the site."

"But surely you couldn't keep it down here," scoffs Crabtree.

"Course you could," retorts Williams. Then he explains what I already know. "TNT don't dissolve or absorb water. It could melt if it got hot enough, but it never would be, down here. It'd just sit down here quietly until they boosted it with the tetryl and made it go up." He walks straight into the back of me, for he has not seen that I have stopped. He adds his torch beam to mine, and then Crabtree does the same.

"Bollocks," mutters my assistant.

"Yep," says Williams. For we are standing in a central junction, with at least six tunnels leading off in various directions.

We round everyone up and send them down into the tunnel system. Finally I feel that we might be achieving something, but the situation is still far from ideal. I have no idea how extensive the tunnels are to which our saboteurs have gained access. They also have the advantage of having had months to learn their way about. We found one brick with the year 1684 etched into it. The system is old, and there is no plan for what we have located, and so our men are merely wandering in circles with pistols raised under H's supervision, hoping to find a pile of TNT. We are in a filthy mess, and not only because of the sewage on our shoes.

"And where are we going?" Crabtree is skipping behind me as I walk quickly back down Avenue E from Building 22.

"Hopefully we are going to take a shortcut. Get that plan out; the one in your book."

Crowds jostle us as we make our way along; the working day is now in full swing at the Royal Arsenal; and the sheer volume of people terrifies me. So many lives that are currently our responsibility to protect. I have been so focused on the danger to the King and Lord Kitchener, even the likes of Fitz; not to mention Crabtree and I, that I have not really stopped to consider the fate of all of these workers; these innocent people slaving towards the war effort in an environment already fraught with risk. The thought is depressing, to say the least. So many thousands of husbands, brothers, fathers, sons. Not to mention a significant number of women workers too. And what about those just outside? What about the children going too and from school, then shopkeepers, delivery drivers, the old man sitting on the step at the Pyro with his tuneless mandolin. All of their lives could be in danger at this very moment; and it is down to the likes of Crabtree and I to ensure that no harm comes to them.

The coal bunker that has become the focus of my attention is accessed from within something called the '*South Forge 40 Ton Hammer Shop,*' via a narrow, ancient staircase in its southeastern corner. Crucially, it is just a few steps from both D.78, the boring facility where Remington was discovered spread between two guns, and from D.73, when the radial crane is located; the one to which the gruesome remains of David Palmer were lashed. The bunker itself is about twenty feet by twenty, with a hatch at one end into which I assume supplies are dropped. A few shovels sit leaning against the wall. The air is thick with dust and a hint of yet more damp. If I survive TNT today, I am sure that pneumonia will get me after all of this scampering about underground. "Who in their right mind offers to blow themselves up?" Asks Crabtree, using a poker of some description to prod some piles of coal. "You've got to be willing to top yourself to set it off deep inside

the arsenal like this. Are they so bonkers, that they would be willing to die to see Britain lose the war."
I am shining my torch up and down alongside Williams, looking for anything out of the ordinary, and a point of access. "Absolutely. Once you have betrayed your country; anything is possible. You are no longer the person you were, when you have become a traitor. You must give up some elementary part of yourself, I think."
"If you're in charge you don't need to do nothing," yawns Williams. "You find some idiot willing to do it for you. Some lost, delusional soul like that woman. Someone might be about to blow himself sky high, but he's a nobody. 'They,' whoever they are, have a mission, as they see it. This is just the beginning."
A miserable idea, but probably quite accurate.
"Sir." Crabtree's prodding has borne fruit, for at the bottom of one pile his poker has vanished almost completely underground. We kick the surrounding coal away to reveal a small opening in the floor, hacked out from below, it looks like someone has placed a simple metal grill over it and covered it with coal to disguise it.
"I'll go first," volunteers Williams.
As we drop down in turn, we spy a rudimentary ladder up against the opposite wall of yet another ancient looking tunnel. The place wasn't called '*The Warren*' before its military days simply on account of the bunnies. There is only one direction in which to go, and we are able to walk three abreast; though I am still hunched over. I suppose we fare slightly better than we did out by Warren Lane. There are only three tunnels branching out from this one. One, on the right, looks particularly decrepit, and so I suggest that we eliminate that one first. It is uncomfortably narrow and full of cobwebs, and I doubt anyone has been down there. More so when after a few yards we are obliged to crawl for a short while to get further on. Our reward is astonishing, for we locate a strong room; reinforced on

all sides and on the floor with oak planks that have withstood their environment well. The Tudor wine cellar might still be evading us, despite our proximity today already to the site of the original house, with its octagonal tower; but this is a significant archaeological find. There are wooden carvings; all ornate and religious in nature as well as elaborate crosses. There is gold plate too. "Bloody hell," cries Crabtree. "What's all this doing down here?"

"I imagine being hidden from the King," I say, opening one large chest to find more catholic idolatry.

"What's any of this got to do with King George?" He says blankly.

"Not the current King; fool. Henry VIII. I imagine this was all stashed down here in the 1530s or 40s; when the monasteries were being pulled down."

Another chest, this one lead lined, has yielded a pile of wooden panels. "They can't be worth much," Williams says, leaning over my shoulder to gaze at numerous falcons interwoven with red and white roses.

"You'd have done well to put these out of sight at that time," I reply. "The falcon was Anne Boleyn's mark. And then of course the Tudor rose. Some poor dupe has had these done to celebrate her marriage to the King and then probably had to hack them down a couple years later after he whacked her head off. Either way, it's clear our saboteurs haven't been in here. At the very least they would have pinched the gold."

We crawl our way back out to the junction and then stand and survey the remaining two options. There is no sight, nor sound of Keyes's group, who have entered via the sewer, so they must be some way off. Perhaps they are not even in the same system as us. I shrug and make for the opening in the middle this time. The entrance to this passage is tiny. I don't think it was originally part of this system; but when we reach the tunnel behind it, it is much taller and wider; not to mention newer; though damp pervades. We pass several alcoves, all of which are stuffed with what looks to be eighteenth century furniture, and a big staircase hewn into the earth and reinforced that leads up to a hatch that is now welded shut. There are rotting bed frames, old paintings where the images have faded away and only scraps of canvas remain hanging in the frames. There is even a hulking great wardrobe with one door hanging off. The passageway ends abruptly. Whilst Williams and I look in and about the remains of someones house, Crabtree wanders off to the far wall with his torch. I am wading through various wooden detritus when I hear him make an exclamation of horror. Williams and I run to him, at which point he apologises effusively. "Sorry, Sir, it's not that."

"Well what is it?" I ask in a bad temper.

Comically opened mouth, he shines his torch onto the earthen wall. Sticking out of it are all manner of haphazard human bones: skulls, femurs, scapulas; everything imaginable. Also present are scraps of rotten woollen fabric. "What are they doing there?"

I crouch down and pick up the bent remains of what looks like it might have been a wooden cross at one point. "I would imagine, given the jumbled nature of them, and the age, that as they cut further and further into the ground beneath the arsenal a couple of hundred years ago, the authorities happened across a plague pit and decided to stop cutting."

Crabtree jumps back as if there might still be some contagion in the air. "Come on, idiot," I say without ill-feeling. "Let's try doorway number three."

We needn't have bothered. The tunnel contains plenty of old crates, full of rotten papers and ledgers. Abandoned bureaucracy. Within fifty feet we come upon a vault door that has quite obviously not been used in decades; owing by the rust to the hinges and the bolt. We've now spent nearly two fruitless hours walking into dead ends and getting nowhere. I pick up an abandoned, rusty metal bar and vehemently swear as I batter the locked door, the crumbling brick walls, old barrels and soggy paperwork around us.

"He's lost it." Finally, Williams is actually perturbed by something; goggle-eyed, as if the earth has shifted on its axis.

Crabtree nods and sighs at the same time. "I'm afraid so," he says in a ridiculous posh voice. "You see, mate, Lieutenant Stanley here is the very incarnation of British temper roused. He will stand a good deal with silent grace and not a titter, stoically he will carry on. Stiff upper lip and all that. But woe betide anyone that pushes him too far. See this? For him it's like the Germans have stomped into Belgium all over again." He scampers off back down the tunnel in search of daylight as I threaten to chase him with my improvised weapon; ready to batter him too.

XXXIX.

Crabtree, Gaylor, Bailey and I sit on the steps of Building 22, with Kitchener's men nearby. It is half past nine, and we have one hour left. We stink. We can barely keep our eyes open. Passing workers are actually adjusting they paths to steer away from us. Williams emerges from inside with a tray of enamel mugs steaming with coffee. "Made it as strong as I could."

As soon as we are revived we will join H and the others back underground; but so far they have found nothing. I barely have the energy to glance up as a motor car rumbles up and stops by the steps. Superintendent Gibbs has been out supervising preparations for the royal visit. His face is a picture of worry; I'd go so far as to say stricken. I suppose apart from the prospect of everyone dying, even if he was lucky and survived a giant explosion, having your command made extinct beneath your feet is not favourable in terms in one's career. "Anything?" He asks.

I think my body language says it all. "No." He stands there for a moment, looking at me intently as if he hopes I may expand on my one word answer and provide him with some insight to calm his nerves. I have nothing for him. His nerves can go to hell with mine.

An officer much my own age, with overly bushy eyebrows and a coat buttoned up wrong, pushes through the main doors of the building. "Is there a Lieutenant Stanley out here?" I drag myself to my feet and raise my hand. "There is a telephone call for you, War Office."

This will either be very good, or very bad. I follow him along a dismal ground floor corridor; painted in an institutional ochre and olive green colour scheme; into a tiny room that is being used as a telephone exchange of sorts. There are three other men squashed around one big desk. "Can I have the room, please?"

Obediently they all leave. The voice on the other end of the line belongs to Fitz, but it is feint. "I have something for you from our friend downstairs," he says proudly.

"How?" Is the first question out of my mouth, for that seemed like an impossibility.

"We sent in one of Lord K's favourites," he says, "giant of an Egyptian fellow with one eye. When he told him that they'd sniped Hahn he evidently surmised that he is just as dispensable as she was, and that being nice to us might be his best chance of survival."

"What have you got?"

"A.25. He would say nothing else. Does that mean anything to you?"

It does, but I cannot think why. "I need to know exactly how they got underneath that building. Can you ask him? He will know what I am talking about. It is imperative."

"We're just about to leave, but I will set our Egyptian friend to it. I'll have someone ring you up if they find anything. Good luck, old man."

"Same to you," I say as I drop the receiver and flee for the door.

"Take my motor car," Gibbs says as I go bumbling past on the way out of the building. Crabtree is already standing, ready to move as I burst out of the main doors and nearly knock two female clerks over. I point him towards the car while I make a sham apology and descend the stairs.

"I'll meet you there," Williams says as he runs in front of a motorcycle, orders the perplexed rider off and zips away towards the river.

I have long since given up trying to fathom how his mind works. "You can collect it from A.25, shortly." I pat the poor, perplexed motorcyclist on the shoulder as we jog past and jump up into Gibbs's army car.

As we pull up outside a weathered looking factory with dozens of workers milling about, I recognise it immediately. I was there the other night, I ran through it. Williams and Stan roll up on the motorcycle. Now I remember. This is his building; the bullet factory. He's a foreman and he can show us anything out of place. I'm glad that Williams is awake enough to have strung this together in his mind. A truck full of soldiers also rolls to a stop next to us, Army Service Corps men; I presume, from the barracks nearby. A young officer, painfully enthusiastic, bounds up to me. "Superintendent Gibbs had us on standby for an emergency protocol. He just made the call. What can we do?"

"Sweep the building," I tell him. "Quietly though, get everyone out, just tell them it is a drill because there is a dignitary visit later. Then calmly surround the factory. Let nobody in."

"Kitchener really is coming then?"

"Yes." I see no harm in telling him that much. It is a decent cover story for what is actually going on. "Nothing serious," I lie, "but it is imperative that we make sure certain buildings are safe, that's all. And tell your men to touch nothing." He nods and bounds off again, barking orders. He is efficient, I'll give him that. His slightly unfit, slightly too long in the tooth band of troops have the building emptied in less than five minutes; and he seems to have done it well, for as they emerge, the workers are laughing and joking amongst themselves; lighting cigarettes and looking expectantly about as if Lord Kitchener might suddenly appear from behind a workshop nearby.

"How are we going to do this?" Gaylor asks once we are inside the now empty factory."

"Spread out in a line, this end," I say to him, as well as Crabtree, Williams, and Bailey. Stan, you go in the middle, you know this building better than any of us." Half a dozen of Kitchener's reprobates are raring to go behind us. "You fellows sweep the perimeter walls inside, three clockwise; three anti-clockwise. If anybody sees anything that looks remotely odd you are to call out and raise your hand immediately. Stan here will then confirm if anything is out of the ordinary."

The shop floor looks smaller in daylight, menacing shadows cast aside. The two thick rows of back to back, low bullet-making machines run down the middle of the room; silent for now. Crabtree and I search either side of one pair of lines as we pass through the hangar; Gaylor and Williams the other. Stan Bailey walks directly between the two, gazing back and forth between both. I can't think how the TNT would be in here. There's nowhere big enough to hold it. Perhaps our prisoner is making fun of us. Perhaps this is his last effort at helping his mad cause from within the depths of the War Office; distracting us during what little time we have left. I am just pondering this new, awful possibility when one of Kitchener's men lets out a simple "Hey!" And raises his arm.

He is down in the far corner with a torch. He has noticed something odd about a desk that has been pushed up against the wall amongst a pile of old equipment. "Might be nothing," he shrugs, "but the floor down here is filthy, don't look like anyone comes up here?"

Stan nods. "They don't. We keep meaning to get rid of all this shit."

"Well around this desk, the floor's clean. Not like someone's scrubbed it, but no muck has accumulated. Or if it had, it's been kicked away again. Someone's been walking about here."

"Excellent observation," I admit. Where does Kitchener *find* these people? "Stan, what's on the other side of this wall?" I ask.

"About eighteen inches of clearance and then the back wall of A.35."

"Is it possible for someone to get out there?"

"Can't think why they'd want to. It's just a strip of dead space. Be uncomfortable even 'aving a crafty fag out there. I think whatever building was behind this originally was slightly bigger and that's why they don't quite match up."

I take one end of the desk and nod at Stan to take the other. "Carefully now." My bandaged fingers protest as we lift it slightly and carry it out just a few inches and place it gently back down. If there are explosives inside, there surely cannot be enough of them to cause much damage to this building, let alone the whole arsenal. But best to play it safe. Crabtree gasps and points at the wall. Moving the desk has revealed a hole that leads to the useless gap between two buildings described by Stan. I crawl through it, dignity be damned, and then groan as I climb back to my feet. In the meantime Bailey, Williams and Crabtree follow. I instruct Gaylor to keep watch on the other side. We have to walk in single file as we make our way up the gravel strip to the other end of the gap; a dead end. Besides us there is only one other thing out here: a small, metal box with two thin spokes sticking out of the top. "Stan?"

"I've never seen it before."

"It has no function in this building?"

He is firm on this. "No. I can't even tell you what it is." I have no idea, either. From the box, a wire runs down to the floor and then up to and along the edge of the building. We follow it to where it vanishes underground through a tiny hole, no bigger in diameter than something made by an ordinary screwdriver.

"Williams?"

He strides up to the box and bends low for a look. "Not a clue, but if I had to hazard a guess? We're looking at M14."

I give him a few moments to consider the problem. "What do we now?"

He puts his hands on his hips; breathes in deeply. After what seems like an age, he says, "I'm not touching it till I see what is on the other end of the wire."

"You think it might be connected to explosives?" I ask.

"I'm not sure it isn't, and so I want to find the other end."

"You think it might be some sort of device to detonate the TNT?" Asks Bailey.

He shrugs. "Never seen anything like it in my life, which means I don't like it."

"Urgh!" Crabtree cries. "But how do we get down there?" He points to the hole and the disappearing wire.

I take a short few seconds to consider this. "It would be easy. They would want to be able to access this, whatever it is, without too much trouble. Stan, where is the nearest building with underground access?"

He looks baffled. "Come on, think." It is still a tall order for him, I know, but it is nearly half past ten. We are out of time. I wonder how often he sees anything of the arsenal apart from his own building.

"There's a Carpenter's shop next door, I know there must be something like a cellar there, because they put some new machinery in it a few years ago and it went right through the floor; it was too heavy."

"Show us." As we climb back through the hole in the wall, place the desk back and depart A.25, I motion to the ASC Officer. "Lieutenant? Is it?"

"Second Lieutenant Abraham," he answers proudly. He cannot be more than eighteen, I'll be amazed if he has been in the army more than a few weeks.

"Well, Second Lieutenant Abraham, take these half a dozen men of mine," I gesture to Kitchener's collective. Add them to yours and widen the perimeter as much as you possible can around this building without it becoming vulnerable. Do you understand? And let nobody in, even if they outrank you."

He salutes again, like this is the most exciting day of his life so far. Oh to be that green again.

The carpentry shop backs right on to the bullet factory and is accessed through a rectangular courtyard almost overlooking the river. A chief poo-bah chippy is outside having a cigarette with one hand and spinning some sort of chisel in the other. Stan calls out to him while we are still running. "How do you get into your cellar?"

"You don't," he says after a moment of bewilderment and some clarification on having Crabtree's black pass waved obnoxiously in his face. "We filled it in after an accident a few years back." On observing the bereft reaction of half a dozen madmen, including an officer, to this news, he attempts to offer us some consolation. "Next door still have theirs though. The stairs are right over there." I don't know how we missed it. Off to the left is a painted iron staircase dropping down to a subterranean door. The carpenter follows us with some of his men and leans down over the railing as we descend. "Nobody's been down there in years, I don't think."

"Someone has," says Williams, pointing to the hinges. "They have been oiled. Recently. They'd not want to make a noise."

He prepares to perform his magic on the lock, but there is no need. For no reason that I can articulate, I reach out and try the handle, expecting it to be unlocked, and it moves. "Gaylor, would you please stay here and guard the door; anyone that isn't one of us coming out of it, nab them. If you could assist him?" I ask, looking up at the workmen. The burly carpenter is already nodding. He shouts to one or two others and within moments there are a group of woodworkers, armed sporadically with axes and other sharp things on either side of our chauffeur. As we disappear through the door, I hear a surge of noise distantly; the honk of car horns, clanging of bells, excited voices cheering and screaming, then merging into a slightly incoherent version of the National Anthem. The King is here.

XL.

Once in the cellar we can see above where the floor has been reinforced to hold up more modern machinery. We can also see a bricked up doorway, undamaged, that presumably was an entrance to the now filled in space underneath the carpentry shop. It is almost empty, save for a few barrels stacked in the far right hand corner, back in the direction of A.25. As we begin hefting them out of the way, it transpires that part of the wall has been removed. There is a passageway of sorts, but no bricks to reinforce it. Soon enough there is not even that, just a space to crawl. Perhaps they wanted their own cellar, to make absolutely sure that it did not appear on any plans.

This time it looks as if they have tunnelled for themselves, for having crouched down and struggled through a ten foot passage we emerge into a rough-hewn chamber. On one side is a great pile of dirt, the spoil, I would assume, from their endeavour. It holds my attention for merely a second, because directly in front of me is a large pile of pale yellow blocks.
"Bugger me," says Crabtree, amazed.
"I'll say," responds Bailey.
Williams pushes past me, his only interest being finding the wire and where it leads to. "I need light!" He shouts from behind the explosives. I hesitate to follow him, then realise how stupid that is. That I am concerned about being ten feet closer to a pile of explosives that might destroy a large portion of London, when I can already almost reach out and touch them. We crowd around him, shining our torches onto what he has found. It is another large case, and the wires run down into it from a hole in the ceiling. There are also more wires running into the blocks of TNT.
"Well?" Whispers Bailey over his shoulder.
"I'm thinking! Give it a rest!" Williams probes the wires gently, examines the box. That he is panicking now makes me even more concerned. Eventually he straightens up slightly. "I think, *think,* we're looking at a device that enables them to detonate all this without being anywhere near."
I puff out my cheeks. "That is something. To kill people in absentia. How does it work? How do we break it, more importantly."
'I won't know much until I take it apart, but in the meantime, I think," he says, drawing out a small set of wire cutters "that it is as simple as this."
There is no time for me to stop him as he bends over and attacks the wire arrangement with his tools; making two neat snips. For a moment I duck and wait to be engulfed in a ball of fire. But then as I stand up

again the only sound is Williams laughing like a rabid hyena.

I hit him on the back of the head. "How sure were you?"

He shrugs, still laughing. "Little over halfway?" He shoves his wire cutters back in his pocket and sobers up a bit. "Here," he points. "So far as I can tell, the circuit needs to be complete. The trigger is upstairs, waiting for a signal of some sort, the tetryl will be in this case, and then there is the TNT. I've broken the circuit. They'll activate whatever they've got that operates it, and nothing will happen. Probably."

"Probably?" I want to strike him again.

"I'm as certain as I can be without looking at it all in bits."

"It 'ardly seems real," says Crabtree. That that was it. We've snipped it and got the better of them. It's too easy."

"He's right," I agree. "There will be a contingency."

We all turn at the sound of sarcastic applause coming from behind the spoil heap. Three men emerge from their hiding place, one of them at the front holding a revolver. The others are armed with knives. "Our employer told us you would run us close, Lieutenant." The accent on the lead one is German. "My friends here are due to leave, but I was going to remain in case anything went wrong, to see to things, I suppose you'd say, the old-fashioned way. You have a saying I like in English. More than one way to skin a cat. But in this case, it is skinning a king."

I have begun edging round to place myself in between them and the case on the floor. I know that if they shoot at the TNT, it will probably remain intact; but that is where my chemical knowledge ends. If they shoot at the detonator, I have no idea. If our talkative Teutonic friend wasn't so fond of his own voice, he would have tried that already. Williams seems to have caught on, because he is edging too, the pair of us forming a human shield of sorts. "You're outnumbered, in case you hadn't noticed." I say this with a calmness that belies the fact that my heart is thumping against my ribcage.

He raises his revolver and shoots. The sound is deafening in the enclosed space. Stan Bailey drops to the ground clutching his chest, gasps for air and then goes worryingly quiet and almost still. The German shrugs. "How are my odds looking now?"

Aside from wanting to kill him, my only thought is to get them away from the explosives, so that no disaster befalls the arsenal. To that end I grab for my own revolver, throwing my torch at him in the process, hoping it will either hit his weapon, or at least the beam will blind him momentarily. I drop to my knee and fire, pain shooting from my bent trigger finger up my arm to the elbow. Williams does the same. One of us appears to hit him, for he drops the revolver and Crabtree leaps at him in a flash and kicks it away. They grapple with each other in the dark, falling to the floor, but I have not time to stand by and idly strain my eyes to watch, because another of them has thrown himself at me, swishing his blade back and forth. The last has made a dash for Williams. All hell breaks loose. I am dimly aware of a stinging in my cheek as he very nearly takes my eye out, and pain in my left hand. In retaliation I kick him hard between the legs. He falls to the floor, clutching his manhood, "You may have broken my hand, but I can still use my foot," I say, stamping on his wrist and relieve him of his weapon. Then I kick him in the face and he goes limp. I was a laughable, fat schoolboy and so my brother taught me to fight dirty.

Armed with something that won't blow us all to kingdom come, I glance across at Williams, blade in hand, but he seems to be doing fine on his own. Crabtree however, is in a chokehold and desperately trying to bite the German's hand off. I take great pleasure in coming up behind his assailant and kicking him in the head. As I boot him in the chest and stab him in the hand, pinning it to the ground, I say: "It's not so much fun when you are the one lying on the floor, is it?" He screams pitifully and rolls over clutching his side. He is beaten.

But the last one is not. "Stanley!" Williams cries as I feel someone rush by and spy the last of our saboteurs go flying behind the spoil heap. I feel a sudden sinking feeling in my chest. I sprint behind the large pile of earth and swear loudly. There is another hole in the wall, and our man is gone. And so, as far as I can see when I grab my torch and throw the beam around wildly, is one of the revolvers that should be lying on the ground.

"We don't know our way around. We'll never find him!" Crabtree is exasperated.

But I have no intention of following him. I make for the tunnel and the exit to the courtyard. "Williams, secure these two, we'll send in Gaylor," I shout. "Crabtree. With, me."

"How are we going to find him?" My assistant wheezes as we climb the stairs.

"We'll try and cut him off," I call over my shoulder. "There is only one place he'll be going. We're going to follow the cheers."

XLI.

The King and Lord Kitchener are making their way through a collection of buildings up by the river. The crowds are immense, a seething mass of humanity ebbing and flowing in their direction as they attempt to get closer to fame and fortune. It has turned into a fine morning, and all of the spectators are rushing from their buildings without their coats; climbing on walls, up lampposts, on top of motor cars to get a better look.

The thing about wartime London, you are never too far from bunting or allied flags of some description, and these are beginning to appear and add a red, blue, white and black flurry of colour to proceedings. There are hundreds of individual shouts as Superintendent Gibbs guides his distinguished guests past the wharves. *Long Live The King, Hurrah for Lord Kitchener.* His Majesty nods his head appreciatively as things are pointed out to him, smiles and engages in conversation with people along his route. Kitchener is less effusive, but walks slowly behind the King, smiling politely and scanning the crowd, talking to the arsenal's hierarchy who have turned out in their best uniforms. He hardly seems to be listening to them, though, and I know that he has only one thing on his mind.

I spy Superintendent Gibbs halfway up a tall staircase attached to the outside of a large factory building, watching their progress intently. He spots me, with a look of alarm, and beckons for me to join him.

"You look bloody awful." He says as I am still climbing up to him. I am in the act of wiping blood from the cut on my cheek with my handkerchief. "Explosives?" He says brusquely.

"Found and dealt with."

His eyes widen. "They were really planning to do it?"

I nod curtly. "The danger has not passed."

"A personal attack?"

"One of them got away, he's armed with a revolver. If it is mine it should still have five bullets in it."

He jogs down the stairs, motioning to several of his men, using hand signals that mean nothing to me. I simply follow with Crabtree. "What does he look like?" He asks as we pace towards the centre of the pandemonium in front of us.

"I cannot say, it was almost black down there, but he is big, I know that much." Quinn pushes through the crowd, making a way for us both, nominally informing any complainants that he is a police officer. None seem particularly placated by this, though some are so excited by the visit that they do not even notice. We reach within twenty feet of His Majesty but can get no closer, there are just too many people. And these last ones are at the front for a reason, they have used their elbows well.

The King is smiling and shaking hands with a particularly old worker, engaging him in conversation. Kitchener has his hands clasped in front of him, listening intently. But his eyes flicker up and wander. He is still alert, thank goodness. He is obscured by a giant of a woman who is doing her level best to be as close to His Majesty as possible. "The big girl in the front," Quinn says, "I was worried about her at first, but she is harmless. Terrifying looking, but harmless, she's been glued to the King since he got here. You get 'em like that sometimes." He has pointed out a fanatic who stands well over six feet tall, clad in working clothes and an old-fashioned bonnet and doing her very best to stay next to His Majesty and the War Secretary. "She stroked Kitchener's hand a while ago. I thought he was going to have a heart attack. I think he might have met his match, finally."

"She's just excited, I think," I say vaguely.

We edge along with everybody else as the King progresses towards a locomotive, waiting patiently to carry them on a joy ride back towards the Beresford Gate. He and Kitchener engage the driver, standing by his miniature cab, in keen conversation. Once again the large woman looms over them, fanning herself and making various exclamations of glee about her proximity to His Majesty. "I can't quite believe it!" She says for the fifth time. "And me a blacksmith's daughter, hob-nobbing with the King!" Several close by pat her on the shoulder, also thrilled with this unexpected adventure. Strangers are talking freely with each other, shaking hands. Someone has stuck up a rousing attempt at Rule Britannia, and more and more people are joining in. The slightly tuneless rendition of the chorus comes again and again; the crowd carried away with the spectacle, growing louder and louder.

Suddenly I see a woman come toppling out of the crowd, as if she has been roughly shoved. Behind her there are more exhortations of surprise and dismay, and out of the bustle bursts our man, gripping my revolver and less than five yards from His Majesty and Lord Kitchener. Please god, don't let him do it with my own weapon. My father will never forgive me. Neither have seen him, the noise of the singing is so loud that unless you are watching the disturbance behind them, you would not even know that it was taking place. He seems to move in slow motion. As he wrestles to get through the crowd, Crabtree and I try to do the same from the other side. Some people roughly shove him back in protest, but he keeps coming. I can hear Quinn shrieking at The King, but is voice is lost in the din. We are not going to get there first, the barrel of the revolver is pointing directly at His Majesty. Then I am watching as the large woman pulls something out of her skirts and shoots at the assailant's chest. Two wires fly from the end of what looks like a deformed revolver and suddenly our man drops and convulses on the floor like he is having a fit. "Not today matey," she cries in a pantomime voice that cannot possibly be real. Then she kicks him daintily with her foot. And the crowd cheers.

By this time, Quinn and Crabtree have reached the King and Lord Kitchener and placed themselves in between both and the prone man on the floor. They are quickly augmented by more policemen. For my part, in case he had any ideas about getting up, I have my knee on his back and another man; Special Branch, possibly, or just an alert bystander, is holding his face side on to the ground and has no intention of letting go. A policeman joins us and handcuffs him, at which point I reclaim my revolver. I stand up and make my way over to His Majesty and Lord K, but not before I stop to talk to the woman who has saved the day. They watch in surprise as I shake her by the hand and cannot stop myself from laughing. She proceeds to remove the silly bonnet, peel off a long, curly blond wig, and remove a hooked, pretend nose, before pulling out a large handkerchief and wiping off a thick layer of stage make up to reveal: Bunny. The army's very own pantomime dame, who never can resist the chance to dress up and be the centre of attention. He laughs suddenly. That ear-piercing, machine-gun rattle laugh, and I see Kitchener wince in surprise.

XLII.

Outside Building 22, the King is preparing to climb into his car and depart with Clive Wigram. As I approach, he is pulling his gloves back on and conversing jovially with his assistant secretary. Without looking up he says: "So you have saved my skin once again, Lieutenant. The explosives were always here."

Wigram is obliged to put his hand over his nose as I stand next to them. "Yes, Your Majesty. But they have been made safe, and will be removed from their hiding place under cover of darkness, tonight. Williams will oversee it. There is more than we thought. This saboteur, the man in command. He wanted to make quite a statement."

He grimaces. "I do dislike a show off. You've lost another cap I see?"

"Yes, Your Majesty" I have no idea where it is.

"And you smell revolting."

"Yes, Your Majesty, I do."

There is a hint of a smile on his very red lips. "Did you give them a good biffing?"

"We did, Your Majesty."

He laughs. "Well done, Stanley," now hand us both one of those rather fetching cigarettes of yours, will you?"

I look at him in admiration as I take out my case. I'm not stupid. He was no more certain that I could find the explosives than I was, but he knew if a King told me that I would do it, it would make me believe. At least a little. To be alert to such things all day, every day, in such a time of crisis; the weight on his shoulders must be crushing when the constitution forbids him from any direct influence on the conduct of the war.

Kitchener remains after the Sovereign has departed. He claps me on the shoulder.

"Well done. Lieutenant."

"Thank you, Sir."

"What was it? The invention?"

"M14? Williams says it was a way to detonate a bomb wirelessly, when you're nowhere near it."

"Remarkable."

"And terrifying."

"Yes. I think this war is quite horrific enough. We will keep the device locked away."

"I am glad." I have no desire to see what something like that could do on a grand scale.

"Have you thought about staying in the army, after the war? I could make use of you, Will. And that man of yours."

"If it's all right, Sir, I'm just going to concentrate on surviving it first. Though I think Crabtree rather has his heart set on being a police detective."

"I'm sure something can be done." He grins. "What was that curious weapon that your friend pulled from within his skirts?"

"Another of Carrick's inventions. He designed it to stun, not kill. Something to do with electricity and a gunpowder charge. He thought it might be useful in catching enemy troops on trench raids in order to glean information from them. I had Williams assemble it from one of the doctor's notebooks. Thought it might be a useful contingency for the King's protection."

"And so it was. Very clever of you. You say he is a Guards officer?"

"Yes, Sir."

"It explains a lot," he says wryly. "You look rather glum for a man who has just saved the Empire from ruin." He sighs. "But you are right to be concerned, of course. They still have the plans for this invention; and you did not get your man. The one in charge."

No, sir. Crabtree has taken to calling him '*The Professor.*' My assistant has argued that we can hardly refer to an arch enemy as 'The Dolphin.'

"Ah! As in Moriarty."

"You have been reading Holmes, Sir?"

"It is hard to avoid when you have that chap of yours quoting it at every available opportunity. He seems to make some valuable deductions based on his knowledge, though, so I thought I would see what all the fuss was about. This Professor. We have not seen the last of him by any means."

"I think not. *The soul that has conceived one wickedness can nurse no good thereafter.*"

"Who said that?"

"Sophocles."

"A Greek? I hope he was more reputable than their current crop of politicians."

"He was a playwright, Sir," I smile. "In ancient times."

"Perhaps I will read something of his in due course. He sounds like a sensible fellow." I try not to laugh. And fail.

Williams is leaning on a lamppost smoking by the Beresford Gate as we depart in the Daimler with Gaylor. The full extent of my exhaustion has hit me and all I want to do is lie in a bath, then sleep for a week. I leave Crabtree snoring in the back and jump down to

say goodbye to him. "Well done." I put my hand out to shake his.
"You're all right," he grins, looking at it outstretched.
"I'm glad you think so. I don't suppose there is any chance you're going to salute me this week, is there"
He scrunches up his face "There is no need is there?" I ask. "Sir?"
He points his lit cigarette at me and smiles. "I knew you'd guess in the end. Too sharp for your own good." He shakes my outstretched hand. "Major Slater. So yes, it's you that should be saluting me, Stanley."
"You might have told me."
"Got to get my fun where I can."
"So you keep an eye on things, from the ground up. It's a good ruse. People behave differently in front of authority. How long have you been doing it? You play the part very well."
He shrugs vaguely. "Trust you to keep that to yourself? After all, you struck me in the cellar, I could court-martial you for that." I give him a casual salute as I get back in the car.

As Gaylor drops me home I shut the passenger door and lean back into the King's Daimler one final time.
"You're not bad, for a miserable bugger," I say.
He grins. "Neither are you, for a spoilt toff."
Touché.
"Till the next time," I laugh as I jog up the stairs to the house.
"Stay out of trouble," I hear him shout. If only.

EPILOGUE.

Detective Chantler has had no luck in locating Carrick's assistant, Mr. Giles, though he is currently the most wanted man in the north of England, so surely he cannot run for long. Dredging the water did not yield Mrs Carrick's body, but her mother has buried little Millicent with the doctor. Stan Bailey is recovering in hospital. The bullet hit nothing vital, and he is very proud to have been involved in saving the arsenal, even if he cannot tell anyone about it. He was well enough to be able to attend Fred George's funeral and hold his sister's hand. One of Lizzie's charitable endeavours is going to help the family. Crabtree and I attended all of the London funerals. It is a nasty part of the job, but an essential one, I think. Our friend in Room X is doing hard labour somewhere, along with the others that we caught at the arsenal, which so far as I am concerned is letting them off lightly; but Lord K is adamant that they may be of use. Because we still have to get to the bottom of who this *"Professor"* is. We may have won this battle, but the war is not over, in more than one sense. Who is keeping a watch on me? On Crabtree? What will they try next? We may have smoked out Giles, but infinitely more worrisome is the fact that there is a high level leak; either at the palace or the War Office. I think I know who is responsible. For now, Lord Kitchener has opened a file and placed it in his office. Not even Fitz knows that it exists. Dr. Scully has conceded that there was nothing bizarre about any of our deaths. That is a small victory, and finally, I had Lynette Hahn buried with her family and bought a stone to mark the grave. I can't explain why I've done it; killer that she was, but there was something so pathetic about her story. And her husband certainly deserved a headstone. Beneath his name it reads: *"An Englishman."*

So far there is still no sign of John. He has no grave, we have no more news. I think that he is probably dead, but as a family we are not ready to accept this yet. My mother has written off to Red Cross in Switzerland and asked the American Ambassador, Mr. Page, to help her to try and trace his whereabouts if he is a prisoner. In the meantime, Josephine remains with Lizzie and her husband; both of whom have fallen madly in love with her. I can do little with the clues that I have: *Agnes,* and *perhaps Bedfordshire,* in terms of tracing her mother. So for now we will have to wait and see, I suppose.

The breakthrough we sought at Neuve Chapelle did not occur, and now as I write this we are now embroiled in a tragedy of a campaign at Gallipoli. Warfare is already unrecognisable and we've barely been at it six months: pumps for clearing trenches, mines, catapults for chucking little bombs. If you can fashion something out of odds and ends lying about the trenches that would make somebody's life easier, then there is every chance that the army will be mass-producing it within a fortnight. And people like Dr. Carrick have a license, now, to invent the most elaborately despicable things. We may have stopped one ghastly creation from seeing the light of day, but there will be many, many more before we are at peace again.

I feel sick when I think of what Britain did to people like Willy Hahn last summer. Perhaps we are every bit as bad as the Hun, but just better at hiding it. Wars are all about lies. They begin with them, then as everybody dies they continue, and then when there are finished they end with ludicrous promises of never letting it happen again; that none of the perpetrators believe. The only truth is that the victors will be equally as miserable as those who have been defeated.

If you have read this far, then I thank you for getting to the end and I hope you have enjoyed this second instalment of my war-time recollections. Of course, I was born in the reign of Queen Victoria so I have no idea what Kindle, Amazon, or even the internet is; but I would appreciate it if you would share your thoughts on RED DAWN by way of a review in order to spread the word. Unless you hated it, of course, and intend to tell the world it is vile. In such an event, I would heartily approve if you reviewed one of my competitors instead. Until the next time, Crabtree and I thank you.

F.D.P.S

Author Notes

The King and Lord Kitchener really were friends going back many years. They did visit the Royal Arsenal in Woolwich together on 17th March, for the reasons described. To my knowledge, though, nobody tried to kill them that day. The King then progressed all around the country attempting to galvanise workers into action. He did so again in 1917 amidst industrial unrest and a spate of republicanism; at the request of the Cabinet. Both tours are detailed in my biography of King George V during the Great War: *In the Eye of the Storm*.

1915 was, in all, a disastrous year for the allies as they sought to find their feet. The munitions situation that His Majesty and Kitchener describe to Will at the beginning of March 1915 is historically accurate, as is the description of the naval campaign at Gallipoli and the impending arrival of Sir Ian Hamilton with a land force. The argument between those favouring a western war philosophy and fighting somewhere else, raged bitterly up and down the country as it did amongst Will and his friends. Hamilton did go to the palace to bid farewell to the King on 13th March. The campaign was a disaster, and it destroyed his long career.

The description of Britain's treatment of enemy aliens was also real. They were rounded up indiscriminately in 1914, and the three ships mentioned existed. The plight of families involved was also as described. As the clerk tells Will, by the spring of 1915 the response to the presence of aliens on British soil was far more measured. British civilians were also detained in Germany.

The description of the Battle of Neuve Chapelle was as described for John Stanley's battalion. Beginning on 10th March, it was indeed Britain's first offensive on the Western Front. It was the first step in puzzling out how to fight an entirely new form of industrial warfare. Initially things went well, but then the British Army began to realise all kinds of issues that would plague operations in the Great War. Further attempts in that sector as spring continued were disastrous.

The issue of missing men was by 1915, proving to be on a scale hitherto unthinkable. The experience of Will's family and the uncertainty relatives faced in not knowing what had become of their loved ones was real. In cases where no witnesses were to be had, they sometimes waited for years; desperately trying to find out if they were prisoners of war. A standard letter was devised and eventually sent out, which told the next of kin that on paper, at least, the army now considered their man dead for a want of evidence to the contrary.

Prince Louis Napoleon did indeed spend a night in that guard hut by the Thames, and the story of his demise at the hand of the Zulus is true. This really was the incident that brought John Bigge, later Lord Stamdfordham to royal attention. The ghosts stories are genuine ones told in and about the Royal Arsenal. You can do an excellent ghost tour there if it takes your fancy. Williams may have embellished the tales a little, but I have been into the tunnel in which the forgotten girl perished. Visiting men have actually had their trousers undone, and to add to the overall creepiness of the tale, this only occurs with a traditional fly. She is apparently baffled by zips.

Lord Kitchener has been my hero since childhood. I've tried to present a more rounded view of him. He was indeed exhausted at this time, and mistrustful of the rest of the Cabinet and of politicians in general. Perhaps too much so. He was trying to expand his literary horizons, and was preparing a house at Broome Park for his retirement after a lifetime of Imperial service. The photograph of JuJu Grenfell in a silver frame on his desk was real. He was a good friend of Ettie, Lady Desborough, who was Julian's mother. A few weeks after the events of Red Dawn, Julian was wounded on the Western Front. He looked to be recovering, but worsened and died as a result of shrapnel penetrating his skull. He had the rare privilege of his family at his side when he died at Boulogne. They moved heaven and earth to get to him. Kitchener, who withstood a wealth of disappointment and bad news at this desk without a pause, on this occasion apparently got up, left the War Office and went for a long solitary walk. Julian's brother, Billy, was killed a few weeks ago during the first liquid fire attack on British troops at Hooge. Small mercies, but he was killed by a bullet, not a flame thrower. Julian is buried at Boulogne Eastern and remembered for his war poem: *Into Battle*. Billy's grave was lost in subsequent fighting in the Ypres Salient and he is remembered on the Menin Gate in Ypres.

Doris Rosalie, the dancer at the London Palladium that Will has his eye on, is real. She was my great grandmother. She was a tiller girl during the Great War. My Great grandfather, who she had yet to meet, was so far as we can fathom, a boy soldier, being only 17 when the war ended. They married in the early twenties. She did have a stack of brother's that would have boxed his ears.

A security/bomb disposal expert who gives the most excellent of cuddles helped me construct the bomb and placed "M14" as an invention out of the scope of reality in WW1. For that he's going to get a big sloppy kiss next time I see him. The device that Bunny uses to incapacitate the final saboteur is, of course, a taser, which was not invented by a NASA man until 1969. Room X is a figment of my supposedly overactive imagination, and I have no factual knowledge regarding any secret access to Buckingham Palace. Of course an evacuation plan for the Royal Family from Buckingham Palace exists, but even if I knew about it, I would not compromise anyone's safety by writing about it.

Coming Soon:

BLUE MURDER

Spring 1917.

"Never trust the French. That's what my grandfather has always said. But then he is demented and was born at a time when we Englishmen shot them for fun."

Now Britain is bound to France as her ally, and their mutual survival is dependent on winning the war. After a monumental failure on the battlefield, the French Army is in turmoil. Discipline is falling apart, and mutiny threatens to spread to the British ranks.

A gruesome discovery at the front threatens to tear the allies apart and defeat them from within.

Summoned by a public figure that he has little time for, Captain Will Stanley is compelled to resolve the mystery.

All of this would be taxing enough on its own, without the appearance of a voice from beyond the grave.

Printed in Great Britain
by Amazon